THE
hero's
JOURNEY
home

FIONA TULLE ∘ E KAY SIMS
TIFFANI LYNN ∘ TARA L.AMES
∘ CD BRADLEY ∘ BT URRUELA

DEDICATION

This anthology is dedicated to all the men and women in
the Armed Forces, past and present

CONTENTS

ACKNOWLEDGMENTS

The authors would like to thank the following members in partnering with us in bringing you the stories within this anthology.

Christopher John from CJC Photography

Gideon Connelly - Cover Model

Tiffany Black from T.E. Black Designs

Cat Parisi from Cat's Eye Proofing and Promos

Aubree Valentine from Forever Valentine PR and More

To learn more about Military Romance Author's United, join their reader group:

https://www.facebook.com/groups/militaryromance/

CHASING FEATHERS

BY FIONA TULLE

CHAPTER ONE

Emma

"Thank you for helping me bring down the rest of my stuff. That was a huge help!" Emma wrapped her arms around her friend's neck, giving her a friendly peck on her cheek, making sure her makeup didn't smear on hers.

"Absolutely! We all need to help each other, right?" Kaitlyn smiled, sorting the boxes out in front of Emma.

"Let me know if I can help you during the signing. You're going to have lines, girl. That cover is going to burn your table." Emma grinned, her hand resting on Kaitlyn's arm affectionately.

"No, you will be having lines. You're the one with a new release this week, remember? I've got to get something from the check-in table, watch my table for me?" Kaitlyn winked at Emma as she stepped over a box to get to her own table.

"Absolutely, it's not like the doors are open yet," Emma laughed, shaking her head as she popped the lid of her box open to start setting her signing table up. The room's low hum and bustling kept her mind busy. This was her first signing without her husband, and usual assistant, in a long while. Her nerves were on fire. The start of every deployment set her feelings ablaze. She was thrilled one second and in tears in another. This was the life of a Marine wife, an emotional roller coaster. Worry consumed her night and day and there was nothing she could do, but pray for his safe return home.

After setting up the stands for her books, she turned around to take a look at how the room was coming to life. As her eyes scanned the room, a smile appeared when she saw her fellow authors, models and other professionals bustling to set their tables up. There was always a high that came with signings. Seeing old friends, readers, and new fans all in one day. It was always a good weekend to spend with like-minded people. Only one thing would make her heart fuller today and that was an embrace from a man she knew she couldn't see for well over six months. It had been fourteen days since their last kiss, but who was counting?

While Emma took the room in, she felt a chasing light sensation up her arm, like a feather running across her bare skin. Looking down, she saw a familiar hand, a familiar silicone ring holding one of her feathers grazing her skin. Shock held her frozen in place for a split second. This wasn't a mirage. Austin.

Twirling around quickly to wrap her arms around his neck - nearly falling over her table. His arms wrapped around her body as fast as her arms wrapped around his neck. She didn't care how ridiculous she looked, the tears were flowing, but it was as if a miracle had poured down from heaven. They embraced, never wanting to let go. All she could feel was his arms, his breathing and his face in her neck. "Austin."

"Emma," Austin broke their embrace to kiss her forehead, but he continued to hold her close around her waist. Emma gripped his side tightly with her arms, leaning back to look up at his handsome, sun-kissed face. His thumbs caressed her cheekbones, wiping the surprise tears away. He knew to be gentle to not smear her eye makeup, but she didn't care if she looked like a raccoon, she had her Austin.

"How? How is this even possible?" Emma was speechless, refusing to let go of him.

Austin laughed, sliding his hand from the tears to tucking a loose strand of hair behind her hair, "Well, it's not like I can tell you where I was headed for pre-deployment. But, when I heard you were in Norfolk for a signing when I was here, I started pulling a few strings with the Colonel and Brigadier General and they gave the whole unit 36 hours of Liberty time before we pushed out. They claim they were going to do it anyway, for morale and all." He shrugged with a mischievous grin on his face. " I reached out to Kaitlyn's husband and he filled me in with where you all would be and Kaitlyn pulled some strings over here. I wouldn't miss this if I could help it. Showcase author and all." Austin's bright and proud grin beamed as he stepped back to motion towards her table. "Ma'am, I'm at your service." he bowed, before pecking a tender kiss on her cheek.

Emma covered her face with her hands taking all of what just happened in. Emotions continued to wash over her as Austin protectively wrapped his arms around her sobbing form. He had an amazing way of calming her when she needed it. He kissed the top of her head and whispered in her ear, "Let's get you shining, girl. No more tears. Just laughter and kisses. I have you for the next day and a half and all I want you to remember is happiness."

Emma nodded into his chest, giving him one more squeeze before regrouping her emotions. Her face had to have looked ridiculous with smeared makeup, but she would fix that. First, though, she needed to find Kaitlyn, who was not standing far, with her cell phone up. Damn her, recording the reunion. Emma broke the steady grip when she grabbed her friend giving her the biggest hug a human their size could do, "Thank you, babe. I don't know how to repay you for your kindness. How did you manage to pull this off without spilling it to me?"

Kaitlyn's laugh filled the room. She clicked her phone off and wrapped her arms around Emma. "What fun would that be? I'm glad we could do it. Tristan was game when he heard we could surprise you. You're the one always surprising everyone else."

Emma kissed her friend's cheek once more, giving her the warmest hug she could give someone who was a part of her miracle. "Where is Tristan so I can hug him?" Kaitlyn turned around so she could see their men standing shoulder to shoulder watching their tender moment. "Come here you big teddy bear!"

Emma stepped closer to her friend's husband, giving him an equally appreciative hug, squeezing him once before stepping back into Austin's grasp. "I can't tell you how amazed I am you're able to pull it off."

"There were a few more hands at play here. Lisa and Amy were in on it. They even planned for him to be here for SaSS and made sure he was on the lunch tab and gave him a name tag." Kaitlyn grinned at them, Tristan having moved around to wrap his arms around his wife smiled brightly at the two of them.

Emma turned to look around for the event coordinators that were her dear friends. She knew they were hustling to get the event started, but she owed them a weight of gratitude that could not be described. Her search was interrupted by Austin, who leaned down to whisper in her ear, "They're at the registration table. Let's go see them before it gets crazy."

Emma looked up at him, his eyes were twinkling, and she could swear his eyes watered by their reunion too. He wouldn't admit it, at least not here and now. "Watch the table? We're going to go say thank you and I'm going to go fix this makeup. Since you know, you were just getting something from the registration table, before right?" She nudged Austin teasingly.

"Absolutely." Kaitlyn waved them off as she turned to get her table going after the surprise went on without a hitch.

As they walked around the tables and to the front of the event, she wrapped an arm around Austin's lower back pulling him close. "I can't believe I have you for a day and a half."

"Let's make the best of the time we have," Austin rested a hand around her, and Emma felt complete.

Emma heard the squeal before she saw the faces of her friends Lisa and Amy. "Oh we're so sorry we missed it, but we had to get something straight here. I am so excited this worked out so well." Amy squeezed her way around the close tables to wrap Emma in a huge hug.

Lisa came around the other side and gave Emma her hug, "Kaitlyn told us he was trying to surprise you and we had to get involved."

The tears began to flow again. She cried into her friends' shoulders. Her appreciation was hard to define. "You know we got your back. We appreciate your hubby's service and your sacrifice. If you ever need anything, you just holler at us and we will do everything we can to rally for you, okay?" Amy said as she gave Austin a welcoming hug.

"We appreciate everything you do for us, including dropping in a last minute personal assistant," Austin chimed in, chuckling

"You could technically come as a model," Lisa teased as she hugged Austin as well.

"No, no I can't. You won't find this ugly mug in front of a camera any time soon," Austin jibed back, laughing.

"I've been trying to tell him that the girls would fawn over him, uniform or no uniform." Emma winked.

"Hell, like you'd share," Austin wrapped his arms around Emma's waist pulling her close in an affectionate hug from behind.

"They can look, but not touch," Emma added, leaning into her husband. She was in awe that he was even here.

"Well you two lovebirds go sort yourselves out, the readers are about to come in and we gotta get this show on the road!" Amy waved at them as they rushed to get their last-minute errands done before the signing opened. "Drinks later?"

"Yes definitely! We'll see you there!" Emma waved back as they made their way to the elevators. She turned to Austin lacing her fingers into his hands. "I feel like this is a dream."

"It's not. We're here, together," Austin pressed the elevator up button.

They both stepped in together, and she pressed the

17

sixth-floor button and turned to face him. It was then she felt his embrace pin her to the wall of the elevator, his lips on hers, stealing the air from her lungs. It was this. This that she desperately missed. His passion for her, his desire for her. Everything about him seeped his love for her. She missed him, ached for him.

She pressed a heel against the side of the elevator as she felt the weight of Austin press against her, his one hand around her waist and the other hand pressed above them on the wall. It was the ding of the elevator notifying them that they had reached their floor that broke their kiss.

Breathless, Emma followed Austin out, her hand entwined with his. "We're in 621," was all that she could say. Her heart was fluttering, and goosebumps lined her skin. His effect on her was powerful.

She pulled her room card out of her back pocket and handed it to Austin who swiftly led her into the hotel room. As the door closed behind them, he had her against the wall once more. This time, the kiss unrestrained with passion. She melted against his body. His familiarity, his power made her drunk for him. She traced her fingers into his side, pulling him into her.

"How much time do we have?"

Emma glanced at her watch on her wrist, not lifting her hand from his body, "Doors open at 10. I have to set up, that'll take about 30 minutes, so .."

"Enough time." Austin pulled her body against his, pressing his lips against hers once more. Emma followed, wanting every minute with him they can have together.

Leading her to the bed, the one she didn't think she would be sharing with her husband today. Crossing his arms, he pulled his shirt off. He leaned down and pressed one of his magical kisses against her lips once more, his hands moving over her body. It took everything in her to restrain herself and play this moment out with him. They were going to have lots of these moments in the next 36 hours. That is if she had anything to do with it.

CHAPTER TWO

Austin

Watching her do her thing was what made Austin proud of Emma. She was in her groove, signing, hugging and taking pictures with her biggest fans. He didn't think his heart could grow in pride much more. She deserved every moment of this glory. He had witnessed her toil into the evening when she wrote. He stood by her when she doubted herself and was almost always the one that hit the submit button for the book when it was time to publish.

After the last set of fans came by the table, Emma slid into her chair, laying a hand on his knee. He smiled at her hand. It was decorated with the rings that he gave her the day they got engaged and the day they got married. Out of the dozens of rings he looked at, this was the one he picked. It was perfect. It was a modest size diamond adorned with two smaller diamonds that were hugged by two feathers engraved into the platinum band. It was his Emma in ring form. He knew the instant he saw it. His thumb ran over her hand, and the ring, squeezing it close.

She smiled at him, her face relaxed and content. "Looks like we're done." He leaned into her and cradled her face in his hands and pressed a tender a kiss to her lips. It was maybe their hundredth of the day, but he was going to savor every bit of his wife that he could. "There's nothing like that feeling after a signing." He watched her reflect as she gazed around the room to take the last few moments in. "There is this glow that happens, almost like a runner's high. I'm addicted to this."

"I'm addicted to you," Austin whispered in her ear, traced his fingers on her low back as she sat taking everything in. Her laughter made his chest want to explode. She was everything. Everything his heart, soul, and mind ever desired. Six months was too long to be away from someone you loved. There they sat for a few more moments, basking in their affection for one another and the success of the day, before he stood, letting his hand fall around her waist, "I'll take care of the banner, you want to start with the swag?"

"Sounds good." Lingering with their hands on each other's body just for a moment longer. Taking a deep breath he turned from her to help her get her things together. They were an old hat at this. A team. That's what made their relationship work. He would help her as an author and she was there for his military career in the Marines. He knew the sacrifice she faced when he was away, but she did it with honor and she made him proud.

Working in sync with one another they were swiftly done with packing the signing gear. He placed the two heavier boxes on top of each other, leaving the rolling cart with her plastic box of personalized white feathers on top for Emma. "Ready?"

"Yes, I can't believe the day is done," Emma smiled back at him as she led them down to the entrance.

"Well, not quite. We still have that after party, remember?" Austin teased her. The Sexy and Sassy Signing always had a concluding party that let the fans, authors, models and other professionals mingle and have fun. He knew they would get there early to leave early.

They both stopped in front of the elevator where a crowd of authors began to gather. Emma, being the socialite of the two of them, engaged in the chatter so he didn't have to. Although social settings never bothered him, this was Emma's space and she shined. He filed in behind her as they filled an elevator. He placed his boxes in front of him and wrapped his arm around her waist just so he could feel her. Even as she talked to those in the elevator, she leaned into him, acknowledging him.

They worked their way back to the hotel room. As he opened the door and pushed the boxes in, he heard Emma gasp behind him. He quickly turned around to watch the box of feathers scatter right in front of their door, releasing them everywhere. The white flutter covered Emma from head to toe, and Austin's side.

He grabbed the cart Emma was pushing and took it in so he could help her gather the precious items back into the box. There were dozens and dozens scattered around them, and still more floating down the hall. The laughter was matched with more because the faster they gathered the feathers, there were more that seemed to flit away or attach to their clothing.

Emma directed him to chase the escaping pieces as she diligently picked them off the floor, tears streaming down her face from laughing. It took them at least fifteen minutes to gather each piece back into the box, but it took longer to gather themselves. Austin watched as the unfortunate delight that took over Emma, she had to prop herself against the wall so she wouldn't tip over from her rounds of amusement. Plucking feathers off each other in the doorway, they leaned into each other, breathless, their faces creased with near permanent smiles, all while still tidying themselves.

"I look like a plucked chicken," Emma said as she pulled a feather caught in Austin's shirt.

"But you're my plucked chicken," Austin kissed the tip of her nose.

"Hey!" Emma slapped his arm playfully.

"Wait, no. You're like a glimmering angel in this fluorescent hotel lighting," Austin chirped mischievously.

Emma threw her head back in a new wave of laughter, "Nice save, buddy."

He sat on the end of the bed, leaning his weight over his hands that were on his thighs. He was trying to catch his breath from the rolls of laughter that kept coming when they tried to figure out how the box slipped off the cart since it was secured when they left the ballroom. He felt Emma move in front of him, her arms wrapped around his neck, pulling him into her. His laughter softened to silence as he rested his face in her torso, his arms wrapping around her waist while taking her scent in. The light and sweet scent of coconut, strawberry and vanilla floral glued to her, it was what emanated off her constantly. They could be out running and sweating and she would still smell immaculate.

"Thank you for chasing feathers for me," her whispers broke the silence between them.

"I would chase feathers every day, and forever if it means I can be with you."

CHAPTER THREE

Emma

"What uniform are you wearing for service?" Emma lifted the garment bag to hang on a different hook, making room for the uniform of Austin's choice.

"Charlie's," Austin called from the bathroom. There was a hush in the hotel room. The last day and a half was about Emma, but these last two hours were about Austin. He was returning to base and service and she was going to do everything she could to make his departure as smooth as possible. Emma opened the garment bag to find the khaki short sleeved button up and green trousers hanging in the front.

"Got them, I'll make sure they're pressed," she pulled the uniform out, ensuring the belt and headgear were also included. She had already unfolded the hotel's ironing board and was prepared to work out any fine wrinkles that may have set while the uniform was hanging in the bag. Austin took meticulous care of his uniform so this act was nearly futile. There wasn't a wrinkle to be found, but she did it anyway, to keep her hands and mind busy.

Austin met her in the room wearing only his greyish silver Under Armour boxer briefs. Emma looked up, biting her lower lip while taking in her husband one last time, in all his glory. The lines of his muscles, sinewy and firm, showed his discipline to his career and to himself. He took pride in his health and fitness and it showed. She took pride in his dedication, and there was no shame in admiring her husband.

"What are you staring at?" He winked at her as he slipped his dark green trousers on after donning his socks.

"My hot husband getting dressed," Emma said while biting on her index finger, her cheeks blooming with pink.

"I love when you blush. Nine years and it never fails to make me happy." Austin stepped closer to Emma, his trousers still unbelted. He cradled her cheeks in his warm hands. "I love you to the moon and back, Emma Carter."

"I love you to the moon and back, Austin Carter," Emma replied before feeling his lips close in on hers. She memorized how he felt, the warmth of his body, his hands, and the way he smelled after a shower. His masculinity secured in her heart and all she ever wanted was to spend eternity with him.

He broke the kiss, only to lean in and kiss her forehead, "Not enough time."

"Never enough time, babe." Emma sighed turning her attention to the khaki service shirt. She offered it to him so he could slip it on as she pulled out the khaki colored web trouser belt. She let her fingers linger over the cool gold colored buckle before also handing that over to him. She admired his uniform process, but she didn't want to let him go.

Once she knew he was satisfied with how he looked, she rose from the end of the bed, dressed in a tank top and khaki shorts. He was leaving to serve and she was left to wait. And wait for him she would. Her heart fluttered as the time ticked away. There was only a finite amount of time left.

She laced her fingers into his hands when they both faced the door and they walked to the elevator, the garment bag casually thrown over his other shoulder. He had ordered a Lyft to take him to the base, and they would have to say goodbye in the lobby. Being a Major had its disadvantages. It meant he had to arrive before the rest of the unit. Leadership, he once said to her, was built by example. She honored him for that.

The elevator doors opened into the lobby and that's when she saw the small crowd sitting at the cluster of couches and loveseats. Their hands wrapped around cups of coffee or water bottles. Her friends. Her book world friends were here to send Austin off with her. The tears she had been holding back all morning began to well up.

She brought her free hand up over her mouth as Austin now led them into the lobby. She was moved.

As they approached the crowd, he squeezed her hand before pulling her into his side. "I didn't think you all would want to join us in the lobby for this?" Austin only let go of her hand to offer a handshake and a friendly embrace to Tristan and Kaitlyn. He intermittently touched a shoulder and shook a hand to show his appreciation. She watched as he set his bag down and was drawn into the conversation, eventually sitting on an ottoman across from a friend.

Emma. Emma remained silent. Her heart was beating faster than she could brace. While she was enamored by the fact her friends came to support her, it wasn't lost on her that she was about to say goodbye to her soulmate and husband. She was entrusting in fate to bring him home safely.

It was Kaitlyn who stood up and wrapped her arms around her. She rocked her back and forth and whispered, "You're not alone in this. He may be gone, but look..." She turned and pointed to the group. "You have a tribe holding you up until the big guy comes back, okay?"

Emma nodded, as she hugged her friend closely. The pair joined the group as they talked superficially. No one wanted to address the obvious elephant in the room until Emma did. "I think the car is about to pull up." It was her sad attempt to pull her husband away so she could steal his last few minutes selfishly. The group realized this and stood to send Austin off with a grand farewell. A moment Emma, even in her need to be with him alone, made her heart swell. Her community defined the word kindness.

"I'm going to secure her in your hands guys, don't let her get into too much mischief while I'm gone." Austin teased as he stood up to move out of the gathering.

"We got her, we promise. If you need anything just let her know and we'll be on it." Kaitlyn waved, then rested her hand on Tristan's shoulder who was still seated.

He nodded as he maneuvered around the group to finally reach her on the outside of the circle. Wrapping his arm around her, he picked up his garment bag and looked at Emma. Her heart skipped a beat. The eyes that watched her were the eyes that stole her heart and soul and she couldn't imagine letting him go when she had only had a day and a half with him. They walked towards the automatic double door. His hand pulled her closer and closer with each step, eventually forcing them to stop so they could embrace right outside the glass doors.

"I know we had this a few weeks back, but remember what you promised, take care of yourself." He rocked her. "Don't worry too much. We know what we're doing." He pressed a tender kiss on her forehead.

She closed her eyes, just taking him in. "I know. And you take care of yourself and don't worry too much. I know what I'm doing." They shared a moment of brief amusement before she paused. "Come back home to me."

"I will walk the Earth to come back to you, Emma."

"And I will search the ends of the Earth, for you." Emma rested her forehead on his chest.

He dropped his garment bag on the bench before Emma felt him wrap an arm around her shoulder and the other around her head to pull her closer into his chest. He kissed the top of her head, letting her embrace him. There weren't words for this moment. All the words were used, except for the three they saved for the very last moment.

Emma knew it was time to let him go when she heard the car arrive and when she felt him take in a deep breath. Her throat began to close, and it felt like she couldn't breathe. She gripped at the front of his shirt, one last time, for that one last moment. He felt her and he didn't move. He only squeezed her tighter.

Emma didn't know how he managed to signal the driver to grab his bag but it bought them just a moment longer. She clung to him as if she was drowning and it was that, she was drowning in her own emotions. She felt him shift and move her. His hands went around her face, cupping her cheek and chin.

"I love you, Emma Carter."

"I love you, Austin Carter."

He let go. She knew that once he turned to get in the car he wouldn't look back. They made that pact early on that each time he left, there was no looking back after their I love you's. The world was beginning to collapse around her but she had to remain steady to watch the car pull away. She begged for the car to not leave in her mind, but it did.

She stood outside of the lobby, with one hand clutching her chest and the other covering her face. When the car disappeared from sight she felt the implosion. She doubled over hugging herself. There were no sobs for this, it was a moment of sheer terror. A world without Austin shook her and she could not survive, let alone fathom it.

SHE GASPED FOR AIR AND IT WOULDN'T COME IN. IT WAS THEN THAT SHE FELT THE RUSH OF COLD AIR FROM THE AUTOMATIC DOORS OPENING. KAITLYN'S ARMS SWIFTLY WRAPPED AROUND HER. SHE WAS HER SAFETY NET WHEN AUSTIN WASN'T THERE TO CATCH HER.

CHAPTER FOUR

Austin

Five months. Five months away from the person that made him complete. The sun beat on his face as he leaned against the cement wall reading the letter she tucked in her most recent care package.

Austin,

I hope you're doing okay. I absolutely loved talking to you on the phone last week. I know you're remote right now and super busy with your patrols, but know I think of you constantly. The weather has been beautiful and the leaves are changing. The cool air is refreshing. Kaitlyn and I are going apple picking. I'll save some for you since you should be coming before they become sawdust. Mom is up to her usual antics. She's already gathering Thanksgiving goods and wants me to pick up our turkey already. I think I'll wait a bit longer. Maybe we can get it together? I have one more signing, it's in two weeks, the first weekend in November. Then, maybe? Not long after that, I get to kiss you. I love you always. I love you forever.

Your Emma

My Emma. He ran his finger across her name and the ink. She was always so conscientious in her choice of stationary and ink. The paper felt like fabric and the ink looked like she wrote with a quill. He loved her attention to detail and he knew this helped her cope too. Writing was her escape, even if it was a letter to him. She must have already gotten the apples by now, and she would be at the signing tomorrow if he had the timing down right.

He lifted the paper and brought it up to his nose. Her. It was all her. He pressed the paper to his chest for a moment before he peeked into the envelope. She always left a small feather in the letters she sent in her packages. They were his good luck charm. He pulled this one out and examined it. Pink.

He twirled it between his fingers before he reached into his breast pocket of his utilities and pulled the small bundle he was making out of her feathers. He smiled as he gingerly maneuvered where the pink feather would fit in his mini bouquet. He loosened the tiny rubber band that held it together and slowly weaved the tiny stem in place. When he was happy with it he tucked it back in his pocket, patting it for good measure.

He folded the letter and pushed up against the wall to pull himself up into standing. She was right, there wasn't much time left in this deployment. He had to stay focused just for a few more weeks and then he could feel her again, the woman that kept him going. He ducked into the officer's tent, scanning the room for his locker, even though he knew exactly where it was located. He slid the letter into his trunk before ducking back out. He was going out of the wire today with his men. He was going to see how patrols in the area were running. The convoys were coming in regularly but he hadn't been out with them in several weeks. The command wanted to chart new roads but the danger was real with an influx of IEDs being found. He wanted his men and women to be safe and the first thing he wanted to do is ensure the paths they were securing regularly were solid.

He greeted his Captain with a friendly pat on the shoulder. They chatted for a brief amount of time, talking about which patrol they would share and what direction they typically make. Any changes to the plan would have to be approved, simply because convoys only traveled in paths that were patrolled. Explosives were placed within minutes sometimes of a patrol walking and driving by.

He moved on to shake the hands of the Lieutenants of the unit moving out for this shift. He went on their inspection and discussed their strategy and what their concerns were. They were the front line team and he needed their information to formulate the safest plan for new routes. This unit's patrol team were considered the perimeter patrol team. They were the faces the locals met and the deterrent for insurgents to engage. Their job was dangerous and he appreciated each of them for the risk they took. Over the last five months, they had lost three men, all due to undetected explosive devices on foot patrol. Their names and faces never left him. He knew every time they left their remote camp, they were facing more and more danger than those who were inside the wire.

"I'm going to be taking the foot patrol today," Austin said as he patted the hood of the Humvee.

"Sir? No disrespect, but are you sure? The Scouts passed by with 24 suspicious finds," the young Lieutenant said. "Any of these humvees will gladly have you on board."

"Thank you for the consideration, but the foot patrol is what I want to see."

"Yes, Sir."

Moments later the team mobilized. With a gun slung over his shoulder, he took to the foot patrol with Staff Sergeant Lopez and Sergeant Lincoln. He recognized these men as being the up and coming enlisted force. Their work was exemplary and the example they set for their unit was recognized in the officer ranks. He wanted to see how they worked together.

"Over there, under the rock." Lopez pointed over the eastward horizon, where a stack of stones sat, a small projectile sticking out in the opposite direction.

"Looks fresh," Austin commented.

"Looks too obvious." Lincoln turned around and began scanning the horizon line, looking for snipers or any hidden figures. Hand signals began to fly, everyone honed in on the potential threat.

Their silence and vigilance was answered by a fast approaching white pickup truck. All guards went up. The Marines riding in the vehicles jumped out and opened their doors to use as a shield. Guns raised commands and yelling ensued. The front team waved the white pick up down, to stop its approach. Not only was the pick up a risk to the patrol, but the closer another vehicle got to the pile the more at risk they were to detonating a potential IED.

The pick up didn't stop. The only reason why Austin's eyes shot upward and back was when he heard the barrage of bullets enter their field. The Marines ducked and took cover near the closest surface they could. He found cover sitting up against the closest humvee. He was sharing the surface with Lopez. They shared quick words on how they would take down the gunmen in the tree that had aim on them. The other teams split off and began addressing each threat. Lieutenants were calling out their commands. The ambush was being messaged back to camp. They were not far, the camp had to have heard this pursuit.

Bullets rattled the Humvee. He prayed they wouldn't penetrate the vehicle's armor and so far they hadn't. Breathless he timed his turn and aim of his gun between barrages with Lopez's. He flipped over from his seated position to a near crawl aiming upward at the tree that held their target. Rolling back into his defensive position for Lopez to step in.

Confusion and chaos broke out. Every time Austin took aim he was watching men fall. The bullets were piercing their armor, even behind cover. Calls for assistance were being rattled through the radio. He was pinned behind his hiding spot and all he could do was continue calling his position out to the others as others did the same. Lopez had shifted to the other side of the Humvee to change his aim and draw the gunmen out of the tree.

Then all things went black.

Austin's eyes fluttered open. The acrid smell of burning flesh mixed with fuel woke him. The ringing buzzed in his head. He spit out the sand, debris and the metallic taste in his mouth. Blood. He quickly patted himself for his gun, but it was lying right next to him, he grabbed it and pulled it to himself. Slowly lifting his head, he looked through the settling dust. Silence. His hearing was gone. The blast robbed him of one of his two "security" senses.

Disoriented he sat up looking around, waiting for the sand to settle some more. As the dust cleared, it was then that he saw the body thrown haphazardly to his right. Lopez. No. Not Lopez. It can't be, but it was. His head darted from one side to the other. Bodies. Bodies everywhere is what he saw. The sand was stained a maroon color, the blood of his comrades being soaked into the earth.

The remaining haze didn't let him see who else went down. He did a self-check of himself, and all he could figure out is that he may have a concussion from the blow, but he didn't see blood on his body. He tasted it, but that still meant he was, for the most part, intact still. Alive. He was alive.

Suddenly, he felt hands under his shoulder, on his chest, shoving him down, grabbing at his gun. He hollered, struggled, rolling back and forth, kicking his legs, trying to free himself from the attackers. He counted four sets of hands and then he lost his gun, all without getting a clear view of who they were.

He was utterly frustrated by not hearing them approach and then things got worse. They robbed him of his vision. A rough sack had been thrown over his head. He continued to struggle and fight back. He was being taken captive and he was using every bit of training to keep oriented and safe. The ringing in his head was dulling but his hearing was still poor. He used the little sensation he had to figure out the direction he was being taken.

His hands weren't bound, but they were being gripped tightly behind his back. He pulled a hand free, just for that split second to pull his name patch off his chest. He needed it to be dropped. He needed to leave that behind. Although he was on the roster, whoever came back would know he was here when shit hit the fan. They'll know to look for him, for potential others. He lost that struggle soon after letting the patch go. This time his hands were pulled back obscenely fast, he cried out in that instant pain. They only relented once his wrists were bound. He wasn't going down yet, he was determined to fight his way to freedom.

Austin felt his body slam against the bed of a truck. He kicked and struggled, for a purpose. He wanted to feel how many he was dealing with. Two pairs of hands grabbed his arms and shove him into a seated position, against what he assumed was the back window of the cab. The ringing was distracting, but he forced himself to focus as the pickup started and began rumbling over the road. Straight. They were going straight. Memorize the route. That is their way back to camp. He swayed, counting the turns and shifts, repeating them in his head.

His internal clock, as accurate as it could be if he had a concussion, told him they were on the road for about an hour before he felt the jolt of the vehicle as it stopped. The sun was blistering, the heat seeped through their uniforms. They weren't undercover. His hearing was improving but had not completely returned. He did hear the opening and slamming of doors. The language being spoken was familiar to him; it was the local dialect. He wasn't fluent but he knew the cadence and tone of the voices. They must've taken him to a nearby town.

Hands. Hands again. Two sets once more. Gripping him under his upper arms, aggressively pulling at his shoulders from the back of the pickup. The soreness from the blast and the rough handling made him holler out. He struggled his way off the pickup. Their grip cutting the circulation off to his lower arms.

He was trained to survive, evade, resist and escape. He would never surrender, especially if he knew there were others in his charge still alive, and potentially captured. His life was directly in danger now, but he fought anyway. It was once he felt the cool barrel of a gun, directed at his spine, that he stopped. Survival above all else became the main game. He must have appeased his captors enough because they released the tightness of their grip. Blood, returning to his limbs. They each had an arm linked on his arm to guide him blindly into whatever structure they wanted him in.

He heard the shuffling of more feet. He was attempting to figure out if anyone else was captured, or if he was alone again. The terrain he felt under his boots changed as they marched him forward. It was smoother but still felt sandy. After having his head forced downward, he was shoved down. With no way of protecting himself, he landed face first on a hard, sandy floor. Stars, stars are what he saw. The pain was minuscule due to the adrenaline surging through his system, but he felt the gush of blood. His nose was broken. Small things still. He was still alive. He felt the rough surface of the sack pulled off his face and his hands freed. He instantly planted his hands on the ground and pushed back, finding a wall to keep to his back and scooted his way up into a defensive crouch, looking around getting the first glimpse of his surroundings.

The room was filled with black veiled insurgents, with large automatic weapons slung over their shoulders, many of them carrying sidearms hung at their waist or hip. Their robes and clothing clouded with dirt and sand. They stood in staggered stances and it was clear they weren't formally trained. His captors were local insurgents, and not of the military sort. Formal training would have them strategically standing at the exit points and protecting their hostages from escape.

They were in a cement-like structure with two open-air windows and one entrance. There was four of them. Sergeant Lincoln was in the corner, his arm in a makeshift sling. He was unable to defend himself very well, but he was also positioned defensively. The other two men he recognized from the patrol but didn't know their name by memory. They were also crouching up against the wall. Their faces beet red and their nostrils flaring as they shifted their weight to their back leg, ready to lunge.

It occurred to him that he was the highest ranking member here and he was going to need to take command. There was no way he could escape and manage to get the rest of them out without being killed. There was no honor in running away and leaving three of his men, his comrades, behind.

Yelling ensued. Guns were lifted and pointed at them. He lifted his arms up, in an instant sign of non-threat, moving forward slowly. He had to get himself and his men out of here. "Major Austin Carter. 55432. October 15, 1980."

His men knew the routine. This was a part of their code of conduct. They were to provide their name, rank, service number and birthdate. No other information needed to be disclosed. He heard the three men step up from their positions and do the same thing, calling out their name, rank, number, and birthdate. Their vocalized rank and six-digit service number cued him that he indeed was the highest ranking member. This was either going to work for or against him. No matter what, he would do everything he could to get out and get out with them.

A united front, the men stood shoulder to shoulder, with barrels sitting at forehead height. The cold metal pressing against their skin, threatening their journey home. They were going to face the guns and captors together. This was going to be a start of a long trek home. A journey back to Emma.

CHAPTER FIVE

Emma

"Are you sure you want to balance your mini-banner on your table like that?" Emma had her hand on her hip, leaning to the side as if to get another view.

"No, I'm not sure," Kaitlyn collapsed in her chair behind the table, clutching her shirt in laughter.

"Give it a stable foundation," Emma moved closer to the display, lifting it with one hand, and removing the stack of books it was sitting on and gingerly poised it on top of the table itself, with the stack returned to the front of it. "There. You'll be less likely to knock it over."

"Yea, except when Tristan comes barreling through." Kaitlyn grinned as she came around the table to meet Emma. "Why didn't I just stick to the big banner?"

"Author troubles, m'dear. Author troubles. These are so much easier to travel with, and people can still take a picture with you in front of it." She leaned into a side hug with Kaitlyn before taking a step, cocking her head to make a final judgment on the rest of the setup. "I think you're set."

Emma looked over at her friend to see what she thought of her table. She nodded looking back at Emma and smiling, "Yeah, I think I'm good now. Are you still good at yours?" They turned around in unison to look at her table that was facing hers.

"You always have this amazing table. You like wave your hands and poof, the table is perfect and here I am trying to balance a damn table banner." Kaitlyn gestured with her hands wide in the air drawing a feigned spell in the air and exploding it in front of them.

They shared in a moment together, as Emma shook her head at her friend, pushing her away playfully, "You're ridiculous."

"I love you, girl." Kaitlyn wrapped her arm around

her friend. They leaned their heads to the side and together. "I don't know how I would do this without you."

"Girl, my love for you is fierce," Emma teased, returning the side embrace once more. "If it weren't for Austin, I'd be sister wives with you, but you get Tristan all to yourself and Tristan and I share you."

With that, Kaitlyn was forced to break their hug and bend over, laughing so hard, she had to cover her face. Conveniently, Tristan appeared from around the corner and entrance with three coffees balanced on a carrier, pausing only to chuckle and shake his head at the two of them. "What are you two up to now?"

Kaitlyn shook her head, wiping her face with the back of her hands to prevent makeup from smearing, pointing at Emma, "She wants to be my sister wife so you could share me."

Tristan set the coffee on the table before arching his brow, a sheepish grin on his face, "Well, I'm game, but I'm too afraid of Austin. He'd kill me. He's a Marine and all. Not sure I could hack that."

Emma had an arm around her own waist with a hand up covering her face in the absurdity of what was happening. "I don't want you, Tristan. I want Kaitlyn. We'd share Kaitlyn."

"Oh." Tristan paused for a moment.

"But it isn't happening." Kaitlyn chimed in with the obvious.

"I love me, my Kaitlyn, but I love Austin too much to be in a sister wife situation with the two of you." Emma shook her head waving her hand at them as she stepped closer to Kaitlyn's table, ready to grab the coffee Tristan got them.

"I get it. Not sure how I'd feel if Kaitlyn said she'd want to share you with Austin." Tristan raised his hands up in surrender. "Mr. Captain America would have my ass if I defied it though."

"You act as if Austin and you don't have your own

damn bromance." Kaitlyn laughed as she grabbed her iced coffee from the carrier.

"True, true. That's my man, right there. Captain America and all. Maybe he'd pull the jealous card and take the two of you down and we'd escape into Neverland together." Tristan laughed. "Heard from Peter Pan himself, as of late?"

"I can't with you right now and no, it's been a while but he did tell me on his last call it'll be awhile. Not much longer now. I can't wait to see him. We should be getting the return date soon. Stop ship on mail is coming up." Emma hugged the paper cup to her chest wondering what Austin was doing right now.

"Well, let us know when, so we can start the homecoming party planning. We need to top the last one," Tristan raised his cup to his lips, as he sat at one of Kaitlyn's chairs at her table.

"Absolutely. So you can figure out how to actually play beer pong with a bunch of Marines that just got home." Kaitlyn ribbed her husband as she elbowed him in the chair next to him.

"Ladies and Gentlemen, the doors are about to be opened. Have fun and sell those books!" The announcement forced their conversation to end. Emma shot Kaitlyn and Tristan two thumbs up as she headed towards her table across from them.

"See you on the other side of this," Emma laughed as she settled herself at her table. The room had a soft murmur to it, it was the anticipation of the oncoming crowds of readers. Even after dozens of signings, Emma felt the nerves rise to her throat. What if she doesn't sell any books? What if no one recognized her? What if she made a fool of herself? All questions that never disappeared until the first fan walked up to her and that didn't take long.

"Emma Carter! I love your books. I especially love Winston in your Lovers series." The excitement is contagious as Emma got up to give her fan a warm hug.

"I'm so glad. That was such a fun series to write. My husband was my inspiration," Emma lifted up one of the Lover series books up to show the fan. "See this man? This was a stock photo Austin found when we were looking for potential cover ideas."

"That's so funny that your husband helps you with your covers. Is he still overseas?"

"Unfortunately, yes. But home soon." Emma pressed her lips together, she felt a tug on her heart.

"Oh great! For the holidays, I hope?" The reader handed her her selection from Emma's table.

Emma took the book and the cash the reader had added. "We hope so, but we never know with the military." She selected a bright blue pen to sign the book. The weight of Austin's presence, or lack thereof pressed against her chest. He sold her books as much as she did at these events. There was nothing more rewarding than feeling your husband's pride in your work.

"Can I get a picture?" The reader grinned as Emma handed her the signed book.

"Sure!" Emma pressed her hands against the table to rise and sweep herself around. Wrapping her arm around the reader's waist she posed for a smile and another hug in front of her banner. "It was so nice to meet you. I really hope you enjoy the new book in the series."

"I think I will! Thank you so much, Emma! I hope Austin comes home soon." The reader waved as she walked away.

Emma nodded a 'thank you' as she made her way back behind her table. The growing murmur filled the room. The attendees were filling in with bags hanging from their shoulders. Her eyes moved over to Kaitlyn's table across from hers where several fans had begun to line up, she smiled. That was another fantastic feeling, watching your best friend succeed.

It didn't take long before Emma's table had a steady

stream of fans, new readers and bloggers file through. Tending to each person with devoted attention, Emma gave all she had to the people who came to visit her. These were the people that made her successful, it was the least she could do.

As each hour passed, Emma diligently refilled her swag; the bookmarks, lip balm and the array of colorful feathers that was her brand on the table. She held onto a long pink feather in her fingers between guests. The silky softness trickling between her digits. It was soothing. The memory of chasing feathers in the hallway of Austin made her smile if it weren't for a sudden visitor she may have broken out into a spontaneous laughter, recalling the feathers splayed along the hallway. Her Marine husband jogging up and down the hallway to gather the stray runaways. Oh, how she missed him.

The constant hum began to lower as the event closing time approached. She had done well. Relieved, that she wasn't going to need to haul boxes of books home with her, she stood up and stretched to take in the last view of the book signing. There was that high again. There were people who wanted to read her words and wanted to hug her and take pictures and that alone caused elation, but to watch her peers, and even more so her best friend, succeed made her heart swell.

She felt her hip buzz. Someone was calling her, and it was unusual. Most people in her circle knew she was at a signing and wouldn't be readily available, but if it were Austin it didn't matter. Recognizing the phone number as base area code she rapidly swiped to pick it up.

"Hello? Austin? Is that you?" She grabbed her money bag and wallet and weaved her way to Kaitlyn's table as fast as she could so she could find a quiet place to talk.

"Ma'am? I'm looking for Major Austin Carter's wife, Mrs. Emma Carter?" An unfamiliar voice garbled back, the reception was poor.

Signaling to Tristan to watch her table, her brows

furrowed to the voice, "Sir? This is his wife, Emma." Her heart felt like it was about to stop. If this wasn't Austin, then who would want to get in touch with her? Was this the casualty unit? Wouldn't they come to visit? Wait. She wasn't home, they would have to call. Her mind racing, she panicked, finding the closest door and pushing through, making no regard to where she would end up. "Is he okay? Please tell me he is okay."

"Ma'am? I can't hear you well...wait, that is much better," the voice becoming clearer as she entered into a vacant hall leading into the ballroom for the event. "Can I get the confirmation that you are Major Austin Carter's wife and next of kin?"

"Yes, I am his wife. What has happened?" The words barely escaping her lips.

"My name is Lieutenant Colonel Mason, I'm assigned to the Department of the Navy and work with the United States Marines at the Pentagon. I'm calling to inform you that your husband has been captured as a prisoner of war during an ambush on a routine patrol..."

The rush of blood to her face and brain forced her to press against the wall, and simultaneously slide down. Raising her hand to cover her mouth in disbelief, the rest of the words became seared memories in her mind. Confirmation of details and privacy were demanded. Mindlessly agreeing to report to their base for more information and protect the identities of the others until next of kin was notified was made.

She scrambled for a scrap of paper. Searching the hallway she found a loose hotel pad of paper with a pen. Scribbling the contact name and number, before having to say goodbye.

"Ma'am, we here at the Pentagon, Department of Defense, Homeland Security and the Armed Forces are doing everything we can to recover Major Carter and bring him home safely." The monotone voice did not satisfy the ache that was forming in Emma's chest.

She gasped out her response, "Thank you." Her voice breaking at the end. Hanging up she clutched the phone to her chest. Crouching against the wall, all she heard was the muffled murmur of the signing to her right and the deafening silence in the hallway.

Covering her face in her hands, the emotions broiling in her core. What was happening? Was Austin okay? Will he be okay? How did this all happen? The overwhelming sense of fear crept up to her throat, she threw her head back and leaned it against the wall, letting out a wail that rose from her soul.

The hallway became a blur as tears streamed down her face, her shoulders rising and falling with the hiccuping sobs that escaped. Her husband was taken hostage and all she could think of was the cruelty and savageness the insurgents displayed on former hostages. She racked her brain and she could not recall ever hearing that those taken in captivity had ever found freedom.

Her world was falling apart as she let out another cry. The door she entered through cracked and the familiar voice called out her name, "Emma? Are you in here? Are you okay?"

Kaitlyn and Tristan rushed into the hallway when they saw the looks of Emma crouching against the wall. Wrapping her arms around Emma, Kaitlyn rocked her for a moment. A friend who didn't care what was wrong but just loved her where she was in that moment.

She wept into her shoulder, the hiccups and sobs breaking her voice, "Austin…." Sitting back with her hands wiping her face of the tears that continued to stream. "...was taken captive in an ambush."

Silence took over. Tristan lowered himself next to Emma and wrapped an arm around her shoulder, pulling her and Kaitlyn into a hug. "He's coming home, Kaitlyn. He is going to come home." He understood the greatest fear that Emma clung to at that moment. "Austin is the most badass person I know. He will do everything he can to come home to you. You know that, right?"

Emma covered her face with her hands, the grief overcoming everything she had control over. "He has to come home. I don't know how to do life without him."

CHAPTER SIX

Austin

The metal bars slammed shut behind him. The only thing Austin focused on was his breathing. As long as he was breathing he was alive. Blood streaming down his side, staining his uniform blouse. He found it ironic the captors had allowed them to keep their uniforms on. Rustling sounds from the dark kept him aroused.

He whispered, "I'm okay. Stay down, but I think they're gone for a few days."

Cold hands gingerly helped him into a sitting position, forcing a groan. Today's round of chosen torment was particularly painful, but he was alive and he hadn't disclosed any information about his unit or his men. He was calling that a success.

"How do you know, Sir?" Lincoln ripped a strip of cloth from the meager blanket they shared and started tending to the bleeding. The strip of cloth was not sufficient for the wounds, but the action itself was soothing. These were his comrades and they were experiencing hell together. He was going to do anything he could to get them out of here with him.

"It's Carter or Austin. I think we can move beyond rank here," he couldn't help but chuckle at what was now a meaningless formality. "There was a phone call. It interrupted this," motioning to his back. "I don't even think they left their women. We're here on our own."

"What? That makes no sense." Lincoln slid back, the scraping sound of the sand and gravel making him cringe. It was the same sound as the tool of torment made right before each strike.

"No it doesn't, but I don't think that matters right now." Austin adjusted his position to find the comfortable sitting position to face the three men. The lights streaked in through the small window that was strategically designed to be out of reach, the bars hogging the whole area of the opening. It oriented the men to the changing of the days and offered cool rain when the rare but most desired storm came through. "I know how we can get out of here."

"What? Are you nuts? They'll kill us before we even get out of the cell." Shepherd remarked, he was one of the two men he didn't know prior to their capture.

"I just have this feeling, they're gone for a little bit. The call seemed urgent, they were cleaning their shit up fast and when did they ever just drop one of us off and not take another?" Austin motioned with his hands, he was only dimly lit but he could see their expressions. Fear and curiosity pressed on their faces.

"Go on," Lincoln waved Shepard down from his defensiveness when he saw him about to respond.

Austin pointed up towards the window, "We're underground here."

"Yeah, we figured that out early on," Shepherd's voice was annoyed. Austin knew it was fear and hesitancy.

"But when we get taken to that back room, that door that leads outside? It is ground level," Austin motioned behind him as if the room was directly there. "Today, I saw that the door didn't have a lock on it. It's just a wooden door with a latch for a knob. Better yet, I saw that whenever one of them left, it opened up into a field, tall grass, and I saw trees. There is cover out there. Anytime someone would come they would come from around the building, coming from that way." Austin pointed out towards the window. "I suspect the market or city or civilization is that way."

"How did you figure that out? They have us blindfolded in there." Tozer remarked, breaking his silence.

"They didn't cover my eyes. They were threatening a brand, and I guess they thought seeing it would scare me more," Austin shrugged. "They've done worse I figured, brand away."

"You're a strange motherfucker, Carter," Shepherd said, running a sand-caked hand through his hair and then scratching at the beard that was coming in. At this point rank was useless and they were in this together, to survive. Each of them having their own draw home. Emma.

"It's what I do. You know that. With the three of you, mostly intact, I think we have a good chance of running away. In the last five weeks that we have been here, they've never left us here alone, with no woman or child for a guard," his breath was raspy, the deep ache centered over his back was setting in.

"Okay, fine, we'll run straight out the door, but how the fuck do you think we are going to get out of here?" Shepard motioned towards the cell door.

"Easy," Austin reached into his blouse and pulled out the small bundle of feathers he had tediously bound together. The feathers Emma had sent him in every letter.

"Did they bash your head or something?" Shepherd asked puzzled and itched with annoyance.

"Settle down guys, let's hear him out. This may be our only chance to get home. I want to go home." Lincoln sighed, running his dirty hands across his blouse while leaning in to look at the bundle of feathers.

Austin refused to hand the feathers around, he had diligently formed them in the way he wanted them, "Every time they've opened the lock I've watched them use a three-prong key. They're not huge and have small indentations."

"Oh fuck. You think it would work?" The mixed expression of surprise and mild excitement pressed on Lincoln's face.

"Are you crazy? How the hell are feathers going to open the lock?" Shepard snapped back, but his voice had softened, as he stood from his place to make his way to the locked cell door.

"Help me up?" Austin offered his left arm. Both

Lincoln and Tozer came alongside him and helped him in a standing position. The world spun for a moment, and he braced into his companions until he felt his gaze and stance steady.

Toying with the soft flecks of the feathers in his hands, he did not want to ruin the feathers that were gifted to him, but these were his good luck charms, and he knew, that if they got this door unlocked, they had a chance to get out, a chance to get home.

"Easy now. Don't hurt yourself worse, we've gotten lucky with my shoulder. If we're going to get out, we need to all get out. No one left behind." Lincoln's voice was soft. Of all of them, Austin was the leader, Lincoln was the uniter, Tozer was the solemn problem solver and Shepard was the one with the temper of the group, but he was also the tallest and had the brute strength the others couldn't compete with.

"So, if I estimated this right, this lock should slide open if I aligned the feather stems right. The strength of the feathers comes in the fact they're in a bundle. They won't snap…..I hope." Austin said as he wrapped one hand around one of the bars above the locking mechanism and slowly slipped the bundle of the feathers, stem first into the keyhole on the outside of the cell.

Silence fell in the cell. Each of them held their breaths as Austin worked the feathers.

Time after time, Austin pulled the pack out and adjusted the ends, being careful not to split the stems that were weakening with each attempt.

After the ninth or tenth attempt, Shepard threw his arms up, "This is ludicrous. You're going to get us killed Carter."

It was then that Austin stood from his awkward crouching position and tucked the bundle in his pant pocket. With measured steps, he walked directly at Shepard. He had his hand outstretched towards him. "You listen here, Shepard. I will not rot here. I will not die here.

48

I have to go home. My wife was not meant to bury me on this deployment. You have two little boys that need their father. You have a beautiful wife that needs you too. Do you hear me? We need to get out of here, and we are going to go home. If it means we open the fuckin' lock with these feathers, we do it!" Austin rarely raised his voice but he needed Shepherd to change his perspective. He needed Shepard to step out of fear and find the courage that made him a Marine. There was no shame in trying to survive, but survive outside of fear, and not cower in it.

Silence again, but this time, no one clung to the cell door near Austin. They let him work it independently. Adjusting the stems again, he bundled them with the rubber band. *Please work, please work.* The stems slid into the lock one more time and he turned his wrist and click.

The most satisfying sound in the last five weeks was that click. Austin wasn't sure if he should holler out in sheer bliss or just step away. He slipped the bundle out of the locking mechanism, still partially in disbelief that the lock may have actually been unlocked.

Tozer must have noticed the change in his stance, "Did you get it?" The three men quickly crowded over Austin.

With bated breath, Austin looked up to Shepherd, "You do the honors."

Austin braced himself against the bars and took a step back so Shepherd could take his place. He watched him press his forehead against the bars, a silent prayer was said, the same prayer that each of them was saying at that moment. Stepping back, to unblock the slide of the door, Austin watched as Shepherd tested the door. Ever so slowly, the sound of metal scratching on metal echoed into the cell. The door was opening. Success! The feathers worked.

Cheers between the men were exchanged. It was Tozer who quieted them down. "How are we going to do this? We will be spotted in our utilities out there."

"We wait until night," Austin said as he slowly slid the

door open further. "We need to gather whatever supplies we can carry. They didn't take everything, they took a lot but not everything."

"How do we know everyone's gone?" Lincoln asked as he slipped out of the cell.

"I got your six, let's clear the place and look for weapons." Tozer followed with Shepherd soon after.

"Clear the place, and I'll go up into the room and try to sort out where and how we need to get out." Austin followed the men, leaning against the wall. Clenching his teeth as he bore weight on his leg that he was convinced was broken. Brewing thoughts of doubt, he had to figure out how he was going to get the men out, while he also escaped, without weighing them down. Emma. He had to get home to her.

Hours passed. They had resettled back into their cell with small pockets of food between them. The days were long in the summer here. They were waiting for darkness to move in. Two kept watch while two slept, conserving as much energy as they could. Shepherd and Austin sat shoulder to shoulder near the cell entrance, anticipating the dusk.

"Carter?" Shepherd whispered, straightening his bent knees from his chest to out in front of him.

"Hmm?" Austin turned his head to listen to his watch companion.

"How do you do it?" Shepherd's fingers dug into the sand and gravel on the floor, keeping his hands busy.

"How do I do what?" Austin absentmindedly drew a tic tac toe game board on the ground.

"Just keep going. This is hell. Don't get me wrong. I want to get back to Stacy and the kids. I desperately want to, but how the fuck did you sum up the courage to stand in one of our places when they come for us? How do you just keep going without batting an eye?" His voice was raspy, cracked with fatigue and stress.

Shepherd was courageous for being himself. Being

captured wasn't something anyone could just survive, let alone follow trained protocol. Austin admired him and the others for the honorable way they were serving their country in captivity.

Austin reached into his side pocket and gently pulled out the bundle of feathers and handed them over to Shepherd. The fateful bundle that released them from their cell, and hopefully into freedom. "It's Emma. I see her face in everything. If the fuckers are trying to pull information from me, all I do is focus on her face, her voice, and the way she felt the last time we were together. She saves me because she completes me." Shepherd handed the feathers back to him silently. Kissing the bundle of feathers, Austin tucked them safely back in his breast pocket this time, over his heart.

For a few brief moments, the men traded turns in tic tac toe, before Shepherd broke the silence, "I don't think Stacy loves me like that."

"I doubt that's true. Your mind is blinding you right now. Focus in on how sweet her hair smelled, or how that kiss felt when you said goodbye. It'll make it easier."

"That's special." Shepherd sighed. "I hope she will be as excited to see me return home as Emma will be to see you."

"Son, she will be. I promise." Austin nudged his shoulder in camaraderie.

"Thank you for dealing with my angry ass in here." Shepherd's voice grew lower, near a whisper.

"I wouldn't want to serve next to anyone else." Austin offered a fist to pound with him on. "We got this. We're going home."

"Why do you think they left us like this? It's like they abandoned us, it makes no sense." A new board was drawn into the sand after the fist bump.

Austin didn't answer the question. He knew the answer but the last thing he needed was to instill more fear or panic. Panic would lead to confusion and chaos and somebody would get hurt. The number one mission tonight was to get everyone out, before….before whatever was about to happen.

Darkness crept into the cell. The witching hour was approaching. Rustling the pant leg of Tozer, he whispered loudly, "Let's go. It's time. We gotta get out of here before it's too late."

With that statement, all four men rose. Austin required assistance, but he was stronger and more focused now than ever before. Time was running out and he needed to get them out of here and into the brush and trees quickly. They would deal with the dangers of the brush when they got there but their lives were in imminent danger if they stayed.

Slowly, and silently, they crept like they practiced earlier, ensuring each passageway was clear for the next to follow. No guns were found in their earlier search, but each of them was paired with a dual set of knives. The moon shone clear into the desert sky; it flickered in through the windows as they made their way through the small compound. When they approached the door, it was Shepherd who swung the door open and cleared the zone so that they all could step out.

Silence. Austin was getting used to silence, and this silence was golden because it also meant they still had time. They each took cover under a planter, large stone or wall until they were sure there were no roaming guards. The small compound and the buildings around them were abandoned, and silent.

It was then that they heard the familiar sounds of engines, low flying engines. The acrid smell of fuel began to permeate the air.

"MOVE! Move into the closest brush! Move, move, move, move!" Austin made the signal to go. They had to move out of the span of the compound or they would be caught between the air strike and freedom.

Austin rose from his place to watch the three men

disappear into the trees and long grass as he worked his way around the wall, attempting to jog. He raised his head to look back to see how far the planes were and to see how much time he had to make it to the wooded area.

He heard the men calling out for him in the cover of the darkness. Knowing he must be cutting it close, he turned, and he braced himself and he bared down on his injured leg and broke into a hobbled jog, crying out with each step. He began to hear the succinct sound of bombs and blasts, approaching closer as the planes had dropped them overhead. He counted as he continued the feeble run. It was the heat he felt first, and then the sound of the blast sent him into blackness.

CHAPTER SEVEN

Emma

"Now, let's all go around the table and share what we are thankful for," Emma's sweet Aunt offered. The long dark wood heirloom table was surrounded by all the people Emma loved, all except one. Five weeks had passed, and there was no news on the whereabouts of Austin and the three men he was captured with. Every day Emma prayed for it to be the day that she received the call that he was coming home, and it never came.

Toying with the cloth napkin in her lap, she folded and unfolded it. She wasn't present to what was going on around her, all her mind could do is imagine Austin starving, tortured, hurt or, worse yet, dead in the desert without her. Here she was, sitting at a table, covered in gluttonous overdoing of her family. How could she be thankful when the man she loved was held captive a whole world away?

Her thoughts were quickly interrupted, "Emma? Emma, dear? Are you ok?" Her mother reached under the table and grabbed her hand.

"Oh? Mom? I'm sorry, I was just thinking." The tears began to well up, her chest tightened. Pushing her chair out, Emma ran from the table and into the kitchen. She clutched the front of her shirt as if it was suffocating her, and the sobs did not stop. Finding herself curling up into a heap on the floor, Emma hid her face in her hands, letting every tear of sorrow and pain go.

The familiar embrace of her mother wrapping her arms around her soothed her for a moment. "Shhh, now. I knew this was going to be too much. I'm sorry, baby, for making you come, but I thought it was best, maybe I was wrong."

There were no words for Emma to say, it was sorrow that she felt, and in those moments, her mother consoled her, whispering supportive words. All Emma could do was to repeatedly mutter, "I'm sorry" and "I miss him."

"I know you do honey." The words of her mother being the most consoling when he was gone. They had shared many of these moments and she needed her mother right now, right here.

It was the familiar buzz of her phone in her pocket that broke their moment of solitude together. She had trained herself to quickly grab any phone call she had, she didn't know when it could be anyone from any department that could call her about her husband. The previous weeks dozens of reporters and journalists had acquired her phone number and their calls had become a nuisance but picking up a nuisance was better than not picking up the call.

Emma wiped the tears from her face as she swiped to pick up the phone, "Hello? This is Emma Carter."

"Hello? Mrs. Emma Carter? This is Lieutenant Colonel Mason from the Department of the Navy."

CONNECT WITH FIONA TULLE!

Website
https://fionatulle.com/

Author Facebook Page
https://www.facebook.com/FionaTulle/

Reader Group
https://www.facebook.com/groups/koffeehaus/

Book Bub
https://www.bookbub.com/authors/fiona-tulle

HOME SWEET HOME

BY E KAY SIMS

CHAPTER ONE
GOING HOME
THE BLUEST EYES IN TEXAS ~ RESTLESS HEART
MAREK

The yellow lines blurred as my truck ate up the pavement, the sunset on the horizon, a bright, glowing orb of hope and new beginnings in the distance. It represented my future, at least, I liked to think of it that way. I'd been on the road for the last two days straight, heading west for home, well what would be my home from now on, anyway. Gunner hung his head out the passenger window, his tongue lolling in the wind, dripping dog saliva along the side of my big Dodge diesel. Cowboy Cadillac, we called them back in Texas.

The early September air was cool here in the evening. Especially driving over the Cascade Range, a blessed relief compared to the heat of San Antonio. The leaves were just beginning to change and soon the winter rains would come. It was my favorite time of the year, late autumn, early fall. I hadn't been back here in years and years, not since my gramp's funeral. That made me think of another, more recent funeral. Those thoughts overwhelmed me, although time had taken away some of the sting.

I watched the sun sink and disappear behind the mountains just ahead, taking all but the last of the light. Shadows of dusk forced me to turn on the headlights. This area was notorious for elk and deer crossing the road. I cranked up the radio when the oldies station started playing The Bluest Eyes in Texas. The lyrics were so appropriate for what I was feeling. The memories flooded my brain, and the tears flowed freely down my cheeks. Gunner must have sensed my mood, for he scooted across the seat and put his head in my lap.

"It's all right buddy," I soothed. "I'm good." I patted his head and scratched behind his ears.

The buzz of my cell phone startled me as the song

came to a close. I reached to adjust the volume as the call connected with my built-in Bluetooth.

"Hey, Grandma," I answered the call, recognizing the number on caller I.D.

"Hey, sweetie," her rough voice came through the sound system filling the cab of my truck. "How far out are ya?"

"About an hour or so, I guess. You don't have to wait up," I started, but she cut me off.

"Of course, I do! Been so excited all day, there's no way I can sleep. I made all your favorites in case you're hungry when you and Gunner get here. I even baked him some special dog treats!" she chuckled.

"Thanks, Gram, you didn't have to do all that," I paused, "I appreciate it and so will Gunner."

"Drive safe and watch out for those dang deer!"

We ended the call and I turned the radio back up.

Gunner fell asleep beside me as I hummed along with the music. I was grateful for his companionship. He was my dog now. We'd had a rocky start though, in the beginning. At first, he hadn't liked me for whatever reason. Territorial, I guess. Gunner was Ryker's bomb-sniffing K9 partner. After only six years of service, Gunner had been retired due to injuries sustained while they'd been deployed in Afghanistan.

Ryker had fought to adopt him. Not long after, Ryker and I had been introduced through mutual friends and we immediately clicked. By this time, Ryker had become a dog handling trainer at Lackland Air Force Base with the 341st Squadron. We were both active duty. I was stationed at Randolph Air Force Base North of San Antonio, in Civil Engineering as an HVAC Refrigeration Engineer. I was the only female in my shop.

Maybe it was the smell of ammonia and Freon that clung to my skin and clothes that Gunner had hated, his nose being so sensitive as a bomb-sniffing dog. That, and he was very protective of Ryker. He seemed to be jealous of our budding relationship. We'd dated only six months before getting married. Sometimes you just know. Gunner got used to me over time, but he was never my dog. It was a running joke that he only tolerated me to make Ryker happy. I swear, that dog worshipped Ryker.

We'd only been married two years and half of that time we'd been separated because I got deployed to Afghanistan for six months setting up the air conditioning and refrigeration systems at a forward operating base for the Army. Ryker had finished his enlistment, separated from service and hired on at a private security company overseas by the time I had gotten back. He left for his new job three months after I got home to the States. I never saw him again. He and his team had been ambushed and killed one night. To this day, I've never been able to find out the details.

Gunner was heartbroken. I knew Ryker was dead before I got the call. The day Ryker died I'd been home on a Sunday morning reading the paper and drinking coffee at the dining room table. Suddenly, Gunner started whining, then barking, his eyes fixed near the front door. I thought someone was about to ring the doorbell, but when I checked no one was there. When I turned back, Gunner was sitting at attention, staring at something I couldn't see.

It was then I knew. I can't really describe in words how I knew, but it hit me like a wave coming up behind me, an overwhelming sense of unexplained grief washed over me. I couldn't shake it. Gunner was acting so strange. He'd started whining again and then he laid down at my feet and covered his muzzle with his front paws. He wouldn't leave my side for the rest of the day. A few hours later, filled with a sense of dread when I saw the caller I.D., I answered the call from Ryker's boss, Dylan. That had been one of the worst days of my life up to that point. And then there had been the funeral. Gunner had been inconsolable. He laid under the casket all night. I was there right beside him. The next day, I had to put him in his kennel so I could attend the funeral.

We'd been on our own the last three years, Gunner and I. My buddy was getting old. He was coming up on his twelfth birthday. The average lifespan for a Belgian Malinois is twelve to fourteen years. I knew I didn't have much time left with him. I wanted to cherish what time I did have left. I'd served my country for the last twenty years and retired at the age of thirty-eight. And now I was going back home to Grandma's farm in Oregon. Gunner would spend the rest of his days happy and loved on the farm with me and Gram.

CHAPTER TWO
Echoes in my Head
A Thousand Miles from Nowhere ~ Dwight Yoakam
MAREK

I slowed the truck down coming out of the sharp 'S' curve at the bottom of the hill as I approached the driveway to Grandma's farm. When I rolled down the window to punch in the gate code, the cool mountain air laced with the clean scent of pine, filled my nostrils, taking me right back to my childhood. Home, I was home. I'd spent most of my young life here, up until I'd graduated from high school and enlisted in the Air Force when I was eighteen.

I'd never gotten along with my parents. They'd been really young when they'd gotten pregnant with me. Some people should just never have children, and my parents were the perfect example of unfit. Grandma took me in full time when I got emancipated at the age of sixteen. I just couldn't take it anymore. All the drunken fights and threats of divorce. It went in cycles. They'd kiss and make-up countless times and things would be okay for a few weeks, sometimes even a few months and then out of nowhere, they'd be at each other's throats. The violence escalated to the point the neighbors started calling the cops. I was mortified to go to school. I'd already been spending entire summers and every weekend I could get away at Gram's. And then came the day my mother beat me to a bloody pulp in one of her drunken rages.

She'd found out Dad had been cheating on her and she'd accused me of covering for him. I hadn't had a clue. I told her as much, but she hadn't believed me. I'd turned my back to go upstairs, tired of her antics and she'd caught me from behind, knocking me to the floor face first, breaking my nose. But she didn't stop there. She'd grabbed handfuls of my hair and begun bouncing my head off the floor. I managed to roll out from under her but she was out of control, kicking, slapping, clawing and tearing at my clothes. At some point, she'd knocked me unconscious and thought she'd killed me. I came to with her begging me to please not be dead. I packed a bag, called Gram, and walked three miles to the truck stop where I'd waited for her to pick me up. My sixteenth birthday was the following week. And school started two weeks after that, so Gram had all my records transferred and I started my junior year at Sweet Home High School.

I pulled the truck forward past the old two-story barn that had been built in 1905. The driveway curved to the left and continued up toward the old house that was even older, built around 1890. Grandma owned twenty acres or so, up here on Marks Ridge. She'd lived here for over forty-five years. She and Gramps had sold their place in California back in the early seventies and moved to western Oregon with their four children to make a better life for the family. Every one of their children had grown up to be successful, all but my mother, the youngest of the brood. Uncle Jared said it was because she'd been spoiled since she was the baby. Aunt Maddie disagreed, however.

"I'm telling you, it's the Bipolar. All the signs were there since she was little. It didn't help that Daddy coddled her," I overheard Aunt Maddie telling Grandma one Christmas Eve back when I was twelve.

It's funny how the mind works, one thought flowing into another and another. In the short space of time that it took for me to drive from the gate up to the main house, I had practically relived my entire childhood in memories.

I parked the truck near the gate to the front yard and there stood my grandmother. The moonlight shone brightly on her silvery mane of hair making her look like some ancient Viking goddess. My grandmother was a badass in her day. Actually, she still was. Ever since Gramps died eight years ago, she'd been on her own up here. She chopped her own wood, mowed ten acres of lawn herself on the old tractor and took care of all the farm animals by herself at the age of seventy-eight. Not to mention, she maintained a half-acre vegetable garden and the other half acre of yard that she'd landscaped herself.

"Hey, girl!" she opened the gate and walked toward the truck just as I opened the door and climbed down.

"Hey, Gram," I stepped into her warm embrace, the exhaustion of the last two days catching up to me. I'd driven straight through, stopping only to refuel, eat, feed Gunner and take a bathroom break when necessary.

She hugged me a long time, smoothing my hair back from my face, then finally she stepped back, letting me go. "It's good to have you home," she sighed. I hadn't seen her since Ryker's funeral.

"It's good to be home," I replied. "C'mon Gunner," I turned back toward the truck. "You remember Gram, don't cha boy?" I helped him jump down so he wouldn't hurt his lame leg. He'd taken a bullet, saving Ryker's life back in Afghanistan.

"Hey there, big fella," she held her hand out for him to sniff. "I got some goodies for you, boy," she patted him on the head. "And I made you a blueberry-peach cobbler, Marek."

"Oh, you know how I love me some cobbler!" My mouth was watering just thinking about it.

I grabbed my bag out of the truck and walked with Gram up to the house along the brick pavers that I distinctly recalled pulling weeds from in between the cracks for hours and hours in the summer when I was young. Gunner walked along beside me, alert and ready as always, his ears perked, keen eyes scanning the path ahead. His limp was more prominent than ever.

"Where's Maggie?" I asked, wondering where the old chocolate lab had gotten off to.

"Aunt Maddie came and got her today. We weren't sure how she'd take to Gunner so she said she'd take her a few days until you get settled in.

"Oh, that was nice of her. Gunner will be fine, though.

He's trained to ignore other dogs and people unless I give him a command to do otherwise. But I understand Maggie might feel a bit put out by another dog invading her territory."

We climbed the steps up to the large wooden deck and entered through the mudroom. I took my shoes off before stepping into the open space, which consisted of a small sitting area in front of a large fireplace. The brick chimney divided it from the kitchen which was to the right of the small sitting room that opened into the living room straight ahead. Previously, there had been a wall separating the kitchen from the sitting room and another wall between the sitting room and the living room. Gramps had taken them out and remodeled the kitchen, opening everything up. Otherwise, the spaces would have remained dark and cramped.

The cobbler sat steaming on the island, fresh from the oven. Gram had set out two, small china plates from her mother's collection.

"Wow, that smells amazing!" The scent of baked peaches, blueberries and a hint of cinnamon filled the air.

"Drop your bag there and pull up a stool," Gram went to the sink and washed her hands before scooping out two huge portions of cobbler for each of us. She went over to the large stainless steel fridge, pulled out a can of whipped cream and covered the tops of our cobbler with a mountain of white, fluffy goodness. "There ya go," she handed the plate to me with a fork from her mismatched silverware drawer.

"I better wash up too," I set down the plate and went to the sink, Gunner on my heels.

After drying my hands on the dish towel hanging from the front of the oven's door handle directly across from the sink, I sat down on the old 1950's metal stool in front of the island. Gunner laid down at my feet.

That first bite of cobbler was always the best, in my opinion. "Oh, my God, I've missed this so much." The flaky, buttery crust melted in my mouth. It was really more like a pie than a cobbler.

"It's always best fresh and still warm," Gram smiled with her whipped cream mustache.

A little while later, I was showered and ready for bed. After taking Gunner out to relieve himself one more time, Gram had us settled in the upstairs guest room for the night. The old farmhouse was quiet, there up on the hill. No wind stirred the tall pines and oaks that surrounded the property. It was dark there in the woods, with only the stars and moonlight lighting the clear September sky. The bedroom window was open to let in the cool night air. I pulled the fabric softener scented quilt up to my chin and snuggled down into the comfortable mattress of the four-poster queen-sized bed. Tomorrow I would unpack and figure out what the hell I was going to do with the rest of my life.

CHAPTER THREE
Roots in a Small Town
Born and Raised ~ Hunter Brothers
MAREK

That first day on the farm, I'd slept well into late morning having been wiped out from the long drive. The sound of the neighbor's cows mooing in the distance had finally woken me. Gunner had not been at my feet as I'd expected. I'd found him following Gram around in the garden as she watered and pulled a stray weed here and there. I was shocked at how quickly he'd taken to her, and a bit miffed. The traitor! I guess I was a little jealous because he hadn't taken to me so quickly back when Ryker and I had first started dating.

It only took a few days to get settled into our routine and soon I was waking up with the chickens. I'd taken over a lot of the chores, but that didn't stop Gram from working. There was always something on the farm needing repairs. By the fourth day, I was out watering the tomatoes, just finishing up when I heard a truck pull up the driveway. Voices drifted over the massive Rugosa rose hedge and then I heard the sound of Maggie barking excitedly. The chickens squawked and scattered into the thick nearby woods that lined the back side of the property.

I shut off the hose and walked along the path up to the front gate to greet Aunt Maddie and her partner, Gina.

"Gunner, stay," I commanded. "Hey Aunt Maddie, Gina. How are you ladies doing?" I lifted the latch on the gate as Aunt Maddie tried to hold Maggie back from jumping up on me. I'd have to break her of that behavior right quick. "Maggie, sit!" I commanded firmly. Maggie complied, but she sat pouting, her head hung low as if I'd chastised her without cause.

"Hey girl, it's been a long time," Aunt Maddie wrapped me in a bear hug and Gina gave me a nod and a big grin.

"Yes, it has. You look good, both of you look good." I stepped back so they could enter the gate into the front yard where Gunner waited patiently for me on the cool grass near the brick path.

I grabbed Maggie by the collar and lead her into the yard, latching the gate behind me. "Gram is up at the house making lunch," I waved my free hand toward the house.

I guided Maggie over to Gunner so I could introduce them as Maddie and Gina headed for the house to help Gram finish cooking lunch. I knew Gunner would behave perfectly as he'd been trained, but I wasn't sure about Maggie. I needn't have worried. She did fine. I let them sniff each other for a few minutes and gave them a few basic commands so they could get used to one another and to make sure Maggie knew who was in charge, then bade them to follow me up to the house.

Ryker had taught me a lot about dog training and discipline in the short time we'd had together. Good thing too, since I wound up being the one to take care of Gunner. Gunner was a soldier dog. He loved training even with his bum leg, though he couldn't run like he used to or jump as high. But I knew without a doubt, that he'd protect me with his last breath if it came to it. And I knew he had arthritis in his old age, poor fella. Maybe Gram had a homemade tincture I could rub him down with later.

We had lunch out on the back patio in the shade under the canopy of the wisteria vine that was out of season, yet still thriving with its thick branches, heavy laden with green leaves. Gram's place was like a fairy garden with hidden treasures to be found around every corner and in every nook and cranny.

"So, Marek, what are your plans now that you're retired from the Air Force," Aunt Maddie asked, around a bite of fried chicken.

"Well, I'm still technically on terminal leave for the next sixty days. But after that, I was thinking about starting my own HVAC and Refrigeration business here in town maybe, or over in Lebanon," I answered her, taking a swig of Gram's homemade hard cider from last year's crop of apples.

"Oh, that's a great idea," Gina smiled. "You know my friend owns Dottie's restaurant over in Junction City. She's been complaining her ice machine quit working and she can't find anyone worth a crap to fix it."

"Tell her if she's interested, I could take a look at it— no charge. I could probably even fix it for nothing," I said, "No promises, though. I'd have to check it out first. I don't have all my tools here yet. Still waiting on the movers to arrive sometime this week."

My household goods had all been packed and shipped, courtesy of the Air Force. Gram said I could store most of it in the barn until I figured out where I wanted to live, though she offered for me to stay here as long as I wanted. The house had four bedrooms upstairs and a master suite for Gram downstairs. She used one of the rooms as her sewing room, which had been my old bedroom when I'd lived here before. She'd taken it over because the natural light from the windows was better in there for her to see now that her eyes were failing her. I'd been staying at the back of the house in Uncle Jared's and Uncle Jack's old bedroom, that was now a guest room.

Yesterday, Gram had suggested that I could remodel the five thousand square foot upper level of the barn, which included a hayloft, and I could then move in there if I wanted. I admit the offer was very tempting. Gram spared no expense when it came to upkeep on the house and the outbuildings. That barn was damn near in mint condition. It already had running water and plumbing. She'd turned it into a dance hall complete with kitchen and bar, a few years ago. Maddie and Gina had held their wedding reception there when Oregon legalized same-sex marriage a while back.

The more I thought about it, the more appealing it

became. Gram was getting up there in age and I could be here to help around the farm. Plus, I think she didn't want to admit how lonely she'd been up here all by herself since Gramps passed. I was her only grandchild. The Uncles had married, but neither had children and Aunt Maddie certainly had no children. My mother had only me and then the birth had been so difficult, she hadn't wanted any more children, which was a blessing, really.

"Mom, let Gina and I clean up. You sit here and relax a bit in the shade and catch up with Marek," Aunt Maddie had started clearing our lunch dishes and packing up what was left of the fried chicken, potato salad and the green salad I had made with vegetables from the garden earlier today.

"Thank you, Maddie," Gram got comfortable on the chaise lounge near the ten-person in-ground, swim spa she'd had installed with the inheritance money she'd gotten when her father passed away a few years before Gramps. Great-Grandpa had been at least a hundred and three when he died.

Gram had lowered the heat way down in summer so that she could 'swim' against the current without getting overheated. The spa acted like a Jacuzzi but could also be used as a small swimming pool. Back in her day, Gram had been quite the athletic swimmer and had even tried out for the Olympics but then she'd become pregnant with Uncle Jared and quit the swim team.

"You know, Marek, this will all be yours someday," she said quietly, closing her eyes as she turned her face up to the warm afternoon sun.

"What do you mean, Gram? What about your children, won't they object?"

"Nope. They all know. It's in my will. They don't want the hassle of the farm. They all have their own lives and property. You're more like a daughter to me anyway, since I practically raised you. And you're the only one who's ever shown any interest in farm work. This is your home as much as it is mine, so when I'm gone, I want you to have it all." She took a deep breath and let out a sleepy sigh. "As, for your mother, she hasn't had contact with any of us for years. She's been cut from the will. Last I heard, she'd been shacked up with some biker over in South Dakota."

I was so overwhelmed about inheriting the farm, I had no words. I guess I'd never really thought about what would become of the farm when Gram's time came. I'd never thought about Gram not being here. I felt tears sting the back of my eyes and I tried to cover a tell-tale sniff.

Gram cracked open one eye at me, "It's okay, you don't have to think about it for a while. I don't plan on 'buying the farm' anytime soon," she snorted at her own joke.

"Gram!" I burst out, barely hiding my own snort of laughter. "Don't joke like that! I don't even want to think about such a thing."

"Well, I ain't going to live forever. I'll be lucky to live as long as my Daddy did," she closed her eyes. "'Sides, you can't take it with you. Best to leave it to someone who'll care for it."

"Great-Grandpa lived a long time. If you're anything like him, you've still got lots of years left," I said, joining her near the pool.

My skin was still tan from the years I'd spent in Texas, but I knew the sun here in Oregon would disappear when the rains began next month so, I figured I better enjoy these weeks we had left before the long gray days became endless through the winter.

"Perhaps I will take you up on your offer to remodel the barn." I settled back in the lounge chair and closed my eyes as Gunner nuzzled my hand to get me to scratch behind his ears.

It was about time I put down roots somewhere. Sweet Home, Oregon was a good place for that, I thought, before drifting off for a short nap.

CHAPTER FOUR
Close Encounters
Winds of Change ~ Scorpions
MAREK

"I'll be back soon, Gram," I called. "You wanna go with me, Gunner?" I patted my hip for him to follow.

"Don't forget to pick up some of that lactose-free milk," Gram called after me as I shut the gate.

"Yes, ma'am! Text me if you think of anything else." I opened the driver's side door to my truck and helped Gunner hop up into the cab.

I hadn't changed my work clothes to go to the grocery store since I was coming right back to finish mowing the lawn. I was dirty and sweaty from riding the lawn tractor since sunrise. It was around eighty-six degrees and not a cloud in the sky by noon. I had on my old Air Force T-shirt with the logo on the back and a pair of cut-off digi camo pants leftover from my time in Afghanistan, and my old lineman boots from when I first enlisted back when we used to wear the black leather that had to be spit-shined nearly every day. I pulled out my loose ponytail and gathered up my long, sun-bleached, blonde hair into a messy bun. I hadn't bothered to put on makeup —what was the point? I looked a sight, but I didn't care. I wasn't trying to impress anyone.

I started the truck and slid my Ray-ban Wayfarer sunglasses onto the bridge of my nose. After waiting a minute, I backed out. I rolled the windows down so Gunner could hang his head out and catch the breeze. The wind picked up as we headed down Ridgeway Road. The town was about four miles away, down in the valley.

A few minutes later I pulled into a slot that had some shade in the parking lot of Safeway, one of two grocery stores in town. I left the windows all the way down for Gunner and poured a bottle of water in the metal bowl I kept in the truck for him. No one would dare mess with my truck with him pulling guard duty.

"Stay here, boy. I'll be back in a jiff," I climbed down out of the truck and headed into the store.

The air conditioning was bliss compared to outside on the hot blacktop parking lot. I pushed my sunglasses up on top of my head, grabbed one of the small hand carry baskets and pulled out my phone to read the list Gram texted me.

Provolone cheese
Salami – the good stuff
Red grapes – get the seedless if they have them
A bottle of Cab-Sauvignon
Vanilla ice cream – Tillamook is my favorite
And don't forget my lactose-free milk, thank you <3

I walked around the store looking for the items. It took less than five minutes. I made my way down the aisle where the cheese was located, which was the same aisle as the ice cream, probably the coolest place in the store. As I stood perusing the different brands of ice cream I heard laughter behind me as a couple of guys came down the aisle and stopped in front of the cheese, across the aisle about ten feet or so away. I glanced up for a split second to see that they were both dressed in dark blue uniforms with Sweet Home Fire emblazoned on the back of their shirts.

"So, Colt walks into the station the other day responding to that structural fire call, you remember that one over on the east side of town? Anyway, he'd just come from the gym still wearing his work-out clothes and Stephens says 'Hey chief, did someone order a Ken doll?' I about lost it!" he laughs.

The second guy busted out laughing, "We can't all be pretty like Colt!"

I felt a smile form on my lips as I turned my attention back to the task at hand. I quickly located the Tillamook ice cream Gram wanted and put it into my basket, then turned to leave.

"Hey! I heard that!"

A third guy came around the corner just as I headed out of the aisle and crashed into me. The impact of his body colliding with the basket caused the cheese, salami, and grapes to fly out onto the floor.

"Ooff! Excuse me, ma'am. I'm so sorry," he reached out to steady me. "Are you okay?"

As soon as his hands cupped my shoulders I felt a jolt. Startled, I looked up into gorgeous, hazel-green eyes staring back at me. I had to tilt my head way back to meet his gaze. He had to be over six-feet tall and somewhere between twenty-five to twenty-eight, I surmised. His dark hair was cut in a military style. It suited him perfectly. His biceps bulged from the short sleeves of his shirt and I couldn't help but notice his well-sculpted chest. Holy hotness! He was way better looking than a Ken doll. He was magnificent! And way too young for me! Wait, what? I hadn't so much as looked at another man since Ryker. I hadn't dated anyone since Ryker. Guilt washed over me immediately. What was I thinking?

We stood staring at each other to the point of awkwardness until one of the other guys broke the silence.

"Jeez, Colt, look where you're going, why don't cha?"

It took me a second or two to gather my composure before I took a step back from the one named Colt. "I'm fine," I said in my scratchy voice, my throat suddenly dry. His hands dropped to his sides, but I could still feel where they had gripped my shoulders. I broke eye contact first. Looking down at my stuff on the floor, I bent to gather it up at the same time Colt knelt to help me. We barely missed knocking our heads together which caused both of us to start laughing.

"Here, let me help you," he reached for the salami that had rolled away.

"Thank you," I put the cheese back in the basket and

stood up as he picked up the grapes.

"Oh, no. A few of these got smashed. Let me go get you some more," he turned to head toward the produce aisle taking the grapes with him.

"No, no, that's okay. It's only a few, no big deal. Besides, that was the last decent bag of red grapes. The rest are in worse shape than those," I smiled, holding out my hand for him to give me back the grapes.

He looked disappointed as he held out the grapes, "I'm so sorry. How can I make it up to you?" His gaze locked with mine as he waited for me to answer.

"Don't worry about it," I gave him a shy smile. "It's totally fine. I really have to go now. My dog is waiting for me." I took the grapes from him as I walked by, heading for the check-out line.

As I rounded the corner I overheard one of the guys whisper loudly, "Wow! She was fucking hot, dude. Why does pretty boy here, have all the luck?"

"Yeah, Ken doll here is so smooth crashing into the ladies," his partner chuckled.

"Will you two clowns shut up?" Colt's deep voice carried to my ears, sending tingles down my spine.

A few minutes later I walked out of the store with my stuff in two grocery bags. Gunner saw me coming and greeted me with a woof as if to say "it's about time."

"I know, buddy, I tried to hurry." I reached my truck and saw there was a big red truck parked on my driver's side with the Sweet Home Fire Department emblem down the side. Go figure.

As I climbed into the driver seat, I saw the three firemen exit the store heading my way. I hurried and put on my seatbelt and started the engine. It roared to life, but unfortunately, I had to let the diesel engine run a bit before I could just take off. Shifting into reverse, I had to wait as the three men walked behind my truck to get to theirs. Finally, I backed out cautiously, then shifted gears, easing out the clutch. I had to drive past the guys to exit the parking lot. Colt, the magnificent, saluted me as I drove past. I barely nodded and slid my sunglasses into place.

Suddenly, I had butterflies in my stomach. I couldn't get out of there fast enough. Something in the air had changed. I couldn't really put my finger on it, but somehow, I felt different. Perhaps, I was finally starting to move on after three long years of grieving for Ryker. The thought made me sad. A tear slipped out of the corner of my eye and slid down my cheek. I'll never forget you or stop loving you, Ryker, I thought, as I headed for home.

CHAPTER FIVE
Windswept
Drops of Jupiter ~ Train
COLT

"Don't look now, Ken, but there's your lady getting into that badass truck parked next to us," Derek said, elbowing me in the ribs.

"I wish she were my lady," I elbowed him back.

I casually let my eyes scan the parking lot and sure enough, there was the stunning blonde I'd crashed into and made a total fool of myself over, all in front of my two best friends, Derek and Terrence. My heart skipped a beat when she happened to notice us coming out of the store. She seemed to be in a hurry as she buckled her seatbelt. I caught myself straightening to my full height and puffing out my chest. Damn, I got it bad, I thought, as she backed out after we passed by the rear of her truck. As she pulled out of the parking lot, we made eye contact for half a second when she drove by, causing my pulse to jump up a notch. I saluted her before I could stop myself and that was when I saw the badass Malinois sitting in the front passenger seat and the Texas plates. I also took note of the Department of Defense decal affixed to the windshield on the lower driver's side corner, as she pulled out onto Hwy 20 heading west. The decal said it was for Joint Base San Antonio, Texas.

Was she just passing through? Of course, she wouldn't be from here. Maybe she was visiting someone here in town. I sure hoped it wasn't her boyfriend. Hell, I hoped she didn't have a boyfriend or significant other of any kind.

"Whew-wee! That is one fine female," Terrence watched the truck merge into the light, afternoon traffic.

I felt like kicking myself for not at least asking her name. I'd been so addle-brained the moment my hands landed on her shoulders, that I had forgotten my own name as I stared into the most incredible eyes I'd ever seen. I couldn't decide what color they were, somewhere between blue and violet, with thick long lashes. She hadn't been wearing anything on her face aside from the streak of dirt that shadowed her right cheekbone.

I'd been so taken back by her natural beauty, I was surprised I remembered how to put words into complete sentences. She was slender, not too tall and slightly muscular in all the right places with curves that would keep a man lying awake at night for hours thinking about her. If I had to describe her, I'd say she was a cross between those movie actresses, Margot Robbie and Charlize Theron. Yeah, she definitely had an edginess about her like Ms. Theron.

I felt disappointment as we climbed into the type six brush engine and headed back to the station. I'd most likely never see her again. I'll be damned, but I couldn't get that blonde out of my head. Couldn't stop replaying the encounter over and over, remembering my hands on her shoulders. The loose tendrils of long hair that had escaped her messy bun, had felt like silk brushing my knuckles as I steadied her after nearly knocking her down in the aisle.

Her odd attire coupled with the military decal, had me thinking she might be former military, like myself. I recognized the digi camo on her cut-offs. And those had definitely been older, military lineman boots she'd been wearing. I hadn't seen boots like those in quite a while. I'd served four years as a medic in the Army, right out of high school.

Upon my honorable discharge, I'd used the G.I. Bill to go to college and obtained my degree in Fire Science and then pursued a degree in the Paramedic Program at Chemeketa Community College up in Salem. I applied for a paramedic job in Sweet Home after finishing my internship with Chemeketa. With my military medic background, I had excelled quickly through the program, gaining the attention of my instructors, one of whom was old friends with the fire chief in Sweet Home. It got my foot in the door, so to speak. I'd bide my time until a full-time firefighter position opened up.

The drive back to the station took less than ten minutes. Once we got back, we brought in the groceries we'd picked up and headed toward the kitchen.

"Oh good, you're back," Chief Barlow looked up from watching TV. "What's for dinner?" he sat on the big brown leather sofa in our breakroom.

"Yeah, what's Ken making for dinner tonight?" Stephens chimed in.

I rolled my eyes at their harassment, "It's barely past lunch!" I slowed my pace and stopped near the couch, "But, I've got a special dish for you, Stephens." I wagged my brows at him and blew him a kiss.

Stephens flipped me the bird and turned back to the TV. The Mariners were playing.

I headed for the kitchen. When on duty, it was just expected that I am the resident cook since I owned and operated The Sugar City Saloon and Restaurant down on Main Street. The former Sweet Home Inn had been in foreclosure when I'd moved here. Sweet Home had a long history as a wild west, logging town filled with nothing but mountain men, cowboys, loggers and almost no women, other than the soiled doves that inhabited the brothels that lined Main Street. Thus, it had acquired the unofficial name, Sugar City, due to the high number of prostitutes and saloons.

Eventually, the town had become incorporated and the city board members had voted on a new name. In keeping with its somewhat seedy past, they elected to name the new city, Sweet Home, as in 'Home Sweet Home,' in hopes of drawing in a higher class of citizens to the area. The town was nestled in the valley along the Santiam River to the north and tucked into the foothills of the Cascade Range that ran north to south from Washington state as far south as California. Nowadays, it was referred to as the 'bedroom community' north of Eugene. It was situated inland about two hours from Newport, Oregon, and about eighty miles southeast of Portland, and ninety miles east of Bend.

According to city records, the Sweet Home Inn had been one of the few legitimate businesses back in the early days of the town and had never operated as a brothel. But, rumors abounded, to indicate otherwise. When I'd acquired it a few years ago, I remodeled it and changed the name. I had bought it with the insurance money I'd inherited when my dad had passed away. I'd had no idea he'd even had the life insurance policy, let alone, named me the sole beneficiary of five-hundred-thousand dollars upon his death. He'd passed away while I was in Afghanistan.

I barely made it home in time for the funeral and then had to report back for duty a week later. Dad had died of smoke inhalation trying to put out a fire at my grandparent's restaurant. The investigation had found the fire was caused by arson but no one was ever caught. There had been a string of fires that year, all set by an arsonist.

I'd grown up in the restaurant business that my grandparents had owned up in Spokane, Washington. I'd worked part-time after school and full-time in the summer ever since my mom had passed away from breast cancer when I was fifteen. I'd learned everything from cooking to bookkeeping, pretty much everything there is to know about running a family-owned restaurant and bar. My grandparents helped to raise me, especially after mom got sick and then after she'd passed. They'd assumed I'd be the one to take over when they retired. Things hadn't worked out that way and I ended up enlisting in the Army. I'd wanted to serve my country after my older cousin had been killed in Iraq serving in the Marines.

Funny how life turns out. I was now the sole proprietor of one of the most successful restaurants in town, a volunteer firefighter and part-time, sometimes full-time paramedic.

CHAPTER SIX
Every Time I Close My Eyes
Dark Paradise ~ Lana Del Rey
MAREK

After a dinner that consisted of Gram's homemade artisan bread, wine, cheese, salami and a salad made with everything in the garden, we sat out near the fire pit to watch the sunset. We didn't light a fire because we were still in a 'no burn' fire season, especially with the high temperatures of late. We sat near the pit in the middle of the front yard facing the west. This location on the property was closest to the highest point, which afforded the best view for watching the sunset over the mountains in the distance.

I'd showered before dinner and put on a thin, white summer dress that I wore as a nightgown, made of some sort of soft, crinkled fabric with a flowy skirt. My hair hung loosely in waves down my back. The air up at this elevation, cooled off quickly as the sun made its slow descent, sinking on the horizon, sliding down behind the mountain tops. It was a relief after the heat of the day. Despite using sunblock, I'd felt the sting of a fresh sunburn when I'd showered earlier.

I leaned back in the wooden outdoor chair as my thoughts drifted. I'd thought about the guy at Safeway who'd crashed into me earlier, at least a dozen times since getting home from the store. And each time it felt like a betrayal to the memory of Ryker. Even though he'd been gone for three years, I'd remained faithful. I still felt his presence all around me. I still talked to him in my head all the time. Many times, after he was gone, I'd caught myself reaching for my cell phone to call him on my way home from work to ask him what he'd like me to pick up for dinner.

It had gotten to the point that I'd had to sell the house back in San Antonio and moved into a rental because I couldn't bear to walk into the empty rooms of the three-bedroom ranch house anymore. Alone, it felt like the walls were closing in on me, even with Gunner by my side. Everywhere I looked, something triggered a memory of Ryker. His clothes still retained his scent after all this time. And every place I went in town or on base, reminded me of a time when we'd been there together, either during our marriage, or back when we'd first met and started dating. I stopped going to our favorite restaurants and hangouts.

I knew when I retired, I had to get the hell out of Texas as much as I loved it. It had been 'our' home, but without him, I couldn't bear to stay. It hurt too much. My therapist agreed that a change of scenery was what I needed to begin the process of moving on. A fresh start. And anyhow, Gram needed me here on the farm.

"What's on your mind, Marek?" Gram interrupted my thoughts. "You've been melancholy all afternoon and evening. Is something bothering you?" She set her empty wine glass on the wooden end table next to her Adirondack chair that she was sitting in.

I sat less than two feet away from her in an identical chair, swirling the remainder of the cab-sauvignon in my glass. I took a sip before answering, "I've been thinking of Ryker, is all." I let my gaze drop to my lap.

The delicate scent of late, summer roses filled the warm evening air, sweet, but not overbearing. It reminded me of our wedding. Damn, there I go again.

"Honey, I know you're still grieving." She reached out and patted my hand. "It takes time," she cleared her throat, "believe me I know. I still miss your Gramps every day. The first few years were the hardest. We'd been together nearly sixty years. Hell, I knew him better than I knew myself. But, that old saying about time healing all wounds is sort of true. Time does soften the sting, but you never truly forget. There's always an ache that never goes away. I cherish all the memories, some more than others, but after a while, it becomes bittersweet, I guess." She squeezed my fingers. "You'll move on in your own way and in your own time when you're ready."

"Thank you, Gram. You don't know how much I needed to hear that right now."

She let go of my hand as she stood and stretched, "I'm going to get that other bottle of pinot up at the house. You want anything?"

"Nope, I'm good," I smiled.

Later after we'd finished off the pinot, I put the chickens to bed and then helped clean up the dishes before we settled in for the night. The day had gone by quickly with the endless list of farm chores. I welcomed the exhaustion, hoping to get some sleep. But my brain wouldn't shut off once I laid my head down on the pillow with Gunner beside me in the big comfortable bed.

I kept seeing a pair of hazel-green eyes twinkling at me above a broad expanse of heavily muscled chest, every time I closed my eyes. I could not get that guy out of my mind. My body began to tingle at the memory of his strong, capable hands gripping my shoulders. To my chagrin, I began to imagine what it would be like to have his hands roaming my body. Before long, I drifted off to sleep, but it was Ryker who visited my dreams.

~*~

I awoke to the sound of Gunner barking furiously and pawing my chest. It was still dark out and at first, I couldn't remember where I was. I thought I was back in San Antonio in the old house I'd shared with Ryker. It took a minute before my groggy mind sorted it all out and I sat bolt upright, sensing danger. That's when I smelled the smoke drifting into my open bedroom window. Shit! Was the house on fire? No, I thought, the smoke was coming from outside.

I leaped from the bed and went to the window which faced the back of the property and the neighboring property. To my left was the fence line between Gram's property and the neighbor's driveway. There was a stand of tall pines on this side of the fence, less than fifty feet from the house and they were engulfed in flames. The flames reached twenty to thirty feet above the treetops. The noise was like the dull roar of a freight train in the distance. Holy Hell!

"Oh, God!" I shouted, turning toward the door. I grabbed my cell phone on the nightstand and ran down the hall toward the stairs, shouting, "Fire! Fire! Gram, wake up!" I dialed 911, putting it on speaker, as I tried not to fall down the stairs in my haste in the dark with the glare from the screen messing with my vision.

Gunner was hot on my heels still barking furiously when we burst into Gram's bedroom to the left at the bottom of the stairs. I found her sitting up in bed, rubbing her eyes. I could see the raging inferno outside her bedroom window which faced the fence line.

"What? What's all the commotion about?"

"Fire! Gram, the woods are on fire not fifty feet from the house!"

"Damn him! I told him not to burn those blackberry bushes until after fire season was over! That dumb son-of-a-bitch!" She swung her legs out of bed, slapping her bare feet to the floor.

"C'mon, Gram! Get up!" I went to help her stand, knowing she was stiff and having trouble moving with her old, achy bones. I wrapped my arm around her waist as I heard the call go through.

"911, what is your emergency?" The female operator's voice was crisp.

"Fire!" Gram and I both shouted at once.

"What is the address of the fire?"

I took over and continued to answer the dispatcher's questions as I helped Gram out of the house. Once I got her to a safe distance out on the south side of the house and the dogs in the outdoor kennel, I grabbed the hose on the north side of the house closest to the fire and started soaking everything, including the roof as stray embers floated through the air.

My heart was pounding in my chest as I watched as the fire roared through the trees, burning down the old growth oak with the tree house that my aunt and uncles had built when they were kids. I had played in that old tree house myself many summers in a row. The smoke was thick and black, drifting toward me. My eyes began to burn, but I kept spraying everything down even as I heard the sirens of the fire truck barreling up the road. Finally, they pulled into the long driveway and quickly got to work, first containing it, then eventually, putting out the fire.

The damage was extensive. Several trees and a thirty-foot section of neighbor's fence were gone. And of course, the oak tree with the treehouse was reduced to a pile of steaming, glowing embers. There was minor damage to the roof of Gram's house from stray sparks and floating embers. But luckily the firemen had acted quickly to put it out, so the damage was mostly superficial.

CHAPTER SEVEN
The World Comes Undone
The Start of Something Good ~ Daughtry
COLT

After the smoke cleared I saw the woman in a flowy, white dress, like a ghost flitting through the ruins left by the fire. Tears tracked through the soot on her face as she took in the damage. An older woman with long white hair walked by her side, openly sobbing as they made their way toward me and the chief.

"Ma'am, are you the one who called in the fire?" Barlow addressed the older lady. "I'm Chief Barlow, by the way."

"No, I did," the younger woman spoke up. It was the same woman I'd crashed into at the store earlier in the day. "Nice, to meet you, sir," she shook hands with him.

I couldn't help the jolt of elation that shot through me upon recognizing her. But then, I felt guilty because of the circumstances.

"Are you the owner of the property, ma'am?"

"I'm the owner," the older lady sniffed through her tears. "I told Greg not to burn those blackberry bushes till after fire season!" She waved her hand toward the neighbor's property and up in the direction that I assumed the neighbor's house must be. It wasn't visible from the intertwining driveway.

"You'll want to call your insurance company, ma'am. We will be citing him for negligence and fining him for illegal burning. You'll want to get a copy of the police report come Monday morning. You can hold him responsible for the damages. Your insurance agent will be able to walk you through the process of filing a claim." Barlow explained.

"Oh, I hadn't thought of that. He'll be pissed if I do that."

"I don't care if he is, Gram! He is responsible. I hate to

think what would've happened if Gunner hadn't woken me. We both could be dead right now. You see the roof?"

"I know, I know," the old lady shook her head. "Thank you for coming so quickly and getting it out." She addressed the chief. "I'll go down to the station and get the police report on Monday. Do I need to call the police?" she sounded worried.

"We've already let them know and an officer is up there talking to your neighbor, right now." Chief Barlow patted the older woman on the shoulder. "Glad everyone is okay. We're going to head out now. The O.D.F. guys are going to stay behind and finish mopping up just to be sure nothing sparks up again." He turned to head back to his truck, "Good night, ladies."

I couldn't just walk away without saying anything. "You be sure to call us if your insurance agent has any questions," I held out my hand to the blonde, "My name is Colton Emerson. I'm really sorry to meet you under these circumstances."

"Marek," the blonde held out her hand, her eyes sparked with recognition. "I think we met earlier, didn't we?" her voice had a low, sexy, Demi Moore-ish rasp.

"Yeah, at Safeway," I felt my face flush slightly at the memory. "I'm sorry about that too, by the way." I didn't want to let go of her hand but forced myself before it became awkward.

"This is my grandmother, Sophia." She turned toward the older lady who was now gazing at me with curiosity and something else I couldn't quite define.

"Nice to meet you, ma'am," I gently shook her hand, mindful of her gnarled, arthritic fingers.

"Likewise," she gave my hand a squeeze with her surprisingly strong grip. "Colton Emerson, you said?" She was sizing me up with her measured gaze.

"Yes, ma'am. My friends call me 'Colt.'" I let go of her hand, my gaze slid over Marek quickly before giving Sophia my full attention.

I could tell nothing got by this old bird. Her eyes were sharp and wise as she scanned me up and down. Oh shit, I thought, she's onto me! She totally knew I was into her granddaughter and I sure as hell hoped I'd passed the 'grandmother test.'

At last, she smiled, boosting my confidence, "Thank you, Colt. We sure appreciate you boys coming up here and taking care of us." She barely stifled a yawn, "This old lady needs to get back to bed before sunup. Good night," she turned toward the house, leaving Marek to stand in front of me by herself.

"I should try to go back to bed myself but I doubt I'll be able to sleep," she looked down at her bare feet shyly as she folded her arms across her chest. I could just make out her nipples in the dim moonlight through the thin material of her dress before she covered them.

I could hear the rest of my crew finishing up and knew I had to be on my way before they started calling for me to get my ass in gear.

"Again, I'm real sorry to have met you under these circumstances, ma'am," I started backing away. "I hope to see you around," with that, I gave her an abbreviated salute, touching my fingers to my helmet and headed toward the truck, feeling her eyes on my retreating back.

"Good night," she called after me, in that unintentionally, sexy voice of hers.

I was on top of the world as I climbed up into the fire engine. This woman was my destiny. I don't know how, but I knew without a doubt, my boring, neat and orderly world had just come undone. It just goes to show, in a moment, you never know who you might meet. And now I knew her name, Marek. It sent tingles down my spine just thinking it.

CHAPTER EIGHT
Young and Alive
Don't Let Me Be Lonely ~ The Band Perry
MAREK

"Hey, Marek!" My grandmother called to me, waving her sun hat trying to get my attention as I finished mowing down by the pond in the late afternoon sun.

I stopped the tractor and shut down the engine so I could hear her.

"What's up? Is everything alright?"

"Oh, yeah, it's fine. The insurance agent called me back," she walked toward me and lowered her voice, "she said the dumbass is going to have to pay —well, his insurance is, anyhow."

"Woohoo! That's great news, Gram," I climbed down from the big mower to hug her.

"It doesn't cover the sentimental value of the tree house," she sighed, "but it does cover the loss of all the trees at market value and the cost of the fence."

"I'm sorry about the tree house. I loved playing in that thing when I was little." It saddened me to no end that it was nothing but a memory.

I'd spent the last four days running the chainsaw, cutting down what was left of the burnt trees and cleaned up as much of the debris as I could with help from old man, Tate from down the road. Gram sometimes hired him for odd jobs around the property when she wasn't able to handle things by herself.

"Let's go out and celebrate tonight," Gram shrugged her shoulders as if she was shaking off her mood. "I know just the place. The drinks are great and the food is even better," her eyes sparkled with mischief.

"Oh really?" I laughed, "You lookin' to get lit tonight, Gram?" I teased.

"Nope, but you are," she grinned, "put on something pretty. Dinner is on me."

"Okay… I've got about a half hour left of mowing and then I'll get a shower." I climbed back on the mower as Gram turned to head back up to the house with a bit of a swagger.

She was up to something, I just wasn't sure what.

~*~

A little while later, I drove Gram into town in my big Dodge after we'd both showered and made sure the dogs were fed and watered before we left. Gunner and Maggie had free range in the fenced-in yard that surrounded the house. They made a good team pulling security detail and had become fast friends.

After my shower, I'd found a dress and my favorite pair of sandals I hadn't worn in years, in my household goods that had finally been delivered two days ago. The Mexican peasant style dress was a shade of light purple that set off my eyes, turning them more violet, than blue. I'd even applied a little eyeliner, mascara and lip gloss. The broomstick skirt of my dress billowed around my legs in the gentle autumn breeze as we climbed up the wide front porch of the Sugar City Saloon and Restaurant.

There were bright red and white geraniums with some kind of blue flowers in huge terracotta pots on either side of the double doors that led into the old-fashioned looking establishment. A large American flag hung from a pole in the front flower bed, planted with red, white and blue flowers. Very patriotic. The old wooden building had a fresh coat of white paint. It looked like an old Victorian, two-story, farmhouse with a wrap-around porch. It reminded me of a wedding cake with all the fancy, scrolled trim-work.

The place was already crowded even though they'd just opened and it was Wednesday night.

The sign said to seat yourself as we entered, but we didn't see any available tables, so Gram and I headed toward the large bar in the center. The bar was a gorgeous, giant slab of redwood, with a polyurethane, mirror finish.

It was L-shaped, extending into the dining room on one side and the 'bar only' side where pool tables had been set up. This side also had a stage and dance floor area and tables around the perimeter. The sign above the archway indicated it was for over twenty-one patrons only. There were two bartenders working to keep up with the crowd.

Gram and I found two barstools open and claimed them before someone else did.

"Hello, ladies," the older woman behind the bar turned to greet us. "What can I get you tonight?" She gave us a friendly smile and handed us the drink menu. "Can I interest you in dinner tonight, or are we just doin' drinks?"

"We'll look at the dinner menu, please," Gram piped up, "and I'll have a virgin Piña Colada. My granddaughter here will have a Moscow Mule." Gram elbowed me, giving me a wink. "I'm driving."

"Oh really?" I rose my eyebrows at Gram. "Are you sure you can handle my big ol' Cowboy Cadillac well enough to get us home?"

"You bet your sweet ass I can, girl! I've driven trucks bigger than that in my day," Gram set her pocket-book on the bar.

"Alright, I'll get those drinks started, but I'll need to see some I.D. first," the bartender looked at me as she handed us the dinner menus.

I laughed, "For real?" I reached for my purse, thinking she was joking. "That's the best compliment I've had in a long time."

I showed her my I.D. and when she handed it back to me, the other bartender came up to inform her the ice machine had quit working again.

"There's enough ice to get us through the dinner rush, maybe, but somebody is going to need to call Colt," the second bartender said. He was tall and young looking and vaguely familiar.

Speaking of familiar, there was that name, 'Colt,' again. For the past few days, I hadn't been able to stop thinking about the firefighter, Colt Emerson, from the other night. What would be the chances it could be the same guy? I gave Gram a sidelong glance and noticed the smirk on her face.

Yep, she was definitely up to something and now I had a pretty good idea what that was. She was trying to find me some work to help me get my business started. At least, that was what I'd thought at the time, as I perused the menu.

"Everything is good here, so get whatever you want," Gram was looking at her own menu. "I usually get the Brisket Mac and Cheese with the coleslaw and sweet potato fries on the side," she said, as the male bartender set our drinks before us. "Thanks," Gram took a sip of her drink right away.

"Oh, that sounds yummy! I wonder if their brisket is as good as it was in Texas, though?" I scanned the menu again to be sure that's what I wanted.

"I can assure you, ma'am, it is every bit as good as Texas-style brisket. I'm originally from Texas and Colt's brisket tastes just like home," the familiar looking bartender smiled and then I suddenly remembered where I'd seen him before —Safeway.

He'd been one of the firemen with Colt the other day at the store. He must've noticed the look of recognition on my face because he reached his hand across the bar toward me.

"I'm Terrence, by the way. You're the lady Colt crashed into at Safeway, right?"

"Um, yeah," I responded, shaking his hand. "I'm Marek. Nice to meet you."

"The pleasure is all mine, ma'am," a grin spread across his face, crinkling his blue eyes at the corners. He couldn't be more than twenty-five and he was openly flirting.

Once he walked off to tend to another customer, Gram whispered, "You got it going on, girl. First, you get I.D.'ed and then you got that young pup there, practically drooling." She chuckled.

"More like, they all need glasses in this town," I took a sip of my Moscow Mule, which was delicious, by the way, "and he was not drooling... okay, maybe flirting a little," I admitted, "but he is way too young, Gram."

"He's over eighteen and that's all that counts. Age is just a number, anyway," she laughed, "I still feel seventeen, inside!" She took another swig of her non-alcoholic beverage.

"Gram! You dirty bird!" I let loose with a deep belly laugh, forgetting we were in public.

"Well, hello again!" That voice resonated right through me, sending tingles throughout my entire body. I didn't have to turn around to know it was him. Someone must have called him about the ice machine.

Gram turned at the greeting, "Hi there, young man. Nice place you got here."

"Why, thank you. How are your drinks?"

"Mine's great! How's yours, Marek?" Gram was over-exaggerating the cheerfulness, in my opinion, which further clued me in that she was up to something.

"It's very good, actually," I finally turned toward mister magnificent and immediately wished I hadn't or at least wished I'd taken another moment to prepare myself to gaze upon that much hotness in all its glory.

Holy hell! He was dressed in tight wranglers that emphasized his bulging quads, narrow hips, and tapered waist. My heart jumped in my chest, causing me to catch my breath. I forced myself to drag my eyes upward to meet his gaze. The moss green button-down shirt he was wearing brought out the green in his gorgeous, hazel eyes. I took in his square jaw, high cheekbones and the slight dimple at the corner of his sexy, full lips. The cuffs of his sleeves were rolled up as if he were ready to work. I took note of the fact that he wasn't wearing a wedding band or jewelry of any kind other than the Swiss Army watch on his left wrist. My cheeks flushed when he held my gaze.

There was an unmistakable twinkle in his eyes.

"You let me know if you need anything else," Colt walked around the bar over to the ice machine in the corner. "I'll be over here trying to fix this thing." He smiled as he reached under the bar and brought out a small toolbox.

Gram nudged me with her foot, giving me a none-too-subtle look with a slight head tilt in his direction. I tried to ignore her and turned my attention to my drink. Unfortunately, she wasn't going to let it go.

"My granddaughter is a refrigeration engineer. I betcha she could have that thing fixed in a jiff. Isn't that right, Marek?"

"Gram! I'm sure he knows what he's doing," I shook my head, feeling embarrassed.

"Actually, I don't!" Colt laughed, setting down the toolbox. "I fired the guy who's been working on it. Turns out he's been nickel and diming me ever since I opened the place. I can do the upkeep and maintenance on it, but I don't know what's wrong with it when it breaks down." He gave me a sheepish grin.

It was too much. He was irresistible and I caved, "I guess I could look at it for you if you want," I gave him a shy smile. "No charge. And I can't guarantee anything. I've only got a few tools out in my truck," I nodded my head toward the parking lot.

"If you could look at it tonight before the band gets here, I'd sure appreciate it, but I don't want to impose," Colt walked behind the bar to where Gram and I sat.

"You have a band on a Wednesday night?" Gram asked.

"Not usually, but a local kid asked if he could play with his band tonight, sort of like an audition to see how the crowd reacts and if he does well I told him I'd give him a chance on a weekend."

"Oh, that was nice of you," I said.

"I like helping out the locals and he seems like a pretty

good kid. His dad is a pastor at one of the churches here in town and he already has a bit of a following."

Before I could reply, Terrence returned to take our dinner order.

"What are we having tonight, ladies?" He gave us both a broad smile.

"Their dinner is on the house," Colt interrupted before we could respond. "That's the least I can do if you're willing to look at the ice machine."

"You don't have to do that," I said. "I'd be happy to look at it for you. I can even do it now while we wait for our food if you want." I was pretty sure it was something simple.

"No, no, it can wait till after dinner." Colt put his hands up, "Anything you want is on the house tonight."

"Well, if you insist," I gave him a shy smile.

"Absolutely! Now if you'll please excuse me, I've got to check on the kitchen staff. Terrence will take your orders now." With that, he stepped back and went through the double swinging doors that led into the kitchen just to the right of the bar.

"Okay, ladies, what can I get you?" Terrence held a notepad and took a pencil from behind his ear.

Gram and I both ordered the Brisket Mac and Cheese with Sweet Potato Fries to share since the portions were huge, and we split a Thai salad with peanut dressing.

"I'll get this going for you." Terrence smiled as he headed for the kitchen.

"Nice place," I nodded and let my gaze roam around the bar and seating area. "Looks like business is doing pretty well." I scanned the room noticing the place was even more packed than when we'd arrived. The over twenty-one side didn't have any open seat left as someone started setting up onstage.

"It's become more and more popular with the locals and now we even get the folks from Brownsville, Lebanon and as far away as Eugene and Albany. Most of the out-oftowners who come to the lake on the weekends make it a point to stop in here either on Friday night or Sunday, before heading home." Gram took another sip of her drink.

"I remember this place was all boarded up when I was a kid. We used to think it was haunted, so we crossed the street to avoid walking by it." I paused to take a sip of my Moscow Mule, which was very refreshing after the heat of the day. "I'm glad someone finally did something with the old place. It really is beautiful in here."

"Yeah, Colt did a good job. I didn't realize he was a firefighter till the other night when he showed up at the house."

Just then, Terrence brought our salad and an extra plate, "Here ya go, ladies." He set it down between us. "How are we on drinks? Can I get you a refill?" I could hear just a touch of a Texas drawl in his voice.

"I'm good, thanks," Gram spoke up, already reaching for the salad.

"I'm fine, just some water, please?" I asked. I still had about half of my drink left.

"You got it." He topped off our waters and moved away to help the next customer in line for drinks.

Gram and I dug into the salad as we continued with small talk for the next few minutes. For some reason, we both seemed to skirt around anymore talk of the fire. We were more than halfway through our salad when Colt brought us our dinner himself.

"Here we are. Be careful—hot plates," he set the bubbling Mac and Cheese layered with BBQ Brisket and a large plate heaping with Sweet Potato Fries down in front of us. "Let me know if I can bring you anything else." He smiled, causing his irresistible dimple to make an appearance. Lord, the man could melt butter with that smile.

"Thank you," I said, inhaling, "it smells and looks divine!" I adjusted my napkin on my lap, feeling self-conscious with Colt's eyes on me.

Damn it, but if he didn't make me feel sixteen again. Did my heart really just flutter in my chest?

"Okay then, enjoy your dinner." He headed back to the kitchen and I caught myself checking out his shapely rear end, exquisitely delineated in his tight-fitting jeans.

I quickly averted my eyes before Gram caught me. I took a bite of the piping hot macaroni covered in creamy, cheesy, cheddar sauce and closed my eyes, savoring the flavor. "Oh. My. Gosh. This is divine!" I said around a mouthful of yumminess.

"Told ya! It's my favorite!" Gram laughed as she scooped up a huge bite and shoved it into her mouth.

"Sorry, Gram, but this is even better than yours and yours is the best... or it was the best I've ever had. Wow, just wow." I swallowed and took a bite of the brisket and once again, closed my eyes. It was so delicious. Terrence was right —it did taste just like Texas-style brisket, maybe even better.

To say we devoured our meal, would be an understatement —more like, inhaled. There wasn't a crumb left between us. Afterward, Gram leaned back on her seat and rubbed her belly.

"Whew! That was so damn good. Too bad I don't have room for dessert. They make a mean apple pie." She grinned.

"Really? I thought you didn't like anyone else's pie but your own." I grinned back, my left eyebrow cocked upwards in question.

"I don't, but theirs is pretty good, I have to say." She leaned her elbows on the bar after sliding her empty plate away.

"That's a hell of a compliment coming from you, Gram. I just may have to try this apple pie you speak of, but I think I'll order it to go. I don't have room left for another thing." I slid off the barstool and stretched. My shoulders and low back ached from riding the tractor all day.

"I'm going to get my tools from the truck," I headed toward the exit. Out of the corner of my eye, I caught a glimpse of Colt coming from the kitchen and suddenly I felt young and alive, ready for anything. I even had a little spring in my step.

For the first time in a long time, I let myself feel optimistic about the future. I was looking forward to my new life in my old hometown. And who knows, maybe I would even start dating. I'd been alone for a long while now and I was tired of feeling lonely.

CHAPTER NINE
Sparks Fly
I Don't Want This Night To End ~ Luke Bryan
COLT

"Well, here's your problem right there," Marek said, pointing to the crimped copper water line. "It can happen sometimes when moving stuff around but this looks deliberate —see the teeth marks? Those are made by channel locks." She tapped the line where it was damaged.

"I knew it! Son of a—" I stopped myself from cussing in front of her. "I had a feeling he was screwing me over. Can you fix it?" I looked into her eyes when she turned her head toward me just inches from my own and waited for her reply.

She was the most beautiful thing I'd ever seen. Her hair was like silk glinting in the bar lights and she'd worn a little make-up which enhanced her natural beauty. I loved that she'd only applied a clear gloss to her full, pouty lips. For a second, I imagined what it would be like to put my mouth over those luscious lips. She was sexy as hell without even trying.

We were jammed into tight quarters between the back of the ice machine, the wall, and the bar. The light scent of her perfume filled my nostrils, wreaking havoc on my senses as I stood behind her. I had to tear my eyes from hers to look over her shoulder at the water lines coming out of the wall, which then ran into the back of the machine.

Earlier, after taking off the front panel, she'd determined from the indicator lights that there was a problem with the water flow, which I had figured out on my own. But the code had also indicated a high discharge pressure. I wasn't a technician, so I had no clue how to proceed. At that point, she said she needed to check the water line. I'd helped Marek pull the big, bulky machine out from the wall so she could check the lines.

"It's an easy fix, actually. I'll have to cut a three-inch section out here," the sound of her voice brought my attention back into focus as she placed her thumb and index finger on the copper pipe above and below the damaged section, "so you'll have to shut the water off to the line. I have some compression couplings in my toolbox on the truck and I just happen to have some three-eighths-inch copper tubing." She turned her head away from me as she explained.

She was close enough, that if I leaned down any further I could have kissed her bare shoulder. And man-oh-man did I so want to! She was wearing an off the shoulder dress in a lovely shade of purple that only enhanced the color of her eyes. With her blonde hair and tanned skin, she was a stunner! She was easily the most beautiful woman in the place. Hell, in the entire town, as far as I was concerned. I was so attracted to her for obvious reasons, but more than that, I felt drawn to her like a moth to a flame. My stomach was doing flips just being near her. She made me feel like a punk kid in high school with his first crush.

"Um, I'll need to go get a few more tools and things from my truck," she interrupted my thoughts again, looking up at me expectantly, "that is if you still want me to fix it?"

Oops, I'd lost focus again.

"Uh, yeah," I recovered, backing up to let her pass as she turned toward me, the skirt of her dress brushed against my jeans as she eased by. I cleared my throat, "Yes, I would sure appreciate it, thank you." Did my voice really just squeak at the end? Dammit! I tried clearing my throat again. "Let me know if there's anything you need or if I can help." I watched her head toward the exit to retrieve the items she needed from her truck.

"Just shut off the water, please," she called over her shoulder. Her hips swayed naturally, enticingly. I found I couldn't take my eyes off her until she'd disappeared through the front door.

Shaking my head to clear it, I looked up to see her grandmother eye-balling me with a lopsided smirk. I turned to shut off the water line as my face heated up with embarrassment at having been caught by old eagle eyes. She'd been watching me, watch her granddaughter. Son of a bitch! I'd have to watch my step if I wanted to stay in grandma's good graces.

Now that I thought about it, I knew I'd seen her before the night of the fire up at her place. In fact, right here in the restaurant a few months back. She'd come in a couple times with some of her friends for lunch and one time when we'd had a local band play in the bar on a Friday night.

I recalled thinking they were a fun bunch of elderly ladies, dancing and singing along with the band most of the night.

"I thought you looked familiar the other night when you showed up with the fire department at my place," Marek's grandma said as I grabbed a bar rag and wiped down the bar. "I didn't realize you were a firefighter besides being the owner of this fine establishment." Her smile transformed her face. There was a definite family resemblance between Marek and her grandmother.

"Yes, ma'am. I've been here about three years now, here in the restaurant and with the fire department. Can I get you anything else?" I nodded toward her empty glass.

"Just more water, please," she slid her glass over to me, "You single?"

I looked her in the eye, "Yes ma'am, as a matter of fact, I am." I refilled her glass.

"Good! You should ask my granddaughter out," she grinned.

I chuckled, surprised at her boldness, "Ma'am, yes ma'am," I dropped the bar rag and mock saluted her just as Marek came back in.

"I'll bet money you were once in the military. Am I right?" Sophia didn't skip a beat.

Marek walked around the bar with her tools toward the ice machine. I stepped back as far as space would allow to let her pass in front of me.

"Yes ma'am, I was." I didn't elaborate.

I began clearing the dirty glasses left on the bar from the previous patrons and started rinsing and stacking them in the mini dishwasher nearby.

"I thought so," she continued. "What branch and what did you do in the service?" Her sharp eyes pinned me.

"Army," I paused. I didn't enjoy talking about my time in service. "I was a combat medic," I said reluctantly.

"Thank you for your service, young man," Sophia reached her hand across the bar toward me.

I shook her hand, feeling uncomfortable, "No thanks necessary. It was my honor to serve."

"Yes, thank you for your service," Marek gave me a nod, tools in hand ready to start repairing the copper line.

"Marek was in the Air Force," Sophia continued. "I'll bet you two have lots in common."

Marek gave her grandmother a sharp look before turning her attention back to the copper line she was cutting. "Big difference between a medic and a Reefer Tech, Gram."

"I know, girl. But you were both military so I'm sure you can relate." Gram was undeterred. "Marek was deployed for a while over in Afghanistan."

"Thank you for your service," I said, giving her a nod. I'd been right about her from that very first encounter when I'd suspected she was military.

"No thanks required. Like you said, it was an honor to serve," Marek kept her attention on the task at hand.

She seemed as reluctant as I was to talk about her time in service, so I let it drop and went back to clearing and rinsing bar glasses.

"Aaaaarrrrhhh," Sophia let out a long drawn out exaggerated yawn. "I'm tired. Farm work kicks my behind." She stretched her arms overhead, then rested her elbows on the bar. "How much longer will you be, Marek?"

"Should only take me fifteen minutes or so to repair the line, but then I have to sit through an ice harvest or two to make sure it's working properly and that could take another hour or so depending on what else may be going on with it." Marek didn't take her eyes off her work.

"That long, huh?" She yawned again.

"I could take you home and come back, Gram," Marek was almost finished cutting through the pipe.

"Or I could give you ride home," I offered.

"Yes! That's an excellent idea. I'll drive your truck home and Colton here, can give you a ride home later when you're done," Sophia said, grabbing Marek's keys off the ring attached to her purse sitting on the bar.

Marek and I both turned to look at Sophia, "Uh, yeah, or I could give Marek a ride home later." I put my hands on my hips, turning my gaze back and forth between them wondering what just happened. Pretty sure Sophia had just maneuvered the whole thing deliberately.

Before Marek had a chance to reply, Sophia slid off her bar stool and waved goodbye, "I won't wait up. Thanks for dinner, Colton." With that, she was out the door in a flash. Considering her age, she moved pretty quick.

The freshly cut three-inch piece of copper line dropped to the floor with a clink and rolled toward me.

"I'm sorry about that —" Marek started.

"No, it's the least I can do," I interrupted. "I appreciate you fixing this beast for me. I'd be happy to drive you home." I gave her a shy smile, but inside I was grinning from ear-to-ear thanking my lucky stars for this unexpected turn of events.

"Hey boss, we're ready to start." Spencer leaned across the bar from the other end. "Band is all set up but we don't seem to have power."

"Okay man, I'll be right there," I turned back to Marek, "Please excuse me for a moment." I gave her an apologetic grin and followed Spencer to the stage to see what was going on with the power.

Fifteen minutes and one blown fuse later, I returned to the bar to find Marek had completed the repair job on the line with brand new compression fittings. She was reprogramming the machine as I approached.

"Wow, you weren't kidding when you said it wouldn't take long," I barely hid my disappointment that our time together was ticking by way too fast for my liking.

She turned, giving me a smile that made my heart skip a beat. "Yes, but now we play the waiting game. I needed to reset the machine," she pointed at the panel on the front of the ice machine. "And now I'll have to wait for it to go through a harvest, possibly two to be sure it's working properly."

"Hurry up and wait," I chuckled. "Been there, done that—Go Army! Can I get you another drink while we wait?" I grinned back at her, excited that she'd be here for a little while longer.

"Oohrah!" She said enthusiastically. "I'll just have a seat if you don't mind."

As she squeezed past me to make her way around to the other side of the bar, her elbow brushed my forearm causing a zing of electricity to spark between us. We both jumped at the contact.

"Sorry," we both said at the same time.

"It must be my electric personality," she joked.

"It definitely is," I trailed off.

We locked eyes for just a moment before she continued around the bar and found her seat again. But at that moment, something passed between us. There was a definite connection and suddenly I didn't want this night to end.

CHAPTER TEN
Turning Point
Think A Little Less ~ Michael Ray
MAREK

The band was really quite good I thought, as my foot bounced in time with the music. I knew I shouldn't have had that second Moscow Mule, but it was too late, I was feeling it already. My lips were numb even as they curved into a smile. I sat waiting for the ice machine to do its thing when Colt asked me to dance. I'd said yes maybe a little too eagerly. I could blame it on the alcohol, but if I was being honest, I knew better. I'd been secretly wondering what it would feel like to be held in his strong arms as I watched him wait on customers not five feet away.

When there was a slight lull in the lines at the bar, Colt told Terrence to takeover. He was so damn gorgeous sauntering toward me with those deep, hazel eyes, square jaw, and those sexy as sin lips pulled into a smile giving me a glimpse of his perfect white teeth. For the first time in years, I was actually fantasizing about kissing another man other than Ryker. Not just any man, but this man who stood before me. I could not deny the mutual attraction between us. I could see it plain as day on his handsome face. He wanted me.

God, it had been so long since I'd felt a man's touch. I couldn't fight this longing that was quickly turning into a deep ache in the pit of my stomach and inflaming the lower regions of my body. Ever since that first encounter with Colt a mere few days ago, I hadn't been able to get him off my mind. My growing attraction to him took my breath away and made me feel guilty at the same time even as I thought about my late husband. I missed him so much. Still, I had slid off that bar stool and followed Colt willingly to the dance floor.

I'm still alive and human, I told myself, trying to

absolve my guilt for wanting to be with Colt.

Out on the dance floor, Colt expertly twirled me into his arms as the band played Sippin' on Fire by Florida Georgia Line. And boy, did I feel like I'd been sipping on fire when his arms went around me for a brief second each time he pulled me into his body, then spun me out in a circle again. I loved the feel of the calluses on his hands as he held mine. I loved how he sang along with the band as if he was singing directly to me, without ever missing a step. The richness of his voice resonated through my body and gave me goosebumps.

I hadn't danced in a very long time so I was surprised at how well I'd kept up. I tried to attribute the fluidity with which I moved in his arms, to the two drinks I'd consumed earlier. But I had to admit it was Colt himself, that had made me feel light on my feet, almost weightless.

The next song the band played was a slow number, Think A Little Less by Michael Ray. I found myself melting into Colt's arms when he whispered the lyrics in my ear, something about thinking less and kissing more. My head dropped to his chest as he waltzed me around the dance floor. It felt natural and for a while I did think less, enjoying the respite from all my thoughts. I breathed in his scent, like mountain air in the early morning and freshly laundered clothes drying in the sunlight. I wanted this moment to last forever, wrapped in his strong embrace. We moved as one, gliding across the dance floor as if we'd been dancing together forever. Our movements were totally in sync with each other and the music as if our bodies communicated on some other plane of existence. I'd never danced so well with someone before, not even Ryker.

The song came to an end way too soon and I reluctantly moved to step out of Colt's arms but he held me for a moment longer, his eyes locked with mine, my chin tilted up. My lips were inches from his and for just a moment I thought he might kiss me, but then he smiled and let me go.

"Thanks for that," he stepped back. "I haven't danced with anyone in a long time." His hands dropped to his sides. "You're really good."

"Thank you, so are you," I ducked my head, shyly. "I really enjoyed it." Before things got awkward I turned to head back to the bar. "I should probably check on the ice machine."

"Yeah," he followed behind me. "I should help the bar staff out now that there's a line again," he laughed self-consciously. "My work is never done."

I checked the machine and was glad to see it was harvesting ice like it should be. I'd give it one more cycle then call it good. I packed up my tools, placing them neatly in my tool bag then turned to ask Colt for help pushing the ice machine back into place when someone in line let out a low whistle.

"Damn, Colt! Who's the new help?"

I ignored the owner of the voice and stood up straight, tossing my hair over my shoulder.

"Hey, Jack. What'll you have —the usual?" Colt's voice had an edge as he ignored Jack's question.

"Aren't you going to introduce me to the new barmaid?"

I glanced at the guy out of the corner of my eye. He looked to be in his late forties, early fifties.

"She's not a barmaid. She's a refrigeration engineer. So, what are you having?" I noticed he deliberately hadn't introduced him to me. Clearly, Colt didn't like this Jack person.

"Refrigeration engineer! Ain't that a man's job?" he sneered at me. "That's the problem with the world these days. A woman's place is in the kitchen," he paused to wave his hand in my direction, "or behind the bar serving drinks." He laughed, then slapped his hand down on the bar top.

"And that would explain why you're single... again,

Jack." Colt retorted. "Now, either order a drink or move on out. There are folks waiting behind you."

"Alright, alright," he held up his hands, "no need to be rude." He laughed as he pulled out his wallet. "I'll have a Ninkasi, or whatever you have on tap tonight."

I turned back to the ice machine and started scooting it back against the wall by myself.

"Hang on, Marek, I'll get that. Go ahead and have a seat. I'll be done here in a second." Colt poured Jack's beer and took his money.

"It's okay, I got it," I finished sliding the machine back into place.

I'd been dealing with assholes like Jack my whole life and especially throughout my Air Force career. It didn't faze me in the least. I didn't give two shits what the Jacks of the world thought about me. I didn't have a point to prove, either. I moved heavy equipment all the time in my line of work. Yes, there were a limited number of women in my career field but it was definitely not a man's world anymore.

I grabbed my tool bag and set it on the bar next to my purse before moving behind Colt as he helped the next customer in line. Jack had stepped back sipping his beer while staring at me as I made my way back around to my stool. The second I sat down he moved to stand next to me since there were no more seats open.

"Hey pretty lady," he sidled up to me a bit too close for comfort, "can I buy you a drink?" He leaned his elbow on the corner of the bar near me. "I'm Jack, by the way."

"No thanks," I refused to look at him, "I've had my limit." He could take my words however he liked. I didn't bother introducing myself. I figured he'd heard Colt call me by name just a few minutes earlier. The guy made my skin crawl. I'd hoped he'd get a clue and move on, but I was wrong.

"Well how about a dance, then?" He moved as if to grab my hand but I reached for my glass of water.

"No thank you," I replied, enunciating each word then took a sip of water.

"Just one dance won't kill you," he reached for my hand again, grabbing my wrist causing me to spill my water on my lap. His breath reeked of alcohol other than beer, which lead me to believe he'd imbibed elsewhere.

I narrowed my eyes at him, "Let go of my wrist if you plan on keeping yours, Jack," I said in the most menacing voice I could muster without losing my cool.

His eyes widened for a moment before he reluctantly let go of my wrist. I guessed he thought better than to press his luck with me. I can hold my own if necessary. Over the years, I'd taken some martial arts and women's self-defense classes when they'd been offered on base wherever I'd been stationed.

My gaze was unwavering as I stared Jack down, waiting for him to leave me alone. There were deep lines on his weather-beaten face as if he spent all his days in the sun or outdoors. His hair was streaked with grey at his temples and for the first time, I noticed the comb-over covering the bald spot on top of his head, which made him look even older than I initially suspected. Our gazes locked as we stared at each other for a couple seconds more before he blinked first.

"I was just being friendly, is all." He sneered, "Apparently, you think you're too good for folks around here, Miss refrigeration engineer!" His voice raised a few notches, "You can take your uppity attitude right the hell outta my town and go back to wherever you're from," his words slurred.

"Not that it's any of your business, Jack, but I'm from here." Normally, I don't feel the need to explain myself, but I was in a mood. "And you weren't being friendly at all. You are downright rude and pushy. And apparently so inebriated that you couldn't take a hint. I thought I'd made it pretty obvious that I'm not interested in making small talk, let alone dancing with the town drunk. Now, before you make an even bigger fool of yourself, I suggest you call it a night."

I was never one to mince words. It was then I realized that we had the attention of everyone at the bar, including Colt. Some of the people nearby started sniggering, not bothering to hide their amusement to Jack's obvious chagrin. His face turned beet red and he started sputtering unintelligibly.

After having come around the bar, Colt made his way toward us, "Jack, you heard the lady. It's time you called it a night. I should never have served you. I'll refund your money and call your brother to come pick you up." He put his hand on Jack's shoulder, taking the half-finished beer from his hand. "C'mon back to the kitchen and I'll get you a cup of coffee." He led Jack away, "Sorry about that. I'll be right back," he said over his shoulder before disappearing through the swinging doors that lead to the kitchen.

I grabbed my purse and headed to the ladies' room. Suddenly, I was tired and just wanted to go home. But the ice machine hadn't finished its cycle. I'd ask Colt to take me home as soon as the machine dropped another batch of ice in the bin.

I used the facilities, washed my hands and finger combed my hair then reapplied my lip gloss. I held my hands under the dryer then let the hot air blow dry my dress where Jack had caused me to spill my water. Then I found some mints in my purse and popped a couple in my mouth to rid it of the lingering taste of vodka, ginger, and lime before heading back to the bar.

I found I had butterflies in my stomach in anticipation of the ride home with Colt and wondered what that could possibly mean. Had I finally reached a turning point in my grief? Was I ready to start moving on?

CHAPTER ELEVEN
What if?
What Ifs ~ Kane Brown ft. Lauren Alaina
COLT

I helped Marek up into my brand new, Chevy Silverado 2500HD parked out back. My heart was racing at the prospect of being alone with her for a few minutes even if it was just to drive her home. I'd barely been able to hold back from kissing her right there on the dance floor in front of the crowded bar, earlier.

"There ya go," I handed her the seat belt, then shut the passenger door as she buckled up.

I climbed up into the driver's seat, put on my seat belt, then looked over at Marek as I started her up. The Duramax diesel engine roared to life.

"Nice truck," she grinned at me. "What color is it?" It was too dark outside for her to get a good look.

"It's Cajun red," I grinned back.

"I like it," she nodded and settled into her seat as I backed out of the parking space.

"That's right— you have a big ol' diesel Dodge if I remember correctly."

"My Cowboy Cadillac. Yeah, Gram drove it home tonight." She wrinkled her brow. "Pretty sure she maneuvered this whole setup." She turned in her seat toward me, "I hope you aren't mad—"

"Of course not! Driving you home is the least I can do. You got me out of a pickle with the ice machine tonight. By the way, did I say thank you for that?"

"Only like ten times, but that's okay. I was happy to help." She laughed. "And the food was so worth it!"

"Glad you enjoyed it."

We sat in silence for a few minutes as I drove through town heading west on Highway 20. After the stop-light, I made a right turn onto Pleasant Valley road. It was a dark and winding road that climbed in elevation the further we went. I kept my pace slow to avoid hitting a deer or some other wildlife. Once in a while, elk crossed the roadway up here. The scent of pine filled the cab of my truck through the open windows. The stars shined brighter up here away from the lights in town. A full moon glowed pale orange, lighting up the September sky, reminding me that summer was over in spite of the recent heat wave. Though the chill of fall hadn't quite reached us yet, it was considerably cooler here in the mountains compared to in town.

"Thanks again for the dance," her voice was barely above a whisper.

"It was my pleasure... trust me." My voice had become rough around the edges at the memory of holding her in my arms.

The drive out of town to her place took less than fifteen minutes, tops. All too soon we were pulling into the driveway. I stopped just in front of the electric gate.

"Oh, here, let me get the gate code," Marek unbuckled her seatbelt and opened the passenger door before I could get out to open it for her.

The headlights illuminated her form as she passed the front of my truck and for a moment I got a glimpse of her gorgeous figure before she punched in the code. I got out of the truck to walk her back to the passenger side and helped her back up to her seat as the gate opened.

"Just pull up there to the barn on the left," she said. "It'll be easier to turn around down here and I don't mind walking the rest of the way back up to the house. I need to go through some boxes in the barn anyway."

"You're going to go through boxes now?" I asked. "It's after midnight."

"I know, but I can't sleep." She brushed her hair back over her shoulder. "Hey, you wanna see the inside of the barn? It's pretty cool. I'm thinking of remodeling it and moving in here, now that I'm back for good."

"Back for good?" I asked, intrigued.

I parked the truck on the gravel drive directly in front

of the barn.

Yeah," she jumped down out of the truck, not waiting for me.

I shut down the engine, exited the truck and met her near some steps on the side of the barn. The motion lights came on and illuminated the door at the top of the steps.

"Now that I'm retired from the Air Force, I'm back here for good." She continued where she'd left off.

"So, this may be none of my business, but you look awfully young to be retired," I said, squinting at her in the semi-dark. Her face was in shadow with the motion light behind and above her. Even so, I had seen her in the bright light of day when I first met her and she had not looked a day over twenty-seven or eight.

She laughed, "Oh, honey! I'm thirty-eight." I watched as she climbed the steps. "Well, c'mon then," she looked down at me over her shoulder.

"Thirty-eight?" I followed after her. "And here I thought you were my age. But that's okay, I like older women."

"Ha! How old are you?" She'd reached the door and pulled the lever back so that it swung out toward her.

I had reached the top step and stood behind her grabbing the door as she entered the darkened barn. "I'm twenty-nine, but I hope that won't stop you from robbing the cradle." I chuckled.

"Robbing the cradle!" She scoffed. "Watch your step," she reached above her and pulled a cord attached to an overhead light, or rather a bare bulb hanging from the ceiling just inside the door. It illuminated a set of stairs that led up to the second story of the barn. "Follow me."

Once we reached the top, she flipped a series of switches on the wall. Mason jar lights hung from the rafters on long cords along with string lights wrapped around the exposed beams and support columns lighting up the entire structure. The cathedral ceilings were outlined in lights making the whole thing look like the inside of a church. It was gorgeous.

I stepped further into the large space that had to be over five thousand square feet. There was a bar with a tap system, refrigerator, and industrial-sized sink. On the wall behind the bar, there was a flat top griddle with a huge range hood and a wall mounted oven. The bar was to the left from the entry near the stairs and ran the length of the wall. Directly in front of me, another staircase led up to the large loft in the back half of the barn. I could see moving boxes stacked up there and assumed they belonged to Marek.

Toward the front of the barn, there was a twenty-four by twenty-four-foot dance floor centered between four support columns with cross beams above it. Giant, white Japanese lanterns hung down from the cross beams, softly illuminating the dance floor.

"Wow! This is truly impressive." I said in awe, lifting my hands, I spun around to encompass the entire space.

"Gram had it done a few years back for my aunt's wedding. I and my late husband came home on leave that year and helped make those mason jar lights. There's over two-hundred of them."

Marek walked over to the bar and reached under it to flip another switch, I assumed. The space was filled with the strains of a country music song as the sound system came on. I didn't miss the fact that she'd mentioned her 'late husband.' I'd had no idea she was a widow.

"You said, 'late husband.' I'm so sorry for your loss," I said solemnly as I walked toward her. "Was he military?"

"He was... but he'd been a private contractor working in Afghanistan when he was killed just over three years ago while providing security for some of our troops over there. I've never been able to find out the details of his death. The mission was top secret.

"He was a K-9 dog handler when he'd been in the Army. My dog, Gunner, was his bomb-sniffing dog." She looked down, smoothing the wrinkles out of the front of her dress with one hand, then looking back up at me she continued, "We'd only been married about two years and half that time we were separated by our deployments."

"I'm really sorry." My heart ached for her. I couldn't imagine what she must have gone through, never having been married myself. I reached the bar and put my hand over hers where it rested on top of the bar. I gently squeezed her fingers, "You don't have to talk about it if you don't want."

"Actually, you are the first person besides my grandmother, that I've talked to about Ryker. I hardly know you and yet it feels like I've always known you. Is that weird?"

"Not at all. Is it weird that I've been feeling a strong connection to you since the first time I laid eyes on you?"

"You have?" Her violet eyes locked on mine. "You know, I haven't been able to stop thinking about you. I've been feeling so guilty about it. Like I'm betraying Ryker in some way. And yet it feels like the universe put you in my path for a reason."

"I feel the same and I don't even know your last name." My thumb drew circles on the top of her hand.

"It's Dietz. Marek Rollins Dietz. My maiden name was Rollins."

The blood drained from my face and suddenly I felt faint. No, it was too weird. It couldn't be, could it?

"What is it? Are you okay?" Marek's voice was filled with concern.

"Ryker Dietz, K-9 dog handler in the Army?" I could barely get the words out. "Then he worked for a private contractor in Afghanistan?"

"Yes, why? What is it, Colt? Did you know him?"

"Not exactly, but I met him." I choked out. I had goosebumps and my skin was clammy. "A couple times, in fact." I couldn't believe this was happening. "I was a medic in the Army. I got out three years ago after my last deployment." I tried to pull myself together.

"You knew him!" The color drained from her face. "How?"

"Come sit down." I pulled a wobbly Marek from behind the bar and led her to one of the stools that lined the front of the bar. She sat, her eyes wide, staring up at me expectantly.

"I don't know if you really want to hear this, Marek." I cleared my throat. "I'd met Ryker once when we were both Army and then again when we were called to medivac out wounded troops along with some private contractors that had also been wounded while deep in enemy territory." I gave her a moment to absorb that.

"Oh, God! What do you know?" She grabbed my forearms as I sat down in front of her. "Tell me! I don't care how bad it is, I need to know!"

"I don't know anything about the mission they were on. All I know is that I was there with Ryker on the bird when he passed. He was so brave. He refused treatment until we had everyone taken care of and even then, he provided cover for us. I finally had to drag him into the helo as we were lifting off. He kept shooting bad guys on the ground even as he was bleeding out. By then it was too late to save him. He was mortally wounded. I held his hand until the end. All he talked about was you."

I'd never forgotten him, or any of the men I hadn't been able to save. But this guy stood out among all the others.

I can't believe I didn't make the connection when I first learned her name. But, how could I have? Marek wasn't a common name but, what were the chances I'd meet the wife of a man I'd met only twice, both times under horrendous circumstances, who then died in my arms— three years ago in a godforsaken land thousands of miles away?

Marek burst into tears, as she tried to stand but fell forward into my arms when her legs gave out. I held her close to my chest and let her cry as gut-wrenching sobs escaped her throat. I didn't care that her tears soaked the front of my shirt. When she calmed down a bit, I finished telling her what I knew, which wasn't much else.

"He said you were the love of his life and you gave him his greatest joy. He told me your name meant 'war' and then he said, 'how ironic is that? A gorgeous woman with a man's name that means war with the sweetest disposition of anyone I've ever met.' He said he had no regrets except the grief that this would cause you. Then he closed his eyes and faded away." My voice choked up at the end.

"He said all that?" She lifted her tear streaked face to meet my gaze.

"Yes, I've never forgotten it." I cleared my throat trying to loosen the lump that had formed, "Unfortunately, I've held the hands of dying men more times than I want to think about. But, Ryker stood out for me more than the others. Maybe it was because of his heroic actions all the way to the end or maybe it was your name. Or maybe, I was meant to meet you someday and tell you about his last words, I don't really know." My hand rubbed her back soothingly.

Her tears streamed silently down her cheeks as she placed both of her hands on either side of my face. "Thank you, Colt. You've no idea how much this means to me." She leaned up and kissed me on the cheek before sliding her arms around my neck, hugging me.

"You're welcome," I really didn't know what else to say. Hoping to convey what I was feeling, I simply hugged her back.

After a while, she unwound her arms from my neck and made as if to stand. I helped her to her feet. We stood facing each other for a moment, both of us at a loss as to how to proceed.

"If you're okay, I should probably head out now," I couldn't help the disappointment that seeped into my heart.

This was a woman that I could fall for, but now I didn't

know if there was even a glimmer of a chance. I was still extremely drawn to her, in fact, even more so.

"I'm okay. In a strange way, you gave me the closure that I needed." She reached up and touched my cheek. "What if it was the universe or what if it was Ryker himself, that made us cross paths? I don't know, but I do know that I'd like to get to know you better, Colton Emerson." She let her hand drop from my cheek back down to her side.

"I would like that, Marek. I would very much like that, indeed." Hope soared in my chest. Perhaps I had a chance, after all. I reached for her hand and brought it to my lips and gently kissed the back of her hand. "Good night ma'am." I reluctantly let go.

"Good night, sir." She smiled softly, "I'll come down tomorrow and check the ice machine again— just to be sure it's still working."

"I look forward to it," I smiled back at her before turning to head down the stairs and out to my truck.

Suddenly, I couldn't wait to find out what tomorrow would bring.

The End

CONNECT WITH E KAY SIMS!

Website
https://kaylene0069.wixsite.com/ekaysimsauthor

Facebook Page
https://www.facebook.com/AuthorEKaySims/

Reader Group
https://www.facebook.com/groups/
EKSpecialOpsReaderGroup/

Book Bub
https://www.bookbub.com/authors/e-kay-sims

SAVING SHAY

BY TIFFANI LYNN

This story is dedicated to my MRAU sisters; Fiona Tulle, E. Kay Sims, Tara L. Ames and CD Bradley. I've found each of you to be supportive, kind and generous within our group and out in the world. Thank you for all you do!

CHAPTER ONE

Shay

"Boom!" I can still hear her little voice in my ear, saying that word with all the theatrics of a six-year-old looking for attention. "Shay, did you see that? I nailed it!"

I wish I could turn back time and answer, "Yeah, Munchkin, I saw it. You did great!" Instead, I can only have the memories of that day, and today, instead of bringing me comfort, they are irritating me, making me feel uncomfortable in my own skin and in the quiet of my solitude.

Her voice rings out in my head again. "Come on, Shay! It's too hot to work on the garden. Let's go swimming!" I smile a little because she said that every day during summer break, and since it's hot enough to be considered summer I think I might listen.

I set the rake against the fence and lift the hem of my ill-fitting sundress to wipe the sweat off my brow. Then I turn and head for the creek. The crickets silence as I walk past them but start back up once I'm farther down the path. The squirrels and birds are noisier than usual for some reason and I hope they quiet down closer to the creek. Peace is harder to find today than most days and I need a few minutes of it. Mother's Day, Father's Day, all the birthdays, Christmas, Thanksgiving, and Fourth of July... They all suck. Unfortunately, today is Mother's Day and the ghosts seem to be close. Maybe it would be better if my family disappeared from memory. Of course, I'd be lonelier than I am now because my memories seem to keep me company as much as they haunt me, but it wouldn't be as painful.

I go right over to the big old oak that's been on the bank of the creek for as long as I can remember and strip down to my birthday suit, leaving my clothes folded neatly against the trunk. There hasn't been anyone other than me

135

on this land in the five years since my grandma died, so there's no need to wear anything. The sand on the creek bottom is soft as I wade out to the one spot deep enough to dunk under the cool water. Relishing the relief, it brings, I spend several minutes just floating and relaxing, trying to clear the thoughts of my sister, Morgan, and her sweet little-girl voice forever stuck at six.

With one last dip under the water I'm ready to get out and go back to work, but when I surface, the hair on the back of my neck stands on end. Something is off. I turn around in the waist-deep water, toward the path I used to get here, straining to hear if something sounds different, and just as I'm coming full circle I spot him. After a loud shriek, I drop back into the water and do my best to cover myself.

The man startles and steps back. "Holy shit!" he barks and turns around, away from me. His hands go up above his head like the police are commanding it. "I'm sorry. I didn't know anyone was here. I won't hurt you."

"You're trespassing!" I yell. My clothes are all the way over by his feet so I'm completely naked and vulnerable.

"Not really. Well kinda." He glances back at me until he catches my glare, and then he turns away again.

"This is my land and I'm the only one who lives here so there is no way you aren't trespassing."

"You're right. I own the land next door and we don't have creek access, so the family that used to live here would let me come through to use it. I haven't been here in years. I should have asked if it was still okay. I'm sorry."

"What land is yours?" I ask, not understanding. The people who owned the property next to us went to jail years ago and I assumed the state took possession of the property. There aren't any other plots close to here since our two farms took up all the nearby acreage.

He looks back to me again and I try to duck lower to hide. "Don't turn around!"

"Okay, how about you get dressed and then we can

talk. It's hard to concentrate with you naked only a few feet away."

"Well, that would be nice, but you're practically standing on my clothes!" I snip at him. I'm completely freaked that I'm naked and a strange man is only a few feet away. Who the hell is this guy?

It's not that I haven't seen anyone in the last five years. I have, but it's usually delivery people or the night clerks and stock guys at the grocery store. No one hangs out here and no one my age has been here since I was a kid. A few times as a teenager, but not since.

"I'm going to lower my hands and move forward a few feet to give you room. You can get dressed."

"How can I trust you?" I ask, my voice thick with suspicion.

"Well, you don't have to. I don't mind having this conversation with you naked." He kind of chuckles and glances back. I catch sight of a dimple before he turns back around, and that damn cheek indent rustles something deep in my memory, giving me the distinct impression, I know the owner of that dimple.

"You stay where you are. Don't turn around! I will freak out on you if you do," I boss him.

His hands go back in the air as his body shakes with humor. "Don't worry, I don't have a death wish so I'll keep staring at this nice oak tree over here." The little chuckle that follows irritates me. I'm naked and he's laughing.

I hurry out of the water, tug my clothes on uncomfortably over my wet skin, and squeeze the water out of my hair. I should have brought a towel.

"You can turn around," I tell him as I place my hands on my hips, annoyed by this whole thing.

His close-cropped, light brown hair is a little messy and damp with sweat. Little crinkles flank his brown eyes, giving the impression that he smiles a lot. This guy has shoulders so broad that they pull his T-shirt tight across his chest. His shorts hang low in the front and brown deck shoes cover his feet. I mean for my eyes to give him a quick once-over, but I must linger a little too long because when I turn my gaze back to his face his dimple is deeper, and his smile is wider than the one I saw a minute ago. My gut churns a little as my mind fights to reveal something buried within.

When our eyes lock for the first time, his smile falls and his Adam's apple bobs as he swallows hard. "Shay?" he whispers. Something about the way he says it makes my gut clench tighter. There's a familiarity in his voice that I can't place and it's unsettling.

"Shay Baird." He says it with a bit of reverence and the dimple returns. Damn, it's frustrating knowing I should know that dimple and not being able to place it.

He takes another step closer as his eyes scan me from head to toe, returning quickly to my eyes. I stay rooted to the spot as my brain sifts through hazy places, trying to locate the dimple.

"You don't know who I am, do you?"

I have no idea why, but words escape me, so I shake my head.

"Paxton Jones. Well, it's Pearsal now, but when you knew me it was Paxton Jones."

Now it's my turn to swallow hard. Memories break free of the haze and tumble through at warp speed.

Paxton and me.

Running through the cornfields with him on my heels-both of us laughing the whole time.

Paxton and me.

Swimming in the creek in the middle of the day when we were supposed to be working.

Paxton and me.

Picking blackberries from the bushes that stretch the entire length of the two-mile road that runs in front of our properties.

Paxton and me.

Sneaking out late at night so we could catch fireflies and put them in jars like lanterns.

Paxton and me.

Inseparable.

I had so many happy years with Paxton Jones until I made him go away. He was my best friend from the time we were about four years old until we were eleven years old. We did everything together. How did I not recognize him? Sure, it's been probably 15 or 16 years since I last saw him, but we were closer than close. I loved him in a way that only a young girl can love her best friend.

"Paxton." It's my turn to whisper.

His eyes soften and without another thought, I step into him, wrap my arms around his waist and bury my face against his chest. I've obviously stunned him because it takes him a second or two to wrap his arms around me in return.

I haven't touched another human being in five years and the sensation is both comforting and foreign. I didn't realize how much I've missed it until he squeezes me a little tighter and kisses the top of my hair.

"I thought you'd be long gone from here," he mumbles against my hair.

I shake my head but don't say anything. How do I elaborate on why I'm stuck in the same place that I was when he left when we were kids? I can't. Not without totally losing it, embarrassing myself and making him seriously uncomfortable.

"I didn't see anyone at your house. I thought maybe it was abandoned until I saw the rake by the fence and the back door open at your granny's. I just never dreamed it would be you here."

I redirect him. "Pearsal?"

"I was adopted by my foster family and I took their name. They were better to me than Brenda and Jared Jones ever were."

My heart warms briefly, knowing that the next stop for

him was better than what he had to live with next door. I worried about him for years when he was taken away.

"Oh. I'm glad." I glance down, thinking about his parents who should never have been parents in the first place.

He breaks my thought process when he asks, "Any chance I can get a glass of water from your place? It's hot and the well is broken over at the farm. That's why I headed toward your farm in the first place. When I didn't see anyone there, I figured I should get a drink from the creek for now."

"Oh, okay. Yes, of course."

I slip past him and head down the path toward the house, my dress sticking to my still-damp body in the most uncomfortable places. I can hear his footfalls behind me but he stays quiet. When I reach my parents' house, I veer right to my granny's old house. The thump of his feet stops and I turn back to see what he's doing. He's paused, looking between me and my parents' old house.

"I thought we were going to your house." His brows are drawn low over his eyes.

"We are. I live at my granny's old place."

He opens his mouth like he's about to say something, but he must think better of it because he closes it and nods before following me the rest of the way. When we reach the porch I gesture toward the rocking chairs on one side. "You can have a seat, and I'll get the water."

He nods but continues staring at me like he has some questions, ones I don't want to answer. I ignore the churn in my gut at the thought of discussing anything about me and go inside, allowing the old screen door to bang closed behind me. I get two glasses of ice water and return to the porch to find him rocking in the brown chair with his head resting against the back and his eyes closed. There's a thin line of sweat above his upper lip and more above his brows.

Paxton grew up to be handsome. He was a cute little kid, but I wasn't at an age to think of him in any sexual way. Well, not past having a first kiss. One of the last nights we snuck out to chase fireflies we ended up sitting by the creek. We were accustomed to talking about everything and I had seen a television show about a first kiss. After a few minutes of conversation about it, we decided to try it. Of course, it was just a peck on the lips, but neither of us could figure out what the fuss was about so we didn't bring it up again.

Now, Paxton's all man. The perfect variety I'm used to seeing on television. He's tall with broad shoulders, a trim waist, that deep dimple on one cheek, and long legs. There is one tooth, next to his eyetooth, that's a little crooked, but otherwise, he's movie star material, the kind you can look at all day and not want to blink.

I clear my throat, unsure of what to say. His eyes open and he reaches out toward the water in my hand. A slow, easy smile spreads on his face. "Thanks," he says as he takes it from me. A little shy still, my eyes flicker away and catch a glimpse of a tattoo that looks like it could be a skeletal frog peeking out of the shirtsleeve on his thick bicep.

Instead of walking over to the other rocker I stand there like an idiot and stare at him as he downs the whole glass in one long drink. His Adam's apple bobs as he swallows and I can't help but be mesmerized by it. When he finishes it off the ice clinks back in the glass and he gives me a sheepish look. "A little more, please?" The dimple is in full effect and I realize the potency of it. That one dimple is lethal.

I nod, take the glass to refill it and return. Once again I stand in front of him like an idiot as he drinks, not quite as aggressively as he did last time. When he lowers the glass, I ask, "More?"

"Nah," he replies, and the dimple comes to the forefront again. "Thank you though. I'm already feeling better. I'll have to go back to town and get a case of water to get me through for the next day or two until I can get someone out here to fix the well. The electricity is on to the property, but I can't stand to stay in the old house so I'm in a tent."

"A tent?"

"Yeah, the house is nasty inside, and besides, I don't have good memories of the place so I don't want to stay inside before I do a major overhaul. Brenda and Jared left the place a filthy mess before they were dragged off to prison. I doubt anyone has been in the place for at least 14 or 15 years. Unless you know any different."

"No, I don't think anyone went there after your parents were arrested. I don't remember much about that time period. Not many people come out this way though. Just the sheriff and some delivery people. I've got no-trespassing signs up all over and people already think I'm nuts, so no one usually bothers."

He stops rocking and leans forward, elbows to his knees, glass in hand, and looks closer at me. "Why are you out here alone? This place used to be full of your family. It was the happiest place I knew before I moved in with the Pearsals."

"I just like the quiet. My family has been gone for years." I stand, hoping to cut off the questions before they continue to a place I can't return to.

"You're welcome to go in and get more. There is a milk jug that's empty next to the sink if you want to fill it up for later. I need to get back to work on my garden. We're supposed to have rain in the next day or so and I need to be ready."

"Shay—"

"Hey, listen. It was good to see you. We can catch up another time, but like I said, I need to get back to work," I tell him as I back away, practically running for my life. I'm actually running for my sanity. I don't want to talk about the missing years from when he left up till now. That's why I go to the grocery store in the middle of the night and have anything else I may need delivered out here. I try never to run into people who might talk to me past casual conversation. A man like Paxton, from my past, is certain to ask questions I don't want to answer.

Without another glance, I hurry down the steps and out back, not realizing I carried my water with me until I reach the garden. I take a big gulp of the water and set the glass by the fence. Then I retrieve the rake and get back to work. Although I'm cooler than I was before I went for my swim, I'm not relaxed. It wasn't just the appearance of someone new on my property, but the fact that it was my old friend Paxton has unnerved me.

I can't even think about the hug I forced him into or the comfort I found at touching another human being after all this time. If I think about how handsome he's grown up to be I will only be more mortified. I just need to block today out of my head and go back to work. I wish it were that easy though. How do I forget strong arms surrounding me and holding me close or the natural scent of his skin mixed with his deodorant? My body tingles just thinking about how masculine and beautiful he is.

I haven't really had that feeling past the times I've seen handsome actors on television. I went on a few dates with a boy in high school and had some excited butterflies, but then I had a nervous breakdown and lost any hope of dating in this town again. I just assumed that I'd never have those feelings myself and that I'd die alone out here on this property.

CHAPTER TWO

Paxton

That was the strangest reunion I've ever had. I didn't expect to see her at all, much less naked in the creek like some version of Eve from the Garden of Eden. She was a cute little girl, but she has grown into a stunning woman. Of course, she's not the kind of pretty I'm used to seeing—the kind with perfect dyed hair, a ton of makeup and the latest clothing styles. Shay's auburn hair is long and probably hasn't been cut in years. Her face is fresh without makeup and by the look of the dress she tugged over her head, she hasn't been shopping recently. It was a little out of date and didn't fit her very well.

What is she doing living out here all alone, and where is her family? It seems wrong to have such a beautiful young woman living in virtual seclusion. The other strange thing about it all is that she's not living in her family home; she's living in her granny's home on the back of the property. Weird.

I spend the rest of the day trying to air out my parents' house and clean it up. They weren't just terrible parents, they were major slobs too. I don't have many memories in the house that don't involve some kind of abuse I suffered at their hands, but I don't remember the house being quite this gross. Sure, they've been gone from here for probably 15 years now so some things just grow, but most of this mess was left behind by them and their nasty ways.

I've thought several times about just tossing a match on the place and burning it to the ground. I could rebuild something on the property that I can live in when I get out of the military in a couple of months, but without water, it's likely the fire I'd set would spread to the field and cause an epic fire event. So, for now, I'm cleaning it out. I'll make changes or tear it down once I move here permanently.

As I'm dumping the fourth bag of garbage into the back of my truck I hear the sound of tires on the dirt road that runs in front of my property. The sheriff, my lawyer, and Shay are the only ones who know I'm on the property so no one should be coming out here. The vehicle reaches my house but keeps going. Shay's surprise to my presence earlier tells me that she's not used to having people around. Do I go over to check on her or leave it alone? She didn't seem very receptive to having me there, but the little voice in my head that has rarely been wrong is telling me to get over there.

I snatch my cell phone off the front porch banister and jog through the mostly overgrown path between the properties. When I break through the last bit of vines into the clearing of her parents' front yard, which is closer to the dirt road then her granny's yard, I see two men in black three-piece suits, with dark, slicked-back hair climbing out of a white Cadillac.

Shay approaches from the side of the yard with a menacing pitchfork and an equally scary expression. I step out a little further so she can see me.

"Shay," I call to her. She turns to me a little and her shoulders relax slightly. "You okay?"

"Depends," she tells me as she turns her attention back to the men approaching. "This is private property, gentlemen," she tells the men while I move over to stand next to her, facing them.

"Are you Shay Baird?" the man on the left asks with a slick smile firmly in place.

She tilts her head. "Depends on who is asking."

He chuckles in a used-car salesman kind of way and I'm on edge more than I was when I heard the car coming down the dirt road.

"Ms. Baird, I'm Joe Angelotti and this is my partner, Leo Ricci. We represent Costa Petroleum. We wanted to talk to you about a few things."

"I don't see what you could possibly want with me." She's rightfully skeptical.

"We're prepared to make you a very lucrative offer on this property if it turns out that you're sitting on an oil reserve like we think you are. Mr. and Mrs. Smith out by the county line just made enough off us to retire at the beach and live high on the hog for the rest of their days." He punctuates his declaration with that shark's smile that makes me uneasy. A smile like that is designed to make her think she's about to be rolling in money. I hope she's not falling for this. I'm trained to read people and situations and nothing about this feels right.

"I don't care if I'm sitting on El Dorado, I'm not selling this land. So I appreciate you stopping by with the offer, but you can move on to the next person. I'm not interested. This is my home."

"Miss Baird—"

"Nothing you can say is going to change my mind," she says through clenched teeth.

"But—" Joe tries again.

I step a little in front of her protectively. "Miss Baird has been clear. It's time for you to go. She's not interested."

Leo clears his throat, drawing Joe's attention, and gives him a quick shake of the head.

Joe takes a deep breath and says, "We'll go, but think about it. We'll be staying at the Plantation for a few more days. The offer stands if you want to discuss it."

Leo walks back to the car and climbs in the driver's side. After a few seconds of silence, Joe follows and climbs in the passenger side. They back out, watching us the whole way. As we wait for them to leave. Once they're gone she turns to me. "What are you doing here?"

"I heard the car passing and had a feeling it was someone unwanted. I was checking to make sure you're okay."

"I've been living alone for a long time," she says quietly.

"I figured that too, but something just felt off. I didn't mean to overstep my bounds."

She sighs and hangs her head. "I'm not trying to be rude. I've been alone out here forever it seems, and I'm not used to having people around."

"And I'm not trying to be intrusive, only helpful. I don't think that's the last you'll see of those guys. When I was at the diner I heard about the Smiths taking a crazy offer from some oil company, but I thought it was just town gossip."

"Apparently not," she says, sounding tired.

"Alright, well I'll get out of your hair. If they show back up, just yell. I forgot how great the sound carries out here." She nods slightly, staring off into the distance. I guess I'm dismissed. I'm not sure what happened, but the friendly little girl I spent all my free time with as a kid is long gone, along with the one who gave me a hug by the creek.

I trudge back to the house, not ready to go back inside to continue clearing shit out. The place is a dump and my insides feel raw as it is; I'm in no mood to make that worse. Something about seeing Shay again has messed up my head. I fire up my truck and head for town.

~*~

A few hours later I've been to Walmart for water, a cooler, ice and some non-perishable food to get me through. I went up and down every aisle trying to kill time and I'm still not ready to go back out to the property. So, I turn into a little restaurant on the water called The Lobster Lounge to grab a bite to eat and a beer. This place wasn't here when I lived here as a kid, but I heard a couple behind me in line at the store talking about it and decided it was worth a try. The building on the outside is nothing special to look at, but the smell in here is incredible.

Once I'm settled onto my stool at the bar, the

bartender approaches. "Hey, man, what can I get for you?"

"Do you have any local brews? IPA preferably."

The guy next to me says, "You should try the Marker 48. Good stuff."

"Thanks, man." I lift my chin at him and tell the bartender, "Marker 48 it is."

For the next 15 minutes, the guy next to me and I carry on a conversation about beer and travel. His build is similar to mine, but he's taller. From the way he carries himself I wouldn't be surprised if he's military too.

"You live here?" the man asks.

"I used to. I'm taking possession of my parents' old property. I'll move back when I get out of the Navy in a few months."

He sits quietly for a few minutes. "I saw your frog tat." It's all he says to let me know that he knows my frog is a tribute to my SEAL status. Most of it is hidden under my shirt sleeve high on my arm but the legs stick out of my short-sleeve T-shirts and half the body is visible when I lift my arms. Most of the time I keep it covered but being in the Florida heat makes that difficult.

"What do you know about frogs?" I ask.

"My partner, Hudson, has one too. I was Army Special Forces. Hudson and I own a security firm here in town."

"Security here?" I ask, not believing him. This town is too small and quiet to need a security firm for anything other than home security alarms.

"Mostly out of town, but our home base is here. We decided to relocate here last year. We're only an hour from the airport and two major cities. We get plenty of clients. I'd rather travel and come back to this place at the end of a job than stay in the city. You know what you want to do when you get out?"

I shake my head. I don't have a clue about what I want to do, only that I want to live here. Not in that particular house but definitely on that property.

"I'm Mike Wade. Here's my card. If you still don't have

a job when you get out and think you might be interested in security work, give me a call. Will you live here in Crystal River?"

"I'm taking back what used to be my parents' property in the north end of Crystal River out by Gator Creek. I haven't moved anything in. I'm still trying to figure out if I'm plowing the house and starting from scratch or remodeling. I'm in the cleaning out phase."

He regards me closely for a minute. "Isn't that where Costa Petroleum is trying to buy up the land?"

How would he know about that? "They haven't approached me yet, but yeah. They came out to my neighbor's place today. She said no."

"They aren't going to like that." Mike shakes his head and takes a drink of his beer.

"No, they didn't," I mutter.

"You planning to sell?"

"I doubt it. That's the only peaceful place I know and after the life I've lived, peace is priceless."

"I hear you, man." We go back to drinking our beer and I eat a grouper sandwich. When I'm ready to leave we shake hands and say goodbye.

I don't know why it didn't dawn on me that Costa would be coming for my land too. Our properties butt right up next to each other, so it makes sense. Maybe they're tied up in trying to figure out who the rightful owner is. I only found out a few months ago and was as surprised as anyone. My grandpa wrote his will in such a way that no one can sell that property without my consent. He must have figured out before he died what a piece of crap my dad was and tried to protect my interests the best way he could. I'd just returned to Coronado from some crazy shit in South America when I got a notification that my grandpa died in that nursing home he was living for the last 30 years and the property was mine. My commanding officer called me into his office and gave me the paperwork. I was surprised, to say the least. I didn't even know he was still alive.

This is the first time I've taken leave to visit Florida in a long time. My adoptive parents came out to see me in California a couple of times and we all met in Texas one year for Christmas at my sister's house, but I haven't been to Florida for a long time.

Once I realized that the town hadn't grown up much I decided I'd like to build there. My issues were never with the city of Crystal River. They were always with the birth parents who had custody of me until I was 11 years old. Now that I know Shay is on the land next door still, has no plans of leaving and is unmarried, I'm even more certain it's where I want to be.

CHAPTER THREE

Shay

How did my life turn upside down again in one day? First Paxton Jones—I mean, Pearsal—shows up for the first time in over 15 years, while I'm swimming naked. Then some slick oil company guys show up to try and buy my land out from under me. There is no way I will sell it and the thought of it makes me feel ill.

As angry as I was to have those men here, though, I was equally pleased to have Paxton at my back. My fear wasn't as great as it would have been had he not been with me. I'm wary of strangers, considering my history, and my greatest fear is having to leave this place for any reason. I have a hard enough time just going to the store in the middle of the night for fear something will keep me from getting back here.

I've been in bed for two hours trying to fall asleep and I'm nowhere close. For the first time in my life, I'm having sexy thoughts about a man to the point of sleeplessness. I know what sex is. Between the birds and the bees conversation I got from my granny—which was super awkward—all the sex in the movies and television shows I've seen, and the brief dating history I had when I was 16 years old, I get what it is, but my lack of exposure to the opposite sex has left me relatively dormant in that department. Well, that was true until Paxton showed up here reeking of testosterone and handsome goodness. I didn't realize real-life men could look like him.

The nighttime stockman at the grocery store looks like he could be my dad and the few delivery guys that have shown up out here haven't looked any way that made me feel like a woman with working hormones.

It's the craziest feeling. Every time I think of Paxton, a little buzzing starts in my sex and my nipples turn hard as rocks. I hope he doesn't come back over because I'm not sure I can curb my body's reaction to him and I'm afraid he'll notice. The embarrassment will kill me, I'm certain of it. I mean, a guy like him probably has a different sex partner every night or maybe even a wife. Crap! Was he wearing a wedding band? I didn't even notice. If he shows back up, that's the first thing I'll look at after I'm done being hypnotized by that damn dimple. God, why am I even thinking about this?

I throw the covers off and walk out through the living room. The nightlights I keep in every room have it bright enough in here that I can see without any issues. I unlock the front door and slip outside. The night is warm and a little humid but not too uncomfortable considering I'm in a tank top and little sleep shorts. I settle on to the porch swing and push off with my feet. It's a new moon so the sky is darker and the stars are brighter than usual. I love these kinds of nights. The crickets are loud and off in the distance, I can hear the coyotes crying.

Although I'm lonely more often than not, I do enjoy moments like these. It makes me think of being a little kid, staying at my granny's, which I did about once a week, and sneaking out here on sleepless nights. I always thought I was being tricky, but my granny could hear the old screen door squeak and would give me a little time before she'd come out and join me. She was a sweet woman and I miss her more than I ever would have thought possible.

The crickets silence suddenly and goosebumps rise along my arms. I stop the swing from moving and sit quietly, waiting to see if they'll start back up. Sometimes a fox or a larger animal moving through the field causes them to quit for a little bit. The cracking of sticks draws my attention toward the east side of the porch and I climb off the swing and move back toward the door.

"Hey!" a familiar voice calls out. I pause and squint into the dark as a tall shadowy figure comes out from the path between the houses.

"Shay, it's Paxton."

"What are you doing here?" I ask, a little freaked by the way he appeared but thankful it's him.

"I couldn't sleep. It's too muggy and hot tonight. I just thought I'd see if any lights were on over here. I'm not used to being alone so the quiet was also driving me nuts."

A sliver of sadness slides down into my belly. "Are you married or have a girlfriend? Or boyfriend?"

His head jerks back a little as he climbs the steps to my porch.

"Nah, I'm not gay. No girlfriend and no wife." There is a long pause as he studies my face before he asks, "What about you? Boyfriend or husband?"

I shake my head. "No, neither. I don't get out enough to have met anyone."

"That's a shame," he mumbles.

I want to ask him if that's a compliment or a put-down, but I'm not sure I'm equipped to hear the answer to that. He motions to the swing next to me. "Can I swing with you?"

I smile a little and nod. When we were kids we spent a lot of hours on this porch swing together, usually shucking corn or snapping beans for my granny. Good memories.

"It's weird being back here," he says, shifting me out of my trip down memory lane.

"Yeah, I bet. I've never left so I wouldn't know. What's weird about it?"

"Sleeping in the front yard. The quiet of no one being around. The lack of fear as I stomp around the property. I spent so many years scared of my father's fists and my mother's verbal jabs. I didn't realize what a state of fear I lived in until I moved in with the Pearsals. It took me close to a year to stop freaking out whenever someone would spill milk, slam a door or get a bad grade. Luckily, they were patient with me and helped me get past it."

"You said it's weird being quiet." I don't really ask a question, I just leave it hanging like I want him to

155

elaborate, and thankfully, he does because I'm curious.

"I'm in the Navy and I'm constantly with the other guys on my team. They may not always be talking but I've become accustomed to the sound of them breathing, the general noises they make moving around, flipping pages or whatever. I guess just knowing someone is around is a different feeling than being completely alone."

"I get it. It took a long time after my granny died to get used to being totally alone. For so long it had been the two of us so when I couldn't hear her snoring at night or moving around the house early in the morning or humming in the middle of the day it messed with my head. I miss her."

"She was a cool lady. I always liked your granny."

"Me too." I smile a little at the thought of her.

After that we sit quietly for a long time, swinging and listening to the crickets that have gone back to singing. I yawn, finally getting tired enough that I can sleep. I know it's a bad idea; I have no idea who Paxton Pearsal is now that he's all grown up, but my gut says he's the same person at heart that he was when we were kids, so I take a shot.

"Why don't you stay here tonight? You can sleep in my granny's room if you want. If that creeps you out, you can sleep on the couch. I have the air conditioning going so it'll be more comfortable than your tent."

"I don't want to put you out. I'll be fine once I get settled."

"You aren't putting me out. It won't bother me at all. In fact, I'll probably sleep better knowing someone is nearby."

He hesitates but I can tell he wants to take me up on the offer.

"Come on, let me get a clean pillowcase for Granny's room." I stand and walk to the door and he quietly follows me.

"You know what?" he asks, but he doesn't wait for me

to finish. "I would be more comfortable on the couch. It would seem weird sleeping in your granny's bed."

"Okay, let me grab you a pillow and a blanket." I go to retrieve both items and when I return I find that he's stripped off his T-shirt and shoes and is standing in front of the couch in low-slung basketball shorts. His well-defined muscles are perfectly cut but not too bulging. My eyes trace the lines of each muscle group and snag on the interesting skeletal frog tattoo on his shoulder that stretches down his bicep. There's a scar that runs about an inch above his hip bone all the way around his waist and a smaller, but thicker scar above his right pectoral muscle. I shove the pillow and blanket his way in hopes of stopping my ogling. How embarrassing. He smirks a little and I'm certain it's because he caught me checking him out. I pretend not to notice and turn away. "Goodnight. See you in the morning," I call to him as I slip into my bedroom.

He chuckles a little and I hear his big body drop down on the couch and adjust. I consider closing the door to my room, but I haven't been able to sleep with the door closed since the night my family died. It's as if I'm afraid I will miss an important sound by blocking it out.

Once I get adjusted under my covers I lie there in the semidarkness, listening intently, hoping to hear his breathing.

"Hey, Shay?" he calls into me.

"Yeah?" I yell back.

"Can I turn off at least one of these nightlights?" he asks.

They're bright. I have four just in the little living room alone. I have them in every room. I can't stand the dark, am actually terrified of it, so I keep those all lit every night."

"Um…" I'm not sure what to say. The thought of turning any off frightens me.

"I only want to turn the one-off that's blinding me. I promise it won't be dark in here. Besides, I won't let anything past me. You won't have anything to be afraid of with me here. I'm trained to keep people safe. That's what I do."

I contemplate what he's saying for a little bit. With all that muscle and whatever Navy training he's had I'm sure he can protect me. Can I let go of my fears for one night and trust him enough to turn one light off? It's only one, I tell myself.

"Okay, go ahead. I'm sorry. I'm a little afraid of the dark."

"I figured that out. It's okay. If I can turn this one off right in front of me I can deal with the rest. I promise you're safe with me here so get some sleep."

Oddly, I believe him.

CHAPTER FOUR

Paxton

As I lie here on her uncomfortable couch all I can think of is the fact that she's one room away, close enough that I can hear the squeak of the bed as she gets adjusted, the sigh she releases as her body settles on the bed and the restless slide of her feet against the sheets. I wonder what she's thinking about. Is she feeling the same pull to me as I am to her?

For me, the draw is crazy strong. I don't know if it's because I'm excited to see the person who saved my life all those years ago or if it's because she's grown up to be more beautiful than I ever could have imagined. Or could it be that she speaks to my protective side?

Shay is a woman living alone out here, and although she's handled everything by herself for quite a while, I can tell she needs someone to protect her from the things she can't control. It's just lucky I was here when the Costa Petroleum people showed up. There is no telling how hard they would have pushed her if they thought she was completely alone.

It was obvious that they didn't expect someone like me to greet them when they arrived. They thought it was going to be a single young woman living alone, someone they could intimidate if their lucrative offers didn't pan out.

I roll to my side on the couch and scan the room. Even with a nightlight turned off, it's still bright in here. I counted three more of them in this room. I'm sure there are equal amounts around the house. It makes me wonder why she's so afraid of the dark. Did something happen with her? With her granny or her family? When I asked about her family she shut the conversation down in a heartbeat so I'm afraid to bring it up again, but I'm dying to know.

The Baird farm used to be teeming with life. It seemed like there were always kids running around, adults working, chickens clucking in the yard and some kind of farm equipment running in the background. I loved being in their place. Mine always had the television blaring or one of my parents screaming or snoring. Any chance I could get I was out of that house and over at Shay's.

My favorite sound though was her giggles. When we were kids I'd do everything I could to make her laugh. That was the best sound in the world and I'd give anything to hear it now. I'm not sure she's laughed in a long time, judging by the sadness in her eyes.

***

The next morning, I wake ahead of her and decide that I want to do something for her so I scour her pantry and fridge as quietly as possible and I whip up some eggs and pancakes. As I'm taking the eggs out of the skillet she comes shuffling out of her room. Her tangled mess of auburn hair is down around her shoulders and her eyes are half closed. "What are you doing?"

"Making you breakfast." I grin at her.

She tilts her head. "Why?"

"You were nice enough to save me from the heat last night and let me sleep on your couch. I thought it was the best way to repay you."

"Oh. Did you make coffee?"

"Of course. It's the one thing I can't live without in the morning. When we're in the field I drink this instant shit that tastes horrible, but it's still close enough to coffee that I'll drink it to get through. It's so bad that most of the guys won't drink it. They drink something called Rip It, almost like Red Bull. I prefer crappy coffee to that stuff."

I open the cabinet and grab a coffee cup, fill it up and pause. "Black or do you want anything in it?"

"Two sugars, one cream, please."

"At that point, it's no longer coffee."

"What, you take yours black?"

160

"Yup."

"My granny told me that drinking it black would put hair on my chest."

"She wasn't wrong. I'm just not a hairy person in general."

I turn around and flip the last pancake. While I'm waiting for that to cook I wash the dishes that I dirtied and dry them off. When I turn back to her she's watching me curiously. I ignore the warmth in my gut her attention brings on.

"You do dishes and cook?"

"Of course. I'm amazing." I smirk at her.

"Yeah, I'm getting that. Do you mow grass and clean toilets too?" She's smiling now and sipping her coffee.

"Actually, I do. Maybe I need a superhero costume with a cape and a big fat 'A' on the chest for 'Amazing Man.'"

She laughs out loud. It doesn't last long but the sound is like music to my ears. How did I make it this long without hearing that sound?

"Oh, you think that's funny?"

"Well…yeah. You in tights?" Her head flies back and she cackles, louder and longer this time, and I'm left stunned, staring at her.

When her laughter subsides, and she sees me staring, she sobers a little. "I'm sorry. That was obnoxious."

"Don't ever apologize for your laughter. I've missed that sound so much." She blushes a little and I turn my focus to my plate, so I can finish eating.

When I'm done, I take my plate to the sink and wash it off. "I'm going to town today to meet with my lawyer. Do you need anything?"

"No. Not really. I went to the store a couple of days ago."

"Okay, well if you change your mind you can call me. I'll leave my number on the pad of paper on the counter."

"Okay," she replies quietly.

I have no idea why I do it, but I move over to stand in front of where she's sitting, lean down and kiss the top of her lovely auburn hair. I don't say anything else; I simply leave out the front door and jog back to the tent to grab my keys, wallet and a change of clothes. I'm going to take a ride over to my adoptive parents' house in the next county and then go to my lawyer.

~*~

An hour and a half after I walked out of Shay's house I'm at my parents' kitchen table wearing clean clothes—after probably the best shower of my life—

having another cup of coffee with my mom. Audrey Pearsal is one of the nicest women in the world. She has zero enemies and the most calming personality of anyone I've ever met. My dad, Ray Pearsal, on the other hand, has a tendency to tick people off without meaning to. He's also an awesome person, but he's quick to speak his mind and people don't seem to like that very much. Although he and my mom are so different they have a devoted love for each other like none I've ever seen before.

"Why don't you stay here and drive back and forth? Sleeping out in that tent sounds horrible in this heat," my mom tells me.

"Originally, it was because I didn't want to infringe on your guys' privacy. You finally have the place to yourselves with all of us gone and I don't want to intrude. It is humid as hell though, so I considered it, but then I found her."

"Her?" My mother's eyes light up. She's always wanted me to find someone and settle down. She wants grandkids, but mostly she wants me to have what she and Dad have.

"Shay Baird," I say with a grin I can't seem to fight.

My mother's smile falters a little. "Is she one of the Bairds who lived next door to you growing up?"

"Yes. How did you know? She was my best friend before I came here. I'm pretty sure she's the one who reported the abuse when I was brought to you guys."

My mom lets go of her coffee cup and sits back in her

chair. All happiness is gone from her face and my muscles tense because the expression she's wearing always precedes bad news.

"What do you know about Shay?" I ask, almost not wanting to know what she's going to say.

"Oh, Pax. We tried not to talk about Jared and Brenda. We wanted you to embrace our home and our family and let the crap from your past go. I see now that we should have told you some things."

I sit back in my chair, mirroring her posture, but crossing my arms over my chest.

"Spit it out, Mom. Whatever it is, spit it out," I demand in a low, controlled voice.

"Jared, Brenda, and that drug dealer guy who was at your house all the time got high one night and killed that girl's family. The only two who survived were the girl and the grandma because they were in the other house when the attack happened."

The bottom drops out from underneath me and my stomach rolls. "Killed them? How?"

"Shot them. They broke into their house in the middle of the night and killed the parents and the little sister. While they were out on bail, Jared found out who turned them in for abusing you, and they came for revenge. They were so stoned though that they didn't realize everyone wasn't in the house. That's what finally put them behind bars for good. All three left prints around the house and even tracked blood back over to your property." A tear slips down my mom's face and she wipes it away. "I'm sorry. We should have told you when you were old enough, but I didn't want you to feel the guilt for that."

Shay's whole family died because she saved me. Because of me.

I stand abruptly and hustle to the sink where I throw up repeatedly until my stomach is empty. Her whole family is wiped out and she's alone because of me. I can't wrap my mind around that. My head drops to my folded arms on the sink, and tears that have probably been bottled up for years spring forward and pour out of me. My mom stands behind me and rubs my back, whispering comforting words and doing her best to settle me down.

Too dazed to stand, I turn and drop down with my back against the sink cabinet. She sits down next to me and puts her hand on my knee.

"I'm sorry, Pax. We should have told you."

"I'm not mad at you, Mom. I'm fucking angry at them. They're selfish, horrible people. They tried to kill her and instead took everything from her. I don't even know what to say."

"There's nothing to say. Nothing you could have done differently. Even if you knew. She didn't say anything to you?"

"No, but when I asked about her family she clammed up. She must hate me."

"She was young too. Maybe she doesn't know."

"I'm sure she does. How could she not?"

"I don't know, honey." My mom's voice is so gentle. It's the same tone she used on me for at least the first year after I moved in with them.

"What do I do? She's not going to want me to move in next door." I stand abruptly and pace back and forth.

"I was so happy to see her, Mom. You don't even know. It was like the only happy memory from that part of my life was standing in front of me. I can't explain it better than that." I grab the back of my neck and close my eyes, opening them only long enough to rant again. "You have no idea how beautiful she is. God, she's just... I don't even know how to describe her. Amazing. I knew something terrible had happened. She lives there alone. Her granny died and she's there alone. It doesn't sound like she ever leaves the property except to shop late at night. No one lives out there. She's this beautiful, sweet, strong, lonely, scared, hermit of a woman and I want to take care of her!" I yell, startling myself. Did I just say I want to take care of her? Where did that come from?

"Oh, honey."

About that time my dad comes in from his morning run and stops in the middle of the kitchen, looking between me and my mom, trying to figure this out.

"What's going on?"

We both stand, and I put my hands on my hips and drop my head, unsure if I can say the words out loud.

"Paxton just found out about Jared and Brenda killing his neighbors."

"What?" he asks, his voice jumping an octave.

"When he was out at the property he ran into the daughter. The one who was his friend. I had to tell him."

My dad sighs and sits on the edge of a chair next to the table.

"You've done so well all these years; I wanted to just let the past stay buried. I felt like you've had enough hurt in your life."

"Tell him what you told me about Shay, honey," she urges me.

"Why? It's never going to be anything now that I know what happened."

"You don't know that."

"She's beautiful, Dad. Gorgeous head of deep red hair, a few little freckles on her nose, these eyes… Oh, man, her eyes. You wouldn't believe them. And still just as sweet as she always was. She lives on the property alone and I don't think she leaves much. I ruined her life. She'll never let me near her now."

My dad studies my face for a long time before he finally stands and makes his way to me, stopping close enough to put his hands on my shoulders. "Son, you're the bravest, strongest of our kids. I've never seen you back down from a fight and I've never seen you turn away when things get too hard. It's what makes you a good SEAL. Maybe you should apply that to your personal life. First, make sure she's worth it, and if she is, then you go after her with everything you've got. That's exactly how I won your mother over and we've been together for almost 35 years." He puffs up his chest proudly. "I know what I'm talking about."

"But Brenda and Jared killed her family. That's not the same thing as what you had to do to get Mom."

"Same principles, son. She needs someone who will care for her, fight for her and love her. If you can and want to be that man, then, in the end, it won't matter if your parents were serial killers or Sunday school leaders. It'll only matter what kind of man you are now."

He makes sense, but for me to move forward with even a friendship—and I want that at the very least—she needs to know the truth. I won't lie to her even by omission. Something about that first hug by the creek tells me she has no clue.

CHAPTER FIVE

Shay

When I woke up to find Paxton cooking breakfast in my kitchen I couldn't stop the warmth that spread over my skin from head to toe. It wasn't just because there was fresh breakfast being made that I didn't have to cook. It was because there was someone else to wake up to. Someone else to share my morning with. Someone to smile at me and do my dishes as a bonus. God, that smirk, and that body. Yum.

How is it possible that he's still single? Paxton is a 26-year-old Navy SEAL with a body to die for, a caring heart, and a killer dimple, and he can cook and clean. It seems insane for him to be alone, even if I have very little understanding of relationships and men in general.

I've tried to work on the garden and do some laundry, but it's been difficult to keep my mind on what I'm doing. My thoughts keep straying to him. It seems odd to me that we have a level of familiarity that's held on even with the long amount of time we were separated. I felt a little shy but still mostly comfortable with him. There's no other reason I'd let a virtual stranger stay in my home overnight other than I trust him.

I heard a car come down the road a little while ago so I know he's back over at the property, and I was doing a good job at staying away until I heard a second car. Because my curiosity is peaked, I creep through the path that Paxton has helped to clear again just by using it. When I come out the other side I see a big black pickup truck and a burgundy four-door sedan. I continue forward until I'm a few feet from the steps of the porch and then I pause, wondering if I'm intruding on him. Maybe this was a bad idea. He might be sick of me after hanging out with me last night and today. As I'm getting ready to turn and haul ass, the door opens and a short, petite woman with blond bangs and a ponytail stumbles forward with two full garbage bags. Her eyes widen and she stops dead in her tracks when she sees me.

"Oh, hi," she says in a soft feminine voice. "You must be Shay."

She knows my name... But how?

"Hey, Mom, did you grab the bag in the second room?" I hear Pax call from somewhere in the house.

Her smiling eyes never leave mine as she replies louder than she greeted me. "Yes, honey, I got it."

"Thanks, Mo—" Paxton starts to say as he comes out the front door and finds me face-to-face with his adoptive mother. I glance between the two of them as he sets his bag down. His eyebrows pull together.

"Is everything okay? Did they come back?"

"Um...no. I just...heard a car and wanted to make sure it wasn't those guys coming to your house this time."

His face relaxes and I glance at his mom, who is grinning at me like I brought a suitcase of money over to deliver. She clears her throat.

"Oh, yeah. Sorry. Mom, this is Shay, the girl who grew up next door. Shay, this is my mom, Audrey Pearsal."

I smile back, feeling a little shy, and reach my hand out to shake hers. "Hi, Mrs. Pearsal. It's nice to meet you."

"Oh, dear," she drops one of the bags she's holding and wipes her hand on her leg, "just call me Audrey. It's very nice to meet you too. I've heard some very nice things about you."

I blush to my roots, wondering what he told her. Unsure of what else to say, I ask, "Do you live nearby?"

"Oh, we live over in Ocala. It's not too far. I just thought this guy could use some help. Once he told us what condition the place was in I knew it would take more than one person. I wasn't wrong. It's filthy." She wrinkles her nose and Paxton busts up laughing.

"Mom, you are too much. I didn't ask you to help because I knew it would gross you out. It's bad in there."

"I'm not leaving you to do this alone."

I watch their exchange as a warmth spreads through my belly. Pax deserved to have a family like this. He should have had it years and years ago, but at least he has it now. I can see why he grew up to be such a good man. He finally found support and love and people who believed in him. If my heart could smile, it would.

Before I can really think it through, I blurt, "I can help!" Both heads swing my way. Taking a step back I blush again, realizing they may not want my help. Why did I open my big fat mouth?

"Ohhhh, that would be lovely." Audrey grins at me and then back at Paxton.

"Really?" He squints at me, both questioning my sincerity and giving me an out.

"Well, only if you want me to. I mean, I don't want to intrude or anything."

"No way! You wouldn't be intruding," Audrey says. "Right, Pax? We can use all the help we can get. My husband is even coming over once he gets off the golf course."

One side of his mouth lifts in a half smile and he tells me, "I'd love to have your help. I just don't want you to feel obligated. It's pretty bad in there."

"It's no problem. I don't have anything else to do besides pull weeds and those will still be there tomorrow."

"Great, let me grab you a pair of gloves. I have no idea what you are touching in there so you need to have your hands covered. Also, be careful; I've found a few old needles lying around and I'd hate for you to get stuck with one. There is no telling what's on those."

He jogs down the steps and throws the garbage bags in the back of his truck. I can't help but notice the flex of his arms and his mom must catch my ogling. "He's grown up to be quite the handsome man, don't you think?"

My eyes widen as I glance at her and I blush again. Damn it! Why does my embarrassment have to be so obvious? "I was just waiting for my gloves," I say stupidly. Damn, I feel like an idiot.

A giggle follows her back into the house. She totally caught me.

Paxton returns to the porch with gloves and a couple of garbage bags. "The only things we're keeping are any pictures you might find. Everything else is getting trashed." I can't hide my surprise. I know they were crappy parents, but the fact that he doesn't want to keep anything seems excessive.

He must read my mind because he gently squeezes my shoulder and explains, "Once you go inside you'll understand. I've been in some scary places in my life but never one this filthy. Nothing survived really. I'll be lucky if we even uncover any pictures, but that's about the only thing sentimental that might be salvageable."

I nod to show I understand, but I don't speak. This makes me so sad for him. I can't go in the house I grew up in yet, but I know when I do, everything will be nice and neat, waiting like it was the last time I saw it.

When I walk through the door, I'm hit with a terrible odor. I've never smelled anything like it. "Oh, man! Ugh." I gag a little.

"You get used to it, sweetie. It's bad though. I'm going to go home and rinse my nasal passages when we are done. It's the rats. They pooped all over the place and there were some dead ones. Then there is all the garbage and rotten food in here. Nasty. I think he should just tear it down and forget about it."

"Mom, I told you I would, but I want to make sure there is nothing in here I want to keep. If there is, it will be buried under the layers of filth Jared and Brenda left."

He's right. If there is anything in here he might want, it will be buried.

We work for hours and get quite a bit done. I'm back in what was Jared and Brenda's room when I hear a very deep voice coming from the living room. "What the hell is that smell? Audrey, y'all are gonna die of fume inhalation. Son, didn't I tell you to open the windows in here? Good God, this is horrible."

"Dad, we couldn't run the air conditioner with the windows open and the heat was worse than the smell. We'll be fine. I'm about to send Shay and Mom home and you can go with them. I'll be fine. I only have about another day of work to do."

"Shay's here? Are you trying to scare that girl away?" I hear him ask with humor in his voice.

"Dad," Paxton's tone a warning.

"Okay, okay. Why don't we work for a bit and then I'll take you all out to dinner?"

"Sounds good to me," I hear his mother answer in her sweet voice.

Loud footsteps come down the hall to where I'm working and when I look up, Paxton and Mr. Pearsal are standing in the doorway staring at me.

Pax steps into the room. "Shay, I want you to meet my dad, Ray Pearsal." He gestures between us and me remove the glove on my right hand before I reach out to shake his hand. "Shay Baird. Nice to meet you."

"Good to meet you too." His handshake is warm and firm; it's perfect.

"Listen, I'm not letting him expose you to these fumes much longer. I plan to take you all out to dinner. Do you have any preference on where?"

My mouth drops open. I'm not sure what to say. It's been years since I've been out to dinner. I've been through a late-night drive-thru but not out to a real meal. What if people recognize me and bring up my family or call me 'Crazy Shay' again? I couldn't stand to be humiliated in front of this family that way.

"I haven't been out to eat in a long time so I don't think I would be good for making a recommendation. And thank you for the offer, but I'll just grab something to eat at my house."

My face flames again and I turn away, not wanting them to see my humiliation. How embarrassing that a 26-year-old woman hasn't been to dinner in her own hometown in years and can't seem to get up the courage to go now.

"Dad, can you excuse us?"

"Sure, son. Shay, I hope you'll reconsider. We'd love to spend some time with you."

My heart hurts a little with that. When was the last time someone wanted to spend time with me? At least five years ago, and it was my granny. She was the last one.

Ray's heavy footsteps move away from the room and Paxton's quieter ones move close behind me. His hands land on my shoulders and smooth down my arms in a gesture so comforting I almost cry.

"Shay," his voice is quiet and gentle, "you mentioned that you don't go out unless it's late at night. No one is going to hurt you with me around. We all want you to come to dinner. It'll be a nice change."

"I—" I start to protest, but he cuts me off.

"Believe me, I understand why you're nervous, but think about this: You're 26. You could live for another 50 to 70 years. Do you want to be looking at the same four walls, eating the same things, alone for that long? I'm guessing if I could dig into that brain of yours I'd find out you've been lonely for the past five years since your granny's been gone. Please let us take you out. You won't find nicer people than my parents. Come on, Shay," he pleads softly.

Should I? What if someone recognizes me? What if people whisper about me? What if…

"Quit thinking so hard," he quietly scolds.

"Okay, fine, but I haven't been out in public in daylight for years. I may embarrass you guys."

"Never," he says gently. He kisses my hair and strides out of the room, yelling, "Thirty minutes until we stop for the night. Shay's going to dinner with us."

"Fantastic!" I hear his mom exclaim, and once again I grow warm inside, feeling wanted. Now I have to figure out how to enjoy dinner without having a nervous breakdown in front of them.

CHAPTER SIX

Paxton

There isn't a word to describe what I see in Shay's eyes as I try to talk her into going with us. Skittish comes to mind, but there is a bit of excitement and the fight for bravery at the same time. If you would've asked me prior to looking into Shay's eyes just now if this exact expression existed, I would have said no, but now I know better.

When we were kids, Shay's excitement for different adventures was cute. She would bounce on her toes, her eyes shining with anticipation, ready for whatever we decided to get into. I could see a little of that when I mentioned dinner out with us, but just as quickly fear joined in too. Scared wasn't part of Shay's vocabulary when we were young. Why would it have been? She had a perfect life with a close-knit, happy family. At school, she was liked by both students and teachers, and the rest of her time was spent on the farm where she was protected and adored. The fact that I saw fear cross her face makes me angry and to know that Jared and Brenda made that happen makes me want to hunt them down and kill them both in the most torturous way possible.

When I realized how nervous Shay was about going out I decided to walk with her to her house while she grabs some shoes so she doesn't have a chance to chicken out. As we're making our way to her place I decide to go with my gut and grab her hand, intertwining our fingers. A slight intake of breath is the only reaction she gives me so I glance over at her and see her trying to hide a small smile.

When we reach her granny's house I release her hand so she can do what she needs to.

"Shay, make sure you grab a key to lock up. With those Costa guys running around I want to make sure you're protected. I don't trust them."

"You think they will do something?"

"Probably not, but I don't want to take a chance with you or your granny's house."

She nods and walks away, returning soon thereafter in a clean T-shirt and a pair of sandals in her hand.

Once she's done putting on the shoes she goes to a drawer in the kitchen, opens it and pulls out a key on an old plastic key ring that her granny probably got at a car dealership 30 years ago. She locks up and comes down a couple of stairs so we can walk back to my house and take my truck.

"Will your parents be riding in the truck with us?" she asks quietly, and I can tell the fear is winning again. I grab her hand again and grip it firmly to let her know I have her back.

"No, they'll drive. They are going back home after dinner. They just came to help for a little bit. I think they were worried about me after I told them how crappy the conditions are."

"I can understand that. It is pretty gross. If I would've known it was still going to be yours one day I would've snuck in there years ago and cleaned it out. I still know where the hidden key is unless you moved it."

"You remember that?"

"Of course! It's not like it was in a normal spot like under a fake rock or under the mat. You hid it so it was in a super sneaky spot under the porch."

I chuckle, thinking about us trying to find the perfect spot. My parents were known for locking me outside and forgetting about me. A couple of times they left me outside overnight, so I got smart and hid my key so I could sneak in when I knew they'd passed out.

We are quiet as we approach my parents, who are standing by their cars talking quietly. My dad is the one who turns to us and says, "Ben is over here working at the power plant this week, so he's going to join us for dinner. Is the Lobster Lounge okay?"

I glance over at Shay. "Ben is my brother. What do you think?"

"I've never eaten there, but I'm willing to try it," she says, her voice quiet, unsure.

"It's mostly seafood. Is that something you like?" I ask to make sure.

She nods. "My granny loved seafood so we ate a lot of it."

"Lobster Lounge it is."

She's quiet on the way there and I resist the urge to talk to loosen things up. Glancing her way, I notice her hands clenched together in her lap and I can't help myself when I reach over and pull her left hand into mine as gently as possible. Her head whips around, eyes wide, and I can't tell if I've freaked her out or simply surprised her.

"Is this okay?" I ask quietly, keeping my eyes on the road.

"Um…yes. Um…sure."

When it's time to sit down, my dad and I exchange a look and one nod of my head. He then shuffles my mom to sit on the other side of Shay. My mom's ability to soothe the most battered of souls just by being who she is will come in handy today for sure.

My mom opens her menu and states, "They have the best grouper sandwich here. I think I'll have that. What about you, Shay? Any idea what you want?"

"Maybe shrimp? I haven't had it in ages and I always loved it."

About that time, my brother approaches our table with a big grin on his face. The guy teased me mercilessly when we were kids, making me feel like a member of the family the instant I arrived in the Pearsal house, while also annoying the crap out of me. I can tell by the expression on his face it's likely he will do the same now, even with Shay present. I forgot to warn her that my brother is like that. Shit, I hope it doesn't freak her out.

"Hey, bro!" he says as I stand and embrace him hard. I love all my siblings, but I'm closest to Ben.

"Hey, buddy. Glad you could make it."

"Yeah, they finally released the chains holding me to my chair in that meeting, but from what Dad says it's a good thing I didn't make it out to help at your house. I think his exact words were 'giant shithole.'"

I turn to my dad and raise an eyebrow.

Dad shrugs. "What? It's true. You know you want to just bulldoze it and start over."

"Yeah, I do, but that takes time I don't have yet."

"Who is this gorgeous ginger?" Ben turns his full attention to Shay and right as I'm about to pop him in the back of the head for being rude, my mom smacks him on the butt. "Benjamin Pearsal, use your manners!"

Being the charming, smartass bastard that he is, he turns to Shay and offers his hand. "I'm sorry, my lady." Shay takes his hand, but instead of shaking it she lifts it to his lips. I grit my teeth, thinking of all the ways I could break his fingers. Ben continues, "What did I do to deserve the presence of such a beautiful woman at my dinner table?"

She giggles. "I was invited by your family."

"They do know how much I love a woman with red hair. It's as if they brought me an early birthday present."

She giggles again.

"Hey, jackass, quit ogling Shay. She's a woman, not a piece of meat, and she's my guest. You have a gorgeous wife. Should I call and tell Jenny that you're having dinner with a different redhead?"

His eyes narrow on me. "Jenny knows I adore the ground she walks on. Keep her out of this. I was just appreciating our dinner guest. Now that I know you invited her I think it's safe to say there are some things you left out of our last conversation." He winks at me and takes a sip of my dad's beer.

"Get your lips off my beer, son," my dad scolds, taking

the beer back. Shay laughs out loud and I glance over to find her amused with my crazy brother, and I relax a little, sliding my arm across the back of her chair. Not because I'm trying to claim her. Nope. Not at all. It just seems far more comfortable.

Once we order our food my parents talk about our siblings, telling Shay a little about all of us. The only biological child of theirs in our brood is Courtney. She was born before I arrived but after Ben and Renaldo were already part of the family. After me, Farris and Chris came. Courtney couldn't find another female besides my mom within miles until we hit high school and then magically the girls always wanted to be her friend and sleep at our house.

As our food is arriving, Mom is telling Shay about the time Ben, Renaldo, and I snuck out of the house to swim in the neighbor's pool and got busted…naked. Groaning, I try to change the subject to the food now piping hot in front of us but my mom is having none of it and Shay can't seem to stop giggling. I wonder how often she laughs. It's such a sweet, carefree sound, but she keeps covering her mouth like she's embarrassed by it.

As we eat, things grow quieter, the mood mellow. My plate is almost cleared when I hear a male voice behind me say, "Paxton." I turn around to find Mike Wade coming toward me.

I wipe my mouth with my napkin and stand to greet him. "Hey, man. How's it going?"

"Good. Having dinner with my wife and then flying to Miami for a couple of days for work. How's it going for you?"

"Good. We're a little more than halfway through cleaning the old place out. Still, don't think I can stay in that shithole, but at least it'll be cleaned out and ready to level. This is my brother Ben, my dad, Ray, my mom, Audrey, and my friend Shay."

Mike reaches out and shakes each hand, greeting everyone. About that time a stunning blonde, who I'm almost certain is Summer Arden Wade, saunters up and slides in close under Mike's arm.

Everyone's mouth at the table drops open, but it's Ben who blurts, "Holy shit, it's Summer Arden Wade."

She blushes a little and I swear Mike stands taller. "This is my wife, Summer. You obviously know who she is." He then introduces all of us, impressing me with his memory of names. I struggle with that often.

Summer waves and says, "Nice to meet all of you."

We all mumble the same in return. Summer twirls a lock of hair around her finger and says, "We need to get you fed or you'll miss your flight. You still have to drive to Tampa."

"Oh, shit. You're right." He kisses her forehead and I swear I hear a sigh from my mom and Shay.

"Sorry, everyone. She's right. I need to get on with my date-night dinner before I drive south." He points at me. "You still have my card. Use it. I hope to hear from you."

"Sure thing, man. I'll talk to you soon."

They turn and walk toward the outside deck and I sit back down in my chair. When I turn my attention back to everyone they are all staring at me like I have three heads.

"Why didn't you tell us you know Summer Arden Wade?" my brother asks.

"Because I don't. I just met her husband. Nice guy but I barely know him so I didn't know his wife was a movie star. Although looking at the guy, it makes sense. Nice people." I take a sip of my beer and set it back down.

"I've watched both of her movies and am hooked on her new television show. I heard it's filmed here in Florida but I didn't realize she lives here. That's crazy. This tiny little town is home to one of the hottest new stars." Shay shakes her head, still trying to wrap her head around it.

"Jenny is going to be pissed she wasn't here for that. Maybe a little jealous too. All Jenny talks about is Summer

Arden Wade's hair. She's obsessed with it. I mean, it's gorgeous, but she's out of control."

"I can't say anything against that. I agree with Jenny. I think Summer has the prettiest head of hair I've ever seen," Shay tells Ben.

Abruptly, I shift so I can face her. The squeak of my chair startles her and her gaze snaps back to mine. "You think she has the prettiest head of hair you've ever seen?"

"Well, yeah. Didn't you pay attention?"

"I saw it, but you have a mirror, right?"

Shay's eyebrows scrunch up. "Yeah, what are you talking about?"

"If you looked in that mirror you'd see the prettiest head of hair in the world. It's been that way since we were kids." Her mouth opens but nothing comes out. I grab a lock between my fingers and allow the soft strands to drift over my fingers. "Look, it's beautiful and probably the softest I've ever touched."

Our eyes are locked on each other and the moment is charged with something I can't quite put my finger on, but it's both heavy and electric. We stay like that until my dad clears his throat to get our attention. A pretty pink blush spreads across her cheeks and down her neck and I turn to glare at my dad.

Ben breaks out in loud boisterous laughter and I shake my head. Imbecile.

My mom changes the subject and we make it through another 15 minutes without another awkward moment before we exchange goodbyes.

CHAPTER SEVEN

Shay

I can't believe I got lost in him. How easy am I? I was ready to kiss him right in front of his family and toss him my virginity on a silver platter. All he did was stare at me and pay me a sweet compliment. Lonely and horny make me an easy target for a handsome, kind and thoughtful man. Our history also makes me feel like we've known each other forever, even though there are years of our lives lost to each other. If I'm not careful I'll fall head over heels for him and be lonelier and heartbroken when he goes back to the Navy. He says he's moving back here. Right next door, but I don't think a single, good-looking guy like him will want to stay once he realizes that our population is mostly old people and there's nothing to do here. Not that I ever do anything or go out to know this for sure, but this town hasn't changed much in the years since I was a teenager.

The ride back to the house is quiet until I say, "I can't believe I met Summer Arden Wade here in Crystal River. I didn't even know she lived here."

"I don't think she's been here long. I met her husband at the bar the other night and it sounds like they moved up here from Tampa not long ago."

"They seemed nice."

"He was for sure. I talked to him for a little while. He's ex-Army and his partner is ex-Navy. They have a security firm that's based here, but they travel for most of their work."

The rest of the ride is quiet. Once we reach my property, Paxton drives down the driveway and around to my house, stopping near the porch. I'm surprised when he gets out at the same time as I do. He rounds the truck and reaches for my hand. I know I shouldn't take his, simply to protect my heart from any further damage I know I'll face, but I can't seem to help myself.

At the steps of the porch, he pauses and releases my hand. My heart rate picks up because the tightly coiled invisible cord that seems to be between us pulls tighter. My breath is coming out in short, fast puffs and he smiles a little, bringing that dimple in his cheek back out before running his thumb along my lower lip. "Breathe, honey." His voice is like warm chocolate melting over me. "I'm going to kiss you and I don't want you passing out."

Oh. My. Gosh. That dimple. That voice. That mouth. I'm probably going to pass out before this ever even happens, just thinking about it.

Pax closes the distance between us and our lips meet so gently at first it's almost a whisper. Surprising myself, I allow my tongue to sneak out and trace his lips. With a groan, he opens for me while slipping his arms around my waist and pulling me fully against him. His mouth is warm and welcoming, and I can't seem to get enough of it as he fully engages in the kiss. His whole body melds around mine as I squeeze his neck tighter and pull him lower to me. Breaking the kiss, he pulls back and asks, "Can we take this inside?"

My tummy flip-flops and I nod without thinking this through. It's been a long time since I've been so overcome by hormones that I turned off my brain altogether like this. I nod and pull my keys out of my purse and lead us inside.

As soon as we're through the door I spin and face him, ready for more. I'm not sure if he can feel the heat and the need coming off me, but the feeling is so strong it seems as if it should be flowing out of my pores like water. In seconds we're making out in a crazy frenzy of lips, tongue and even a little bit of teeth. When his mouth moves across my cheek and down my neck I can't help the moan that slips from my throat.

The next thing I know he's leading me to and down on the couch. As soon as my head hits the cushion, he's over me, hips resting between my legs and a good portion of his muscular body pressed to mine as he resumes our kissing. I thought kissing him while we were standing was amazing. This is beyond that. It's unbelievable.

His hardness is pressed deliciously against my center and if I had any room for leverage I would rock against him to alleviate the growing pulse between my legs. It's maddening and wonderful all at the same time and I can't get enough of it.

"More," I break away and whisper. "More. More!" I wiggle a little, needing relief from the burning in my core.

"I don't want to move too fast with you, Shay. I don't want you to regret any of this."

"Please, I need—"

"Shhh. I know what you need. Shift to the side and I'll give it to you, honey."

After a little bit of awkward shuffling he resumes the kissing, but this time he undoes the button on my shorts and slowly slips his hand down along the skin of my belly until he hits the damp center of me. I arch against him when he hits the perfect spot and almost knock him off the couch. He chuckles a little and nips my bottom lip with his teeth before swallowing my moan. Those strong, calloused, manly fingers of his work in a small circle between my legs and way too soon my world explodes into a trillion little sparkles. I cry out and shake from head to toe, unable to control my reaction. I've never felt as relaxed as I do right at this moment.

Paxton shifts slightly and I'm reminded that he's still in his uncomfortable state. I'm such a selfish jerk! How could I forget that he didn't just reach nirvana like I did?

"Oh, Paxton," I whisper. "I'm so sorry. I left you hanging and—"

"Stop," he says, placing a soft kiss against my lips. "Has anyone ever done that for you before?" His eyes bore into mine, waiting for a response. I know my face is beet red again.

"It's okay. I want to know. There are so many missing

pieces, so many lost years. I have no idea what your experience level is but I know it's probably not much."

"No, no one has ever done that to me before, not besides me." Surely my embarrassment will deter him from asking any more questions that will make this worse.

"Please tell me you've been kissed before."

"Yes, I dated a guy when I was 16. Cliff Oleander. He got as far as second base after several dates. We had fun until I had a nervous breakdown at school and became 'Scary Shay.' He dumped me in a note the day those kids gave me that nickname. Then my granny pulled me out of school and homeschooled me until I earned my diploma. I haven't been around people very much since all of that went down so there were no chances for more experiences. Never thought there would be actually."

Tenderly, he pushes my hair away from my face, allowing his fingers to drift over my cheek and down my neck, pausing at my shoulder. "I'm sorry you've been through all of that. You deserve to have a better life and I hope I can help you with that."

I blink, trying to clear my head and wrap my mind around what he's saying. "I don't want to be your charity case because you feel bad for me."

"How could you think that? Were you not standing in the front yard a little bit ago or lying on this couch? There is no charity involved in this scenario. You are beautiful and kind and smart, and you have the cutest laugh I've ever heard. You have a piece of my history that no one else does. You know things about me that I never have to explain or be embarrassed about because you lived them with me."

"So much has changed since you left this area, Pax. I'm the town freak. A hermit. I'm 'Scary Shay,' for goodness sakes!"

"You're none of those things. You're a young woman who has survived some traumatic things and did it the best way you knew how. I've been all over the world. I've seen some serious freaks. You are not one of them." Pax's expression is gentle as he waits for my reply.

Could this really be happening? Could he honestly feel something for me? I didn't think I'd ever be making out on a couch again or have someone look at me like he's looking at me. Or experience the crazy swirl of feelings that I have twisting inside me.

"So, if I'm not your charity case, what am I?"

"Something so special I don't have a name for it yet." His grin is sweet and charming and any other questions I have seem to melt away. That answer will work for me tonight.

~*~

The next morning, I wake up and find myself in my full-size bed, on my side, in my shorty pajama shorts and T-shirt, with one leg hiked up over Paxton's hip, one arm stretched out under his neck and the other wrapped around his middle. I'm breathing my morning breath directly into his face. When I told him he could sleep in the bed with me last night I never envisioned waking up like this. We fell asleep, both dressed, but on top of the covers with my back to his front and he had one arm casually resting across my waist. How do I get out of this position without waking him? It's super awkward and I want to brush my teeth before he even opens one eye.

I begin scooching away as gently as possible so I don't rock this rickety old bed, but I only get about an inch away when he clamps down on my hip with one hand, shifts his entire body with lightning-fast speed and rolls me to my back. Hard as a rock, his cock rests against my clit and I moan. His sleepy eyes roam up from my belly, slowly over my breasts, up my neck, past my lips and settle on my eyes. His eyes are sleepy and sexy and I can't seem to help the involuntary tilt of my hips seeking friction from him.

"That's what I'm talking about," he rumbles, and then he dips his head to take my mouth in a kiss designed to make me forget that neither of us has brushed our teeth.

It's deep, long and so freaking perfect that I forget I'm inexperienced and melt into his kiss, his touch, his everything.

All of his weight rests on one elbow so he can use the opposite hand to push my nightshirt up and up and up until my breast is exposed. My whole chest heaves with the deep breaths I'm taking. His mouth closes over my nipple and I arch as far as I can, ready for his attention. I thought his fingers were in charge of bringing all the bliss, but now I know they are secondary to his mouth, which is currently sending lightning bolts to my core. Pulling back slightly he blows softly on my wet nipple and sparks fly in my chest. I run my hands up under his T-shirt, over the smooth skin of his back, and dig my nails in, trying to pull him back down for more. His body shakes with a slight chuckle before he starts again and it's all I can do to keep from trying to dry-hump him. A quick shift of his weight moves him so he can show the same attention to my other breast as I continue my assault on his back.

"Paxton." I moan and wrap my legs around him, hoping for more pressure.

He must get the idea because he begins to rock against me and the friction is in the perfect spot, in the perfect amount, and I'm climbing closer and closer to heaven. Just before I clench up and lose myself in the second orgasm I've had in less than 24 hours, I open my eyes and they lock eyes with Paxton's. Something about the intimacy of the moment and the fact that he's my long-lost best friend pushes me over the edge and I cry out and shudder and shake. Within a few seconds he tenses, shakes and practically collapses on me. Did he just…?

"I haven't done that since I was in high school. I should be embarrassed, but how can I be when it felt good?" he mumbles against the skin of my neck.

Something about the scenario, like we were in high school, makes me giggle and hold him tighter.

"Seriously, honey, that laugh is the cutest thing I've

ever heard, but it makes me a little self-conscious when I just came like a teenager in my pants while dry-humping you."

My giggle turns into a full-blown laugh and when he tries to pull away I lock my ankles and try to hold him in place. "I'm just deliriously happy and it was sweet, what you just said, and I don't know… I told you I'm a freak."

"Freaks don't look that beautiful when they come, honey."

"You know just what to say, don't you?"

When he opens his mouth to say something he's interrupted by a knock on the door. Who the hell is knocking on my door? I only have company when I order something or the sheriff stops by. He was here two weeks ago so I know it's not him.

"Shit, let me clean up and I'll get it. Put some clothes on, honey."

I jump up when he moves toward the bathroom and start tugging on a bra under my nightshirt, drop my sleep shorts to the floor and shimmy regular shorts on. By the time I'm pulling my wild mane of hair away from my face, Paxton is making a beeline from the bathroom to the front door where the knocking is getting louder.

Pax yanks the door open and standing in front of him are Joe and Leo—the Costa guys. What do they want? "She's already told you she's not interested."

"We heard her loud and clear, but we were looking for you and just thought we'd check in with her. Convenient for us that you're both here," Joe says as he smirks at me.

As I wonder what this is about I slide under Paxton's arm.

"Well, we're here to make Mr. Pearsal—or should we say, Jones—an offer he can't refuse."

"I'm not selling either. The land is about to be my home."

"Did you forget to say, again?"

I glance up to find Paxton's head tilting, quietly assessing these men.

"I didn't forget to say anything, and the last name is Pearsal now, not Jones."

Joe turns to Leo and says, "I think maybe we misjudged them. She's definitely stronger than I expected. Stronger than me for certain. If I knew my parents were killed by my lover's parents I don't think I could ever get past it, much less have a happily ever after."

Did he just say that Paxton's parents killed my family?

For one brief moment, the world stops spinning for me and all the air is knocked out of my lungs. As I double over, flashes of ambulances, cop cars, my grandmother screaming, and that awful silence once they all left us alone burns through me at warp speed. Before I can stop the onslaught of horrific memories, Paxton growls, "You son of a bitch!" and dives out the front door toward them. Vaguely I can hear the crunches of knuckles on bone and the grunts of men in a fisted battle. Instead of trying to stop it I sink to my knees and drop my head to the floor. Paxton's piece-of-shit parents are the ones who killed my amazing, salt of the earth, loving, beautiful family. How did I not know it was them? How? How? How?

The tears and snot flow down my face and drip on the floor as the reality of what happened sets in.

I have no idea how long I've been on the floor when the screen door squeaks and the car the Costa men pulled up in peels out down the dirt road.

"Shay." Paxton's voice is pained.

I glance up to see how badly he's beaten up. It's not too bad. Probably a black eye, split lip, and some bruises, but the look in his eyes has me refocusing on the floor again.

"You knew."

"I'm sorry. I just found out. I've been trying to figure out how to tell you once I realized you didn't know either, but I didn't want it to affect what we're building here.

We've got something special, Shay. I don't want the mistakes of my parents to ruin the happiness we can have."

"Are you kidding me? Of course, you don't want the mistakes of your parents to ruin this. But you've got to remember I didn't leave hell to find the perfect family, grow up in a happy home and get a fabulous career in the military. No. Your parents took my happy home and my future from me, probably because we had you taken from them."

"Don't let them take any more from us," he pleads as he gets on his knees close to me on the floor.

"How can I look at you every day and know that because of you I lost my family? I can't. I'm not strong enough."

"Shay…"

Shaking my head and keeping my eyes averted, I say, "You need to leave. I can't deal with you being here right now."

Not one single muscle moves on either of us.

"Sh—"

"Get out!" I screech at the top of my lungs.

Without another word, Paxton Pearsal stands and gathers his stuff from around my house and quietly lets himself out. As his truck pulls out of my driveway I let out a cry. It's a sound I've never heard myself make before. It's probably the sound of the rest of my soul dying.

CHAPTER EIGHT

Paxton

Days have gone by and she hasn't come out of that house. I know because I've sat and watched almost the entire time. I ate some granola bars and slipped away for water and to handle bodily business, but otherwise, nothing. I would've worried she was dead in there but I did some recon last night and found that she's moved places and even had the television on at one point.

For now, I'm going to have to settle for breathing in and out, being alive physically, because I feel dead inside. I have to fly back to Cali tonight and then right back to South America. My SEAL team is being deployed again. I've got a couple more months to go and I guess this is the best way to spend it, buried in a mission.

Although I'd like to tuck tail and run, re-up and go ahead and make a career of it now that my hope for a future here in Florida is trashed, it's just not in my make-up. I'm a fighter. Always have been. When I get back to Florida I'll fight to win her over, to show her that I'm worth overcoming the past for. I had no control over what happened to her parents. As much as I'd like to blame myself, I was a kid. If the Baird's didn't intervene I would have been dead within a year. My parents' hate of me grew worse the older I got and the beatings were becoming too much to handle. Besides, I remember her parents. They were good people and I know they wouldn't do things any different, even knowing the outcome, because they saved the life of a little boy. They were those kinds of people.

Since it's going to be a few months until I can get back, I've got Wade and Hudson on duty watching out for her. They've been briefed on the whole Costa situation and our falling out. She may not know it, but she needs someone to look out for her. Those Costa guys were just dying to get me out of there so they could find a way in with her.

That's the only reason they told her about my parents. I don't trust them, and I figure they will use whatever means are necessary to get what they want.

CHAPTER NINE

Shay

It's been three weeks since Paxton left my house and I can barely drag myself out of bed. When I'd had the last handful of dry cereal in the house I finally made myself go to the store and even that was a chore. My head is so messed up with everything that I even thought someone was following me through the store, but every time I turned around there wasn't anyone there. Maybe I need to call my old counselor and set up an appointment. I don't want to turn into the lady who went insane after she suffered one too many emotional blows. But I feel like I'm on the verge of that scenario now.

When I get home and am unloading my groceries I hear gunshots in the row of brush and trees that separates my property from Paxton's. Instead of hiding like I should, I run to the door, snatch my shotgun up, and step outside with it up to my shoulder, ready to shoot. "Who's out there?" I yell.

No response.

"Who's out there?" I yell again, louder.

There is a rustling near the path we used for Paxton's house so I aim in that direction and wait. Five men appear, three of whom are struggling to get free of the other two. I squint into the dark, trying to figure out who these people are and what the hell they're doing here.

"Shay, it's Mike Wade. We met at the Lobster Lounge with Paxton Pearsal," says the guy in camouflage gear and face paint who is holding one of the other guys. "This is my partner, Hudson."

Another guy—this one a muscled beast of a man— wearing camouflage and face paint and holding two guys, nods and murmurs, "Ma'am."

Mike continues, "We found these guys with gasoline and lighters on your property. They were hired by Costa

Petroleum. I need you to call the sheriff. Tell him Hudson and I are here but we need him ASAP."

My mouth is hanging open because I have a million questions, but what he just said stuns me.

Gasoline?

Lighters?

My property.

They were going to torch the place and I would've lost everything. Normally at news like this, I fall apart, just like I did on Paxton a few weeks ago. I shut down and hide, but this time fury spreads throughout my body in a tidal wave of crazy and I drop the shotgun, leap off the porch and head straight for the men being held. Everything that's been pent up for the last 15 years comes out in a cat-scratching, screaming frenzy of lunacy in the form of a 120-pound redhead. It doesn't take long for Mike to get me under control and keep hold of his guy.

"Calm the fuck down! I can't hold you both. Go get your phone and call the sheriff. I don't have the extra hands to do it." His tone snaps me back to reality and I stop struggling in an attempt to be free and return to killing this guy with my bare hands.

"Shay, get inside and make the call!" Mike demands.

I back away a little, not taking my eyes off them. "Um… O… Okay." I just charged a couple of large, thuggish grown men, thinking I was going to tear them limb from limb. I've officially lost it. I turn and skitter up the stairs into the house to make the call. Once that's done I step outside and find that all three men are face down on the ground with their hands zip-tied behind their backs. Mike and Hudson are standing over them with their guns pulled.

"He's coming. He said to give him 15 minutes." My voice is shaky and I'm certain that my adrenaline is dropping so I sit on the top step and stare at all the men in my driveway, wondering how my life ended up so crazy.

The sheriff shows up in less than 10 minutes with

several deputies right behind him. He must have been flying. I don't move while he talks to Mike and Hudson. When they're done talking and the Costa guys are loaded up in the police cars, the sheriff comes to check on me. I do my best to assure him I'm okay. Mike sits down next to me and watches the cars all pull away.

"Tomorrow you'll need to go to the station to file a report and answer some questions, okay?"

I nod and then turn my head to face him so my cheek rests on my arms. "How did you end up out here?"

"Paxton hired us to watch out for you. He was afraid the Costa guys weren't going to take your no for an answer and it turns out he was right. They've been sniffing around since he left."

"He hired you? For me?" I ask, perplexed.

"In case you haven't figured it out, that man is in love with you."

"I don't think that's true. We had a nasty fight before he left. We have history."

"I know. He explained it. I don't know Paxton very well yet, but I know that a man like that doesn't spend the kind of money he's spent to keep you safe on just any woman. She has to mean something to him."

"When does he come back?"

"I don't know if he is. He mentioned reenlisting since he had nothing to come back for, but he wasn't certain when he left." He pulls his card out of his wallet and passes it to me. "Call us if you need anything. I should get going. Summer flies back in tomorrow morning and I need to be rested up. Take care."

He stands and jogs toward the woods he came from, where Hudson is standing waiting for him. Right before he disappears, he turns back to me. "If he comes back, don't let him slip through your fingers. You won't find another man like him." Both men wave and vanish down the dark path.

Guess I have some thinking to do.

CHAPTER TEN

Paxton

Nine weeks later...

Getting out of the Navy was the right thing to do. I need to start looking at my life in the long term. The plan is to go back and fight for Shay. If I hang in there long enough, maybe she'll come around.

Because I stopped cleanup when everything went south with her, I'll be returning to the tent and more work. I'm definitely going to plow that place down though and start over. I don't want any reminders of Brenda and Jared.

Turning down the gravel driveway to the house, I see several cars—my mom's, my dad's, Ben's, and one with Texas plates. My sister maybe? What are they all doing here? I didn't tell anyone I was coming back except Mike Wade and he only met them for a minute when I was last here.

When I put the truck in park and climb out, my family starts to file out the front door. It's not just Mom, Dad, Ben and Courtney, but also Farris, Chris, Chris's wife and their little boy, Alex, who all file out the door and stand along both sides of the porch. We haven't all been together in one place since Chris's wedding seven or eight years ago.

"What are y'all doing here?" I ask, striding toward them, ready to get a giant family hug that means I'm really home.

"Shay called and said you still needed some help cleaning up."

I stop dead in my tracks. "Shay?"

"How did—" I start and change questions midsentence. "Why did—"

I don't finish because Shay steps into the doorway, holding a sign that says 'Welcome Home' in handwritten

199

letters. "Shay?" I ask, not believing that she's standing here and that I don't have to go drag her over here.

"Mike Wade told me when you would be home. I called your mom and asked for help to get this finished, so they all came."

"You did this?" I wonder out loud as I make my way to her, ignoring my family altogether.

"Yes."

"Why?"

"It's my way of saying I'm sorry. I was wrong."

Stunned by this turn of events, I stand there, unsure of what to say. I'm really excited, but also afraid this is a dream and I'll wake up as soon as I touch her. I've spent the last three months in hell, both physically—in the jungles of South America—and mentally—worried about Shay.

Courtney's voice chimes in right behind me. "Kiss her, stupid! She's saying she's sorry and she did all this for you!" She gives me a little shove toward Shay and the next thing I know I'm standing within breathing distance of her. Shay's eyes are wide and unsure. Hating that she feels that way I grab the sign, toss it to the side, and before she can protest I pull her against me and kiss her as hard and long as I can until the catcalls of my family become too annoying.

~*~

It's now dark and because it's still somewhat summer here that means it's around nine o'clock. My family left from Shay's house, everyone waving as they pulled away just moments ago.

"That was the best homecoming I've ever had," I tell her as I wrap my arm around her shoulder and pull her close to me. "I loved every minute of it. Thank you."

"You're welcome. I wanted you to know how happy we all are that you're home for good."

"We need to talk. When I left, you wouldn't even speak to me. We'd had an ugly fight and I need you to fill in the blanks on what changed and what you want from here."

"Let's go inside and sit down so the mosquitoes don't carry us away," she suggests as she leads me back inside the house. "I'll grab us drinks and we can talk about all of it."

Once we're situated with our drinks and are on the couch, me in the corner with my arm along the back and her sitting close but sideways with her knee cocked so she can face me, I start the conversation.

"After you left, the Costa guys tried to burn me out of the property."

"What the fuck! I had Wade and Hudson out here! How did they get past them? Why didn't anyone tell me?"

"Mike and Hudson are the ones who stopped it. They didn't tell you because I asked them not to. Although, according to them you couldn't be reached until a later date anyway."

"I was gone but they could have told me when I got back stateside."

"Their visit was a wake-up call for me. I started back to counseling and got a bunch of stuff straight in my head. I'm sorry I freaked on you about your parents. Somewhere deep down I think I always knew but no one confirmed it. I never asked. I must have been afraid of the answer. The reality was that the information opened all of those old wounds, letting feelings out I had tucked inside. Losing my family and later my grandmother, who was not just my only remaining relative but my best and only friend, nearly killed me. Many days I wished I would just die so I wouldn't feel so disconnected anymore. I knew I was wasting the life I had and I knew deep down my family would be disappointed in me. But because of my breakdown in high school and still living in this small town, I didn't have anyone to support me in getting my life back. I didn't feel like I had anyone or anything to live for. When you showed up at the creek that day, looking like a movie star and later proving you were still my strong,

201

sweet friend, I started feeling like I wanted to live again. When I thought I lost you, it snapped me out of it. I got in counseling. I won't lie. I've got a long way to go. I finally get it though. You can thank your friend Mike Wade for opening my eyes."

"So why were you working on my house? Why did you call my family?"

"I knew I couldn't finish that place alone and I wanted to be able to give you something. I want to give you a future…" She swallows hard before she continues, "I'd love for it to be with me, but even if you don't want that I still want to be your friend and help you." Her eyes avert when she says friend. "You can stay here or at my parents' house, whichever is more comfortable, while they clear the land and you rebuild."

"You want me to stay here while I have a house built?" I ask to be certain.

She nods her head slowly and chews on her bottom lip.

Leaning forward a little, I push her hair over her shoulder, noting she's had a haircut recently, and lean in much closer. "Will I be sleeping on your couch?"

She swallows hard and shakes her head.

"Will I be sleeping in your granny's bed?"

Her chest rises and falls with her breath. She's nervous as she shakes her head.

I move in even closer so my lips are almost touching hers. "Am I sleeping in your bed…with you?"

"Yes. If you want me." Her answer is a whisper.

There is no question in my mind that I want her, so I decide it's time to show her. Moving so fast she doesn't realize what's going on until she's already in the air, I scoop her up and carry her to her room and lay her on her bed.

I've been with a lot of women over the years. As a Navy SEAL, they've tended to throw themselves at me, but it was always fast and furious. Obviously only there to take care of our needs quickly. I've never had someone in front of me who meant the world, who needed my patience and attention like she does. Never anyone I wanted to worship with my eyes, hands, mouth, and cock all at the same time. Her heavy-lidded gaze follows me as I round the bed and slide on next to her. Lowering my mouth to her, it only takes a few seconds for things to heat up between us. Her legs shift restlessly against the mattress when I push her shirt up over her breasts and tug the right cup of her bra down, exposing the dusky rose nipple beneath the fabric. When my head lowers and my lips make contact, her fingers slide along my scalp and dig in a little. She likes this. I relentlessly tease the peak with my tongue and teeth and switch sides when her squirming becomes more aggressive.

My gaze lingers on her longer than I intend when I catch sight of the I'm-ready-for-you look she's blazing into my skin as I continue her torture.

"Sit up, honey. I want that shirt off. Need you bare."

Shay doesn't hesitate; she peels her shirt off and tosses it carelessly to the floor, followed by her bra. I grin at her devilishly. Her breasts are the perfect handful I thought they'd be when I saw her swimming in the creek a few months ago.

As I concentrate on giving her breasts plenty of much-needed attention she tugs on my shirt. "If I lose mine, you have to also."

I don't have to be told twice. I sit up and whip mine off and toss it toward hers. Then I yank my shorts off too. Now I'm only in my boxer briefs, which are clearly at the limits of their stretch capacity because I'm so hard for her. When I lean back over her, pressing our bare chests together, she wiggles a little and I slip my hand below the waistband of her shorts and panties, into her amazing heat. She's so warm and wet, ready and willing.

"How far do you want to go, Shay? We can stop here if you want."

It's probably not fair, but I can't help it when I press

my pointer finger against her clit as I ask her. She can't respond right away as I swirl my finger on the pulsing nub.

In the middle of trying to catch her breath, she says, "Don't you dare stop. I want all of you. I want to give it all to you."

"Push those shorts down."

Shay does as I ask and now she's lying in front of me in nothing but a pair of light-pink satin panties that were crafted to make men stupid. A red halo of lush hair is spread out around her head. Between the feminine curves of her almost naked body, all that amazing hair and the look on her face, she could be painted into a masterpiece. Sexy, beautiful and breathtaking.

I climb off the bed, pull a condom out of my wallet, drop my boxers onto the floor and move back into position next to her, completely naked. Those steel-gray eyes of hers widen. "Is that... Is that going to fit?"

A small chuckle escapes. "Yeah, honey. It just may take a little patience." Her throat bobs as she swallows hard. "You sure you're ready for this? We have plenty of time." The fear slips away as softness spreads over her features.

"I want it to be with you. I want it to be now."

"Slip those pretty panties off." Her eyes never leave mine as she does as instructed. I don't give her a chance to get embarrassed; instead, I rearrange so my face is between her thighs.

"Paxton," she whispers, lifting her head to stare at me with wide eyes.

"Close your eyes and enjoy." I don't wait for her to respond or react. I run my fingers along her auburn curls and open her. Before she can protest I taste her. How can one woman be so perfect? The feel of her, the taste of her...amazing.

Licking and sucking and swirling, I work her until she's crying out unintelligible words. Then I crawl up over her body, knowing she's ready for this. I slip the condom on expertly. "Wrap your legs around my waist."

"My legs feel like rubber; I don't think I can."

I chuckle a little and she lifts her legs and wraps them around my back, locking at the ankle. "This is probably going to hurt, but I will do my best to go easy. The pain will go away shortly, but if it's too much just say so and I'll stop."

She nods and closes her eyes.

"Don't close your eyes. I need to see you."

When she opens them I smile at her, so ready for this. She lifts her hand and touches my cheek, pausing at the indentation. "That dimple. That sweet, sexy dimple. I love it."

Unable to stop myself I lean down and take her mouth with mine. As I flex my hips, pushing at her entrance, I break the kiss to see her face. With each inch she takes, her eyes widen and I worry it's too much, too soon.

"Want me to stop?"

"No, no, keep going," she whispers.

I thrust hard one time to push past that barrier and then hold still. Her bottom lip quivers so I lower my mouth to hers and kiss her softly. My thighs shake as I fight to stay still. Eventually, her body relaxes and I begin to move. Slowly, carefully. After several strokes, her tension smoothes out and her body relaxes. Her hips begin to move naturally to meet mine. When her fingernails dig into my back I increase the rhythm and when I get close to losing it, I slip my thumb between us and find her clit. She's so responsive—thank God—that it only takes a few seconds for her to clench up tight and let it all go. My hips power into her, my mind no longer controlling my body as nature takes over. I throw my head back and call out her name when I come. Her hand snakes out around my neck and she pulls me down to kiss me long and hard. Once I'm spent I roll away, peel off the condom, toss it in the trash, and move in next to her. This time though, I pull her onto me so she's straddling my hips with her head lying on my shoulder.

A year ago today I was covered in camo and paint, doing recon on a drug cartel in South America. Today I'm home, with Shay, building my future in a way I know is going to last. Tomorrow I will be seeing Mike and Hudson for a job with Sunset Security. Life doesn't get any better than this.

CONNECT WITH TIFFANI!

Website
www.tiffanilynn.com

Author Facebook Page
https://www.facebook.com/Tiffanilynnauthor/

Newsletter
http://tiffanilynn.com/newsletter-signup/

Book Bub
https://bit.ly/2rFdA0q

Twitter
https://twitter.com/tifffanilynn74

FLOWERS FOR A HERO

BY TARA L. AMES

CHAPTER ONE

In about fifteen minutes, Brogan Malloy would reach Blowing Rock, a historic town tucked high above the Blue Ridge Mountains in North Carolina. It'd taken him a year to get his shit together to make this trip. Too bad it wasn't a vacation instead of a personal mission.

Tomorrow he'd meet with the parents of one of his men killed in action. He had to deliver to them their dead son's letter. Brogan shifted his weight in the seat and clutched the steering wheel tightly, feeling guilty as hell for not doing it sooner. He owed their son so much. Not only was he a damn good SEAL, but his best friend, too.

Beyond anxious to get tomorrow over with, Brogan navigated the SUV along a suspension bridge snaking around Grandfather Mountain, a famous peak named after one of its cliffs shaped in the face of an old man. He couldn't help but laugh. If he hadn't gone through rehab, he'd end up looking like an old man in no time, too— either that, or he'd be dead.

Yeah, Brogan had to admit the view was magnificent, with its stunning long-range vistas and pastoral landscapes. Everywhere he looked he saw green. It was so unlike the rocky skeletal ranges in Afghanistan or the jungle canopies in—a sudden onslaught of shouts and screams echoed inside his mind and bloody image of his dead friend's head blown off flashed before him.

No!

Dammit.

Not now.

Taking several short breaths, Brogan turned up the volume on the radio and blasted the inside of the SUV with heavy metal, but it wasn't enough to drown out the pain hammering inside his head like a goddamn jackhammer.

Nerves raging, Brogan pounded the steering wheel with his fist and slammed on the brakes as he pulled over onto the side of the road, desperate to silence those cries and erase the visions. Mouth dried, palms sweaty, he licked his lips and reached for the bottle of whiskey lying next to him, wrapped in a brown paper bag.

Inhaling and exhaling sharply, Brogan yanked his hand away and swallowed back the endless thirst assaulting his throat. "C'mon, you, dumb bastard," he muttered, "you don't need it." Just get your sorry ass through today and tomorrow, he told himself, and then he'd be all right.

Taking some more deep breaths, Brogan shoved those shouts and images aside and merged back onto the two-lane highway. Relieved he hadn't caved in and drunk himself into a stupor, he navigated the SUV around another curve and fired off a quick smirk at the bottle lying there next to him, still sealed and unopened. He took it with him wherever he went to test his resolve to stay sober.

Unlike all the other tests he'd passed in his life, fighting his addiction would challenge him until the day he died. There'd always be something in his path—whether it be a flashback, a sound, or a fleeting thought—to trigger his urge to drown out the pain in whiskey or to pop a pill to forget the guilt.

Finished coming around the bend, Brogan was about to accelerate when he noticed a Ford pick-up truck parked on the side of the road facing the opposite direction. A chick inspected the engine underneath the hood. He did a double-take at her long, slender legs. The drive up to Blowing Rock was breathtaking, but oh man, this sight was mouthwatering radiant, making his own engine rev.

Glad for the distraction, especially by a chick with mile-long legs, Brogan drove onto the shoulder and parked, so his vehicle's front end faced the truck's. With her head still underneath the hood, he'd have to be dead not to notice her cute butt cheeks peeking out of a pair of shorts.

Eager to find out if she looked just as good in the front as she did from behind, Brogan hopped out of the SUV and strode towards her. "Hey there, do you need any help?" he called out.

"I checked all the fluids, the spark plugs, and the alternator," she rattled off over her shoulder. "Nothing's wrong with them. I think it's the battery."

Brogan had never thought auto parts could sound so sexy, but when she spoke about them in her southern accent, it was like listening to a sweet, country song. If only she'd come out from underneath the hood. He really wanted to see her face.

At last, she wheeled around.

With short, curly hair pulled back in a headband, creamy white skin, and the sun on her cheeks, she greeted him with a smile as bright as the day's spring morning with clear skies and a soft, cool breeze.

His heart skipped a beat.

The chick was definitely gorgeous in her tight shorts and t-shirt. Even her eyes were vivid and green, like the Arabian Sea on a peaceful summer afternoon. Surprisingly, she didn't seem at all hesitant to be talking to a stranger. Maybe because he was in a southern rural area and she was being true to the region—friendly and hospitable.

"Could you give me a jump?" she asked.

Brogan would love to give her a jump, and for the first time in his life, he found himself struggling to speak. He couldn't believe it. Eventually, he found his tongue and managed to spit out a few words, "I sure can help you out with that."

"I really appreciate it." She gave him a look filled with so much gratitude, it made him shift his feet where he stood. "I'll go and get the cables."

His heart skipped another beat as he watched her hurry to the back of the truck. If given the chance, he could easily stand there all day and just stare at her.

She soon returned with the cables and handed him one end. Her soft fingers brushed against his, giving him one heck of a jolt. Brogan blew out a breath, not wanting to imagine what she'd do to him with a soft peck on the cheek, he was barely surviving the mere touch of her hand.

Recovering from that jolt, Brogan popped the hood to the SUV. After they both hooked the cables up to their respective terminals, he started his vehicle and revved the engine. Then, he joined her where she leaned against the side of the dusty blue truck and waited for the battery to charge.

"Thank you for stopping to help me." She folded her arms across her chest and gave him another one of those sunny smiles. "You're a real lifesaver."

Yeah, that was him all right, and she was sweeping him away with her sweet southern charm.

"You seem to know a lot about auto mechanics," Brogan mused.

"My dad taught me." She broadened her smile, showing off a spot of grease on her lower left cheek.

Brogan clenched his hand, fighting off the urge to wipe it off. What the hell was the matter with him? He was the one who swept chicks off their feet, not the other way around. The guys on the team even nicknamed him 'the sweeper' because of what he could do with his Californian charm, but this chick was unbelievable. She had his heart skipping, his tongue tied, and his hand aching to touch her, and he'd just met her.

"Do you live around here?" Brogan asked, curious to know more about her.

"I used to but not anymore. I came—I came to visit my parents. How about you?" She tilted her head and stared.

All Brogan wanted to do was drown himself in those green pools. Man, this chick was really turning him on. He couldn't believe how much he was attracted to her and shoved his hands in his jean pockets and rocked on his heels, back and forth. "I'm just passing through. So, if you're not a mechanic, what do you do for a living?"

"I work at a VA outpatient clinic."

Brogan scrubbed his face with his hand. He had enough hospitals, clinics, and pills to last him a lifetime.

"I'm a physical therapist," she added.

A PT? None of his therapists had ever looked as good as she did. The chick had the whole package going for herself—pretty, independent, and smart. Assuming she was single and available, she'd be a great catch for any man, except for him. He'd be a devout bachelor until the day he died.

Before he could give her a chance to ask him what he did for a living, he quickly asked, "Can you recommend a hotel in Blowing Rock?"

"There's several, but my favorite is Mountainaire Inn. They have these neat, little cabins you can stay in off Main Street."

Man, he wouldn't mind shacking up with her in one of them. It'd be heaven compared to sleeping under the stars with a bunch of guys in the middle of a battle zone, or on a jungle floor crawling with leeches, scorpions, and snakes. "The place sounds cozy." Maybe she'd be interested in joining him.

"It is." A shade of pink rose up her neck. By the time it reached her cheeks, it turned red.

Amazed she had actually blushed, Brogan offered her a grin and then glanced over her shoulder at the truck's cargo bed filled with an array of colorful plants. "I see you like a flower or two," he said jokingly.

She laughed, sending another jolt through him. He eased out a breath. He didn't know which of the three he liked better, her smile, the sound of her laugh, or her touch. If he didn't have to choose one, then they'd all come in first place.

"I love flowers," she said excitedly. "Do you?"

"I've really never thought about it." The only ones Brogan knew about grew between cracks and sprouted up on overgrown lawns. He believed they were called weeds, and they weren't the kind he could smoke. "What types do you have back there?"

"Let me show you." She led him to the rear of the truck. "See the ones with the black center and yellowish petals."

"Yeah."

"They're called Black-eyed Susan. They mean justice."

Brogan chuckled. He'd given out a few black eyes, and they were all justified. "I didn't know flowers had meanings."

"These sweet, clear blue ones over here are called bachelor's buttons. Supposedly, if a bachelor liked someone and wanted to date them, he'd wear one in his buttonhole. If the bloom thrived, it meant his love was reciprocated."

Well, he wouldn't be wearing one of those any time soon. However, this lovely chick was tempting him to change his mind. "What are those over there?"

Her eyebrows lifted with excitement and their eyes caught and held until she darted her gaze away and spoke in a soft voice, "The yellow ones are daffodils. And those red ones are tulips."

"Oh yeah. What do those mean?"

"The daffodils usually have reference to the sun, like the sun is always shining when I'm with you."

Anyone who stood around her long enough could easily find themselves feeling the same way towards her, she certainly was brightening his day. "And the tulips?"

"Oh, those sometimes mean, uh, perfect lover," she said quietly, her cheeks matching the same color of those tulips.

Brogan imagined she'd be a perfect lover with her perfect breasts, tiny waist, slender legs... Ah, hell, he sighed. Well-trained in reading body language, he could tell she wasn't the type to have a short hot affair or a hookup. Whenever she mentioned something related to intimacy, she'd turn redder than a beet.

And he found himself liking it.

It'd been a long time since he'd seen blushes like hers. In fact, he hadn't seen any since he lost his virginity at age fifteen to a girl one year younger than him. Living in and out of foster care as a kid, he had to grow up fast. He was constantly messing around and getting into trouble. If it hadn't been for the Navy, he would've probably ended up in jail or dead by his eighteenth birthday.

"Do you think my battery is charged yet?"

Her question pulled him out of his spiraling thoughts. Much to his surprise, he didn't want their time together to end and scrambled for an excuse to make her stay longer. "Give it another minute. So what's that plant called?" Brogan pointed to a potted plant with bright, yellow buds.

"That's a rose bush. Each rose color has a different meaning. Yellow symbolizes friendship, joy, and good health."

He'd never thought he'd have any joy on this trip to North Carolina, considering what his personal mission was, but she certainly brought him some and he was grateful for it.

She reached over the side of the truck and cupped a yellow bud. "Come here and smell this."

Brogan leaned forward and took a breath and inhaled a light, lemony fragrance. If his team saw him now, sniffing posies, he'd never hear the end of it. But he had to admit, he liked the scent of the rose, it was sweet and warm, like the woman standing next to him.

"What are the other rose colors?" Brogan asked, amazed by his sudden interest in flowers, or was it by his sudden interest in her?

"They come in fourteen different colors and each one has their own significant meaning, but the most common are yellow, pink, red, and white."

"And what are their meanings?" he asked, his eyes fixed on her flushed cheeks.

"Pink roses are often given as a token of admiration and appreciation, the red symbolizes love and romance,

216

and white is typically associated with marriage and new beginnings."

"I bet you've been given all four types of roses."

Under hooded eyes, she shook her head and laughed. "Only red ones."

Everything about her was pretty, including her long, thick lashes. "So does that mean you're not married?" Brogan asked, hoping much to his amazement that she wasn't.

"Yes, that means I'm not married." She cleared her throat and then peeked around him. "I think my battery should be charged by now," she said quietly.

His battery sure was, but he could tell the conversation was becoming too personal for her, and she was getting uncomfortable with it, and Brogan couldn't blame her. In spite of the small town, low-crime-rate appeal, she was on the side of the road alone with a stranger, high up in the mountains with very few cars passing by. Yet, if she knew what he did for a living, she'd have nothing to worry about.

Regardless, his intention wasn't to make her uneasy, and he realized it was time to say goodbye, much to his regret. "I'll turn off my SUV, and then you can see if your truck starts."

Relief washing over her face, she nodded. After the cables were removed, she hopped in behind the wheel as he sat behind his and cut the engine.

"Okay," Brogan called out. "Start it now."

The hum of a powerful V-8 filled the air.

She slammed the door shut and poked her head out of the truck's window. "Thank you so much for your help. I hope I didn't bore you too much."

That was the last thing she did. "Not at all." Brogan smiled. "I'm glad I was able to assist you."

"Well, enjoy your visit to Blowing Rock."

Brogan sat in his SUV and watched her pull out onto the causeway and drive south down the road until the truck disappeared around the bend. Dammit, he should've gotten her number. Granted, he'd told her he was passing through, but it would've been nice to have asked her out to dinner or meet him for a drink of lemonade, later.

Or, maybe it was better he hadn't.

He could tell she was a bit apprehensive, and he didn't need anything right now that could distract him from carrying out his personal mission. It took him a long time of getting here, but he was there now, and he had to see it through to the end, no matter how much it pained him. He owed it to his friend and family.

Resuming his journey, Brogan started the SUV and pulled back onto the causeway and headed north towards Blowing Rock. His mind roamed back to thoughts of that lovely chick, of daffodils and tulips, of her bright smile and charming laugh. He thinned his lips and shook his head. He should've asked for her number.

CHAPTER TWO

Fully naked, Brogan used a hand towel and wiped the steam off the mirror, his wet chest glistening under the bathroom's lights. Yesterday, he'd decided to take the pretty chick up on her suggestion and checked in at the Mountainaire Inn off Main Street. Today, he was finally going to face his demons and meet Mr. and Mrs. Harrison. His hand shook. He took a breath and leaned forward and stared at his reflection staring back at him, or more like the hollow shell of a man he once was.

Hair, damped and short, Brogan wore a day's worth of stubble on his chin and jaw and six months' worth of pain, pills, and booze on his brow. He'd been clean for three months. Three long months. It might've well been for a day. He was constantly fighting off his endless thirst for whiskey.

"You can do this," Brogan said aloud to himself and frowned at the small chunk of his upper left arm missing, taken out by a piece of shrapnel twelve months ago. Then, he lowered his eyes and gazed at the scars on his outer right leg where he was grazed by a bullet almost two years ago.

A sudden image of his buddy's headless body bombarded his mind, reigniting his unquenchable thirst for whiskey. Heart pounding, Brogan cupped his ears with his hands and shut his eyes tight.

God, make it stop.

Make it stop.

Desperate to return to that ever peaceful stupor where he didn't have to relive seeing his friend die, he flung his eyes open, raced into the bedroom, and yanked that whiskey bottle out of the paper bag. He clutched the damn bottle hard until his knuckles turned white.

Palms sweaty and shaking, Brogan shook his head and exhaled sharply through gritted teeth. No! Goddammit, no! He couldn't let his thirst win. Not now. Of all days, not now. Chest heaving, he licked his lips and swallowed back the devil's thirst and set the bottle down, then returned to the bathroom and splashed cold water on his face. The freezing spray yanked him out of his frenzy. Taking deep breaths, he calmed himself down, ever so grateful he'd won that battle but not the fucking war. Hell, it would never be over.

After a quick shave and a fast comb, Brogan took his time and dressed, tending to each detail with a SEAL's care. Clad in neatly pressed blue trouser-pants and a white starched shirt, he slipped on a pair of polished black oxfords and then a service dress blue jacket. Once again, he was Chief Petty Officer Brogan Malloy, a highly trained operative who could think fast on his feet and lead a team in and out of danger until that fateful day twelve months ago.

Brogan clenched his hands and glanced at himself in the mirror, at the shiny gold Trident pinned above three miniature rows of badges and insignias. Hell, he'd gladly give them all back if he could change the past and return his dead friends.

Enough sad shit.

He slung his backpack over his shoulder, tucked a white envelope inside his breast pocket, then shoved the whiskey bottle back inside the brown paper bag, and checked out of the cozy cabin.

Still mad at himself for not getting that chick's number, Brogan hopped in behind the wheel and pulled out onto Main Street. Last night, he could've gone for some company, not that he was looking for a hookup. But if he had been, it wouldn't have been with her. She definitely wasn't the type, not with those sweet, flushed cheeks.

In about ten minutes, Brogan would arrive at the Harrisons. He played out in his mind what he planned on telling them over and over again until he reached his destination. Parked in the driveway of a two-story, old farmhouse, he blew out a breath and glanced at the brown paper bag still lying next to him on the front seat. Even though the house looked warm and inviting, surrounded by lush, green mountains and acres of growing Christmas trees lined up in neat rows, he couldn't help but be nervous. What he was about to do was worse than engaging with the enemy. Grabbing his officer's cap, he slipped it on and then opened the door to the driver's side and stepped outside.

At a calm and steady pace, Brogan strode up the paved walkway and knocked on the screen door. Standing tall and straight, on a veranda that wrapped around the house, he took a breath and inhaled the sweet aroma of freshly baked apple pie. In all his thirty-five years, he'd never had anyone make him a homemade pie, and it sure as hell smelled good.

An older man in his mid-sixties hesitated at first then opened the door. "Is there something I can help you with?"

Brogan swallowed. There was no going back now. "Are you Mr. Harrison?"

"I am." His eyes latched onto him with heightened curiosity.

"Sir, I'm Chief Petty Officer Brogan Malloy. Your son and I served together."

"Oh yes, Will talked about you often. Please, c'mon in," Mr. Harrison's southern accent echoed off the veranda's wooden floorboards.

Fighting to remain calm, Brogan removed his cap and stepped inside.

"Martha," Mr. Harrison called out. "We have a visitor. Bring a couple of glasses of your fresh lemonade and come join us."

Quietly, Brogan followed Mr. Harrison into the living room and took a seat in a floral upholstered chair. The older man closed his newspaper left on a cushion, then sat on the sofa across from him. He stared anxiously at Brogan, his crow's-feet tightening around the outer edges of his dark eyes.

Brogan could only assume a part of Mr. Harrison desperately wanted to hear what he'd come to say while another part of him didn't want to relive through the nightmare of losing a son. As both men waited for Mrs. Harrison to join them, Brogan glanced around the room at the light, yellow-painted walls and woven, oval-shaped rug.

The old farmhouse definitely had a welcoming feel to it. A myriad of family photographs lined the mantel above a stone fireplace. Books and knick-knacks filled shelves, including a folded American flag encased in a glass-shaped-triangle. It had to have been the flag draped over Will's casket. Brogan took a breath to steady his nerves.

At last, Mrs. Harrison, an attractive, slender woman in her late fifties, strode inside. She set a fancy tray down on the coffee table and offered him an inquisitive smile. No doubt she wanted to know the nature of his business, just like her husband who still stared at him with an anxious look on his weathered worn face.

"Martha, this here's Chief Petty Officer Brogan Malloy."

Brogan rose. "Ma'am, it's a pleasure to meet you."

"I feel I already know you," she said softly. "Will had an enormous amount of respect for you. He talked often about you and the team."

Her kindness only added another layer of guilt onto his golden striped shoulders. "I'm sorry I hadn't come out sooner to meet with you both."

Hands a bit shaky, Mrs. Harrison poured them each a glass of tall lemonade and then handed Brogan one. He took two large gulps, one to wet his throat, and the other to give himself the courage to continue. If it'd been whiskey, he would've finished it in one swallow. He returned to his chair and sat across from Mr. and Mrs. Harrison, sitting on the sofa, wide-eyed with their backs straighter than a vintage washboard.

Brogan took a jagged breath then selected each word

carefully before he spoke them. "I'm really sorry I wasn't able to attend Will's service, but I was in bad shape back then. The hospital didn't release me until three months after that mission. Then, I was redeployed before I could come and see you." Which was cut short because he'd been strung out on booze and painkillers.

"Go on, son," Mr. Harrison said in a low voice. "We're listening,"

My God, the man had called him son. Nobody had ever called him that before, but it felt comforting to hear it now as strange as that sounded. "I think it's important for you both to know Will did die a hero," Brogan said proudly. "He loved his job. He loved his country and family. He was well-liked and admired by the guys on the team. He was damn good at what he did."

"I—we would both like to know the truth about what happened to him on that day," Mr. Harrison said flatly, his eyes never leaving Brogan's face.

Brogan shifted in his seat and let out a breath. Then, he took another sip of lemonade, his mouth begging for a taste of whiskey. "That mission is still classified, so what I'm about to tell you must stay only among yourselves. Understand, there'll be parts I won't be able to share."

"Anything you can tell us will be greatly appreciated." Mrs. Harrison glanced at her husband. He patted her hand and finished his drink in a few gulps.

Brogan squared his shoulders and spoke in a low voice, "We were dropped behind enemy lines. Our mission was to go in and rescue a group of peacekeepers captured by an unruly group of rebels. Everything we did had to run like clockwork and with expert precision. One false move, one bad mistake, and we'd not only jeopardize the operation, but we'd also put the hostages at risk."

Brogan glanced at Mrs. Harrison who sat there quietly and clung to every word he said. He finished his lemonade and refilled both his and Mr. Harrison's glasses. The man leaned forward, took a sip and then waited anxiously for

Brogan to continue.

"We could hear their captors, shouting and laughing. They were high on drugs and alcohol, which didn't help matters. The hostages were being held by these heavily armed lunatics. We could tell those poor people were getting slapped around and experiencing horrific, mock executions. If we didn't get them out soon, we feared they'd be killed."

Mr. Harrison spoke in a shaky voice, "Will always said, if he had to go into a hostile situation, he didn't want anyone else to lead them but you."

Brogan shut his eyes briefly and heaved a sigh. He wished to God Will hadn't been with him on that mission. Against his demands, Will had insisted on volunteering for it instead of going home to enjoy his leave. Damn, stupid bastard.

Desperate to remain in control and not lose it in front of them, Brogan continued, "Our initial plan was to go and get the hostages out in one single sweep. But it quickly became obvious there'd be casualties if we did that."

"So what did you do?" Mrs. Harrison sat on the edge of her seat, her face riddled with apprehension.

"We didn't have much choice. As we encroached upon the rebel camp, we quickly became under enemy fire. It sounded like the Fourth of July with rocket launchers going off, grenades exploding, and bullets whizzing by everywhere. Needless to say, we stormed through the camp's buildings, capturing rebels who surrendered and killing those who didn't. The hostages were secured, the area, for the most part, had been neutralized, but a few rebels managed to escape. At that point, the team hadn't lost anyone."

Brogan shifted in his seat and took several more gulps of lemonade. The hairs on his back stood up as he was about to relive once again that fateful scene. He took a few breaths and clenched a hand, fighting to keep his shit together and not unfold in front of the Harrisons.

After clearing his throat, Brogan spoke in a smooth voice, "The surviving rebels had regrouped and launched a counter-attack or more like a drug-fueled rage. Bullets sprayed everywhere. We thought we had all the hostages until we spotted a young woman being used as a human body shield." Brogan's mouth dried. "Will, your son, raced up from behind and killed the rebel, saving her life."

"In exchange for his own," Mr. Harrison said more to himself than to him.

Brogan nodded. "He was hit."

Teary-eyed, Mrs. Harrison let out a low sob. "And then?"

"I tried—I tried to save him," Brogan choked on his words, his tears streaming down his face. "But a grenade exploded."

Briefly, he shut his eyes tight, desperate to block out the image of his friend's head being blown off, of all the bloody shredded pieces of bone, brain matter, and helmet flying everywhere, one of which Brogan learned later had torn off a small chunk of his arm. "The blast was so powerful it had flung me on my back onto the ground where I slammed the back of my head hard against a rock. I don't remember anything after that. I had blacked out."

Brogan placed his sweaty palms on his knees and swallowed the knot wedged deep inside his throat. It was sheer torture retelling this story, but he had to go on for their sakes. "Two weeks later, I woke up in a hospital in Germany where I learned the team had gotten the hostages all out safely, but that we had lost Will."

The pair of them sat there across from Brogan quietly, taking in all that he'd said. The pain streaking across their faces mirrored his own. The sudden sound of Mrs. Harrison's sobs was devastating. He had to say something, anything, to offer the poor woman some comfort.

"Will was very fortunate to have parents like you. Most of the guys on the team, including myself, grew up under different circumstances. I'd never had a brother until I met your son. We would've died for each other." Brogan wiped the tears off his face, with the back of his hand, and cleared his throat. "There are many things I can take, but losing Will wasn't one of them. His death affected me more than I'd realized. I developed a strong taste for whiskey and got hooked on painkillers."

"And now?" Mrs. Harrison sniffled and dabbed the corners of her eyes with a hanky.

"I've been clean for three months. But I won't lie to you, it's been a struggle." Brogan stood and retrieved a white envelope from his breast pocket and then handed it to Mr. Harrison. "Will wanted you both to have this in case anything happened to him. I'm sorry I couldn't deliver this to you sooner."

On wobbly legs, Mrs. Harrison stood and took Brogan's hand in hers. He could tell she was trying to be brave for his sake. God, if only he could've saved Will.

"You have nothing to apologize for," she said softly. "I know this had to have been very hard for you to tell us what had happened."

Brogan nodded. There was nothing else for him to say. He was emotionally spent.

Blinking back tears, Mr. Harrison clutched the envelope to his chest and rose. Brogan could tell he was trying to stay strong, too, just like his wife.

"You're welcome to stay here if you like." He sniffled. "We've got plenty of room. And Martha here is one heck of a cook."

The offer was so damn tempting, but Brogan had to get out of there and get some fresh air before he lost control and unfolded in front of them. "I truly thank you for the kind offer, but I'm afraid I can't."

The grieving couple followed him outside. "Dinner's at six." Mr. Harrison said. "There'll be an extra plate set for you in case you change your mind."

Brogan had never felt more welcome in a home as he did now, but he needed to leave. He was too overwhelmed with emotion to stay, and there was one more thing he needed to do. After shaking Mr. Harrison's hand and accepting a warm hug from his wife, Brogan left the house, hopped inside the SUV and drove away. If he didn't have one more visit to make, he'd pull over, open the bottle of whiskey, and drink himself until he was numb.

Under the late afternoon sun, Brogan rode along a two-lane highway and then made a turn into an old, country cemetery. He continued down a winding road, passing acres of towering green maples and rows of weathered tombstones. Once he found the right row marker, he parked the SUV and glanced around to make sure he was alone.

Confident he was, he slipped on his cap, grabbed the paper bag off the front passenger seat, and stepped out of the vehicle. He took a breath and inhaled the fresh smell of spring, but to him, it might as well have been death and misery.

Eager to finish the last part of his personal mission, Brogan strode down a grassy path until he found the white granite headstone and read—*William Harrison, PO US Navy, Silver Star, Purple Heart, April 3, 1988, May 19, 2017, US Navy SEAL, Beloved Son & Hero.*

Shoulders quaking, Brogan bent down on one knee and bowed his head, his tears dropping in the dirt. In a shaky voice, he spoke above a whisper, "Hey man, it's me. It's been a long time coming. I'm sorry I missed your funeral, buddy. I was in a coma. Can you believe that shit?" Brogan laughed and clutched the whiskey bottle tight in his hand.

"When I woke two weeks later, they made me stay in the hospital for three months and go through a ton of rehab. But after that, I got pretty fucked up in the head there for a while, so I—" —Brogan choked on his words— "so I couldn't get out to North Carolina to deliver your letter until today. Your parents are good people."

"Ah Christ, this is hard." Tears poured out of Brogan

faster than he could fill a shot glass with tequila. "I miss you, man. Hell, the whole team does."

He slapped his palm against his friend's tombstone. "Goddammit, I should've had your back. Why didn't you go on leave like I'd asked—you dumb bastard?" Brogan tried to resist the urge to open the bottle and take a swig of whiskey but his need for alcohol was too great.

Throwing caution to the wind, he grabbed the bottle out of the bag and unscrewed the cap. As he was about to take a drink, he heard a twig snap. Shit. He shot to his feet and wheeled around and gazed into the face of that chick he'd helped out the other day.

Holy crap. Where in the hell had she come from? Bottle in hand, tears staining his fucking face, he stood there frozen, too embarrassed to speak.

Arms full of potted flowers, she stopped midstride and stared. "You're that guy who helped me out yesterday." She looked just as surprised as he did.

Still speechless, he stood there like an idiot and nodded. If it'd been earlier in the day, or another moment in time, he'd lay on the charm and ask her out, but not here—and not now. All he wanted to do was to spend the rest of the afternoon alone with Will and their best friend Jack Daniels.

As he was about to tell her to leave him the fuck alone in a much politer manner, she asked, "Are you—are you Chief Brogan Malloy?"

Ah shit, how did she know who he was? She didn't yesterday. "Yeah, that's me. How did you know?" Mouth drier than the Sahara Desert, he watched her set the potted flowers down by the gravesite.

"By your name badge. Otherwise, I would've never recognized you. The only photos I've seen of you were when you were dressed in full combat gear with your face hidden behind a pair of sunglasses and a thick beard."

Speaking of faces, he dried his quickly, using the back of his hand, and cleared his throat. "Tell me, who are you?"

"I'm Will's sister, Chelsea."

Chelsea. In his frenzy, Brogan had forgotten Will had a sister, but now he remembered Will was so proud of her, he was always bragging about her, and the team appreciated her care packages. He imagined she had to be in her mid-twenties. That'd make her about nine or ten years younger than him. What a shitty way for her to formally meet him when he held a liquor bottle in one hand and his face was wetter than a baby's diaper full of piss.

"What are you doing here?" he asked, wishing she'd go away.

"Every season I plant fresh flowers on my brother's grave, except at Christmas. A wreath is placed instead."

For a few seconds, they stared at one another. Brogan didn't see any judgment or disapproval in that stare, only compassion, and understanding followed by a sympathetic smile.

He winced.

Though he stood there fully dressed, he felt totally exposed and vulnerable. He sure as hell hated feeling that way. He served in almost a dozen tours and was a fucking warrior, not a goddamn mandy-pandy or someone's charity case. Of all days, why did she have to pick this one to come and see him at his worst?

"Can't you come back later?" Brogan asked. "I'd like to be left alone for a while."

"I wish I could leave, but I can't. I've got to get these plants into the ground before they die. Why don't you help me?" Chelsea said more as a command than a request.

Before he could refuse, she took his good friend Jack Daniels out of his hand and placed the bottle on top of Will's headstone. Clearly, she could tell he was hurting. He appreciated she hadn't made any disparaging remarks about his appearance or about his pain, but dammit to hell, why couldn't she have left like he'd asked her? She was stubborn, just like her brother.

"I'll dig the holes," she said, her southern accent floating in the air like a soft wisp of wind.

Normally, he could stand there and listen to her talk all day, but not now, not when all he wanted to do was drink himself into oblivion.

"You can hand me the pots when I'm ready," she added. "I don't want you to get your uniform dirty." She knelt down by the gravesite and looked up at him and gave him a warm smile.

He frowned. His blood was iron, his heart, steel. And this woman was melting their metal edges. The attraction he had felt yesterday for her hadn't left. It was only getting stronger with every second he remained in her company, and he didn't like it. He'd never felt a woman's true affection before, and he didn't want to start now. If he had someone to care about, he might not be able to fight in a clear state of mind. It was better to be a loner and remain dead inside. He had to do something about this fast.

"I think I'll leave you to it." As he was about to reach for the bottle and go, she offered him an even warmer smile, melting those metal edges even more.

"Please stay," Chelsea urged. "I could really use the help."

Shit, how could he say no to her when she looked up at him like that with those vivid green eyes, or when she was Will's sister? With nothing better to do but drink the rest of the day away, he decided to hang around for a while to ease his guilt for not wanting to stay and help.

"Okay," he sighed. "Which plant do you want first, the daffodils or the tulips?"

"You remembered their names," Chelsea sang out in surprise.

Brogan let out a low laugh. "Daffodils mean the sun is always shining when I'm with you." When he was with her, it was hard not to feel that way. "And tulips mean perfect lover."

He watched the shade of pink rise from her neck and color her cheeks a sweet red again. He could almost feel the heat from her blushes penetrate through his uniform and rise up his arm. Yep, no doubt about it, he was seriously attracted to her, and there was nothing he could do about it.

"I think I'll start with the daffodils," Chelsea said, pulling him from his thoughts.

On one bent knee, Brogan grabbed a pot, and as he was about to yank it out, she placed a hand on his and stopped him. "No. Not like that, silly. You'll tear the plant apart. Here, watch me." She lifted a pot and squeezed it, loosening the dirt and roots from the sides. Then, she eased it out gently. "See? Now you try it."

Under her commanding eye, he repeated the steps and then held the intact plant high in the air. "You mean like that?"

"You got it." She took the daffodils from him and quickly covered its roots with fresh dirt. "Have you been to my parents' house yet," she asked and brushed a curl away from her face, "or were you not planning on stopping by to see—"

"I've already spoken to them." Brogan handed her another batch of daffodils and watched her plant them.

"Oh, when did you do that?"

"About two hours ago," Brogan replied

"I just missed you. I left about then to visit a friend on my way here. How were they?"

Brogan eased out a breath and handed her some tulips. The day's emotion had taken its toll on him, and he really didn't want to do a recap.

"Oh, never mind," Chelsea said and planted the flowers. "I can tell it's been a trying day for you. My parents will let me know later."

As much as Brogan appreciated being spared, he couldn't be a completely heartless bastard and not say anything to her about her brother. "Will was really proud of you. He was always bragging about his kid sister."

Chelsea froze. "I never knew that," she whispered.

"The guys on the team sure loved your care packages, too."

"I met a few of them once when I flew out to California to visit Will." Chelsea stopped digging a hole and gazed into his eyes.

"I heard about your visit." They all wanted to take her out and make her their girlfriend. Now after meeting Chelsea, Brogan understood why.

"I wish I could've met you back then," she said, with a smile.

Brogan did, too. "If memory serves me right, I was supposed to hang out with all of you, but couldn't because I was sick as a dog with the flu."

And now, he was sick with grief and sadness, even after a year since Will's death. Too bad Chelsea had caught him at his weakest point. He couldn't help but admire her strength and wonder what the hell she thought of him after seeing him weep like a damn baby.

"Can you hand me the Black-eyed Susan next?"

Beneath a tall, shady maple tree, Brogan continued helping Chelsea plant flowers until all the pots were emptied and the gravesite was covered in an array of colors ranging from yellow, pink and red to purple and light blue.

"This is nice of you to do this for your brother." Brogan smiled, admiring her handiwork.

"Will always said I was sentimental."

And if he were alive today, he'd pull him aside and say, "You're such a wuss. You just met my kid sister, and she already has you wrapped around her little finger."

Chelsea's lower lip trembled and tears pooled in her eyes. "Dammit. I promised I wasn't going to do this today."

Ah shit. He went and made her cry. "I'm sorry. I didn't mean to upset you."

"You didn't," she said in a quivering voice.

Drowning in guilt, Brogan brushed her tears away with the back of his hand, his knuckles warming instantly against her wet, creamy skin.

Shoulders shaking, Chelsea let out a soft sob, "I just miss him so much."

"We all do." Brogan pulled her into his arms, his gut-wrenching with pain and hurt.

Without saying a word, Chelsea placed her head on his shoulder and wept. Her body trembled against his, sending the mother of all shockwaves through him. He exhaled sharply, amazed by the magnitude of that jolt, and glided his hand up and down the swell of her back. Soon, her muscles eased and her sobs quieted, but he continued to hold her, never wanting to let her go, shocking the hell out of him.

About six months ago, he was back in Afghanistan, and now, he stood holding a beautiful woman, listening to birds chirping overhead and insects droning off in the distance in rhythm with his pounding heart. What a far cry from the sounds of gunfire and grenades exploding.

Brogan took a breath and inhaled Chelsea's scent of fresh spring flowers. For the first time in his life, he had intimacy with a woman—without the sex, without his guard up, without the urge to flee at a moment's notice. And he liked it, maybe too much for his own good.

A cool spring breeze swept over them, breaking the magic between them. Chelsea broke loose, and Brogan felt the void instantly. He had no idea how long they'd stood under that shady tree, holding each other, but he wanted to pull her back into his arms. Instead, he dropped them by his side and blew out a breath.

"We better get going." Chelsea collected the empty plastic pots and hand shovel. "We don't want to miss dinner."

"Dinner?"

"Don't tell me you turned down my parents' invite." She blinked, her long, thick lashes still wet from her tears.

"How did you know I was invited?" Brogan brushed a smudge of dirt off her soft cheek, using his thumb, wishing he could do a lot more.

"Because anyone who's a friend of the family, or a stranger in need, always gets an invite." Her smile faded. "Oh no, I can tell by the look on your face, you turned them down. Well, I guess I'll just have to drag you there myself." She slipped her hand in his and gave it a pull. "C'mon. You can't back out now."

"All right, all right," Brogan laughed. "I'll come." He didn't let go of her hand until they reached their vehicles. Much to his surprise, he'd liked holding it. Her long, slender fingers had curled around his palm perfectly. "I'll follow you to the house."

"You're not going to pull a fast one and take a quick turn in the opposite direction, are you?" She gave him a worried glance.

He shook his head. "I won't ditch you. Promise."

"You better not." She smiled. "See you there."

On the drive back to the Harrisons, Brogan found his mind flooded with thoughts of Chelsea. Yeah, sure, he'd offered comfort to grieving widows before, but Chelsea wasn't a widow, and there was a strong connection forming between them that he'd never felt before with a woman until now.

Part of him liked it. A lot. While another part of him didn't like it one damn bit. She was melting those steely edges around his heart, making him feel alive inside instead of dead, making him vulnerable, making him have emotions that could cloud his judgment out in the field if he wasn't careful.

Ah, shit, why did Chelsea have to feel so damn good pressed up against him? It was as if she'd been made for him. They both fit together perfectly. Hell, everything about her was perfect. Brogan tapped his thumbs on the steering wheel and frowned. Falling for Will's sister, a gorgeous, green-eyed brunette, had never been factored in on this trip. He was supposed to pass through North Carolina and continue to beat his addiction and regain control over his life. He didn't even know yet if he wanted to leave the Navy or continue his career and take that BUD/S instructor job offered to him.

Soon, they both arrived at the Harrisons. Chelsea parked the truck in the driveway, and Brogan parked the SUV in front of the house and glanced at the empty seat next to him and reared his head.

Unbelievable.

He'd totally forgotten about the whiskey bottle. He'd left it behind at the cemetery. He'd never done that since he sobered up three months ago. He'd taken that thing with him everywhere he went to fall back on in case he needed it like it was a damn security blanket. And the man had he needed it until Chelsea arrived at the cemetery. Call it luck, but she'd saved him. Otherwise, he would've spent the rest of the afternoon alone, getting trashed under a shady tree, instead of holding her and finding a few minutes of peace.

Thankful he hadn't relapsed, Brogan jumped out of the vehicle and strode towards Chelsea as she waited for him on the veranda, looking pretty as ever in shorts with a smudge of dirt on her cheek. No longer craving a shot of whiskey, he found himself craving for a taste of—Chelsea. Following her inside the house, Brogan imagined one kiss and he'd be addicted to her for life.

"Mom, Dad," Chelsea called out, "look who I found."

Mr. Harrison poked his head out of the living room and broke into a grin. "I see you've decided to join us for dinner after all. Where did she find you?"

Before he could speak, Chelsea jumped in, "We met at the cemetery. When he told me he'd been at the house already, I insisted he come back and have dinner with us."

Mr. Harrison exchanged a glance with Brogan. "You'll have to excuse my daughter. She can be quite persuasive at times. She gets that from her mama."

"I have to shower and change. I've been playing in the dirt all day. Dad, show our guest the downstairs bath. He may want to wash up, too, before we eat."

Brogan watched her disappear up the stairs and found himself missing her already. Ah, hell, he shook his head and frowned. What was she doing to him? He'd never had such thoughts before. And he doubted she knew the effect she was having on him. She was probably being friendly to him because that was the southern way, and because he was her brother's best friend, and nothing more. After dinner, Brogan decided he'd say his goodbyes and head back to California.

CHAPTER THREE

About thirty minutes later, Brogan found himself in the dining room, washed up and seated at a fancy linen-draped table loaded with dishes filled with cooked carrots, mashed potatoes, homemade rolls and roast beef. He'd never had a home cooked meal as grand as this one before. He licked his lips and inhaled the sweet and spicy scents floating around his head, like a heavenly halo. Starving, he wished Chelsea would hurry up and join them.

At the head of the table sat Mrs. Harrison, and at the foot, an impatient Mr. Harrison. "Where's that daughter of ours? If she doesn't get here soon, the food will be cold."

"Be patient," his wife scolded. "I'm sure she'll be down in a minute."

Mr. Harrison gazed up at the ceiling as if he was looking for strength.

Brogan couldn't help but laugh inside. So this was what it was like to grow up in a loving household. It was no wonder everyone on the team was envious of Will. Unlike his lucky buddy, most of them, including himself, came from broken homes, grew up in rough neighborhoods, and were constantly getting into trouble.

"How long are you on leave?" Mr. Harrison poured himself a glass of lemonade from a large pitcher and frowned at his daughter's empty seat.

"Six months. I have three months left." Yeah, three more months to try and stay clean and sober. Man, Brogan hoped he could keep it up. He'd almost lost it earlier today.

The sound of shoes brushing softly against the stairs resonated inside the room.

"Ah, here she comes," Mrs. Harrison smiled.

Brogan watched Chelsea enter and take a seat across from him. He blew out a breath. The woman was outright, breathtakingly gorgeous in her blue sundress, with her hair all curly and face made up with a touch of pink on her cheeks and lips.

The urge to pull her in his arms and kiss her swept over him faster than a F/18 jet could fly. He took a gulp of lemonade to distract him from such tempting thoughts, then eased out a breath.

As Brogan was about to thank them again for inviting him to dinner, Mr. Harrison spoke in a solemn voice, "Let us say grace."

Not much of a churchgoer, Brogan sat in the middle of the table and accepted a hand on either side of him from Mr. and Mrs. Harrison. Then, he bowed his head and listened to Mr. Harrison intone a thankful prayer. Brogan chuckled to himself. The only time he'd said grace was when he was a kid. He had prayed to God there'd be plenty of food on the table to fill his empty belly because there usually was never enough to go around when living in foster care.

"—Thank you, Lord, for the meal we are about to receive and for bringing us Brogan to our humble doorstep. We pray you watch over him and keep him and our brave men and women serving this great nation, safe. Amen."

"That was lovely, dear." Mrs. Harrison gave her husband a smile then passed the platter of roast beef to Brogan. "So what do you plan on doing for the rest of your leave?"

Good question. Part of him wanted to stay and get to know their daughter better while the other part told him to hightail it out of there after dinner.

"I'm not sure yet," Brogan blurted. "When I'm stateside, I usually spend my time in California. I own a small place there on the beach." He helped himself to a big slice of roast beef, followed by a serving of mashed potatoes and carrots.

Mrs. Harrison scowled at his plate. "That's not enough. Take more. I have plenty left in the kitchen."

She didn't have to ask him twice, and Brogan happily

helped himself to four more large spoonsful of spuds and sugar-coated carrots.

"Have you ever been to North Carolina before?" Chelsea bit into a roll and licked a dab of butter off her chin.

Envious of that dab of butter, Brogan shook his head and cleared his throat. "This is the first time. I had no idea Blowing Rock was this beautiful." His gaze locked onto Chelsea's and a shy smile tugged on her plump, pink lips.

Brogan swallowed a gulp of lemonade, quenching his thirst but not his desire to kiss her.

"You should stay and see the sights." Chelsea smiled and took another bite of roll.

Admittedly, it'd be hard to say goodbye to her later when all he wanted to do was drown himself in her sweet scent of fresh spring flowers, or pull her into his arms and kiss her.

"Well, if you're going to do that you might as well stay here," Mrs. Harrison insisted. "We have plenty of room."

Brogan had to put an end to this before it was too late. "I couldn't impose on you like that."

"Don't be ridiculous," Mrs. Harrison said with the wave of her hand. "We'd love to have you."

"I'd be more than happy to show you Linville Falls and take you to a winery." Chelsea stared at him from across the table and gave him another smile that almost melted him like the butter on his hot roll. "We could even ride the trails around Moses Cohen National Park by horseback if you like."

How could he say no to her when all he wanted to do was bask in her warmth? "Are you sure?"

Mr. Harrison tapped the table with the bottom of his fork. The room quieted. All eyes were on Brogan. "Give it up, son," he said. "You won't win this battle, no matter how hard you try, so after dinner go and collect your gear, then come back and stay with us."

Brogan laughed. He knew when he'd been outflanked

and had no choice but to surrender. "All right, ladies, you win. I'll bunk here, but I don't need to go back to the motel. I'd checked out earlier this morning."

Both mother and daughter gave each other a gloating glance. As much as he hated losing, he didn't mind losing to them. Surprisingly, what had started off as a difficult and emotional day was now turning into a pleasant evening.

"How about some more roast?" Mrs. Harrison lifted the platter.

"No, ma'am." Brogan shook his head and pushed his empty plate in front him. "I can't eat another bite." He wiped the corners of his mouth off with a napkin, then placed it back on his lap. "It was delicious. You sure are a great cook, Mrs. Harrison."

"You need to stop being so formal. Call me Martha."

"Yes, ma'am." Brogan gazed at Chelsea. He had to quit staring at her, but it was hard not to when she took his breath away.

Mrs. Harrison rose and grabbed two empty serving bowls off the table. As if on cue, Chelsea jumped to her feet and began to help her clear dishes away. No way could Brogan just sit there and not pitch in.

As he was about stand and reach for the platter, Mrs. Harrison shook her head. "Don't you dare think about it. You're our guest."

"Really, I don't mind."

"Don't even try and begin to change her mind." Mr. Harrison laughed. "You'll lose that battle, too."

Overwhelmed by their hospitality, Brogan leaned back in his chair and took a sip of lemonade. It tasted sweet, just like the way he imagined Chelsea would taste. He clutched the glass tight and shook his head. Every single thought he had was about Chelsea and nothing else. He'd never met a woman before who had such a hold on him and in such a short period of time. He didn't know whether to be happy or angry at himself for not keeping his emotions in check.

Mrs. Harrison returned from the kitchen. "We have apple pie and peach cobbler. I made the pie, and Chelsea, the cobbler. Which one would you like, fellas?"

"I'll have one of each," Mr. Harrison said.

"I'll have the same." If Brogan kept going at the rate he was eating, he'd soon be too big to fit into his trouser-pants. Regardless, he couldn't afford to offend either woman and had to have a serving of both.

After Mrs. Harrison left the room, her husband leaned over and spoke in a low voice. "I miss having another man around the house. You ruffle a feather in the coop, and you end up having two hens clucking at you."

Brogan laughed. However, after being deployed so many times and being with mainly men day in and day out, he liked having women around for a change, especially the Chelsea kind. Man, she sure was sweet. Dammit. There he went again, thinking about nothing else but her.

CHAPTER FOUR

Following dessert, Brogan brought his gear inside the house from the SUV and changed out of his uniform in Will's old room. If there was an award in every sport to win, Brogan swore Will had won them all. The shelves were loaded with trophies similar to the way Will had earned stripes, badges, and medals in the Navy. He had been one badass SEAL.

Brogan's heart raced. Pain flowed through him, like a damn oil gusher. He had to get the hell out of there before he bawled his eyes out. He hurried into his t-shirt and jeans then darted into the hallway and down the stairs.

Chelsea greeted him in the entryway with a smile, easing his mind and warming him instantly.

"It's a beautiful night outside," she said softly. "Care to join me?"

Still miserable, Brogan nodded and watched her take his hand in hers and lead him outside onto the veranda. She sat on a swing hanging from the ceiling, then pulled him down next to her. Other than the low-lights emanating from the house, they were surrounded in darkness, with potted flowers clinging from the eaves and sounds of insects droning off in the distance.

"It sure is a clear night," Chelsea remarked, as they rocked back and forth in the swing slowly. "I wouldn't want to be alone out there if it was cloudy, at least not without a flashlight."

Brogan had his fair share of moonless missions, except he had night vision goggles, a radio, a heavy backpack and an M4 to help guide him through them. But he didn't want to think about that now. All he wanted was to sit next to Chelsea, inhale her sweetness and listen to her charming voice.

"Tell me about yourself."

"What would you like to know." Brogan shifted his weight on the swing. He hated talking about himself.

"How about start at the beginning. Where did you grow up?"

When Chelsea stared at him with those melting green eyes, Brogan found it impossible to say no to her, or deny her anything. The damn woman was reeling him in, hook, line and sinker. It wasn't good. He couldn't be on top of his game, not if he had feelings for someone back home.

But at that specific moment, Brogan would do anything she asked, or give her anything she wanted, and he relented, "My parents were both drug addicts. When they died, I was about seven. I was tossed from one relative to another until I was twelve. Then, I was put into foster care. My uncle said the family couldn't afford to keep me any longer when they were actually tired of dealing with all the trouble I was causing in school." Brogan swallowed back the pain wedged deep inside his throat. To this day, it still hurt.

"Will never told us any of that," Chelsea said softly.

Brogan smiled to himself. His buddy could always keep a secret, and evidently, he took that one to the grave.

"How terrible it must've been for you growing up all alone." Chelsea stared with so much empathy, Brogan could almost feel it flow through his veins.

Glad those days were long past him, he shrugged a shoulder. "As soon as I turned seventeen, I joined the Navy. They became my family. I've never looked back since then."

"Well, now you have another one. You're welcome here anytime." She brushed his cheek with the back of her hand.

No one had ever made such a kind offer or caressed his face with such tenderness like she did. He wanted her to do it—again and again.

Brogan cleared his throat. "That's awfully nice of you to say that."

"My parents informed me you were in the hospital, wounded, and in a coma, and that was why you weren't able to attend Will's funeral." Chelsea gently touched his upper arm, the one with a small chunk missing out of it. "I'm glad you survived. Knowing Will, I'm sure he'd feel the same way."

Brogan sat there, getting drunk on her goodness. The woman was utterly intoxicating. "You have no idea how much I wish I could've been there."

Chelsea pulled out of her pocket, the envelope he had given to her parents earlier. "Thank you for delivering this to us. It meant a lot to my mom and dad, even though it had to have been quite painful for you do it."

He nodded again. "It was, but I'm glad I did it."

This woman was so full of compassion and understanding, it made his heart burst with emotion, like that green creature who stole Christmas. If Chelsea kept that up, there'd be no going back to that life where he felt totally dead and alone inside. He knew he should cut the evening short and hit the sack before it was too late and he lost his heart.

"So what happened after they released you from the hospital?" Chelsea clasped his hand and gave it a gentle squeeze.

"I was redeployed." Brogan stared at their fingers woven together and chuckled to himself. Never in his life had he sat on a porch with a woman before, or held hands with one and just talked. This was all new for him, and he liked it.

"I shouldn't have gone," he added.

"Why?"

"I couldn't cope with all that had happened to Will. I turned to alcohol and painkillers, but eventually realized I had to clean up my act before I got myself killed or someone else on the team, so I requested leave and sought help. I've been sober for three months."

"And today?" Chelsea asked teary-eyed.

Brogan reared his head. Were those tears for him? No woman had ever wept for him before. "If you hadn't come

245

along when you did, I would've relapsed."

"I'm happy you didn't." Still holding his hand, Chelsea gave it another gentle squeeze.

When Brogan was with her, like he was now, drinking whiskey was the last thing on his mind. "It's been a struggle, but I'm determined to beat my addiction."

"Good for you. I believe you will."

It was nice to have someone like Chelsea to believe in him. No one outside the Navy ever did. "Have you read Will's letter yet?" Brogan asked, desperate to not rehash anymore of the past. It only made him feel miserable.

"I haven't." She shook her head. "Have you?"

"No," he said flatly and wasn't sure he wanted to either.

"I was wondering if you'd like to read it."

His hand trembled. Brogan doubted he could hold the paper steady. "I'd rather you read it aloud if that's okay with you."

"I think I can manage." Chelsea unfolded the letter and began to recite aloud, "Dear Mom, Dad, and Sis, I'm sorry you had to be given this letter. I had hoped I would've beaten the odds and had come home to you, starving for a home cooked meal, and eager for another camp out with the family under the stars."

Brogan leaned back and closed his eyes and listened.

At first, Chelsea's voice was calm and steady but soon she was choking on her words. "Sis, all the guys are going to miss your care packages and hearing me brag about you. Just because I'm gone doesn't mean you have to stop though. I'm sure they'd still like to get those treats, especially the chewy nutty bars, and updates on how well you and the family are doing." A quiet sob escaped her lips. "I'm assuming Chief Malloy delivered this letter. I want you all to look out for him and keep him in your prayers. The guy hasn't always had it easy, but that is all I'm going to write on the matter.

"I can't thank you enough for being my family. I had a

wonderful life filled with love and friendship. All I ask of you is please don't grieve for me. I died doing what I believed in and what I loved most. Please bury me in my uniform in that old, country cemetery closest to home, hopefully under a shady maple tree. Never forget me. I'll always love you. Your loving son and brother, Will." Chelsea's voice faded in the soft, spring breeze.

Brogan opened his eyes and saw her tears, mirroring his own streaming down his face. Without thinking, he pulled her into his arms, and they held one another. At that moment, he knew she had drawn him in. Feeling so much alive and not alone, he couldn't imagine going back to that life he once lived and had to do something about it quick before he lost any chance with Chelsea.

"Oh, I have something for you." Chelsea pulled away and grabbed a small bouquet of flowers off a small round table and gave it to him. "They're for you, a true hero, just like my brother."

Brogan smiled at the tulips, daffodils, and bachelor's buttons he held in his hand. Touched by her kind gesture, he spoke above a whisper, "Thank you. They're real pretty, just like you."

Chelsea blushed and broke into a sweet smile. "Who's carrying your letter?"

"I—I don't have one. There isn't anyone to give it to."

"That's not true anymore."

His heart pounded. "What do you mean?"

"You have my family." Chelsea paused. "And me."

Her words gave him encouragement. Maybe she felt about him the same way he felt about her. "Do you really mean that?"

She nodded and kissed his cheek.

Oh man, there was no denying it, not after that sweet peck, Brogan was crazy about her. He set the flowers down and took her hands in his and faced her. "I may not have to write one. I've been offered an instructor's job here in the States."

"Really? Where?" Chelsea asked excitedly.

"Back in California."

"Are you going to take it?"

"Maybe." Brogan pulled a bachelor's button from the bouquet and placed the stem inside the pocket of his t-shirt. "If I—"

"If you what?"

"If I had someone to come home to every night."

"You mean you don't have anyone?" Chelsea asked incredulously.

Brogan shook his head. "But I'm hoping I will."

"Oh," she sighed and lowered her head.

He placed the tip of his finger underneath her chin and lifted it. "You see what I'm wearing?"

"A bachelor's button." Chelsea nodded.

"You told me a bachelor would wear one in their buttonhole if they liked someone and wanted to date them. If the bloom thrived, it meant their love was reciprocated. I'm hoping it'll bloom. Do you think it will?"

She broke into a smile. "Are you serious?"

"I would never kid about something like that. I've never asked a woman before. You're the first." And hopefully the last.

"How would this work? I live here, and you live in California."

"I have to report back to my counselor next week. You could come out and stay with me in Coronado, or I could make arrangements for you to stay somewhere else. We could meet and spend time together and get to know each other better." As much as he wanted her to move in with him and lay in his bed, he could wait for her. She was definitely worth it.

"And if we do, and it does work out between us, what then?" Chelsea asked.

Without any hesitation, Brogan blurted, "We'll get married."

"Holy crap." Her eyes widened. "You are serious."

"I've never been more serious about a woman in life like I am with you. If I lived here, if the circumstances were different, I wouldn't be moving things this fast, but I don't want to waste your time if you're not interested."

"You sure don't mess around. You've given me a lot to think about. Maybe there is something you could do for me that could help me decide."

His pulse raced. His heart hammered. Whatever she wanted, Brogan would go above and beyond to make it happen. "Sure. Anything you want. Just tell me, and I'll do it."

"Kiss me."

Brogan grinned. That had been what he wanted to do since the moment he'd met her. He slid his eager fingers through her silky hair and cradled her ears in his hands. Then, he pulled her head towards him. His mouth covered hers gently. She willingly parted her soft lips, and he happily slid his tongue inside and met hers. Together, they did a slow, country waltz, taking their time to explore.

Brogan savored her taste of sweet peppermint and groaned. The attraction between them overwhelmed him. He couldn't wait to begin their lives together.

Chelsea broke the kiss.

Brogan sat there quietly for what seemed like an eternity and waited for her to speak.

"Has anyone ever told you what a great kisser you are?"

A grin spread across his face while his ego rose a few notches. Yeah, he'd been told that before, and a few other things, but none of it mattered, Brogan only liked hearing it from her. Once again, his heart hammered. "So, did that seal the deal?"

"You have to promise me two things."

"Name them."

"You stick with your rehab program. You relapse more than once and it's over."

"Agreed." Brogan ran his fingers through her short, curly hair and fought back the urge to glide them down past her neck. This woman had really rocked his world—and for the better. "What else?" he asked.

"Take that instructor's job. Please. I've already lost my brother, I don't think I could handle losing you, too."

Brogan let out a low laugh.

Chelsea frowned. "That was funny?"

"No. Not at all. I'll take the job."

"Then why did you laugh?" She gave him a gentle whack on the arm.

"I've never had anyone care about me before the way you do. My relatives were glad to be rid of me. You're the first one who wanted to keep me."

"So do we have a deal then?" Chelsea asked, her eyes gleaming with sheer adoration.

"Yeah." Brogan nodded. "We have a deal."

"Shouldn't we seal it with another kiss?" She smiled shyly, washing him in a ray of light filled with hope for better days ahead.

Brogan pulled her into arms and kissed her. Almost nine months ago, he wanted to end his life with liquor and pills, and now, he was getting himself together and found a good woman. Hopefully, in time, Chelsea would grow to love him. He believed she would. He swore the bachelor's button in his makeshift buttonhole had grown twice its size since he'd put it on.

Without another thought, Brogan deepened the kiss, thankful he'd found Chelsea, thankful he'd found someone to call his own, thankful he'd found—a loving home.

CONNECT WITH TARA!

Website
https://www.taralames.com

Facebook Page
https://www.facebook.com/TaraLAmesAuthor/

Reader Group
https://www.facebook.com/groups/781606672011489/

Book Bub
https://www.bookbub.com/authors/tara-l-ames

WOUNDS OF WAR

BY CD BRADLEY

I would like to dedicate this piece to Master Sergeant Raul "Roy" Perez Benavidez. He is a personal hero of mine and in my humble opinion one of the finest soldiers to ever wear a uniform. When I was first invited to be a part of this anthology I knew I wanted to honor him. This is a work of romantic fiction but is based on his life and accomplishments. It is a fanfiction if you will of a great American Hero.

"For those who have fought for it, life has a special flavor the protected will never know. You have never lived until you have almost died. And it is us veterans that pray for peace most of all, especially the wounded because we have suffered the wounds of war."

–MSG ROY P. BENAVIDEZ

CHAPTER ONE

Growing Up

Roy sat playing with a rusty truck on the faded living room carpet.

"El funeral fue hermoso. The funeral was beautiful." A woman he barely recognized was saying. He said nothing but watched family and strangers come and go on the day they buried his mother. Both of his parents had been sharecroppers and now they were gone. Roy could still hear his mother's persistent cough ringing through the house. He passed the truck to his younger brother Roger who had started crying. Where were their mother's arms to comfort him? Roger was too young to understand but Roy knew. A year prior they had buried his father, Salvador. The same raging cough had wracked his once strong body and left him weak and small toward the end. Roy picked up a small bloodstained handkerchief. It had been his mother's. Roy ached to see her again.

The quiet whispers of his family were all around him sucking the air out of the room. They talked about Roger and himself as if they couldn't hear. When they did notice the boys, they bathed them in looks of sadness and pity. No one seemed to know what would happen to them or where the boys would end up.

"I could take Roger home with me." Auntie Maria said to the group of long-faced women.

"NO!" Roy shouted and pushed the woman before bursting into tears and taking off. He ran past some of his cousins playing in the hall and closed himself in the small bedroom he shared with his little brother. Tears streamed down his face and he hugged the small tattered pillow he had had all of his eight years. He remembered the look of sorrow on his mother's face the day she finally fell so weak they took her to the local emergency room. She knew then she wasn't coming home. He could see it in her hollow eyes.

"Hijo mío, sé más valiente de lo que sientes. Siempre ve con honor, y Dios te dará fuerza en tus días más oscuros. My son, be braver than you feel you are. Always go with honor and God will give you strength in your darkest days." Her frail voice haunts him as he rocks back and forth in the empty room. Tears brimmed in her beautiful brown eyes as she spoke the last words he would ever hear from her lips. Now she was gone. He knew the priest had said she would be in heaven with his father, but Roy struggled to understand why God had to take her. Why with all the angels he had in heaven did he have to take the one bit of love and comfort they knew in this wretched world.

His little heart hurt so bad and there seemed to be no light in the darkness. Just then, his uncle and aunt came looking for him. His Aunt Alexandria pulled him into her lap and held him while he cried.

"Why would God take her? Doesn't he know we need her here?" Roy cried as tear poured from his little cheeks. "He isn't fair. He is a bad God."

"No, mi hijo my son, he isn't a bad God. He loves you just as your mother did. Be strong for her and for Roger. You must be strong. Life will bring you many challenges and it's never fair. But how you handle those challenges shape the man that you will be."

Roy held onto his aunt. Her words sounded big and far away. At that moment he didn't care for being a man. He wanted to hold his mother's hand, hear her sing sweet lullabies and fall asleep in her arms. Surely when he woke this would all be a bad dream and she would be making tostadas in their small kitchen. That kitchen was currently packed with faces he didn't recognize and this was no dream. It was to this point the worst day of his young life.

Roger and two of his young cousins piled into the room. His Uncle Nicholas picked Roger up and explained that the boys would be leaving Cuero, Texas and move in with them and eight cousins in El Campo. As much as Roy enjoyed his cousins, the idea of living with ten children in one house made Roy nervous but they would be together and right now that was all that mattered.

Roy looked around his small room and realized that after today he would never see it again. He grew up immensely that day. He vowed to always look out for his little brother and try to live to his mother's words. He believed that no matter where they ended up as long as they had each other it was going to be ok. When all the visitors had gone, they gathered their few possessions and the boys said goodbye to the only home they had ever known.

Despite crowded conditions and minimal resources, they grew up with love in their aunt and uncle's home. Roy's grandfather often told them stories about heroes of their heritage and they ran and played in the dusty streets of El Campo. In a home with ten children, there is always someone to play with even if there is not enough on your plate. Roy and Roger settled into life with their new family. The elementary school in El Campo was only a mile from their house and they easily walked it each morning and afternoon with the gang of children they now called their siblings.

Roy was too young then to fully understand the slurs of the ranchers and the white children who made fun of them. In Cuero, they had lived in a predominately migrant community but El Campo was bigger and they had more interaction with the other people in town.

"Hurry up Roy," Luis urged as they walked the dusty road to school. "You will make us late. Mrs. Rodriguez will be very angry if we are late again."

Roy struggled to keep up. His short legs were stocky but he never quit, he just ran alongside his cousins and kept going. Roger was still too little for school and stayed home with his aunt and younger cousins.

A pickup truck roared up the dusty road behind them.

Hoops and hollers from the teenage boys in the back sounded like a pack of wolves. The hair on Roy's neck stood on end. His heart began to race. He was only in the second grade but he was old enough to know to fear these guys.

"Just keep your head down Roy," Luis instructed quietly. "Whatever you do don't look them in the face and don't say a word."

The truck sped past them completely covering the small group of children in a cloud of dust. Before Roy could even breathe a sigh of relief, the taillights came on and the rusty Ford screeched to a halt. The gang of football players in the back jumped out and started toward them.

"Look, it's a bunch of dusty field rats." A tall gringo wearing a football jersey and jeans yelled as he led the pack toward the still coughing kids. "What's a matter, beaner? You lose your breath in the Rio Grande."

"They can't even understand what you are saying Troy, they're just a bunch of stupid Mexicans." Another boy shouts and semi steps between Troy and the kids. "Let's get on to school. We're gonna be late."

"Not so fast. I'd swear you had a thing for wetbacks, Greg. No, we're gonna have some fun." Troy sneers and knocks Luis' books into the dirt. Troy circled around the small group like a shark. As instructed, Roy and the other children kept their heads down and remained perfectly still. Roy's heart was about to beat out of his chest. He willed his little hands not to tremble and slowed his breathing. When Troy stopped in front of him, Roy closed his eyes and prayed that somehow he could be invisible.

"Open your eyes, little greaser," Troy growled and pushed the small boy to the ground. Roy fell hard dropping the small sack that contained his meager lunch. The apple that his aunt had given him went rolling in the dust and landed by Troy's ogre-like foot. An apple may not seem like a great prize but to a child, with nothing, it felt like the holy grail. Troy picked his foot up and smashed the piece of fruit into a muddy pulp.

Roy looked up with tears burning to escape from little eyes. His little fists balled up but he did not move, he just sat stewing like a pot set on for boil.

"Come on, Troy, let's get going," Greg urged and tried to reach for Troy's arm, but Troy pulled away and stepped toward Valentina and Lala. The two girls were just a year younger than Roy but they were smaller by about ten pounds. Valentina was his cousin and Lala was her best friend. The girls stood holding each other but looked down as Luis had directed. Troy took hold of one of Lala's dark pigtails and waved it around pulling her hair.

Lala stood with her lips pinched in a thin line, squared her little shoulders and looked him right in the eyes with a scowl. For some reason, this infuriated Troy who grabbed Lala by the shoulders and shook her. The little girl began to cry and scream but the other children did not move. Roy boiled over and could take no more. He got up and charged the bigger boy like a raging bull, yelling as he ran full force into Troy's abdomen and knocked the wind out of him.

Troy dropped Lala and doubled over coughing and sputtering while he tried to find his breath. Roy stood between him and the other children, terrified but defiant. His breathing slowed and he stared the monster down. The next few minutes went in a blur. Troy stood and tackled the small boy and began to pummel him with his fists.

"You're going to kill him!" Greg yelled and he and the other boys pulled Troy back toward the truck. Blood ran from Roy's nose and lip and dripped onto the dusty Texas road as they sped away laughing. Roy slowly stood and Lala took her own apple out of her lunch sack and handed it to him, then threw her arms around him and held on tight.

By the time he was ten he led the pack and often

carried Roger if he was falling behind. He did his best not to get into trouble but trouble had a way of finding him. Roy expected people to act with honor and when they didn't he had no problem standing up to them. His hot-headed temper often landed him in even hotter water at school.

"Your education is the most important thing." His uncle explained time and again. "It is your ticket to a better life. You must get a good education then you can get a job that will provide for you and your family when you are grown." The last thing he wanted was for his brother or himself to be a burden on his aunt and uncle. If they caused trouble, Roy feared they would have to leave. Despite his best efforts, Roy managed to get into trouble with the gringos on a regular basis and he began to look for other ways to be of use.

With that many children in the house resources were scarce, so when Roy was old enough to work he got a job shining shoes at the local bus station. Some of the patrons were kind but most were not and regarded him as a dumb little Mexican. They couldn't see the heart and soul of the young man down on his knees polishing their shoes so that he could help feed his family. They couldn't feel the pain of their words or the lost dreams of a little boy who just wanted a chance in this world.

The rotund businessman barely fit into the chair of Roy's booth. He propped his dusty cap toe oxfords up onto the stand and stared impatiently at Roy. Jumping to work, Roy grabbed his kit and began to clean and polish the man's expensive shoes. The entire time Roy was working, the man sat eating a big pulled pork sandwich with sauce dripping onto Roy and the stand. The smell of the tender smoked meat tore at Roy's stomach. The growling and gnashing of which thankfully was so loud in Roy's mind he barely heard the insults the man threw at him every chance he got.

"Can you even understand a word I am sayin' boy?"

The fat man's southern twang hung in the air thick as barbeque sauce. "I reckon not you, one of them stupid Mexicans. If ya'll gonna be in this here country you gotta learn the language. This here's 'Merica and we speak English."

"Si, Señor. Yes, Sir." Was all that Roy could say. Not that he couldn't speak English, in fact, he spoke English and Spanish fluently but to keep out of trouble with the boss hogs of this world he knew to keep his head down and his mouth shut no matter how degrading the situation.

When he finished, the man stood up, admired the work, then spat on Roy and threw a shiny dime into the dirt. Roy scrambled for the money, sweat and saliva dripping from his forehead in the Texas heat.

Over time Roy began to believe their words and grew bitter and hopeless. He started to get into more serious trouble at school and began to hang around with kids who were just as disheartened as he was. His uncle tried time and again to instill in him that you need an education to have hope for the future, that an education was his ticket out of poverty. But as a twelve-year-old boy of Mexican Indian descent living on crumbs in a very white world, Roy let despair drive him to recklessness and bad decisions.

In the seventh grade, Roy dropped out of school and ran away from home. Later he would state this was a bonehead move that he was not proud of but at the time he could see no other option. He had lost his sense of purpose and felt very hopeless about his future. This boiled in him like a raging lion and he didn't know what to do with it.

Once on his own, Roy realized that he still needed to eat so he took a job as a farm laborer. He worked from daylight until dark across four states as a migrant worker. Picking fruit was backbreaking work, often in intense conditions. Sweat and pain were as much a part of his day as the sun in the sky or the dusty air that he breathed. Roy learned to push through the pain and get the job done at all costs.

His uncle's words played over and over in his head. Without an education, there was no way out. The only jobs available to young brown men without an education were in fields or occasionally factories. The majority of people that he worked with were undocumented so the hours were long and the work was hard for very little pay.

"Roy... Roy. Come on... We need to get paid and get on the truck before it heads out." Rafael called to him and slid down the ladder. The sun had already gone to bed, and they had just finished this field. "if we hurry we could make it to the office."

Rafael was two steps ahead of him the whole way as they raced to the office where the campesinos were paid at the end of each job. They made seven pesos a day for working sunup to sundown regardless of the weather. No work, no pay, so they were out there no matter what. Their bed for the night would be in the back of an old pickup truck on the way to the next field. Occasionally if they were in one area for any length of time, they could use a makeshift tent. Tonight was not one of those nights. A canteen of water and whatever rotten fruit they could carry would be their meal as they rode beneath the stars. They worked seven days a week and sent most of the money home to their families. Roy hoped that the meager amount he was able to contribute would make a difference and keep Roger out of the fields.

He hoped and prayed that his brother was working hard in school. He was finally beginning to understand what his uncle meant by education being the ticket to freedom. Roy knew that he wanted more for his life but didn't know how to go about it. Night after night he would lay in the back of that pickup truck looking at the millions of stars and wonder what it was all for. He knew he was meant for more than just picking fruit.

Roy's body grew strong but his mind grew restless. He needed a sense of purpose but lacked the education and skills to do anything else. One hot Texas night the truck broke down and they were stranded on the way to the next job. Miles from any assistance Roy helped the driver fix the truck and get it going again. When they reached a filling station the next morning the driver bragged about Roy's abilities to the owner of the shop. The station owner took a chance and hired Roy on the spot to work in the tire shop. He learned to change tires and retread them. The work was challenging and physically exhausting but this was nothing new for Roy.

He was able to send a little more money home to his family and the owner of the station let him sleep in the back. The other workers in the tire shop, seasoned in their trade gave Roy a long way to go but were, for the most part, his new family.

"Hey, Roy! We gotta big one for ya." Gus yelled from just outside. Roy stepped into the daylight covered in oil and sweat. At seventeen years old he was the youngest and most agile worker in the bunch. As such it was his job to crawl under vehicles to set the jack when the job started. This time it was a garbage truck that had gotten a flat on the way to the dump. A swarm of flies followed and hovered around it with the fervor of a biblical plague.

Roy groaned inwardly but knew the job had to get done no matter what. They pulled it as far into the bay as it could go and he shimmied underneath the rancid smelling truck with the jack. Streams of putrid liquid dripped from various places down on his forehead and hands. Roy pushed the smell out of his mind and set the jack where it belonged. He was learning that doing a good job often meant personal sacrifice. Roy crawled out from under the truck to a chorus of cheers and laughter from the guys.
"You smell like a pile of dog shit that got left out in the sun to rot." Gus was rolling with laughter. Roy stayed the course and crawled back in with the second jack. There was still a job to do and Roy wasn't giving up. He wrestled with the jacks and fought the massive tire until he got it

removed. By the time he finally got it changed he was exhausted, covered in grime, but satisfied with a job well done.

The station owner paid a bit more than the ranch owners but Roy still made significantly less than the other workers at the shop. He didn't complain, but when he heard some customers talking about the pay from a guard unit they did on the weekends and he decided to check it out. Roy spent an afternoon talking to recruiters and in 1952 he joined the Army National Guard.

CHAPTER TWO

The Army

From the moment he stepped on base Roy liked the moral and honor that he saw from the men in uniform. The time spent working in the fields and lifting heavy tires had prepared him well for the physical training involved. The national guard pay was more than anything he had received previously and he finally felt a sense of purpose with his life. He continued to work in the tire shop through the week and then attended his guard duties on the weekends. One Friday afternoon he was just rushing from the station to the post to mail his pay to his family when he ran smack into a beautiful young woman carrying a small bag of groceries. She dropped the bag onto the wet pavement and apples went rolling in all directions. He scrambled to help her pick them up and when he stood to hand them to her the busy street fell silent. Her dark curls flowed around her petite face and big brown eyes stared back at him. Lips so red that Christ's own blood paled in comparison smiled at him and before she ever spoke a word he knew.

"Roy? …. Roy Benavidez, Is that you?" She asked laughing and crying at the same time and threw her arms around his neck causing the apples to go rolling once again.

"Lala? I… I'm sorry I mean Hilaria Coy?" Roy asked dumbfounded, he hadn't seen her since the seventh grade. Roy still remembered the round-faced little girl with dark curls and big eyes that held his hand that day on the dusty Texas road. She stood like a 1950s pin up dream and he could barely believe the vision before him. Her striped dress had a wide shirt collar neck that was open in a large V shape with a matching Camisole underneath. This was belted around her tiny waist and then became a pencil skirt that moved with each sway of her full Hispanic hips. She

267

was not a little girl anymore.

"You can call me Lala, Roy… I'll always be your Lala." She said with a giggle and they both stooped to pick up the apples once again.

"Are you working here? Are you…" He hesitated, "Married?" Roy prayed her answer would be no. Her fine clothes and shoes worried him. He couldn't provide for her like that. Not working in a tire shop and in the guard on the weekends.

"I'm a secretary at a law firm here in town. And I sew clothes for people on the side. Mostly mending but I made this myself, what do you think?" She stood as they finished gathering the strewn groceries and gave a little twirl.

"Muy bien very good, Lala! You are a very talented woman." Roy stood in awe of the woman she had become. "I need to send my paycheck to my family, then I have a little time before I report to guard duty. Would you like to have dinner with me?"

"Are you a security guard?" She asked looking him over as he was still in his uniform from the tire shop.

They started walking together toward the post office, Roy carrying her bag and Lala hanging on his arm like she did when they were little. Eight years had gone by since he had seen her last but they fell into step as if it had only been eight days.

"I work at Jamison's Filling Station in the tire shop through the week and I report to the National Guard unit on the weekends." He filled her in on his various jobs and travels. When they reached the post, as usual, he sent the majority of his check to his family and only kept a very small portion for himself. He knew taking her to dinner would deplete most of what he had to eat on for the week but he didn't care. It would be worth it.

Instead of the fancy restaurant he had heard businessmen in the shop talk about taking their wives to, Lala opted for the small diner two streets over. Neither one of them owned a car and she said they shouldn't spend money on a place like that when they were both doing all they could to help their families. Over dinner and then coffee she filled him in on all the happenings in El Campo since he was gone and urged him to come home to see his familia.

"Your Tia Alexandria would love to see you. It broke her corazon heart when you went away." Lala explained and took his rough hand in her delicate one. "The money you have sent has helped so much. They know that you love them and your Tio Nicholas is not cross with you for leaving, he is just sad you did not stay in school."

"Do you see them often?" He asked, suddenly missing home for the first time with an ache he couldn't explain. "How is Roger? What is he doing now?"

"I worked with Alexandria through high school, she taught me to sew. I still see them when I take the bus home to attend mass with my family as often as I can afford to. Roger is doing very well. He is working toward his realtor license and did you know... Oh," She giggled, "probably not… He and Selia Zepeda are hot and heavy. It won't be long I expect those two will be getting married." She raised her eyebrows up and down teasing at the salaciousness of the relationship.

"He always did like her," Roy said with a laugh and knew he needed to see his brother. He needed to be there for him.

"What about you?" She asked suddenly becoming serious, "Did you find someone along the way?" She asked and then bit her ruby lip pensively as if she was almost afraid to hear the answer.

"Yes," he answered honestly and her face fell. "I met her a long time ago, I just didn't realize it until today." He gave her hand a squeeze and she lit up like the sky on the Fourth of July. "I have guard this weekend but maybe next I could ride the bus with you back to El Campo and visit our families."

"I would like that very much." She answered still

holding his hand. When they parted ways outside the diner, Roy felt like he was ten feet tall and walking on air. He knew now what he wanted out of life.

The entire weekend at guard he couldn't get his mind off of the glorious girl with the big brown eyes. "Hey Benavidez, what's up with you?" his training officer asked, "You are practically singing this weekend."

Roy filled him in on reuniting with Lala and how he wished that he could do more, be something more. "She deserves so much more than what I can give her. I don't have the education or the skills for a better job. I need to go back to school but now I am too old. I want to be the man that she deserves."

The sergeant had watched him work without fail or complaint for the last three years. "Benavidez, you are a very hard worker. You can read and write two languages. You are a smart man even if your hot head does get you into trouble sometimes. Have you ever considered enlisting in the regular Army? The pay is better and they give you a place to live. It's better than sleeping in the back of the tire shop."

Roy thought about this for the rest of the weekend and Monday morning he reported to the recruiter's office to see if he qualified for the regular army. He didn't have a high school diploma but he was very strong and could read and write in two languages so they said that he could sit for the entrance exam and if he passed he would be allowed in. The pay was eighty-three dollars and twenty cents a month. This was definitely more than he had ever made before and he knew he had to make it. They scheduled his test for two weeks out. Every night after the shop closed he studied with books he got at the library.

Sometimes he met Lala at the library or the diner and she would help him. Roy picked the lessons up quickly. His determination fueled the late nights. This was his chance for a better life. A change to right the wrongs when he left school and ran away. He had learned to work with his back, now he needed to work with his head.

As promised, the following Friday Roy went with Lala back to El Campo to visit his family. Tia Alexandria was as beautiful as ever and he held the woman as she cried the happy tears of a mother welcoming her son home. Tio Nicholas shook his hand and hugged him. Roy couldn't remember why he had stayed away so long. Pride had gotten in the way of family and Roy was sorry to have missed the time with them. Tia Alexandria and the girls had prepared a feast for his return. The smells from that small kitchen made his mouth water and his heart melt. This was home. He was home.

His brother Roger came and brought Selia and they ate and danced long into the night. Cousins, Aunts, Uncles the entire family family celebrated the return of one of their own. Younger children ran around and played games. Roy watched them and remembered it wasn't that long ago that was him and Roger. It seemed like only yesterday and a lifetime all at once.

The next day, Roy talked at length with his brother and uncle about his decision to join the Army. He told them about his service thus far in the National Guard and how he needed the Army to gain skills and education. Roger was interested in the Guard and said he would like to talk to the recruiter with Roy the next time he went.

"I'm proud of you, my son." Tio Nicholas said placing his hand on Roy's shoulder, "You have to keep trying. In this life, you can never give up."

"I know that I paid a large price for leaving school early," Roy confessed. "It was a bad decision on my part, and I will pay dearly for it my entire life."

"It broke your Tia's heart when you left. You have a good mind, but you sold yourself short. This is your second chance to make something of yourself and to take advantage of the opportunity that you threw away the first time." Tio Nicholas counseled as they sat on the back porch steps under the stars. Roy looked up at the night sky. He remembered those were the same stars he looked at from the bed of that truck. This was his chance to become the kind of man his mother would be proud of.

"I will work hard, Tio, I won't give up," Roy promised and meant it.

"I know mi hijo, my son, just don't let that hot head of yours get in the way." His uncle teased and patted him on the back.

Roy attended Mass with his family and Lala and her family. For the first time since he could remember, he was hopeful about the future and knew what he had to do. When he went back to Houston, Roy passed the entrance exam and was accepted into the United States Army. In 1955, he was stationed in Fort Ord, California. Roy began to study Linguistics in addition to his regular duties but no matter how busy he was he made time to write to Hilaria.

My Dearest Lala,

I hope that this letter finds you well. I have completed another round of training and I learned today of an army group that gets extra pay to jump out of planes. I am doing well in my unit, mind the occasional KP duty for having a mouth that is too big for my britches. I asked my sergeant about the group and he said it is called Airborne and he thinks I may qualify. I will talk to the recruiters and see what they think.

This could be a good opportunity for us. May I say "us". I have given up trying to figure out how a man can love a woman his whole life from just a young boy... It just happened. When I saw you on the street in Houston and that apple from your bag came to rest. I picked it up not knowing it would change the rest of my life. Handing it back to you after all those years and seeing the breathtaking woman you had become, changed me. It took me over and I will not rest until I can see you and be with you again. I miss you every day and I pray that someday I will become the kind of man who deserves a woman like you.

How is everyone at home getting on? Please give them my love. I hope that my brother is getting on well and staying out of trouble.

I love you my darling… I hope that it is ok to say that.

Roy

Each letter took two weeks to get to her and then two weeks for the response to return. By the time Lala's letter reached base he had been sent to Georgia for Airborne training. Roy had qualified and began the grueling training it would take to become part of the eighty-second airborne. He continued to send letters home not knowing at first if she was receiving them or if she felt at all as he did.

My Dearest Lala,

I have been accepted for Airborne training. I don't know if my last letter has had time to reach you yet but they have shipped me to Georgia. The recruiter failed to mention just how difficult this school is but I will complete it. Every time we mess up there are pushups. I am here to testify that I am one man responsible for pushing Georgia into South Carolina with pushups alone. My Master Sergeant is firm but I look up to him greatly. We are just completing ground week (Week one) and I look forward to the towers.

Thoughts of you at night keep me going. I want to be a winner for you my love. I hope that you return the feeling. I look forward to your letters. All my love to our families.

Roy

"Benavidez! On your feet!" Master Sergeant Parks yells as Roy slips in the mud beneath the weight of the massive log that he and his partner carried as part of a team-building exercise before moving on to the Swing Lander Trainer.

Roy struggled in the wet mud and slipped again. "Do not give up Benavidez. Winners never quit and quitters never win." The old master sergeant yelled. "What are you, Benavidez?"

"I am a winner, sir!" Roy yelled back and stood with the log and moved forward one difficult step at a time but

273

he never gave up.

Once on the Swing Lander Trainer Roy had to focus on protecting his face, pulling the risers in, swinging his knees so he was not locked up and then land with five points of contact. Roy realized that when he jumped out of planes or helicopters these were the skills that would save his life.

Roy hit the ground like a sack of potatoes and rolled as instructed. "Good work, Benavidez! How'd that feel?" The Master Sergeant asked as Roy gathered himself from the ground.

"As good as falling from a moving truck, sir!" Roy answered and knew there would be pushups as a reward but he didn't mind. He was making it and it felt really good.

On the final week of Airborne training, Roy finally got a letter back from Lala. He rushed back to his barrack after the day was through and tore it open like a rabid dog.

Roy, Mi Corazón, My Love,

I am so thankful to have met you again. My heart is full when I recount the days I dreamed of you when we were young. I have loved you from the moment you spared me from that monster when I was eight years old and I thought I would die when you went away. You don't know this but I tried to follow you. I watched you get in the back of that work truck and stood helpless as it took off down that dusty road. With tears streaming down my face I started to run. I chased you and called out your name but my legs were too short and my steps too slow to keep up. I sank to my knees and I cried because I feared I would never see you again. Night after night I prayed for your safety and for your return to me.

I know that God has brought us together for a reason and I know that he will return you to me now. Wherever the army takes you in this world I have to trust that he who is greater than all will protect you and bring you home safe. I light a candle for your return each Saturday at Mass just as I did when we were young.

Forever yours,

Lala

Roy was on cloud nine through the final week of Jump school. Riding in that C-130 with all his gear strapped to his back all he could think of was the scent of her skin and those crimson lips he was dying to kiss. Each time they reached the target height he would jump willingly knowing he was one step closer to the woman of his dreams.

Unfortunately, the Army already had plans for Roy and before he was able to return to El Campo, Texas to see Lala and his family, he was deployed to Germany. While there he learned to speak German and joked that he was the only Hispanic American to speak German with a southern accent. Roy finally felt proud of the work he was doing and knew that he was gaining skills that would let him take care of Lala the way he wanted to.

Their letters increased dramatically during his deployment, often not waiting for a reply before sending another and she did the same. Every day mail drop was like Christmas for Roy as he waited to see if there was a word from home and from his love.

My Dearest Lala,

I fear this is the first of many goodbyes that we will face if you choose to stick out this life with me. I made grave errors in my youth and did not value the education that was offered so freely. I let my hot head and temper get in the way of the future we should have had, but know this if you are game I will do everything in my power to make you proud. I love you like the sun that rises with the mist over the mountains.

Angel, If I thought that I adored you before, it was but a snowflake before the avalanche. Every thought, everyday dream is of you. I have something to ask of you, and I pray that it is not too soon. I will be returning in the coming months and I pray that you will be waiting for me.

Roy

Days past and Roy continued training and serving with his battalion in Germany. He was a devastatingly hard worker and picked up the language quickly. He spent some time in France and began to speak French as well. He received orders that when he returned he would join the 82 Airborne Division at Ft. Bragg, North Carolina. At that time in his life, he had one objective, to bring Hilaria with him. Days lingered on and he waited breathlessly for her reply.

Just before returning home he received a letter from Lala. He could barely breathe opening the envelope although they had exchanged nearly a hundred letters during the time he was gone, this one he felt would determine their future.

Roy, Mi Corazón, My Love,

I hope that my letter finds you well. The days and hours pass and I watch breathlessly for the postman to bring word from you. I take comfort knowing that this is not wartime but talks of unrest in the world frightens me for you. Know this- I am all in, honey, I love you. Whatever this life brings I will wait for you. There is no other man who will speak to my soul as you do. No other hands I wish to hold me, no other lips will ever find mine. I belong to you, and you alone.

All my love,

Your Lala

At that moment Roy's heart was full in a way he had never dreamed for himself. He immediately went to a shop in Germany and made a purchase he had been saving three months for. He sends the package to his family and made a single request of his uncle and grandfather. Now he must wait. He knew that he would have leave when they returned to the States and he hoped to go to Texas before moving to North Carolina.

His family did not have a telephone and he was en route to the United States before he received word of whether the mission was successful or not. All Roy could do was hope and pray that all had gone well. The long voyage home via ship was as wrought with anxiety as it was with nausea. He longed to see her again. To hold her and know that she would be his forever. He almost couldn't bear to think of her saying no.

When he arrived back in New York, he set out by train for El Campo, Texas. Lying back in the cheapest possible seat he closed his eyes and tried to imagine her face when his uncle, grandfather and their priest showed up at the door to speak with her father. He had sent word by telegram when he arrived in New York of the day and time his train would arrive. Would she be there waiting for him? By her last letter he knew that she would. Roy clutched it in his hands and read it over and over as the train passed through the mountains and valleys on the way to his love.

Would her father say yes? Roy was a devout Catholic as was his beautiful Lala and her family. If the priest had given his blessing, Roy prayed that her father would too. He hoped that he had become the kind of man that her father would accept and welcome for his precious daughter. Would she like the present that he sent her? He wished that he could give her all the finest things that the world had to offer. He knew as a man of his stature, there would be many times he would be unable to but this one time he wanted to give her the world.

The ring he had hidden in the breast pocket of his uniform bore a small opal. He had picked it up in Germany on his last day there. He hoped that she would love it. The details in the engraving were hand done by a craftsman there in his shop. He pictured it shining in the sun against her brown skin. There was never a woman as beautiful in all the world and he knew that this was a once in a lifetime dream.

The train rolled into the station at four thirty-eight in the afternoon. He awoke suddenly as the train whistle blew and it came to a stop. Three days by train had left him a bit disoriented and stiff. He stood and stretched and tried to look out the window to see if anyone was there. At first, he didn't see anyone. His heart sank. Roy grabbed his small suitcase and made his way off the train. By the time he stepped onto the platform he spotted her. There stood Lala, a vision that outdid every fantasy he dared to dream and every last member of both their families.

He couldn't believe his eyes. Roy dropped his case and ran to her. He picked her up and swung her around and around. Roy could barely breathe. He set her down and turned to her father who just nodded and smiled giving Roy his blessing. With that Roy could not wait another moment he dropped to his knees before her and pulled out the ring.

"Lala, love of my life, breath in my soul, fight in my body. You are the reason I wake in the morning and the last thoughts in my mind as I drift to sleep. When my body leaves this earth your name will be on my lips. I pray until then with your father's blessing that you will do me the honor of being my wife. I pledge to you I will work hard every day to be the man you deserve." Roy pledged as he took her hand in his.

"Roy Benavidez, you fool, I have loved you since I was eight years old. You have always been the man I am proud to love with all my heart. Mi corazón My heart, there is no other. There will never be another. Yes, I will marry you. It took you long enough to ask." She said through laughter and tears and bent down to kiss him.

Roy stood and took her in his arms this time and vowed to never let go. He kissed her like there was no one else in the world. All the sounds and bustle of the train station faded away and for a moment they were the only two people on earth.

When he finally set her down the short duration of his leave nearly slapped him in the face. "I only have three days until I have to report to Ft. Bragg in North Carolina."

"That's ok." Tia Alexandria piped up. "We didn't know how much time you would have so when your uncle got your request we sprang into action. Everything is prepared. Tonight we celebrate and tomorrow the wedding." Alexandria gave the signal to the family who began to hoop and holler and whisked the two young lovers back to his aunt and uncle's house.

It looked like his aunt had been cooking nonstop since he had sent the letter. No wonder no one wrote him back, everyone seemed to have been working over time. Paper decorations handmade by his cousins adorned the backyard. Lights and lanterns were everywhere. His cousin Luis' mariachi band played the love songs of Vicente Fernandez and they danced into the night. Nothing could be more perfect.

The next day, in the parish they had grown up in, Roy Benavidez stood at the front of a long aisle aside the priest and waited to see the love of his life. He wondered if she had received his present and if she liked it. When he had asked about it the night before, she had been evasive and refused to talk about it. He was afraid maybe she did not like it.

He looked at the faces of their families. The pews were packed with friends and family on both sides and he knew that he was blessed beyond measure. He thought back to that night in the back of the truck riding from one dusty field to another and thanked God for answering his prayers in a way he could have never imagined. Whatever else you bring in this life. He prayed silently, This is enough. This is more than I could have ever asked for and I am thankful.

Suddenly the doors in the back of the sanctuary open and when he saw her, his knees felt weak and all the air left the room. She had received his present alright. Lala had skillfully made the seven yards of silk and swiss lace into a gown so exquisite Queen Elizabeth would faint with jealousy. The scalloped lace neckline fit just at the edge of her shoulders. Long sheer lace sleeves tapered down her delicate arms to her wrists. The belt around her tiny waist he recognized as his mother's. He remembered the tiny silver buckle from the one photograph he had of his parents on their wedding day. The gown flowed to the ground and she looked like an angel. As she started to move toward him on the arm of her father, Roy felt his heart swell and his eyes brim with so much love he thought he might burst and die on the floor of that church.

When all the vows were said, and the dances danced, and the food was eaten, they finally were able to go home. Her parents had made them reservations at a hotel in Houston as they had to catch the train for North Carolina the next day. She was going with him. No more separation.

"You could stay with your family until I get things settled and find us a place." He urged when they were alone in the elevator to their floor. Roy worried about where they would stay in North Carolina while he sorted out married housing on base.

"You are not getting rid of me that easily. I will sleep in a cardboard box if I have to, but I will not be away from you again. I love you." She stood defiantly with her little shoulders squared as she had when they were eight. Just then the doors opened and they stepped into the hall. They walked to their room. Roy took the suitcases and set them down. He started to protest again, but she put her finger to his lips.

"Stop talking Roy Benavidez and show me what it means to be your wife," Lala said breathlessly and looked up at him with a look he had never seen before in those brown eyes.

Roy threw open the door like it was on fire, scooped her up in his arms and they went inside. Two suitcases sat in the hall forgotten but untouched all night.

~*~

The next day they embarked for Fort Bragg, North Carolina to start their new life. They were lucky enough to get into married housing without too much difficulty and Lala found work on base, while Roy trained as a special forces officer. The years from 1959 to 1965 were everything they had dreamed of. They grew together and welcomed three beautiful children into the world. Both

Roy and Lala remained devout Catholics and visited their families as often as they could. Roy had a few small deployments with his special forces group but nothing for any great length of time. He specialized in linguistics, photography, intelligence, and cross-trained as a medic. He also served as an interrogator when needed.

As it goes with life though just when we become comfortable. Tensions in Vietnam were growing and there was talk of his group being sent.

He held his children and kissed Lala goodbye. This is the way of the special forces soldier. When called, they go. When needed, they rise. There is no holding back, only looking forward until the job is done and they all come home.

"I will love you until the end of time." He whispered in her ear and joined his men on the tarmac.

"I will be here waiting for you. You must return to me." Lala pleaded quietly tears wet on her brown cheeks. Their three small children stood clinging to their mother and waved as Roy climbed onto the plane.

Vietnam was a different animal than anything they had faced or any deployment he had been on to that point. News reports were coming in every day of the deteriorating situation there and the devastation that they faced. Though she always worried about him for the first time since they were married Lala was truly afraid.

Lala watched the plane take off and suddenly she felt like that twelve-year-old girl all over again chasing a truck that would never come back.

CHAPTER THREE

The Long Road Back

In 1965, Roy was sent to South Vietnam as an advisor to an ARVN infantry regiment. They set out on patrol in the thick jungle foliage. Flies and mosquitos swarmed around them. Many of the men became ill from the elements alone but Roy was used to working in the Texas heat and he simply blocked it out. The enemy was everywhere, but you could not see them. Patrols in this area were particularly dangerous because of booby traps left by the Viet Cong in the dense jungle that were difficult to detect.

Roy's team had to keep a lookout for everything they had learned in training. They came to a clearing and the section leader held up his hand for them to stop. Silently he pointed to a thatch frame that was barely noticeable on the jungle floor. Everyone stayed back while he threw a rock to set it off. The frame broke easily revealing Punji Sticks. Roy had read about and seen pictures of these traps made with sharpened bamboo stakes, often smeared with urine, feces, or another substance that would cause infection in the victim. The VC would dig a hole and put the sticks in the bottom, then cover it with a thin frame like this one. The victim would put his foot through the cover and fall on the spikes below.

Carefully they moved around the obstacle and proceeded on with their mission. Roy made the sign of the cross as they passed. He hated to think of one of his men at the bottom of that hole. The Viet Cong had created traps everywhere. They pressed on through grasses so thick you could barely see the man in front of you. Benavidez had heard stories of the three-step snakes or pit vipers that the VC carried in their packs in case they were searched. They were called three step because if you were unfortunate enough to get bitten you would only take about three steps before falling over dead. The men were on high alert as each step could be their last.

They moved another twenty yards and the rains began. Gallons of water pour from the sky soaking everything and distorting the already poor visibility. The men continued to move the best they could through the miserable conditions. Suddenly there was a loud noise and movement to their left, one of the men had stepped in a charge trap and it had blown right through his foot. Benavidez and the other men in his group rushed to the aid of their friend and began to secure the perimeter. Once they got him stabilized they moved out retracing their steps back toward base. Two of the men had Michaelson in a litter carry while Benavidez helped carry his gear.

Back on base, the team reported what they had found and where. They reviewed the dangers to watch out for and rested to prep as they would do it all over again the next day unless they got other orders. Back in his tent Benavidez took time to say a prayer for the injured man and to write a letter to his wife and little ones. Rain beat down on his tent and just about everything he owned was wet.

"I swear this here jungle is trying to digest us," Roberts exclaimed sloshing into the tent and flinging water everywhere. "We are gonna get all covered in sores like C company if we don't figure out a way to stay dry." He stripped and flung himself on his cot.

"Hang your socks up with your uniform." Benavidez suggested, "They may have a chance of drying if you do."

"Good call. What are you writing? That another letter to your wife?" Roberts picked up a small flask and took a swig before grabbing his socks and wringing them out.

"Yes, when you get married, Roberts, you will understand." Benavidez went back to his letter but Roberts was in a chatty mood.

"You hear them talking about the pit vipers?" Roberts suddenly asked. "No thanks. I don't do snakes. They said the VC catch those little critters with their bare hands and walk around with them in their packs. No way!"

"I'm more worried about the IEDs they make with grenades and cans, or the cartridge traps like we saw today. They are small and much harder to detect.

"Did you hear about Jones?" Roberts interrupts, "He got caught in some kind of bamboo spike thing. It was in some of the training."

"You mean the bamboo whip?" Benavidez asked, laying his letter down. He would have to finish later. "The one where the guy sets off the trip wire and it releases a whip consisted of spikes over a long bamboo pole."

"Yup, that's the one. They said it hit his chest going a hundred miles an hour. Swear to God." Roberts exclaimed patting his own chest as if checking for wounds. "Speared him clean through. There's no coming back from that."

Benavidez shook his head, Jones was a good guy. "We need to be extra vigilant tomorrow. This area is loaded they had months of preparation time before we got here."

When Roberts finally fell asleep, Benavidez returned to his letter. He wanted to make sure that Lala knew that he was alright and not to worry. She had enough on her plate taking care of their children, she didn't need to worry about him too. The next time he went to a city he would pick up presents for them. He hoped that would help ease their minds. He didn't know how long he would be here, but he felt strongly that the work was important. While there were snares and pitfalls everywhere, he had also heard about some of the great works that other GIs and units were doing to help the Vietnamese people. There was an orphanage over on China Beach that some of the men had built a playground for and they visited often to help make repairs to the building and bring supplies. Benavidez had already started gathering supplies and when he got his first down day he planned to go with the marines to visit.

The chaplain of their unit was working to coordinate support for the orphanages. Marines donated food, money and as many supplies as they could locate. They even bought toys for the children when they had the opportunity to go to Hong Kong. Benavidez felt drawn to join the effort as he had been an orphan himself.

My Dearest Lala,

I pray that you and the children are doing well. I want you to know that I am safe and working hard. I believe that God has a purpose for me here in Vietnam. I have heard of several good and noble works that the men and the chaplains are involved in outside of our regular duties. I am excited for the opportunity to help with this.

The weather here is wet, most of the time. In fact it has rained every day since I arrived. It's quite a contrast to the Texas heat. This country could be beautiful if it weren't for the fighting and the pitfalls. I want to learn more about the people here and their culture.

There was a short break in the torrential rain tonight and the heavens opened up to reveal the same stars that shined on us the night before our wedding. I think of you always.

All my Love,

Roy

Incoming fire in the distance made sleep difficult but Benavidez and his men rested the best they could throughout the long wet night. The next morning after a delicious meal of powdered eggs they were sent out on another patrol. Roy moved quietly through razor grasses and dense vegetation. Bamboo shoots thirty meters high created a canopy overhead that at times blocked the majority of the light and greenness was all that you could see.

They held their rifles over their heads as they waded through water that was waist deep, trying not to make a sound. Where the trail left the canal they moved into a field of chest-high grasses. This section was somewhat exposed and another patrol had contact with Charlie near here in the last day or two. Tension ran through the men as adrenaline started to pump.

Suddenly, light was everywhere as if the sun had exploded. The incredible sound tore through his ears like a rocket and then there was nothing but an intense ringing so loud he could hardly get his bearings. At first, nothing hurt and Benavidez couldn't tell if he was alive or dead. He tried to pat his body and didn't feel any holes. His men were saying something, yelling maybe but he couldn't understand what they were saying. His vision was blurred and he struggled to make out the scene before him. The only thing he could hear aside from the ringing was the pounding of his heart in his ears. At least he was still alive. He needed to get up. Benavidez tried to move and realized he couldn't. His legs didn't even feel like they were a part of his body anymore. As the adrenaline started to wear off, the feeling returned and his back felt like it was being ripped apart. Pain tore through his spine and shot down into legs he wasn't sure he even still had. Suddenly, he felt himself being lifted and mercifully he passed out.

Roy Benavidez was sent back to Brooke Army Medical Center in the United States. The physical pain was excruciating but it was nothing compared to the blow when the doctor came in. Roy had been lying in the beige room for two weeks. They had x-rayed and poked and prodded him with everything that modern medicine could offer. Roy sat staring at the clock waiting, watching. After what seemed like an eternity, the door opened and a gray-haired man in a white lab coat walked into the room.

"Mr. Benavidez, my name is Doctor Williamson, I want to start by saying thank you for your service." The doctor said as he helped himself to a seat by Roy's bed.

"Tell me doc, how soon can you get me back to my unit?" Roy questioned immediately, the pain was still ridiculous but he needed to get back.

"I'm sorry Mr. Benavidez, but the blast has damaged your thoracic spine. There is nothing we can do." Dr. Williamson said, unable to hide the look of surprise on his face. "You are home now. You are safe. Be thankful for that."

"I need to get back to my unit. We were just getting

started. I haven't even gotten to do anything yet." Roy protested. Why couldn't this doctor understand?

"Your spine is damaged beyond what we can repair." The doctor stressed slower this time as if he was waiting for it to sink in. "You will never walk again."

The words hit Roy as hard as the blast that took his legs in the first place. He felt his soul crumble and he just knew they had to be wrong. Roy shook his head back and forth, angry tears took the place of the words he could not find. This was not the end of his life. This was not his story. He covered his face with his hands and tried to grip what the doctor had said. He barely heard the door close when Dr. Williamson left.

Why God? Why would you send me to that country and give me a sense of purpose and then let this happen before you even let me fulfill it? What kind of test is this?

Before Roy could even process the news his room was filling with family. Everyone talking, crying, and hugging. They talked as if he wasn't there or couldn't hear them. Roy was reminded of the day of his mother's funeral when as a little boy his future was decided without his input. He was not a little boy anymore. He refused to have his fate decided by the limits of others. He insisted that he would walk again and go back to his unit, but they just looked at him with sad eyes.

Brooke Medical Center was located in Houston so it was close enough for family to visit regularly. In no time at all Lala and the children were there and staying with family. Lala was by his side every moment possible.

"Roy, mi corazón my heart." she cried and threw her arms around him. "When they said you had been blown up..." Her voice cracked as she choked on her tears. She sat on the bed with him and he wrapped her up in his arms.

"I am still here, my love. It will take much more than that to get rid of me." Roy assured her and held her tight even though the pain was excruciating. Every movement elicited lightening bolts that sent him out of this world. "They say I will never walk again, but I don't believe that. I can't. I can't believe it."

"Then don't. Don't you believe it, Roy Benavidez. You are stronger than they will ever give you credit for. I know you. I know how strong you are and how big God is. This doesn't have to be the end of your story. You decide that. God decides that. They don't," Lala squared her little shoulders and sat upright as straight as she could on the bed and took his hands. "I will be here with you. Just tell me what to do."

Roy squeezed her hands. The road ahead was going to be long and dark but with her help, it wouldn't be as lonely. They begged the doctors and nurses for therapy, for an intervention of any kind, but were turned down. Everyone told them that there was no hope and they couldn't waste therapy resources on someone who would never walk again. Roy begged them to at least try. When he again failed reflex and strength tests, the doctors told him to give up and except that this was his life. They said they would put in for his medical discharge but that it would take approximately six to nine months to go through. Until then he would stay at the hospital.

Lala stayed by his side. She massaged his feet and moved his legs back and forth. Despite the pain it caused in his back, he instructed her to keep going. She went to the gymnasium at the hospital and watched the therapies they did on some of the other soldiers, stretching and moving each limb and she tried to repeat it with him the best she could. All the while they talked of the children and the life they would have someday when he was able to walk again.

Every day without fail she was there. Her smile plastered on and her voice chipper even though the bags under her beautiful brown eyes told a different story. He could tell by the pinpricks on her fingers that she was sewing again. It killed his soul to know that she must be sewing all night to be here with him through the day.

"Lala, you need to get some rest. The kids need you. I need you to be healthy. You don't have to come every day." He worried that she would wear herself down until there was nothing left. He had watched his mother do the same thing after his father died and he couldn't bear for history to repeat itself. Not now not after everything they had been through.

She worked with him that day and when they were done he asked her not to come the next day. "Please, Lala. You must get some rest. Perhaps you could come three days a week and we can work then. I will think of you every day, my love. Please, I can't watch you kill yourself."

Lala cried and protested at first but eventually, she consented. Roy knew that he must fight this battle and that no one could win it for him. That night after everyone left, he prayed for strength and slipped out of bed. At first, he fell to the floor in a heap as his arms were weak from laying in bed for so long and he had very little feeling below his waist. What he did have was intense blinding pain in his back. Roy took a few deep breaths to keep himself from throwing up. He knew the rest of his life depended on how he managed the next nine months. He could lay in bed and accept this as his fate or he could fight like hell every single chance he got.

After regaining his composure he crawled one painful inch at a time toward the wall. When he reached it he forced himself to sit upright and pushed his back against it. With all the might in his body, he tried to push himself up the wall. He raised a few inches but could not get his legs under him, he buckled and fell. Nurses rushed in at the sound of the crash.

"What are you doing out of bed Mr. Benavidez?" Clara the charge nurse scolded and called for an orderly to come to help put him back in bed. "Did you have a nightmare? Are you having trouble sleeping?"

"No. I'm fine, leave me be." Roy protested, "I need to

stand against the wall. Can you help me stand to build strength in my legs?"

"Oh, Mr. Benavidez, you can't stand honey. Your back is broken. Your legs don't work anymore." Clara informed him softly, her features pinched as she tried to mask the pity.

The orderly arrived, and they pulled him back in bed. Clara stepped out and returned with a sedative to help him sleep. Roy protested again but finally gave in and took the medication. Night after night the ritual continued. As soon as all was quiet Roy would slip out of bed. Eventually, he gained strength in his arms to ease out without making a sound. He would drag himself to the wall at the time crying with the brutality of the pain. Every fiber of his body wanted to give up and lay down, but he could hear his master sergeant in his mind. Quitters never win and winners never quit... What are you, Benavidez? I am a winner! He would shout silently and force himself to keep moving. He reached the wall and used the nightstand and a chair to push himself up with his arms much like an Olympian on the rings. Once up with his legs beneath him, he would ease the weight down on them. Night after night he fell and the nurses would come scolding him and force him to take a sedative.

Each morning they would tell the doctors who would scold him again for trying to get out of bed. They started trying to give him a sedative before bed and he would hide them under his pillow or mattress. When Lala came to visit he would inform her of his progress. Like conspirators in a great cover-up they worked together moving and stretching. When no one was around she would help him get against the wall and ease onto his feet. They cried together at the intense pain but stood firm and did not move until he told her he was ready.

Despite the medication, the pain did not improve, as he began to get some feeling in his legs again they too burned like they were on fire and tingled as though he was covered by a million biting fire ants. He took the new sensations as progress no matter how unbearable they were. At times his will became weak and his heart was heavy. In those times she carried him. Lala crawled into the bed beside him and let his weary head fall on her chest. She recounted all the things they had to be thankful for and all the dreams they would realize one day. She told him stories of their children and his brother's growing family.

Roy would close his eyes and live through those moments. He escaped the pain and fear and helplessness with her hope and love. Night after night he would try again until he got to where he could stand holding on and move his toes back and forth then his feet back and forth.

At times when he wanted to give up, men would come in limbs missing, spirits broken and he knew for them he needed to go back. He remembered on one of the training missions in his Special Forces training, the leader would tell him- Faith, determination and a positive attitude will carry you further than ability. You can do it, Benavidez. You can do it!"

One morning he and Lala sat on the bed, she was massaging sore feet and ankles from standing so long the night before, when the doctor walked in. "Mr. Benavidez, good news, your medical discharge papers have arrived. I just need to complete your final exam."

"Please, No!" Roy begged, "I just need therapy to get back on my feet."

"Roy, we have been over this a thousand times in the last nine months. Your back is broken. Medicine cannot fix it." Dr. Williamson explained yet again. "Even if you could stand, there is no way you will ever walk again."

"But doctor, look what I can do." Roy blurted as he jumped out of bed and held on to Lala's hand forced a small step. Tears ran down his face from the sheer will and devastating pain, but he stood tall.

Dr. Williamson stood open-mouthed for a moment just trying to find the words. Finally, he said, "Benavidez if you can walk out of this room I will tear up these papers."

Roy looked across the ten-foot room that suddenly seemed the length of two football fields. He looked at the doctor and then back to Lala. She said nothing but squeezed his hand and squared her little shoulders. Roy set his sights on the door. Like Peter out of the boat onto the stormy sea, he began to take one shaky step at a time. Pain shot like mortar rounds through his spine and legs with each heavy awkward steps, but he never gave up. The nurses who had put him back to bed so many times stood with tears in their eyes and began to cheer him on.

Quitters never win and winners never quit... What are you, Benavidez?

"You can do it!" they cheered. "Keep going! You are almost there!" Orderlies hearing the ruckus joined them as did patients in wheelchairs and on canes.

What felt like a lifetime later he reached the door frame and took one final step to freedom when he collapsed into their waiting arms. Dr. Williamson took the papers and with tears in his eyes ripped them clean in two.

"I am a winner, sir." Benavidez panted, "I will not quit."

Dr. Williamson changed his report orders to add daily therapy. Six months later Roy Benavidez walked out of Brooke Army Medical Center with a limp headed back to Fort Bragg, North Carolina to be a part of an Elite Studies and Observations group. Lala and the children moved with him and despite the unrelenting back pain, he trained twice as hard as he ever had. Roy had one goal, to get back to Vietnam to finish what he started.

It took two years for him to regain his previous strength and agility. He ran five miles every day and did hundreds of pushups in addition to his schooling. He began to jump again. Landings initially tore through him but he became stronger and stronger and needed less time to recover. Finally when he was able to complete three jumps in one day they said he was ready to go on deployment.

More than anything, Roy wanted to go back to Vietnam. Lala was devastated by the idea. When his orders came in to go to Central America as an advisor she was overjoyed. It was a non-combat area, and though there are always dangers it was not considered a hot zone. This was fantastic news to everyone except Roy.

He needed to get back. He had unfinished business in that jungle and he was determined to see it through. As a non-commissioned officer, he was good friends with some of the higher-ranking officers who had pull for assignments. Roy went to them and pleaded his case. They knew how badly he wanted to go back and what he had gone through to be able to do just that.

"You realize that this may be suicide, Benavidez? That place is a hot mess." The officer asked. "You are passing up a great assignment and asking me to send you straight into hell. Do you realize that?"

"I have to go back. One way or another, I have to go back." Roy stood firm. He was mentally and physically ready. The officer diverted his orders for Central America and in 1968 assigned to Detachment B56, 5th special Forces Group Airborne, at Loc Ninh, a Green Beret outpost near the Cambodian border.

"What have you done?" Lala screamed at him and beat her fists into his uniform. Tears poured like rains over the Vietnam rice fields and he just wrapped her up in his arms. "Why would you do this to us? Why, Roy?"

"I have to go, Lala, I wish that I could explain this to you. This is my purpose. I love you more than life itself, but I can not be the man that I am destined to be for you unless I finish this." He tried to smooth her hair and wipe away her tears.

"Roy Benavidez, you stupid, stupid, man. I love you, God only knows why, but I love you with every fiber of my being." She choked out between sobs. "Mi corazón my heart, do what you have to do, then come home to me. Promise me… Promise that you will come back to me."

CHAPTER FOUR

Six Hours of Hell

In the later part of April 1968, Roy and his partner were sent to gather information deep behind enemy lines. They moved swiftly on foot through the jungle toward their destination. Roy was much more aware this time of the potential hazards pointing them out along the way. He was determined not to get taken out by another booby trap. God had a purpose for him here, he could feel it. It took them six hours to reach their destination. Roy and his partner began gathering information and documenting what they saw. He was trained in photography and captured rolls of film. They communicated with hand signals to remain silent. Several times the VC passed within inches of their position. Two days in they had collected what they needed and were preparing to return home.

Just then an enemy patrol came up the path heading straight for them. They did their best to blend into the surroundings and remain perfectly still. Benavidez's heart raced when he heard the excited voices of the enemy. They had been spotted. Shots opened up and the two men returned fire. They moved as quickly as possible firing their weapons as they ran. He was just clearing a tree when he heard his buddy cry out.

The mission was complete but Benavidez didn't want to leave his buddy behind. He circled back and took out the closest two VC then assessed his buddy. "You are ok. You are going to make it. Just hang on and I'll call for an extraction helicopter." Benavidez instructed. His buddy had been shot through the eye, the back and the legs but he was still breathing.

Benavidez stabilized the wounds and called in the extraction chopper. He held off the enemy until the team arrived with a Mcguire Rig to get them out. The Mcguire Rig was fashioned from a two-inch side, fifteen-foot long tie down strap with a quick-fit buckle on one end. It was used to form a sling that attached to a longer one hundred foot rope that could be lowered from the helicopter. They dropped the rig with a sandbag and Roy helped secure his buddy into the rig. He then stepped into the rope sling and secured himself holding on to his buddy to keep him from falling out.

Enemy fire popped on all sides of them as they were lifted from the jungle. As they began to move through the canopy of the jungle the ropes began to twist and rub on each other. Roy looked up helpless to untangle them. He had to hold on to his buddy as he had slipped into unconsciousness and would not be able to hold his own. The ropes continued to rub and burn and Roy knew just a few more minutes and they would break through.

Just then a non-commissioned officer named Leroy Wright in the chopper saw the same thing. "Hold on!" Leroy yelled down at them as he tied himself off and jumped out of the moving helicopter to physically untangle the ropes. Roy had never seen such dedication. The love of man and country that soldier showed that day saved Roy's life and he vowed never to forget it.

When they landed in a safe zone his buddy was whisked away to the mash hospital for emergency surgery. Roy found the officer and thanked him.

"You saved our lives! Thank you." Benavidez exclaimed and stuck out his hand to the man before him.

"That's our duty," Leroy said with an unmistakable Jersey accent. "I know you'd do the same for me."

Later that night Roy found out that his buddy had expired. With spirits low, he wrote to his precious Lala the last letter he would send from Vietnam.

My Dearest Lala,

My heart is heavy as I write to you. My partner of these many weeks has been killed. It wears on my soul to get to know such a man, and respect him and serve with him, only to watch him be taken away. I know that God still has a purpose for me here. I do not doubt that, but the emotional wounds of this war sometimes greatly outweigh the physical ones.

I do not know the shape this mission will take but I will serve in whatever way necessary. Know that I am well and strong. I have been able to aid in some of the children's missions that we spoke of before. The children here remind me of our own. Coming from such a large family the children in the orphanages provide a sense of familiarity to this strange world. I want to help them in every way possible.

I think of you and the children in all that I do. My love to them and always my love to you. Whatever happens, over here, know that you are my everything. Even as the wind rustles in the trees my love calls to you. I see your face in the rising sun and whisper your name to the stars.

I dream at night of the time when I shall be with you again, hold you in my arms and listen to your sweet voice. I'm sorry that our life together has been filled with more goodbyes than good mornings. I pray that in the years to come that will change. Until then...

All my love,

Roy

He sent the letter the following morning before Mass. He didn't know what was in store for him in this place, but he felt strongly that he was where he was supposed to be doing the work that was needed. The following Thursday, May 2, 1968, Roy sat in a station area waiting for his next assignment. Transmissions came over the radio off and on every day and sometimes they would get called out.

Suddenly there was a pop pop pop like a popcorn machine over the radio. "Come in… Come in…" The radio operator yelled back.

"Get us out of here! ASAP! ASAP! Come and get us out of here! Quick!" The soldier yelled from the other end. The panic in the young man's voice could be felt through the radio waves. Roy's heart began to pound for that kid, he had to help.

"Who are those?" He asked the radio operator.

"I don't know they haven't given a call sign yet." The

radio operator continued trying to reach the desperate team. Roy noticed pilots running to the flight line and he followed them to see where they were going. Just as he reached the line, a badly shot up helicopter was coming in hot. He noticed the door gunner was slumped over the large weapon. He ran over to unstrap him and yelled for the medics. As soon as he lifted him up Roy saw that it was Michael Craig. The boy was just nineteen years old. Their unit had just celebrated his birthday in March.

"Hold on, Michael... Please hold on. Help is on the way." Roy pleaded with the boy as he held him in his arms.

Michael opened his eyes and looked up at the sky. "My God!" He said as a sob escaped his lips, "My mother and father." with that his eyes closed and his body went limp in Roy's arms. Roy held on as the final breath escaped him and the medics took him away.

Roy asked the pilot, "Who are the people on the ground?"

The pilot was the same one that had evacuated Roy and his buddy the other day. He turned and looked at Roy and it clicked. "Hey, you remember that black NCO that saved your life the other day? It's his group."

"Leroy Wright!" Benavidez shouted. He knew that Leroy and Mousseau and O'Connor were always picked for special assignments. He jumped into action instinctively. He had to help those men. Roy saw a medic bag, grabbed it and ran for one of the helicopters that were about to lift off and jumped in.

"Hey, get out of here!" The pilot yelled at him. "You can't go in there, it's too hot!"

The Forward air controller came over the radio warning them to turn back. "You can't go in there. It's too hot! It's too hot!" They pressed on. Those men needed help and they weren't turning back.

When they reached the area, intense enemy fire prevented the chopper from landing. After several attempts, Benavidez instructed the pilot to a clearing and told them he was going in. The pilot did his best to hold the chopper steady about ten feet off the ground. Benavidez realized that he had taken off so quickly he forgot to grab his AK. There was no time to turn back. Armed with only a medical bag and a bowie knife, he gave the sign of the cross and jumped out directly into the chaos below. He immediately started running the seventy-five meters toward the stranded men. Racing through a barrage of enemy fire he was struck in the leg. Pain ripped through his thigh. He stumbled and fell but was able to get up again. I can still move my leg, perhaps it was just a big thorn. He convinced himself and kept going. A few yards further and an explosion ripped into his face, back, and neck with a flash of light and searing pain. His ears rang and his vision blurred, but he called out to God and got back up running through continued fire to the brush pile where Wright's men lay.

Ignoring his own injuries he began to assess the situation. Four of the soldiers were dead and the remaining eight were pinned down in two small groups. He quickly opened the medic bag and stabilized the wounds of the first group the best he could.

"Hold on, I've got you," Benavidez yelled to Mousseau and started wrapping his wounds.

"Where's everyone else?" Mousseau looked around for the rest of the group.

"It's just me... Let's get you fixed up and ready to fight back." Benavidez injected morphine and cinched the bandage tight over Mousseau's wounds to stop the bleeding.

"What the… Either you're stupid or crazy. Either way, I'm glad to see you." Mousseau propped up to fire back but his weapon was out of ammo. Benavidez took ammunition and weapons from the dead and redistributed it among the wounded so they could fight.

He armed himself with an AK and made his way to the second group to tend to and organize them. He gave the men morphine and when they were stabilized and armed, he called in and directed air strikes to help establish a safe extraction zone.

He stood in the clearing to get a signal despite putting himself in direct fire "Herb Thirteen, this is Tango Mike Mike. Got bad guys on three sides, and we have 4 KIA [killed in action] and 8 WIA [wounded in action]. Tango Mike Mike has been hit. I need Dust Off [medical evacuation helicopter], but I don't have a secure LZ [landing zone]. We can hold, but it's going to be close." Another bullet ripped through his right thigh as he made the call, but Benavidez did not slow down. Once a safe perimeter was established he called again for a helicopter to land near one of the groups.

As soon as the chopper neared the ground he sprang into action picking up the closest wounded soldier and hauling tail toward the waiting bird. The door gunner fired into the tree line and Benavidez picked up a rifle from the ground and provided additional support while they loaded the soldier. He ran back for the second man. Enemy fire and grenades landed all around him as he made trip after bloody trip to load each of the wounded and dead from the first group onto the chopper. When that group was loaded, the chopper picked up slightly and Benavidez provided covering fire as he ran alongside the chopper to the second group. When they set down again, enemy fire intensified. As they reached the second group, Benavidez saw the body of team leader Sergeant First Class Wright. Good ole Leroy. He hardly had time to mourn his friend as there was still a job to do. He retrieved a pouch around his friend's neck that contained sensitive information. As he shoved it into his shirt a bullet tore through his abdomen and a grenade exploded right behind him sending shrapnel up his back and knocking him to the ground by his fallen friend.

Just then the helicopter pilot was struck, he slumped forward and the chopper went down hard flipping over violently. Benavidez grabbed his friend and pulled him to the overturned helicopter. He formed a small perimeter. Each breath was forced agony that caused him to cough sprays of blood. He was reminded of his parents before they died of tuberculosis. That last blast must have gotten his lung he reasoned, but he was still able to move so he kept going. Benavidez knew if he stopped now it was over for all of them.

Winners never quit and quitters never win… What are you, Benavidez? "We are winners!" he yelled to no one in particular as he pulled the disoriented soldiers out of the toppled bird. He redistributed ammunition once again and encouraged the men to keep fighting.

"You can do it!" He yelled to the weary men, "Do not give up. Keep fighting." The men held on, battered and broken, they headed his cry and continued to fight. He could see the enemy closing in and knew that time was running out.

He got back on the radio and called the airstrike in Danger Close. He knew that it could be suicide, but it was their only hope.

"Be at your coordinates in two minutes. You got panels [orange fluorescent cloth panels used to mark locations] out?"

"Negative, no panels available. Popping smoke now." Roy yelled into the radio and toss canisters of yellow smoke into the fading light.

"I have yellow."

"Roger, yellow," Roy yelled back

"Got you in sight... where's your incoming fire coming from?"

Roy paused to return fire 32, then resumed the transmission. "We're taking small arms and mortar fire from the line of trees to our south and west, and machine gun, automatic weapon and mortar fire from our east. There is possible a small village just beyond the tree line there I noticed when we flew in. We're dug in just south of the overturned chopper in the brush just to the north of our smoke. Charlie is about to crawl up my nose at the moment I need you, danger close to our location."

"Roger that, Tango Mike Mike...Hold on, we're comin', for ya."

The rolling thunder of sky warriors and Skyhawks ripping open the heavens and raining down God's own fury upon the enemy is both exhilarating and terrifying especially at this close of range. Stray fire flew through their perimeter,-. further wounding some of the men including Benavidez.

The men cheered as the air strikes drove the enemy back slightly and Benavidez called for another strike. Over and over he checked on his men and called again.

"Tango Mike Mike, are you there? Over," A pilot called frantically over the radio after a particularly close strike.

Benavidez scrambled from the man he was helping back to the radio. He could not afford for them to think he was dead as they might pull out and go away.

"Tango Mike Mike, are you there? Over," The voice called again.

"This is Tango Mike Mike," Benavidez answered and all the men on the ground and every man in the sky cheered at the same time.

Back on base, anyone who could not get on a bird or a plane to help were gathered around the call radio. This was their man. This was their brother. Every soul on that base was praying. Every time they made another strike the men waited. The long intervals of static and silence gripped their nerves. Boom boom boom boom, then nothing. The priest made the sign of the cross and prayed. "This is Tango Mike Mike, do you copy?" Cheers erupted from the men. He was still alive. By some crazy miracle in this God forsaken place, he was still alive. No one had seen such bravery or determination or love of man and country before.

Halfway around the world in a little North Carolina suburb, a lovely Mexican American woman was sweeping her kitchen and listening to the radio for news of the war when the doorbell rang. Her heart leaped in her chest and she prayed to God that she would not be one of the thousands of women with a uniformed officer on her stoop to give her bad news.

She cringed each step and walked like a pirate to the gallows. Teeth clenched, she opened the door. Relief flooded her soul when the postman smiled back at her and offered a registered letter.

Lala tore it open and when she read Roy's words somehow she knew he was in trouble. She sank to her knees on that front step and began to pray. She prayed longer and harder than she had in her entire life.

The children came to their mother's side to see what was wrong and she grabbed them up and ran up the street to their church to light a candle. Together with the priest, she prayed for God to spare him and bring him home.

~*~

Roy had been in the thick of the fight for almost six hours when they finally got enough of a clearing for a Huey to land. "Pray and move out," He yelled to his men. Once again he began the dangerous and painstaking process of loading the wounded and the dead onto the chopper. He left trails of blood with each pass- some theirs, but mostly his. They say you leave a part of yourself when you fight in a foreign land. If that's the case, Roy left about two thirds.

Enemy fire and grenades were still going off on all sides and the blood was so caked on his face from head and facial wounds that he could barely see. Trip after trip he ran and stumbled and ran again trying to make sure every man, dead or alive, was onboard safely. Finally, he grabbed Mousseau, who had been providing covering fire but was now too injured to move. Cradling the man in his arms and bleeding profusely from multiple wounds, Benavidez began the last trek across to the chopper. He stepped over the bodies of the VC soldiers that littered the ground. With just feet to go, one of the enemy soldiers jumped up and hit Benavidez in the side of the head with the butt of his rifle shattering his jaw and knocking him to the ground. As Benavidez rolled over, the VC soldier lunged at him with the bayonet and Benavidez grabbed the blade with his bare hand. He let out a blood-curdling scream as he pulled the man toward him and buried his own bowie knife in the man's gut. The bayonet had slashed his hand and forearm in the process, but they were so close and he was not about to quit now.

He grabbed Mousseau up once again and made the final trek to the chopper. Only when Mousseau was secured did Benavidez allow himself to be pulled in. When they grabbed him by the shoulders to pull him in, he noticed something dangling in front of him and reached for it. To his horror, Benavidez grabbed a handful of his own intestines and held them to his gaping abdomen. Far overweight, the chopper dipped side to side as it struggled to take off. Enemy fire was all around them in the distance. Lying there as they flew away he watched the blood run from the doors of the chopper into the green hell below.

Laying side by side with Mousseau he reached out and grabbed his friend's hand. With the saving grace of the chopper blades spinning over his head, Benavidez allowed his eyes to close. He felt Mousseau squeeze his hand tight. Like brothers, they had fought together. The mission was complete. It was finally time to go home. Mousseau's grip tightened and then just like that he let go.

Benavidez drifted in and out of consciousness for the remainder of the flight. By the time they made it back to base, the blood on his face had dried to where he couldn't open his eyes. He had lost so much blood from the thirty-seven separate wounds that he was unable to move. His jaw was broken and he could not open his mouth to speak.

He could hear them pulling off the wounded and the dead and identifying the bodies. He had been in such a zone of collecting men that he had gathered three dead enemy soldiers into the chopper as well. The waiting teams began moving the living to the mash hospital and laying out the dead into body bags.

"What about this one?" Someone asked and Roy felt himself being lifted.

"Damn looks like he got four VC soldiers. Put him with the others."

Roy felt himself being laid on the ground. He tried to move, but his strength was gone. He tried to scream but no voice would come. He could hear the zippers of the other dead as they were placed in body bags and closed up.

I'm not dead! He screamed in his mind. Please for the love of God. As they place him in the body bag and he could hear the zipper closing. He tried his best to wriggle in the pools of his own blood.

"Hey, what are you doing?" a familiar voice yelled. "Hey, stop!" The zipper stopped midway.

"What, it's just another VC piece of crap."

"No! No, that's Roy Benavidez, he is the one that just saved everybody. Please help him, check him... please."

"I'm sorry son there's nothing we can do. Medicine can't save him. Even if he was alive, he's too far gone."

"Come on Doc, just check him." Jerry was yelling now. "Check his heart! Check it!"

The zipper lowered and someone knelt beside Benavidez. A warm hand pressed onto his cold chest.

"Come on Roy! Don't give up now, buddy. Hang in! You can do it!" Jerry sounded like a madman.

With the last bit of strength and fight in his body, Roy did the only thing he knew to do. He spit right in that doctor's face.

"Well now, I believe he might make it." The doctor said and called the transporters over to take him into a triage. The nurses worked to get him cleaned up. He could hear them talking. There was still a long way to go. Roy knew he had to stay alive to see Lala. He had promised her he would come home. That was a promise he didn't intend to break.

The nurses had cleaned him up enough that he could see. Two bags of IV fluids hung beside his bed bringing his pressure back up to at least the minimum to sustain life. He could hear them listing his wounds, condition as critical.

"How the hell is he still alive?" A man's voice rang out through the tent hospital. "Pulse is thready, BP is sixty over palp. That's actually an improvement, so we'll take it. We've got shrapnel in his head and neck. Nurse, where's that O neg? If we don't get some blood pumped in and these holes patched up he doesn't have a prayer in hell of making it."

"Right lung is gone." Another doctor calls out.

"You mean no breath sounds?" The first doctor questions.

"I mean gone. There's a big stinking hole in his back where it should be. Its... its... gone."

"We've got to get him into the OR now. Hang that blood. Move."

They rolled him into the OR and Roy could see a nurse on her hands and knees sobbing, crying out to his creator.

"Why? Why God? Why would you do this to these boys? Why would you let this happen?"

Roy looked over at the operating table next to his, the lifeless body of a young man lay there with no arms and no legs.

The nurse looked up and her big brown eyes met his, but all he could see was Lala. He heard her cry out and the world went dark.

~*~

Lala was hanging sheets on the line in the backyard when the officers came. She watched their dark car roll up in slow motion and she hung onto the line with trembling fingers. This was it. Years of dreading this moment. Years of watching her friends and neighbors get that fateful call. Years of praying it would never be her. The line was visibly shaking when she heard the car stop in front of her house. In silence, she waited. Minutes that seemed like hours passed before the back door opened. Her heart broke into a thousand pieces before they even said a word as the officers followed her daughter into the backyard. As they walked toward her, the grim looks on their faces said all she needed to know. Lala burst into tears pulling the sheets down with her as she fell.

"He promised me…" She screamed, "He promised…"

~*~

He sustained seven major gunshot wounds, twenty-eight shrapnel holes, multiple lacerations and puncture wounds from the bayonet in both arms and his hand. His right lung was completely destroyed and he had actual shrapnel embedded in his head, neck, arms, back, and legs. The back of his skull and his jaw had been crushed by the butt of that gun. No human should have survived what he did. Many young fit men didn't.

Roy faced multiple surgeries to stay alive. He was stabilized, evacuated to Japan for further treatment and then to Brooke Army Medical Hospital in Houston. No one expected him to survive, but they thought a hero like that deserved to at least be close to home when he passed. His Commander wanted to put him in for the Congressional Medal of Honor but didn't think he would live that long so he put in for the Distinguished Service Cross instead.

When a hero staggers back from the filth that is war, in some ways he never really comes home. The firefights, the inhumanity, the degradation plays over and over like a movie in the mind. Roy had been in and out of consciousness for days when he finally reached Texas. Days maybe weeks of restless, nightmare riddled sleep influenced by morphine and repeated surgeries passed before he woke up.

Light streamed in the small room pulling him from his slumber. Roy stirred and struggled to open his eyes. The sun's rays were blinding at first. White hot daggers in his eyes and literally every part of his body hurt. The intensity of what he felt was so great he couldn't distinguish one pain from another. Was he dead? No heaven couldn't have this much pain, perhaps it was hell. No, he'd been there and this wasn't it.

Roy forced his eyes open and held on while they found their focus on the familiar beige room. He couldn't help but laugh. As he came more to himself his eyes fell on the nightstand. A single perfect red apple sat there waiting for him to return. Roy sat up and looked around. His movement startled Lala who was curled up in a chair with her head resting on the foot of his bed.

She looked up at him, her big brown eyes weary and full of tears. "Welcome home, mi corazón my heart."

He wanted to leap forward and hug her, but he still could not move. Roy was bandaged from head to toe. He could only wiggle his toes and move his eyes. The door opened and in walked Dr. Williamson. He had a huge grin on his face. "Nice to see you again, Sergeant. We need to quit meeting like this." Roy tried to laugh. He was home. The road would be long, over a year of surgeries, but he was home.

No one expected a small immigrant orphan who dropped out of school to amount to much, but he became a Master Sergeant of the Green Berets. No one expected a man whose back was blown up by an IED to ever walk again, but he did and he ran ten miles a day. No one expected a man jumping out of a helicopter into a hot enemy zone with only a medic pack and a bowie knife to survive six hours in hell, but he did and saved the lives of eight men and brought all the dead home. And with all the injuries, and surgeries no one expected Roy to live, but he did.

Roy P Benavidez did what no one ever thought he could do with faith, determination, and a positive attitude. He walked out of that hospital a year later with the love of his life on his arm. Three beautiful children followed them running and playing as they went.

In 1981, President Ronald Reagan gave a speech. He told reporters beforehand, "Pay attention to what you are about to hear. If the story of his heroism were a movie script, you would not believe it." He went on to give a speech detailing the unsung heroes of Vietnam and finally reading the citation of Roy's actions. Roys stood tall and at attention. His wife Lala and their children sat in the audience. The whole room sat in awe of this man and what he had done.

"Sergeant Benavidez, a nation grateful to you, and to all your comrades living and dead, awards you, its highest symbol of gratitude for service above and beyond the call of duty, the Congressional Medal of Honor."

CHANGING SEASONS

BY BT URRUELA

Tomorrow Means Nothing
The sun breaches the horizon.
Villagers are stirring.
When light exposes vast desert;
Speckled with dirt shanties;
There's the stink of something shady.

When Mosques begin to sing their praise;
A calm before the storm.
Guttural calls will come to end.
And man must come to terms
See, tomorrow means nothing here.

Handwritten notes and pictures work—
Well enough to calm me.
Just enough to bring home closer.
To help the pain to ease.
Two have gone this month already;

God, how many more have to go?
Bombs they are relentless.
Insatiably seeking a host.
What comes of the pictures?
The notes? And what comes of a soul?

CHAPTER ONE

The convoy from Kuwait to Baghdad took well over five hours and as I sat in the gun turret, my hands clenching the 240-Bravo machine gun and my eyes scanning the dark horizon, I felt like I was an action hero in a movie. It just wasn't real to me yet. It couldn't yet be processed that I was in combat and capable of dying at any moment. I didn't know it then, but I learned quickly: tomorrow means nothing in a war zone.

When I think about it now, my innocence and naivety make me laugh. I had absolutely no clue what was in store for me up north, on the bloody streets of Baghdad, but I'd find out the hard way three weeks later when we hit our first improvised explosive device after a routine route clearance patrol.

An IED using an artillery shell was buried at the start of what was called Chicken Run Road, a stretch of dusty road that led toward the main gate. The area was heavily monitored by tower guards, so whoever planted the IED was not only ballsy but slick as fuck. We were the lead vehicle and I was driving when the explosion rocked the passenger side of our Humvee. At that time, it was unlike anything I'd ever experienced. Like in the movies, time froze for a moment, and then crept back up to speed. I watched as the windshield seemed to splinter in slow motion. The Humvee filled with a plume of black smoke. My ears rang relentlessly.

I patted my chest, scanned my legs, checked my dick… all good. I looked over to find my TC, or track commander, staring blankly from the passenger seat, chunks of shrapnel protruding from his helmet and his eye protection. His bulletproof window is completely smashed, but still intact, and there's a golf ball sized hole near the top of his door frame that let sunlight through.

"Sir, Sir, are you okay?" I asked, my eyes wide and concern thick in my tone.

Still staring out the windshield, he responded in a monotone voice, "I think so." He took a deep, steadying breath before he looked over at me, though his eyes aren't on me, but tracing the sharp edges of the dime-sized shrapnel pieces stuck in his glasses.

He was fine, and the five of us in the vehicle were left with our first war story to tell and a Humvee in need of extensive repairs.

It was a time of rapid growth and maturity for me, as it is for all war virgins. In combat, you learn, and you learn quickly, death is very real, and your actions and reactions can affect whether you or someone else loses their limb or life that day. It forces you to suppress emotions; to become nearly robotic. You train and train and train for that moment, and when it comes, appropriately so, it allows you to operate on instinct and ability alone. When bad things happen, when horrible things are seen, there's no mulling over it, there's no hurt, or regret, or trepidation at that moment. There is only today. There is only the mission.

You get blown up. Nobody gets hurt. You joke about it after.

A little girl's lifeless body is clutched in her sobbing mother's arms, and a blood-soaked cloth separates you from a sight you don't think you could ever bear—the girl's head split wide open, a sniper's bullet to blame—tomorrow the memory goes way down deep. You forget about the blood and the place where the poor girl's head should be. You forget about the devastation in her mother's wretched cries. You put them away for a while, until you're back home and alone, sitting with only the memories and your burgeoning anguish… sometimes with your handgun too, and the quietest of voices saying, 'please, make it stop. Make it all stop'.

It worked the same way March of that year when we were back from a long day's mission, relaxing while we could as our job had evolved into our unit's Quick

Reaction Force, or QRF, at that point. As QRF, when bad shit went down, we were the first ones on the scene unless a nearby patrol could get there first. That night I wish we hadn't been QRF. That night changed me. Not at first, but much later, I'd realize just how badly it did.

Two guys from one of our patrols—Staff Sergeant Darrell Clay and Sergeant Israel Devora Garcia—were dismounted when a buried IED went off, killing SGT Garcia immediately and leaving him in pieces on the road. It took SSG Clay's arm off at the shoulder. I'm thankful that as the driver for that mission, and with another unit assisting already, we were pulling cordon (blocking off the road) and couldn't see the scene from our position. I don't know how I would've handled seeing SSG Clay slowly bleed to death on the street. I only ever heard about it after the fact, the thought alone haunting me so much that I thanked the Lord SSG Clay wasn't in view. And then I thought about his family, his kids. He was the first person I met when I got to my unit in Germany, as it was his job to get new privates acquainted with the unit and surrounding area. He always greeted you with this big toothy smile and had a friendly voice that immediately comforted you. You could tell immediately why dropping knowledge on new privates was his thing. There's nothing quite as scary for a young man as arriving at your first duty station completely fucking clueless. SSG Clay made the process so much easier. It crushed me to find out it was him bleeding out on the street that day.

We held a ceremony for them both when it was all said and done; a heart battering affair known as The Last Roll Call. For The Last Roll Call, the entire company stood in formation, with First Sergeant Thompson presiding. He called out each of our names and we responded in turn. Garcia and Clay were saved for last, and their names were called out three times. Of course, there was no answer. Their bodies were likely already on their way to Dover Air Force Base where morticians would ready their bodies to be put into the ground.

I thought of their families as First Sergeant called out their names; haunting as his voice echoed against the hollow desert air. Tears streamed down my face from behind my protective glasses. I would've been embarrassed, but when I looked around, I realized everyone in formation had their glasses on too. They wiped at their eyes like I did. They sniffled. We were one in that formation; one in brotherhood, one in mourning, and for those of us who were new to combat, we were one in growing, maturing, and hardening. That was our introduction to the realities of war, and the cold hard inevitable truth: not everyone makes it home.

Our squad leader called us new guys over to him after the ceremony, and we obliged, encircling him, and for the first time, I saw emotion in his features. He too had been crying, and for the first time since meeting him a year prior, he appeared to be as human as the rest of us. He told us that he understood what we were going through. That it never got easier, but we had to go back to work tomorrow. We had to drive on for SSG Clay and SGT Garcia's memories. We couldn't let their loss take our heads out of the mission, lest someone else meets the same fate because of it. Our lives were in each other's hands, and it was never as clear to me as it was that day, that a man must come to terms at one point or another: Tomorrow means nothing in a warzone... And neither does yesterday.

CHAPTER TWO

5.5 Liters

Everything is white—the walls, the bed, the sheets—causing a harsh glare to permeate in the room from the sterile fluorescent lights. I turn them off, but the nurses just turn them right back on—doing their hourly checkups or for the frequent "celebrity" visitors wanting to praise me for my service, cameras always at the ready. I just want them to leave, all of them. I want silence, sleep, just a little privacy. To be left alone with my mangled limb and ever-pumping pain meds. I'd sleep for eternity if I could only keep my eyes closed. When I do close them, all I can see is him—burnt beyond recognition—his wife and newborn son left back home to wait for knocking soldiers with terrible news.

I wonder what she'll be doing when they do come. I wonder how she'll react. I wonder if she'll think of me too. I want her to know that I think of her. I've thought of her and that boy of theirs since that terrible day.

Major Taylor took the brunt of the roadside bomb. He saved our lives, four of us total. It's what keeps me up mornings like these; four a.m. watching Home Improvement with one eye closed, the other fighting to focus. Riddled with survivor's guilt and the explosion playing on a loop in my head. The smell of charred flesh and melted plastic still stuck in my nostrils like it was yesterday, and not a week ago already. I pump the Dilaudid every five minutes, and while it does a good enough job of making Tim "The Toolman" Taylor look like a Pixar creation, it does little to ease the severed nerves and cooked muscle in my thigh that burns, freezes, itches, and stings all at the same time.

Five pieces of shrapnel—varying from baseball to golf ball to quarter sized—destroyed six inches of my femur and left a gaping hole in my thigh the equivalent to a fleshy donut. Bandages connect plastic tubes to a vacuum machine that pumps away harmful pinkish-yellow fluid from each open wound. Feeling odd sensations is nothing new as nerves chaotically search for reconnection, but the warmth that overtakes my thigh now is different. It feels too real, like hot maple syrup is being poured over the extremity. I look to see that each hose is now pumping vats of burgundy blood. The adhesive connecting bandage to skin begins to loosen allowing blood to seep onto the sheets. I call to a nurse's aide through the box beside my bed, panicked, and when he responds, he calmly places a bunched-up towel beneath my thigh to put pressure on the bleeding. His nonchalance eases me for a moment.

He's seen this before. Everything's good.

And then I realize the pressure from the towel causes arterial blood to rupture from the bandages and spray from my leg like a lawn sprinkler, several feet into the air, coating the once white sheets and now terrified nurse's aide in buckets of blood like it was the climax of Carrie. His frantic calls for help bring an army of medical personnel into my room, one by one. The panic painted on each of their faces fills me with a fear that breaches any perception of fear I've ever had before.

This isn't good.

In an instant, a year of bullets and bombs on Baghdad streets is evaporated from my memory. True terror now takes hold. I force my drooping eyes onto the television, my vision blurs, my heads a helium balloon, my hands cold and clammy.

I call out to them, "Don't let me die, don't let me die," over and over again. I feel embarrassed by this. Like I'm an actor giving it his all for a chance at the Oscar. This is me. pg 14I'm the action hero and this is my final scene.

A mystery doctor, tall, black Idris Elba look alike, has two fingers and all of his strength pressing down on my leg where the femoral artery meets the aorta. He stops the blood enough for the team to transport me to the OR. The gurney ride is much like a lucid dream. I keep my eyes locked onto mystery doctor and the passing fluorescent lights cast a glow around him that make him look divine.

And then nothing.

I wake moments later to doctors and nurses frantically fighting to get a tourniquet on my leg. Bright operating bay lights blind me. All I can hear are muffled exchanges and the repetitive beep of machines. I force my eyes to focus and set them to the surgeon, the mask covering his mouth, and the last thing I see before my world goes black is the look of terror on his face, given only to those in dire conditions.

Fourteen hours later I wake, opening one eye first, and then the other. I can make out the distorted outline of figures around me. They stand over me as if watching me, waiting. My mouth is dry and the acidic taste of desflurane bombards my taste buds. I wipe the blur from my eyes to see my mom and stepdad, and the surgeon, standing over me, looks of relief on their faces.

"You gave us quite the scare," the surgeon says, resting his hand on my now fully bandaged and ex-fixed limb. I run my eyes along the large metal contraption, much like a barbaric Tinkertoy design, that runs the entire length of my leg, from ankle to hip. My eyes flit to the inside of my left leg, which was initially untouched by the roadside bomb, and find it now has a trail of staples from ankle to groin.

"We had to take the greater saphenous vein from your good leg to create a new femoral artery in your damaged one. We realized when you were in surgery that you had dislocated your knee too. We turned you over and it went back the opposite way, like Joe Theismann." He chuckles. "Not sure how the doctors in Germany missed that one. But, all in all, you were very lucky," he continues with a smile, "the shrapnel initially damaged your femoral artery upon impact, but the intense heat cauterized it immediately. It saved your life."

Approximately 5.5 liters of blood in a one hundred and eighty-pound body. The surgeon guesses about half of that was left to coagulate on the sheets and the tiled floor of my ward room. He's excited, and a little proud, and I force myself to smile as I take it all in, but, really, I don't feel lucky. I'm frightened.

What if tomorrow it blows again?

What if I'm sleeping the next time it happens and I can't warn someone?

What if this is it?

The surgeon leaves a short time later and my parents fill me in on what he left out. They tell me twice during the procedure my heart stopped beating. It got so bad that at one point they readied my parents to say one final goodbye. My mother tells me this as if gossiping with a neighbor, but I only stare into the distance. I can hear her tell me they came again during surgery to warn of my likely amputation, but my thoughts are to a parade field on an Army base in Germany; my comrades getting back without me, jazzed out in dress blues for our welcome home ceremony, drinking German beer and planning their Christmas vacations.

I don't want to hate them, but I do.

My thoughts belong to an obliterated Humvee in Iraq.

They're matted to the interior in thick, fleshy chunks. They're counting the fading beats of a dying heart.

My thoughts are no longer my own but possessed by war, narcotics, and confusion.

Mother doesn't like my lack of attention much. "I'm trying to tell you about your surgery," she snarks, "Are you even listening to me?"

I'm not.

My 21st birthday is in a week, and I'm wondering what kind of cake I can snag from the dining facility after this, and about Frankenstein—on account of all the staples.

CHAPTER THREE

The Day We Met

It was early in the summer of 2007 when I met Lexi, my first girlfriend, after getting blown up. I wasn't walking just yet, having only gotten out of inpatient six months prior. My leg was healing, if not slowly. The skin grafts had taken. The ex-fix removed and replaced with an IM nail, but the femur would need longer to heal. I'd been through three bone grafts already and only the third one led to growth, thanks to the addition of stem cell-infused cadaver bone. I wasn't mentally well, but I also wasn't the absolute mess I had been over the three months I spent in inpatient being poked and prodded, going in and out of surgery, and generally being annoyed by every single person I'd come into contact with.

The first month of inpatient was the worst. Beyond the terrible pain and the sleepless stints in ICU that came in the first month, I also had my mom and step-dad to contend with. They'd spent the entire first month there with me, which both surprised me completely, and annoyed the fuck out of me.

Neither one of them had ever cared before. Not even a little bit. Our household was filled with physical, verbal and emotional abuse from them both. There was no love there. So, when I got wounded, and they showed up at my bedside playing the role of worried, loving parents, it made me sick. I could see my mom Meryl Streep-ing it up in front of the nurses and celebrity visitors, showing them how wonderful of a mother she was. Problem was, it was all fraudulent. And the more those white walls closed in around me, and the more attitude she let slip out, the angrier I became. By the end of that first month, I was ready to slit both their necks and then my own. I was miserable. It climaxed near the end of their stay when my mother got snarky with me, so I shot back angrily, the first time I had done so. She left the room in a huff and my step-dad followed after her. After a few minutes, he returned without her and asked me if I could "take it a little easier on her." Those days were drug-filled—I was on morphine and Dilaudid—so I can't say for sure whether I laughed in his face or not (time seems to chip away at memories like a sculptor, no?), but I like to think I did. I couldn't fucking believe the words that came out of his mouth. And then I could. That was my parents, finally showing their true colors. My mom was a selfish, self-centered asshole. My stepfather was a bigoted lapdog.

They left a few days later and I breathed a sweet sigh of relief.

My dad and sister came next for Christmas that year, my last month of inpatient. I was a psychotic fucking mess. And that's probably an understatement. The rage that filled me was palpable. I could taste it. I wasn't sure who or what I was mad at—George W., insurgents, Osama Bin Laden, my mom—fuck, it didn't matter, I hated everyone. I grew up with anger issues, a product of my environment, but that, that was different, it was all-encompassing. I was a ship cruising right into the perfect storm, turbines full ahead.

The big difference between the visit with my dad and sister and the last one with my mom and stepdad was the existence of genuine love and concern. Though I was an angry nutcase going off on them every second, they understood, they helped, however, they could, even when it just made things worse. See, what I learned early in my recovery, which would suit me well later in life, is that I'm fiercely independent and I hate people taking care of me. I like figuring shit out on my own. So as much as I knew my sister and dad only wanted to help, our constant battle between what I will and won't allow them to do for me was often a point of contention. But, Lord, how I fell in love with them after those few weeks.

My relationship with them both was weird at the

time. I'd spent one semester of my senior year of high school living with them after getting kicked out of my mom's house. I hadn't seen either one of them in nearly a decade before I called my dad up at seventeen and asked if I could stay with him. I was kicked out of his house six months later for dropping out of high school. Over the six months I spent with him, he traveled relentlessly for work, so we really didn't form any type of relationship. My sister and I, on the other hand, spent most of our time together and ended up driving each other completely fucking nuts. At one point, after I called her a bitch upon leaving the house (to this day she claims I said cunt. She is a liar.), she threw a twenty-pound weight at me that nearly caught my heel. We hated each other.

Our problem was, we were too alike, and the town we were living in was Sodom and Gohmorra for teenagers. Seriously. With Pops gone most of the time, we would often throw massive house parties. Alcohol and weed were on constant tap and coming from an area where that kind of stuff wasn't very prevalent, the town ended up swallowing me whole.

I left my dad's house and moved in with my girlfriend after getting kicked out. Thanks to her parents opening their home to me, I was able to graduate high school. Fast forward two years and I was laying on a hospital bed with what felt like two strangers in my room. Yeah, I'd gone home on two leaves and mended both relationships—my pops and my sister even saw me off at the airport before I went back to Iraq—but it didn't feel familial.

After that last month of inpatient, seeing how much they were willing to put up with and go through just for my comfort, it suddenly happened, the bond grew stronger. My blackened heart opened up to them, and looking back on that, having the great relationship that I do now with them both, I'm thankful for those miserable days that brought us together.

When they left, and I was released from inpatient, I

was sent to a place called Mologne House, which was, for all intents and purposes, a hotel, with a front desk, clerks, and even a restaurant. But unlike most hotels with families or elderly couples on vacation, this hotel's occupants were all military, all long-term residents, and each had suffered a debilitating injury or illness. Mologne House is essentially the stop off between the hospital and normal barracks, during the phase when you're still not squared away medically, but you're healed up enough to leave the hospital. Mologne House still ran like a hotel, because most us were very seriously wounded and needed the extra care. There was a laundry service, maids, and even a video rental place in the lobby run by a non-profit; hundreds of movies, all varieties. My love for movies and tv shows was about to be intensified tenfold.

The thing about Mologne House was, even at full capacity—in 2007, both Iraq and Afghanistan were seeing some of the worst fightings—it could feel empty for a patient staying there. Nobody wanted to talk, including myself. When you hang out with other military members, naturally, your conversation will turn to combat stories. At that point in all our recoveries, the last thing we wanted to do was talk about it. Wheelchairs passed in hallways like ships in the night, each soldier or Marine, sometimes an Airman or Seaman, going about their own business, worried about their own recovery, some so worried they just couldn't deal. When you saw an ambulance out front, its lights flashing, your heart would sink knowing the probability of suicide victim strapped to a gurney inside was high.

My only friend, if you could call him that, was my first roommate, a well-mannered and quiet soldier battling testicular cancer, but as he was more mobile, I didn't often see him. I was cripplingly lonely. My life consisted of a few hours of physical therapy each day, three squares at the Mologne House restaurant, and a ludicrous amount of comedy movies and TV shows. Sometimes an action, thriller or horror would make its way in there, but most of the time, I watched comedy to help get my spirits up. Those were the days I fell in love with The Office, Friends, King of Queens and Seinfeld. Those were the days TV characters became my only friends. I look back on that time now and I'm thankful. Humor in writing, especially in a serious piece to kind of level everything out, is very important to me, and I like to think I'm decent at it. I attest a lot of that to those sleepless nights I spent watching Kramer come barreling through Jerry's door or Michael Scott stepping on a George Foreman grill.

That's how my life went for a good six months after leaving the hospital and my family went back to their normal lives. Me? I wasn't living. I simply existed, mindlessly cycling through each day just like the last, and the one before that, and the one before that. It went like that for a while, until one day I opened up my MySpace (yeah, it was still cool back then) and saw the message from Lexi.

We didn't know each other, she wrote, but she found me looking through profiles and loved my story. As a Specialist in the Army Reserves with one deployment under her belt, she could empathize with my situation. We chatted a bit back and forth about Army stuff and her life growing up on Chincoteague Island, a small community on the eastern shores of Virginia known for their wild horses. I didn't dare tell her about my past. At that time, I didn't think anyone could understand. She then asked me out to a hookah bar in Georgetown.

Panic set in.

I had just spent a year in Germany, too busy training up to date (hell, I couldn't speak a lick of German anyway); a year in combat; and nine months recovering from my wounds. I hadn't been on a real date since high school. I looked gaunt, the muscular two hundred and five-pound body I carried around in Iraq had whittled down to one hundred and sixty pounds of skin and bones from months

of atrophy. I hated everything about myself at that time…
but I said yes anyway. The excitement of a possible
romantic connection with someone was too appealing to
let my insecurities win out. Besides, she knew I was
wounded not too long before that. If she couldn't
understand, well then, fuck her.

She picked me up from Walter Reed as I had no car
and she didn't want me having to deal with a cab in my
wheelchair. She brought a friend along, understandably,
though I had to chuckle a little wondering how in the hell
I'd even be able to harm her even if I wanted to. Shit, I
was the one who should've had a friend with me. My ass
was in a wheelchair. Unfortunately, Ross and Joey were
busy.

She was naturally beautiful with chestnut hair, these
cute little chipmunk cheeks, and an electric smile that
brought out one dimple on her left cheek.

Once I finagled my way into her SUV, and she loaded
my wheelchair into the back, her friend looked back at me,
eyeing me up and down for a moment. She could've been
Lexi's sister, though she was curvy and with a constant
look of judgment on her face.

"Okay, okay," she said, finally looking away as she
turned toward Lexi, who was climbing into the driver's
seat. "He is cute. I wasn't sure when you came out." She
added, glancing back at me again. "Your hat was pulled
too low. Why do you wear your hat so low?"

I shrugged. "I don't know."

"Wendy, shut up! You're such an idiot," Lexi scolded.

"What?" Wendy acted surprised, though her lips curled
up into a wicked smile.

The fact of the matter was, I wore my hat low because
of my insecurities at the time. I thought my angular face at
that lower weight made my Italian nose look huge. The
first thing I dug about the woman who would be mine for
the next year was her interactions with Wendy (a spoiled
princess if there ever was one, I'd come to find quite

quickly). Lexi took no shit and had no qualms about setting Wendy straight, especially when it came to me.

I was thankful Wendy and Lexi chattered away the rest of the ride to the hookah lounge as my nervousness sat like a knot in my throat, my mind void of anything but self-doubt.

We sat there in the dim hookah bar for hours talking away. The shyness I came in with was quickly withered away by Lexi's glowing personality and Wendy, as much as I never could stand her, was hilarious as hell. Within that conversation, we talked more about our hometowns, hers sounding much more my style than my own (I found this to be very true. Go to Chincoteague and Assateague. Seriously!), traded more Army stories, and talked about her classes at Marymount University; a small school in Northern Virginia.

I was hooked.

I hadn't felt that spark in so long, hadn't had a woman smile at me like that in so long, that I soaked it all up and she had me hook, line, and sinker.

And that's when I should've walked away and saved that poor girl's heart.

What I was too young to know at the time and would come to learn years later, after repeated self-analyzation, is that I was too broken to be anyone's someone. So broken I couldn't even see past my own selfish desire to fill a hole that couldn't be filled.

In that year, as she would split her time between Chincoteague Island and Marymount University, I developed a taste for alcohol.

Yeah, I had been a partier when I was younger, a mischief if there ever was one, but not like this.

As my femur strengthened, and I began walking again, I frequented the Silver Springs bars just down the road from Walter Reed, a popular watering hole for employees and patients. I can't remember the exact name but think typical Irish bar. We'll call it McFadden's. McFadden's would become a second home to me. I'm pretty sure in the year I spent with Lexi, I likely provided the funds for, at least, one employee's salary for the year. And it's where I had my first drunken fight post-injury.

A mouthy Seaman who worked at Walter Reed (and a complete stranger to me) had been fucking with me all night for whatever reason. I've found in my life that if I'm at a bar with drunk twenty-somethings or military men, the douche bags always find me. And when I drink, I'm not one to be fucked with, even as a timid twenty-two-year-old with a fucked up leg.

I was sitting with the first friend I ever made at Walter Reed outside of my roommate, Jim, a neighbor at Abrams Hall, the new barracks I called home. He was a Sergeant in the Army and had fallen in a pit while on a night mission in Iraq. He was wearing night vision goggles and leading his squad down the road when he took one step too many and tumbled down into the hole, breaking his femur clean through. We bonded over sharing a similar injury, and his 'speak softly but carry a big stick' mentality (he was Montanan after all) was always pleasing to be around.

He tried to talk me off the ledge as, throughout the night, the kid poked and prodded me. "Dude, forget him. Besides, what are you gonna do, beat him with your cane? You can barely walk." He laughed.

I was maybe six or seven beers down at that point and still on a steady diet of oxycodone, which intensified the alcohol's effect. And I was livid.

"Fuck that, man. I will kill that sea bitch."

"You don't need to get into trouble, man. How about we just go?" He tossed a twenty to the bar top.

I glanced around the room but didn't see my new friend.

I nodded. "Alright, I'm good and fucked up anyway." I threw my own twenty to the bar top and stood, repositioning the brace on my leg, which kept my foot upright. After my femoral artery blew, and the fourteen-hour emergency surgery was finished, the stress of the blood flow rushing back into my lower right leg once the tourniquet was removed caused compartment syndrome. My doctors described this as a hot dog microwaved too long. The pressure inside my leg was too much. They had to give me fasciotomies on either side of my calf to relieve it, but unfortunately, it was too little too late. My anterior tibial, which enables the foot to move upward, went necrotic from the pressure and had to be removed. A cane—lined top to bottom with band stickers like a club bathroom—steadied me as I hobbled toward the exit.

After we left the pub and passed through a large group of smokers, we crossed the street when I heard the seaman say, "I knew you wouldn't do shit."

I stopped in my tracks, my breathing heavy, my hand clutching the cane's grip mercilessly, blood rushing to my scrunched-up face.

I turned around, staring at the seaman when Jim grabbed for my arm.

"Come on, Taylor. Let's go, man," he said.

The snide look on the seaman's face far outweighed the pleas of my buddy. I walked toward him slowly, the click-clack of my cane against the ground the only sound as every smoker looked on in anticipation.

I didn't say anything to the seaman. I didn't even stop walking before I swung, hitting him square in the jaw and knocking him unconscious. He crashed to the ground as a few gasps escaped the crowd. My eyes went wide. I hadn't expected him to go down so easily. I'd been in my fair share of fights up to that point but never knocked anyone out. I hadn't even punched anyone since a fight over a weed eater in basic training, but when I hit the seaman, all those old feelings from my mischievous youth came rushing back; the power I felt watching him crash to the ground released a flood of endorphins.

Worried about the frequent police visits to downtown Silver Spring, I turned and hobbled as quickly as my bum leg would allow me toward my buddy, who stood across the street, his mouth gaping and eyes wide.

"Holy fuck, bro," he said, but I didn't stop to conversate.

I jutted into a parking garage as he followed close behind.

There are many things people can be addicted to outside of the usual suspects—video games, shopping, gambling—for me, that day began a five-year streak of violent behavior for the sake of feeding the desire to cause pain. The need to make someone else feel the hurt I had gone through my whole life.

I've never hit a woman. Never would. But the anger and aggression I was feeding into as I self-medicated spilled into our relationship. Lexi was the first in a string of one year-plus relationships that I was involved in, while the tsunami-like PTSD took over my every thought. Three beautiful women. Three beautiful souls. Three broken hearts.

I hate the person I was before twenty-seven. I hate that I let the disease control me, possess me, eat away at what once seemed normal. All that bright eyed and bushy tailed crap I felt after graduating basic training, arriving in Germany to join my first unit, and even shipping off to Iraq to fight for my country, went right out the fucking window. I didn't care about tomorrow anymore. I didn't care who I was or who I'd become, I simply fed my rage, my desires, my addictions, freely and abundantly.

Poor Lexi, she had to deal with me when the nightmare began. She wanted to save me, as did the two girlfriends who followed her. The problem was, I didn't feel my life was worth saving. The suicidal thoughts began that year. Just a few times, and only here and there, at first… the little voice, warm and welcoming, at the back of your brain that tells you it'll feel so much better to just sleep forever. You think about the sleepless nights, the missed appointments from eventually passing out at six in the morning and not waking up, and the shame that comes with them, the loss of the career you once loved, the sports you once enjoyed. With each negative thought, the voice grew just a little stronger, the picture of my death became a little bit clearer. I could see myself on a bridge, swan diving to my merciful ending. I thought about how I could never shoot myself. I didn't hate my face and who would want to leave this world in multiple pieces anyway? Obviously, that removed jumping off a building from the list too. I thought about how carbon monoxide would be too slow, and pill overdose too painful. I knew that far too well from a suicide attempt at thirteen, a desperate attempt to get out from under the scarring clutches of my mom and stepdad, and the first of many growth periods in my life.

Those thoughts tormented me as I forced a smile, pretending every day I could be a good boyfriend even though I was dying inside.

That's not to say I didn't enjoy my time with her. Quite the opposite, really. When she was going to school at Marymount, I spent nearly every night with her in her dorm room. When she was back home in Chincoteague, I'd visit her every weekend. Those drives I will never forget. They're when I felt her love start to change me. I'd be cruising the Chesapeake Bay Bridge, the windows down, the sun shining, and the tunes blaring, and the feeling of immense joy would strike. Mayday Parade's first album, *Lessons in Romantics* will always take me back to the days when Lexi showed me there was true goodness in the world. She showed me that even though my parents were unable to give me love, someone else would and very much could. She showed me even I could love again.

Unfortunately, for us, it wasn't enough. She was deploying, and I was too weak to support her as she deserved to be supported, though, I wanted to, desperately. I wanted to send her the cards and packages I never received. But in the end, knowing that my addictions and desires would ruin us, I made the choice to leave.

When I look back now, I don't regret the choice I made, because I knew I would've ended up hurting her worse than I already had, but I still wish I could've been stronger. I told her years later how sorry I was for how I treated her, for stealing a year of her life, for not trying harder. Married and happy, she accepted my apology.

She met a monster that day at the hookah bar in Georgetown. It took me a long time to realize that. And an even longer time to fix it.

CHAPTER FOUR

Down the Rabbit Hole

After two more failed relationships, much of the burden of blame sat squarely on my shoulders as I felt crippled by the unknown—what the future held for me, who I was without the uniform, what to make of the storm inside my head. I had grown tremendously through the development of VETSports and my much-needed move to Florida, but the key to relationships eluded me. There was still something broken inside me. Something pulling me away from any semblance of good in my life when it came to women. I needed to figure out why. It was the loss of Hannah that did it to me. I had never known true emotional pain until I lost her for the last time.

Accelerated Resolution Therapy, or simply ART, through the Camaraderie Foundation, was initially Hannah's idea. She loved me so much, more than anyone ever had, and she just wanted me to love myself too, to be happy, to give myself a chance. She wasn't pushy about it but subtle at first, before trying to nudge me in the right direction when I became dismissive. I never did go for her. I don't know if it would've made the difference for us anyway. But I've wondered.

I spent three years single and searching for the answers.

Why do I sabotage all the good that comes my way?

Why can't I accept happiness as anything but fraudulent?

Why do I hate myself so much?

It was a hard three years, missing Hannah with every fiber of my being, and loathing myself more than ever because of my inability to keep her. I tortured myself even as I began to make a name for myself in the romance industry, even when I was seeing my books on Barnes and Noble shelves and meeting readers who appreciated my work. I was miserable without her, thinking endless thoughts about my inabilities as a partner... and as a man.

ART did for me what so many psychiatrists, counselors, and cutting-edge therapy programs never did before it. It allowed me to see the good within myself, to accept my past for what it was and to assign blame appropriately, and it allowed me to let go of all the pain I held onto for so long since childhood. For the first time in my life, I felt clarity. I felt the full weight of my potential. And I became hungry for more.

I never did want to do a dating show. I'd never even seen one. I had initially been interviewed for a different show; one in which I'd live in a San Diego mansion with eleven other professionals from different fields while I worked on my next book. It sounded great! They really liked me and had me do another interview with the casting director. After a few weeks with no word, I figured they decided to take a different route, and moved on. That's when they called me about *Coupled*. I didn't see it then, but through hindsight, this was their bait and switch.

I didn't tell them 'no' right away, but in my head, I was screaming it. "Fuck no!"

I, at least, wanted to think on it. *A Lover's Lament* was crushing it in sales, I was working on *Into the Nothing*, and I didn't want to pass up a good opportunity. So, I went to my family for advice. I thought maybe they could help me come to a decision. I don't blame them one bit for telling me I should go for it. They were as blinded by the possibilities as I was. With the success that had come with *A Lover's Lament* and my desire to chase this dream I somehow stumbled into, landing a show on *Fox* seemed like a good move.

After getting the go-ahead from my family, I said yes, and flew to LA for a final interview with all the big-time producers. I was nervous as hell but ended up doing really well. A month or so later I was on a plane to St. Maarten. The excitement was real. All trepidation I had before, gone. I wanted to approach this opportunity without judgment, worry, or expectations.

Seeing the eleven other men who would be my counterparts on the show for the first time was daunting. I've never been one for competition and certainly never saw myself as someone who stacked up against the men I'd just met, but I stifled my nerves and tried to hang my hat on being the only veteran there. No matter what these men had done, no matter how perfect their smile or carved up their abs, they didn't fight and bleed for this country. I had. And I operated those first few days with that thought securely in place at the forefront of my mind.

Over the three nights we spent together, partying in St. Maarten like we weren't going to see the next day, I learned to appreciate those guys for their uniqueness, personalities, and charm. The producers had done a damn good job.

Looking back on this time—the excessive partying, the extracurricular drug use—I can see now it was the beginning of the end for me with that experience. I should've seen it then—as I should've seen when I joined a fraternity five years prior—an environment like that, for a person like me, is like fuel-soaked kindling to a fire.

I had nearly gotten off the show before it even started. On the last day before I was to be on the show, legal went over the contracts with us and I noticed two things: a discrepancy in what they had verbally committed to with me, and, for the first time, I learned what the show would entail.

Before that moment, the details were kept secret, the only thing shared with me being that it would be limited in drama and a unique take on the reality dating genre.

What I found out was, they intended it to be like Tinder in real life. Not only did that idea cause me to roll my eyes hard, I also knew it was way outside of my comfort zone. The thought alone made me ill.

After being talked off the ledge from the person who would become my nemesis on the show—we'll call her

339

Carrie—I decided to go through with it, and off I went.

The important thing to remember here is, I go into most everything in my life with some excitement, no matter how much anxiety it causes me. I try and focus on the good and take the experiences as they come, and that first day, meeting the women, as nerve-racking as it was, I truly enjoyed it. As with my fellow male contestants, each woman seemed to have engaging personalities and unique back stories, a few standing out especially well.

Ashton was a little quiet at first, certainly the girl next door type, but with this effervescent smile and a lively sparkle to her eye that let me know there was so much more going on inside that head than what the first introduction would lead me to believe. Our conversation was short, but a spark was obvious.

Kristen was taller than I normally like and slender, but she was breathtakingly beautiful. I was captivated by her eyes, her energy and what seemed like a true zest for life. She was by far my favorite woman that day, and someone I knew I was going to choose immediately after she walked away.

There was one other woman I was drawn to out of the ten I met, we'll call her Lily. When Lily sat down in the seat, her midnight black hair to her shoulders and the little pools of ocean blue in her eyes that caught glints of the Caribbean sun, I tried my hardest not to smile. She had that curvy body type I love, a sincere smile, and a unique style. I was smitten. And then she spoke.

It wasn't how she spoke that bothered me—I've always appreciated a good New York accent—it was what she said.

"So, I've always had the belief that you can tell a lot about a person by the first kiss," she said, a tension in her shoulders that let me know she was nervous.

"Oh yeah?" I ask, my own nerves stifling anything more than that as I worried what was coming next.

"Yeah, and I figure, why not get it out of the way

first..."

Oh, my God. What the fuck do I do here?

I panicked, not wanting to kiss a complete stranger on a tv show, but not wanting to completely embarrass the girl either.

Noticing my not so subtle hesitation, panic took over her facial features.

"Uh, I mean, if you don't want to—"

"No," I said, forcing a smile and placing a hand to her cheek. I took her in slow, and kissed her with fervent passion, very much aware that the kiss was going to make it on the show.

After our kiss, she smiled, but nothing more was said between us before she was whisked away.

I laughed nervously, shaking my head as I contemplated what had just happened.

Regardless of the awkward kiss, I was still genuinely interested in Lily. She'd tell me later when she was at the couple's villa with another guy, that producers had put her up to the kiss. I let her know about how they had convinced me not to pick her, though I was torn between her and Ashton. Neither one of us were very happy about the new information.

Once the speedboat whisked me, Ashton and Kiersten, away, we were to be taken to the 'other side' of the island to the couple's villa to meet with the first two couples who had gone before us. What looked seamless on TV, was my introduction to the misery that is television production. It was the first time I realized how little 'reality' had to do with reality television. I was sequestered from Ashton and Kiersten after our little speedboat scene and we didn't see each other again until a couple hours later when we ran through our 'entrance' at least ten times, each woman on either arm like I was Hugh Hefner, but I felt like Hughy fuckin' Louie, so completely out of place, and burning up from Anguilla's unforgiving humidity. I'm not even kidding. A/C's weren't allowed outside of our rooms, as they were too loud through the mics, so my forever-sweating ass was miserable anytime I was anywhere but my room. Producers would face a constant battle with the patches of sweat that often took up my shirts, and I was left uncomfortable as fuck. The pool was my best friend. Unfortunately, so was one of the only other things we had to do in our downtime, which was plentiful—alcohol. We asked for board games, musical instruments, stuff to paint with, books…. None of which we ever received. But we could count on there being whatever alcohol we wanted in the fridge and cupboard, stocked full every morning.

I'm not complaining here. I fully anticipated that. It's reality TV after all. I went into the show comfortable with my level of alcohol usage, which was significantly less than my early to mid-twenties saw. I realized that it would be there, and in abundance, and I felt confident in my ability to moderate. What I hadn't accounted for was an excessive amount of downtime with no entertainment but a pool, conversation and the three books I brought and devoured within the first two weeks. I was bored stiff most of the time. Excursions were fun but extremely short in terms of the actual activity. The downtime before and after filming, which is filled with pre and post interviews and waiting around for others to do their own, was by far the most difficult time for me. Out of all the shit, the experience brought my way, the endless waiting with no clear endpoint killed me. It felt a lot like basic training to me. Looking back on it all and analyzing it, which I've done often these past few years, I've come to truly believe military-esque mental tactics are utilized in the reality TV game to fuck with contestants' mental state. There were just too many correlations between the show and basic training.

Before that first dinner with the other couples, regardless of all the waiting around, I was still excited. Still naïve. I was optimistic. I mean, I had two beautiful, bright women with me, of whom I got to pick one to get to know better over the next six weeks on a tropical island.

For fuck's sake, what could go wrong?

That first dinner, I got a light introduction to the world of reality TV production. Much like producers manipulate contestants, they also use manipulation on each other. Not only do the low-level associate producers work incredibly long hours on little to no sleep—with pay that doesn't correspond with work input—but they're also used as puppets in the process. The big-time producers sit in a trailer, watching everything play out on a bunch of TV screens in front of them. Watching all of our ticks, mannerisms, and body language, they call commands over the headset and the associate producers oblige. This is what happened to me that first night.

I had already met the first two guys on St. Maarten before taping but had to pretend like I was meeting them for the first time. The women—who I had just met for the first time— were gorgeous, intelligent, and engaging just like the two I had with me. One, in particular, I'm going to call her Linds, stopped me in my tracks. She was chosen by the first guy, so I hadn't gotten the chance to choose her, but I knew when I first laid my eyes on her—even more so after getting to know a little about her—that she would've been the perfect one for me. She had light brown highlighted hair, these incredible light blue eyes that were just so alive I couldn't help but smile when I looked at her. She had this warm, friendly smile and an air about her that screamed earnest compassion. I've always been attracted to that quality in a woman. I'd find myself from that day on, enamored with her. She turned out to be as genuine and compassionate as she was that first night and one of the few I still keep up with. The asshole that got her on the show dropped her on her ass shortly after airing just as Ashton had done to me. Oh, what could've been…

After an hour or so of fantastic conversation between the seven of us, one of the associate producers came out— he was one of those 'in your face' abrasive types—and he

343

asked if any of us guys had kissed one of the girls during the first day meetings. Knowing they were obviously talking about me, but wanting people to find out on my own terms, I kept quiet. I felt uncomfortable with the situation, to begin with, knowing all of it would end up on TV, and had hoped I would sit whomever I picked down and tell them about it on my own terms. It wasn't a big deal, in terms of what was done, but I was most bothered by how it was done. As the three of us shook our heads 'no' (my bottom lip sticking out and a slight shrug for added effect), the associate producer eyed me with his hands on his hips. I stared back at him, passing him the look that said, 'you ain't winning this one'. He went back inside for a moment as we continued our conversation at the table outside on the patio.

After a few moments, he returned, looking right at me, and he asked, "Hey BT, are you sure you didn't kiss anyone during the meetings? Lily maybe?"

The four girls gasped and giggled as they had all spent a few days with each other before taping like us guys had.

I saw red. My heart pounded in my chest.

Shaking my head firmly, I said, "That's so fucked."

I could barely speak. I felt betrayed. Silly me.

"It's not a big deal," Kiersten said, forcing another laugh.

"No, I'm not worried about the kiss," I said, my eyes locked on the associate producer who had just become my detested enemy. "Shit, she sat down and asked right away if I'd kiss her. What was I supposed to do? What bothers me is, it should have been on my own accord. Y'all are fucked up. Seriously." I sneered at the AP before he departed. The conversation continued around me, but I wasn't a participant. I couldn't think about anything else but that rat fuck in his high-pitched voice saying, 'BT, are you sure you didn't kiss anybody?' It took over my fucking mind.

Realizing I was upset, Linds asked, "Are you okay?"

I nodded as I stood from my chair. "Yeah, I just gotta go to the bathroom."

I proceeded to the bathroom, but before entering, I pointed my finger at the only AP I liked and motioned sternly for her to follow me. She joined me by the bathroom with a concerned look on her face.

"What's up?" she asked, her brows crinkled.

"Are you kidding me?" I tried controlling my anger, but it had taken over me. My whole body felt hot. I jabbed a finger toward the patio though it was out of sight as was everyone else. "What the fuck was that shit?"

"What?" She continued acting oblivious.

"You know what y'all just did. I know what y'all did. Dropping that fucking bomb at dinner. Are you serious? I should be the one to share that kind of shit, whenever I see fit. It's not your right to do that shit to me when I'm meeting most of these people for the first time. It's disrespectful. This is some Jerry Springer shit. I was wary about this from the get-go, and I told you, I told you fuckers—I'm sorry, you know I like you—it's just, I told you I don't deal well with disrespect, and in my book, that's what y'all just did."

"I—I'm sorry, BT. I swear, I didn't know."

"I'm sorry too. I just can't do this shit anymore."

"What?"

I nodded toward the front door down the hall. "I'm out of here."

"Are you serious?"

"Absolutely. I'm not gonna be played like this."

"BT, just stop and think about it for a second."

"I'm sorry, I can't. You know I appreciate you, but I can't deal with these assholes anymore."

With that, I left the villa and walked down the road to my own. I began packing, a feeling of resolve washing over me. My gut was telling me that leaving was for the best. It was the third time I ignored my gut during the process.

The producer on shift—the Carrie woman who had

talked me out of leaving the first time around in St. Maarten—came to my room first, but when I found out she was the one calling the shots and made the decision to drop the bomb at dinner, a fucking fire lit inside of me. I shamed her for a good half hour over her career choice. I'm not proud of some of the things I said, but I carried a lot of anger into that experience. Half of that anger was derived from situations just like the kiss bomb at dinner, manipulation at its finest for the sake of drama. And the other half, I can now say with confidence, was because I was so angry with myself. Three times my gut said no, and three times I ignored the warnings. It was the first time in my life it had happened to such a magnitude. I was ashamed.

Eventually, the producer just below Mark Burnett came to my room. Before I continue, I must note that I have all the respect in the world for Mark. He was a veteran himself, and I bonded with him over that during my LA interviews. We had two phone conversations near the end of my TV experience where he showed true compassion and understanding for my situation and response. I will always appreciate the time he took out of his day for me.

Now, the guy just under him, Timmy… Timmy was an asshole. He was rich, and he made sure everybody knew it right when he walked into a room. He spoke to us contestants with his nose in the air. We weren't people to him but characters he could manipulate at will. You didn't have to know him long to see it. When he came to my room, it was my first time meeting him, but at that point, he was still pretending to be my best friend. I asked him if I'd get in trouble legally for leaving early, and he said no, but spent a considerable amount of time convincing me to stay. He asked me to name my price after wearing me down. I told him I would need a signed document stating the footage from dinner would never be used.

He agreed.

It should've ended there. I should've left that day and

saved myself the torment, the heartbreak, and the re-introduction to the ugliness of alcoholism that the show brought with it. It wasn't an easy recovery, and it hasn't been easy to see the good in that experience over the past two years, but I have finally come to terms with my time on the show. We were given the gift of instinct for a reason. It's a universal feeling: the queasiness in your gut, the little voice, faint but authoritative, directing us one way or the other, a sense of clarity and decisiveness. If we're not in tune, or if our instincts are masked (such as mine were with this show due to desire to get my books out there) we can be led astray. I am more in tune with my gut instinct now than I ever have been and I can truly thank my experience on the show for that. There's something to be said for maintaining perspective.

Though I had my fair share of issues with production, immense boredom, and, for the first time in a long time, the feeling of being the outcast, my biggest issue on the show was that I had genuine feelings for Ashton. She was incredibly kind, always radiant and perky, and extremely bright. It wasn't until after the show was over, and I was back home, that I realized I didn't really know a thing about her. After six weeks together, she was still a stranger to me. I was infatuated with the idea of us; the hardened combat veteran and the girl next door with the big heart. We seemed to fit so seamlessly throughout the process until we just didn't. She was there for me, and we were okay, until that last day. We had bickered previously about my issues with production. How I could see them pulling the strings at every turn. How they were doing their best to fuck us up. She never saw it though, or just didn't want to see it, and it led to some disagreements. On the show, these were portrayed as issues with my PTSD. The problem was, the producers knew they couldn't break that fourth wall. The narrative could've never been, *'BT's pissed at producers'*. So, they had to improvise. I don't blame them for how they edited. I don't blame them for using my own footage against me. I put myself in that position, and regardless of whether I did at the time or not, I should've known how it all would've went down. I allowed myself to be blissfully ignorant and irresponsibly optimistic. This was entirely on me.

Once I finally arrived back home and tried to get back into my normal routine, I found that not only was the ever-present desire for alcohol back but the anxiety I felt knowing they had compromising footage of me and wondering which of that footage would make it on air sent me into a tailspin. I was living in a constant state of fear and worry, which, in turn, intensified the return of my alcoholism.

Truth be told, *Fox* caught me at my absolute worst one night. And it's been a constant fear of mine that the footage would be seen by the masses ever since.

In the simplest of terms, I was 'that guy'. Maybe a week or two in, we had a large group dinner where all of us got tuckered up and producers initiated a few sexually charged topics for discussion. When it got around to Ashton, she was extremely uncomfortable and a few people at the table attempted to prod the information out of her. She ended up leaving the table, which was shown as her leaving because of me. In reality, I had followed her to her room and found her crying in there. It broke my heart. After talking with her, I discovered she was second guessing coming on the show and that she was thinking about leaving. She felt like an outcast due to her virginity, just as I had for my service and injury. She felt isolated just like me. As much as I tried to reason with her, she was too upset to console and asked for space, which I gave her.

That's when my emotional floodgates were opened, thanks to my fair share of red wine, and a kind-hearted cast member named Ben. Ben was a wise, mid-thirties hot shot out of Chicago, and had that natural swagger I'd always envied in a man. His openness, genuine good nature, and communicative ability had me balling like a bitch in about five minutes. I was just so hurt at the thought of Ashton leaving, I had really started to dig her at that point, and with my own issues with producers thrown in, I was an emotional basket case. The second a tear came tumbling down my cheek, cameras were at the ready, their bright lights showcasing my 'weakness'.

I lost my shit.

For the next forty minutes, I first evaded the cameras with Ben so we could continue our conversation, and then, when they'd inevitably find us, I'd then push the cameras out of my face with a mouthful of expletives to follow. I don't ever want to see that footage, nor do I need to. I know what I looked like that night, and I spent the remaining four weeks on that island regretting it. I spent a good hour that night—after everyone had gone to bed and the only sound was the waves crashing against the shore—running up and down the set of seventy or so stairs that led from the villa down to the beach. It was only me and the cameraman, painted by the full moon and smattering of twinkling stars. Every time I reached the top of the stairs, sweat dripping off my body, I cussed the cameraman out. No, not so much the cameraman, as the producers watching from their trailers. I don't remember the exact number of times I scaled those stairs, but I know it was well over fifty, and I know nubbie took a beating. For me, it was a juvenile, testosterone-fueled response to the 'world' seeing me at one of my weakest points.

As it turned out, none of the footage post-dinner was ever shown, but I spent months before that episode aired enveloped in terror.

What if everyone sees me like that and I lose everything I've worked so hard for?

I couldn't even fathom it. The thought alone crippled me. I ended up spending the summer in St. Louis with my sister and brother. I knew that if this show was going to expose the world to my ugliness inside, I'd need to be around family. I was already drowning in my latest bout with alcoholism, and with each day passed, I numbed the anxiety and fear more and more with it. What started as a 'cute' idea to save all my Jameson bottles that summer to make a kind of Jameson bottle sculpture, ended as a rude fucking awakening. The bottles I had amassed that summer would put to shame even the staunchest of whiskey enthusiasts.

I was a full-blown alcoholic in a complete freefall, and I can thank my Jameson Mt Everest for opening my eyes to it.

I made my way back home to Tampa at the end of that summer with a commitment to beating the bottle once and for all. I stopped going out when I got bored. I stopped keeping Jameson in the house. And most importantly, I let go of the pain the experience on the show caused me through therapy and a lot of self-reflection.

Now, I still drink whiskey, and beer, well, I fucking love that hoppy goodness, but I have a handle on it again. I don't know if I'll ever stop for good. I find myself drawn to the bottle when I'm in social situations, especially around people I don't know and in large groups. I find that when the depression and anxiety inevitably rear their ugly heads from time to time, the Jameson comes calling. When I question being thirty-two and single and wonder what kind of fucking defect I must have to not be able to keep a woman, I can almost taste the whiskey on my lips. But, I'm better now. I'm freer than I've ever been before; more self-confident, honest and understanding of my issues. I believe in me these days and I don't know if I could've ever said that before the show.

True strength is most often derived from trying situations. That show was a turning point for me. It was when the scared little boy from my past and the fraudulently positive person from my present, simply became... me. We so often try and hide who we really are from the world, worried that our ugly truths will turn others away, or lead to criticism and judgment. The latter is almost always true, and that's where strength comes in. I'll take every last drop of criticism and judgment that comes my way when sharing the fucked-up sides of me because it's allowed me to connect so much better with others like me. It's inspired others to tell their own truths. At the end of the day, the more honest we are with ourselves and others, the closer we get to true happiness. Happiness isn't a fantasy and it sure the hell ain't automatic. It's a badge of fucking honor. It's a testament to hard work, dedication, and a commitment to a better you. Don't take it from me. Take it from the desperately unhappy motherfucker you saw on that show. You simply can't change your past. You can only learn from it.

CONNECT WITH BT!

Website
http://www.bturruela.com/

Facebook Page
https://www.facebook.com/AuthorBTUrruela/

Reader Group
https://www.facebook.com/groups/492513690944840

Twitter
www.twitter.com/BTUArmy

ABOUT VETSPORTS

The mission of VETSports is to help veterans achieve better physical, mental, and emotional health through sports, physical activity, and community involvement.

Our organization encourages all veterans to participate in physical activity and engage with their community as a member of local sports team. We know the benefits of sports and how participating in team activities can lead to not only a faster recovery, but also a sense of purpose and fulfillment to our lives. VETSports is committed to run an organization built upon the values, teamwork, and the warrior ethos that have been instilled in us since basic training.